The Frederick Sisters

Are Living the Dream

The Frederick Sisters Are Living the Dream

A Novel

Jeannie Zusy

ATRIA PAPERBACK

New York • London • Toronto • Sydney • New Delhi

ATRIA
PAPERBACK

An Imprint of Simon & Schuster, Inc.
1230 Avenue of the Americas
New York, NY 10020

First Atria Paperback edition October 2023

ATRIA PAPERBACK and colophon are trademarks of Simon & Schuster, Inc.

For information about special discounts for bulk purchases,
please contact Simon & Schuster Special Sales at 1-866-506-1949 or
business@simonandschuster.com.

The Simon & Schuster Speakers Bureau can bring authors to your live event.
For more information or to book an event, contact the
Simon & Schuster Speakers Bureau at 1-866-248-3049 or visit our website at
www.simonspeakers.com.

Interior design by Dana Sloan

Manufactured in the United States of America

1 3 5 7 9 10 8 6 4 2

Library of Congress Cataloging-in-Publication Data is available.

ISBN 978-1-9821-8538-1
ISBN 978-1-9821-8539-8 (pbk)
ISBN 978-1-9821-8540-4 (ebook)

*For Davie
and All Who Care*

Part One

✦

Ginny's Castle

We're going against Ginny's wishes, we're going against our big sister Bets's wishes, and, for the record, we're going against my wishes, too. Here we are, Ginny and me, going east on the beltway toward I-95. I'm taking her away from her small house in the small town where we all grew up in Maryland, and I'm bringing her to be near me in my small town, north of New York City. I'm driving her SUV, she's in the passenger seat, and on her lap sits her baby doll Binky Baby. Behind me, on the backseat and facing Ginny, is her beloved old pup, Rascal. Those two have been looking into each other's eyes since we left Rehab for the Stars. I call it that because of all the rehabilitation centers on the hospital's list, it was the highest rated. In the trunk is my small bag, three larger Ginny bags, her TV, Rascal's bed, and on top of all that, Ginny's brand-new wheelchair.

"It'll be like summer camp," I said to her last week. "You always wanted to go away to summer camp, now you finally get to go!" It's April, but I've been trying to present that it's temporary and might even be fun.

"Not over my dead body will I go to New York," said she, her usual flat delivery.

It was a difficult conversation, and ultimately, I heard myself say, "Well, whether you want to or not, your not-dead body is going to New York."

That's right. She's not dead. If you had asked me four weeks ago if she was going to die, I would have said, "Sadly and definitely, yes." If you had asked me four weeks and one day ago if she was going to die, I would have said, "No way! Ginny just retired from her high school janitor job and she's easing into a long and relaxing retirement."

How do I know it was four weeks ago? Because four weeks ago was the official high school full team support meeting for my younger son, Leo, and tomorrow is the one month follow-up full team support meeting. The guy struggles academically. Yes, that's four weeks of trying to manage this Ginny mess long distance, four weeks of juggling and turning down freelance jobs, four weeks of diminishing income.

"Gin-Gin," I say. "It's going to be great. Rascal and her cousins will finally get to meet! You can come to our house for barbecues! The boys are so excited you're coming. And my friends will finally get to meet the legend. They think you're my imaginary friend, you know."

I don't have many friends right now. Not since the separation. Really, I just have the one friend, and that's Theresa, next door. Everyone else dumped me because they assumed that I dumped Bill. Tomorrow night marks one year since the last time I had sex (oops—it wasn't with Bill—but I swear I didn't dump him), and Theresa is going to perform some sort of ceremony involving her new fire pit to honor this, to honor my future not-lonely libido. Or something.

"I can bring Rascal to visit you and we can go on drives, and maybe, well, you know our town has its own little watering hole, maybe we can go swimming together! When was the last time you went swimming? Wouldn't that be fun? Like in the olden days when we used to go to the pool together? And the beach with Mom and Dad and Bets? And of course, Malibu . . ."

Ginny isn't listening. She turns herself away from Rascal to face front. Not easy for a gal of her size. She's not talking to me. She's ignoring me. *Click, click.* I glance over to see that she is playing with her door lock. *Click, click.*

My sister Ginny. She's a large purple-clad woman with badly bleached blond hair. Right now, it's clean and combed, thanks to the rehab. Her T-shirt has sparkles and says *Life's a Beach*. Her fanny pack is pink and sparkly. Her pink boots are sparkly, too. Her face usually wears something that might be mistaken for a scowl, though it's really just concentrating. Right now, I imagine she's considering her escape plan.

She's got intellectual disabilities; she reads and writes at a third-grade level. Sometimes she says her brain takes the day off. She's got type 2 diabetes and a lust for sugar, which is a dangerous combination and ongoing challenge. Still, she's managed to live independently for almost twenty years in a small house that our parents bought for her just five minutes from their own. Our dad died five years ago, our mom followed a year later, and since then, Ginny has continued to manage and even take care of Rascal. Rascal is an old fat rectangular block of a dog with short sticks for legs. She's black and thick and even her fur feels fat. Oily fat. She is Ginny's best friend, mother, child, and bodyguard. Seriously, she has an aggressive streak.

And now I am recalling the phone conversation we had four weeks and one day ago, just one of our daily check-ins, in which she told me she was "Living the dream, riding the waves." I asked her if she was still taking her pills, walking Rascal. She told me she was an independent woman and to stop being a worrywart.

Well East Coast girls are hip

I really dig those styles they wear . . .

We're listening to the Beach Boys because they are Ginny's favorite and I wanted to put her in a sister road-trip, summer-of-beachy-boys kind of mood. She's already asked me to turn the volume up twice and we only just hit the road. She's into surf culture even though she's only been on a board once and she almost drowned on that occasion. Our biggest sister Betsy—now Bets—turned her on to it. Bets just launched Moon Boards, her very own brand of boards, and runs a surfing school in Venice Beach, California.

I wish they all could be California girls . . .

And I, Maggie, live in a small Hudson River town, just an hour north of New York City. I'm a freshly-separated-from-her-husband woman, still living in the house where we raised our sons. I raised our sons. Graham is in college now, but Leo is still there with me, which is why I got to keep the house. I make a living drawing storyboards for TV commercials. These days, it's mostly pharmaceuticals, power drinks . . .

I am bringing Ginny to Sunnyside Nursing Home and Rehabilitation Center, which is in Ossining, just fifteen minutes south of my house. She'll be there until they get that fucking open wound to heal, until she can walk again, until she gets her mojo back. By then, I'll have had a ramp installed at her place and she and Rascal will be able to go back home.

"Sunnyside," I say cheerfully. "Isn't that a nice name? I checked out four places and it was the nicest. Plus, you get your own room!"

"They're gooey."

"What is? What's gooey, Ginny?"

"Sunnyside up."

"Well, if you flip them over and stick a knife in the yoke, it spreads and it's not gooey. I know that because Graham hates his eggs gooey."

Click, click, click.

"I'm going to California very soon," Ginny says.

"Oh yeah?" I say.

"Bets says."

"Huh," I say.

Bets hasn't mentioned this plan to me. We haven't spoken since last week, when I told her that, against her advice, I was bringing Ginny up north . . . Now Bets is not returning my texts. "Just let the girl go home," she laughed. "Let life do what life does . . ." You mean death? I thought. I tried to explain to her what poor shape Gin-Gin is in. "She can't walk," I said. "Which means she can't drive . . . Can't live independently . . . If you could just fly out, you'd see . . ." "Really wish I could, got a lot going on . . .," our eldest sister said to me. "But hey," she said, and not unkindly, "you do you!" Huh?

Huh, I think the last time I went on a trip like this, just Gin-Gin and me, was the time my parents flew us out to LA to visit Bets. Yeah, it was after I graduated from college and before I got a job. Betsy had gone to UCLA and was now an official California girl with no plans to return east. She was a professional surfer, one of the first women. She had sponsors and even got local commercials and modeling jobs. A week was a long time for her to commit to hanging with her little sisters, so I assured her that we'd be fine and she didn't need to play tour guide.

She promised to take us surfing. Ginny could not stop talking about it for the whole month before we left. She told everyone at Roy Rogers where she worked that she was going to go surfing with the Beach Boys and Farrah Fawcett and don't be surprised if she didn't come back because she might become a professional surfer, too.

I was afraid of the waves. I didn't like going past where they broke. Betsy had taught me how to dive into them way back when she was still on the East Coast, and she swore if I could do it there, I could do it here, in the Pacific. But the waves were bigger. The undertow, stronger. I hated the sensation of going against such power with my eyes closed and not knowing when I'd get through it, if I'd get through it, when the next one would come. "Just dive in," she said, "trust, the waves will carry you. Be at one with the waves."

Ginny was fearless, which as far as I was concerned, wasn't a good thing. The only stroke she knew was the doggy paddle. "If it's good enough for dogs, it's good enough for me," she said.

"Maybe she shouldn't go out there," I said to our big sister.

"Stay loose," she said. "She's having the time of her life."

I decided that I wasn't a surfer and opted instead to coat myself with Hawaiian Tropic, sit on my beach towel, and draw. So what if I lost points with our sister's friends? Let Gin-Gin be the point girl. From where I was sitting, I could see forever, while my toes felt safe and warm under the sand. And there was Ginny, giggling with Betsy's friends. They were having a ball with her, too. "Hang ten!" I heard one of them call to her as she wrestled herself up onto the board, beyond the first set of breaking waves. Ginny just lay there and rode the next few waves. I wasn't sure, but I thought she looked scared. She had bought an eyeglasses band so her glasses wouldn't fall off. I could see the water on the lenses.

And there was Betsy. Out past the breakers, riding a wave. She looked so in control, in her element. Her hair flying wildly behind her. Even from my spot on the sand, it was clear to see that our biggest sister was a deeply tan Californian surfing goddess.

But then a scream and an array of panic and two of Betsy's friends went running into the water. Ginny had gone under. Her surfboard was riding itself in and she was still out there. I could see her head popping up from behind the second set of waves.

"Ginny!" I screamed. But Ginny couldn't scream back. "Doggy paddle!" I yelled.

The guy with the braid got to her first, and with the blond girl's help, they pulled her to shore. They were dragging her by her underarms. I was running to her, to them, trying to see her face on the way, calling her, "Ginny! Ginny!" Her face was lost behind all her hair, it was like her head was on backward. Her glasses were dangling open from the neck strap. I caught up with them and the guy with the braid kind of looked up to acknowledge me. He was serious. "Gin-Gin?" I said. "Do you hear me?" He plopped her down on the sand and the blond girl ran around Ginny and squatted down at her head, quickly moving the hair away. Braided guy went in for mouth-to-mouth. The girl did the counting. They seemed to know what they were doing. Our big sister was still out there, oblivious to it all. Finally, Ginny coughed up a lung's worth of the Pacific and came to.

"Gin-Gin," I said, kneeling by her side, "are you okay? Ginny?" She started patting around on her chest and I realized she was trying to locate her glasses. Incredibly, they were intact, and I handed them to her.

She looked up to see our sister's friends there. The girl was now standing at her feet and the guy was still kneeling at her side. He was holding her hand. "I got some sand on your lips, Ginny, sorry about that," he said as he gently wiped it off.

"Ginny, are you okay?" I said over and over.

"I'm fine," she said as she sat up slowly. Disoriented for sure.

"You took a tumble!" said the blondie.

Ginny kept squinting and shaking her head about.

"Maybe you should rest with your sister for a while," the guy said. "That was probably kinda scary."

"You look like Malibu Ken," Ginny finally said. And then to the girl, she said, "You look like Malibu Barbie." They laughed modest laughs. "Mattel's doesn't lie," my sister said.

That night Betsy lit a nice bonfire on the beach and everyone was drinking rum drinks and beer and smoking dope. I had done my share of drinking and smoking by then so I was fine with joining in. Ginny, who never drank and never smoked, had two very large Mai Tais and took some intense tokes and fell asleep on a blanket. From the other side of the fire, I could see her soft and sunburned face catching bits of light. Her mouth was open and she was drooling. Under other circumstances I might have gone over there to wipe the drool away, but in this case, because I was pleasantly stoned, I was fascinated by the show of saliva gathering at the side of my sister's lips, slowly lengthening until it dripped off.

Eventually our big sister and her boyfriend walked down the beach and disappeared behind the dunes. I sat there with her friends singing Cat Stevens songs and the entire album of *Hotel California* in order. The braided guy was not so subtly hitting on me, and I explained to him that

I was still in love with my college boyfriend back in Baltimore, even though we were actually broken up. "Sometimes you've gotta love the one you're with," he said. He was a babe and he saved our sister's life, but the guy was way too old. And I was not a beach blanket girl. He interpreted it in his own way. "Yeah, it would be hard to say goodbye to each other in the morning..."

I went inside Bets's little bungalow to get a sweater and got waylaid by Malibu Barbie, who was basically trying to get the inside scoop on Bets. All the boys and girls had crushes on her, for as long as I can remember. When I got back to the bonfire I discovered that the braided guy had fallen asleep next to Ginny. He was curled up behind her, with his arm around her belly. This was kind of weird. Maybe if I wasn't so lit it would have registered as very weird, but instead, I lay down on the other side of the flames and watched how his face caught glimmers of light.

On our last day, Bets took us to her favorite surf shop and bought us T-shirts and ankle bracelets. When the flight attendant asked if we had had a nice time in California, Ginny nodded solemnly. "I'm bummed out to leave my boyfriend," Ginny said. "He saved my life."

"Goodness!" the flight attendant said, looking over toward me.

"He's one of the top surfers in the state," Ginny said.

❦

"Let me know when you have to go to the bathroom," I say. "There are stops every half hour or so. I usually stop before or after the Delaware Memorial Bridge, but we can stop whenever. I know Rascal will have to do her thing, too."

She turns back to look at her beloved.

Sunnyside is a temporary solution. I really did check out four places, and I had many long phone calls with her insurance company and I worked my best charms to get Sunnyside Nursing Home to accept Ginny even though she is not a senior. I've done this all by myself while working and cooking and cleaning and driving Leo to lacrosse practice and teaching Graham how to change a flat tire via FaceTime.

Bill didn't offer to help. Well why would he? We're separated; I kicked him out of the house, according to him. My problems aren't his problems anymore. I've been dreading doing this five-and-a-half-hour drive by myself . . . But hey, even if he had offered, I would have said, "No, thanks, Bill, I'm good." Because I wouldn't want to give him that. Ex-husband hero flies in to save the day. Sorry, Bill, but you're just going to have to watch me fly. And sorry, Bill, but shouldn't you be putting your energy into getting an actual job so that you, too, can contribute to paying for your sons' colleges? And if you wanted to help so much, where were you back in the olden days when I needed help changing diapers? I should have had him come along and given him Ginny diaper duty.

Oh yeah. That was a discovery . . . a discovery among many other discoveries that I made at Ginny's house. Let's do a quick review:

Diapers. I did not know that our dear sister Ginny, at age fifty-six, wears diapers. Even our parents, in their eighties and nineties, did not wear diapers. To think, she'd been "Living the dream" . . . while wearing diapers? She never volunteered this information, but perhaps I should have known? I discovered this when I entered her house, also known as Ginny's Castle, for the first time after that long first day at the hospital, the day I learned that she wasn't actually dying but going home in three days. I walked in to the smell of shit. I walked in to a growling Rascal. After letting Rascal out back to take a most extended pee, I began to look around, expecting to find a very large dog poop in my sister's bedroom. Rascal growled again at something under the bed. It was round, it was white. I took a broom to it, knowing rightly well that Rascal would protect me from whatever the hell it was. And it was a diaper. A full diaper. Gagging, I ran to Ginny's small bathroom, possibly to throw up, and the stink was harder in there. Diapers in the trash can, diapers in the shower. I had to run out of the house for fresh air.

Ginny's Castle had gone to pot. There was a pot on the stove that had something growing in it. Seriously, the boys and I had visited her at Christmastime, just four months ago, to celebrate her retirement. She wore Holly Berry lipstick and her Santa hat. Her place wasn't so bad then.

Her baby doll collection, over twenty of them, sitting up in my boys' old crib, freaked me out.

Her Official Surfing Museum of Maryland now includes a life-size cardboard banana-hammocked surfer guy. He freaked me out, too, so I shoved him into her avalanche-ready closet. Betsy's Old Yeller surfboard, hanging there on the Benjamin Moore Ocean Blue wall, had accumulated an inch of Cheetos and talcum powder dust. I asked Ginny once why she didn't use her janitorial skills on her own home. "In protest," she said.

I already knew about the dead bolt locks on the doors—she did that after Mom surprised her by cleaning her house when she was at work. Ginny did not appreciate Mom's invasion of her privacy. Now I've discovered that the doors have chain locks as well. The windows are hammered shut. Ginny lives in a safe neighborhood, I think; according to her, though, maybe not.

Lots and lots of empty Jell-O cups. Like fifty. Strawberry flavored, as some still had the foil cover attached. Ginny had told me she'd been eating strawberries for breakfast, and I was surprised because they're out of season.

And finally, rats. Yes, while I was happily chilling with Rascal on Ginny's front porch, drinking cheap red wine from her *Little Mermaid* mug, Rascal started growling at something under the deck. I was a bit drunk, so I was brave. I went down there and turned my phone flashlight on to discover not one, but two rats. They scurried away. Not into the gutter or under the bush, but into a broken window that led to Ginny's basement. I slept on Ginny's recliner to keep myself elevated.

❦

"I've gotta go to the bathroom," my sister says.

"Rats," I say. We just barely got off the beltway. And then, "Okay!" I start looking for the next exit, which I think is Sandy Spring.

So, yeah, I had a cleaning company disinfect her house and I had an exterminator de-rat her house. Ken and Karen have volunteered to keep an eye on it. At the kennel, Rascal received a bath.

"It'll be like summer camp for Rascal, too," I say. "Rascal gets to play outside with Coyote."

Yes, Rascal will stay with us while her mother recovers. It will not be easy, as Rascal does not like other dogs and, according to Ginny, has never met a cat. But I am determined to face these challenges and become stronger. Also, I want to do it for Mom and Dad. And somewhere deep inside me, I believe this is best for all of us.

Now she can finally settle, with the knowledge that I am nearby. She can focus on getting better and not worry about her pup so much. Now I can see her on a regular basis. She'll be just fifteen minutes from me in the next town. It will be so much easier. And it will be good for Rascal, too. Really, I have no idea the last time that dog was allowed to play outside off leash.

I told the folks at Sunnyside that while my sister might at first appear to have a rough edge, deep inside she's a softy. They told me they were all so excited to meet her. Having a younger resident will be refreshing for all of them. Also, they will happily accept full payment by check until Ginny's Medicare goes through. That's cool. It's Ginny's money, which was put aside for her by Mom and Dad, so Mom and Dad are paying for summer camp!

Sunnyside asked all the usual questions, and of course they got her records from the hospital and the rehab. Regarding her intellectual disabilities, they asked if she has a DSM-5, an official diagnosis. I told them

I didn't know, it's just something we know, have always known. "She's high functioning," I told them. "Always worked, drives . . ."

I remember the first time I knew. That something was different about Ginny. It's something I'd rather not recall, something I've been trying to suppress. But memory is a meany that way. It involved our kitten Marble.

We'd been in the backseat arguing when we overheard Mom and Dad saying something about a different school, a special school, and that maybe Ginny should go there. I said that I wanted to go to the special school, too, but they said it wasn't for me. Ginny and I both went to Kensington Elementary School, where I was in second grade and she was in sixth grade for the second time. Kids had been calling her "dumb ball" and "fatso" and sometimes she came home crying. Still, I didn't want her to go to a different school and neither did she. Our parents told us not to worry about it, it was just in the thinking stages.

As they were unloading the groceries from the car, Ginny sidled over to me and whispered, "The Russians are coming. We need to build a fort." We ran upstairs to grab blankets and beach towels and then we ran out to the backyard and draped the coverings over our metal geodome jungle gym. I don't know where big sister Betsy was on that fresh spring day. Skateboarding with the boys, I suppose. She was five years older than Ginny, already in high school. She was so much groovier than we were, so confident and sporty. I was introverted and awkward, and Ginny, well, Ginny was Ginny. Still, she was my most trusted companion and together we were building a fort to protect ourselves from atomic bombs and we were singing! "The ants go marching one by one, hurrah, hurrah," I said, "Follow me!" and she did! And we marched around the fort.

Ginny was my "Sergeant" and she commanded me to gather supplies, which meant running into the house and grabbing Campbell's soup cans and a pot and she even sent me into Betsy's room to steal matches. I remember our mom being there in the kitchen, seemingly oblivious to our mission and the dangers that were coming.

Then I had to go to the outside faucet to fill a bucket with water, which I did, but it was too heavy for me to carry it back, so Ginny had to run out and get it. Even for her, it was heavy. She was splashing water all over the place, leaving tracks for the Russians! When she got back in the fort, she was sweating. She poured the water into the pot. And then Marble appeared. Ginny asked her if she was a spy. She meowed, so we let her in.

We sat knees to knees, Ginny, holding her baby doll, and me, holding Marble. Marble didn't like being held very much, so she started meowing. This was dangerous because of the enemy, so Ginny sent me over by the trash bins to get a box and then she put the kitten in the box and closed it to keep her safe. Marble kept meowing, though, so then I ran inside to get her some food. We put the food in her box and she calmed down.

This is the part that's hard to remember. I remember it clearly and that's why it's hard. When Mom called us in for dinner, Ginny put the pot of water on top of the box to keep Marble from getting out. I pointed out that the top flaps of the box sank a little bit with the weight of the pot, but Ginny said this was normal, she'd done it in school once. I remember wondering, Done what? Put a kitty in a box? Whose kitty was it? Did she get to bring Marble to school? I suggested that maybe we should let her out of the box, but Ginny put her face very close to mine and said, "The A-bomb."

After dinner, we ate ice cream while we watched *Love Boat* and when it was over, we ran back outside to our shelter because . . . the Russians. We were surprised to see that the pot of water had sunk almost completely into the box. Ginny slowly lifted the pot off the box and I opened the flaps to see Marble. She was just lying there, asleep. I reached in and picked her up to pet her, but she did not wake up. Ginny said she was just playing dead. We both took turns holding her and petting her and tickling her but her body was starting to feel stiff and not floppy. I could feel my insides starting to burn up, the heat from the tears percolating.

Then Mom came outside and she was calling Marble. Ginny's and my eyes met. Hers were wide and I could see that her hands, which were still holding our dead kitten, were starting to shake. "Marble!" our mother was calling. I could see her approaching the fort. "She's coming," I whispered to Ginny. "Quick," my sister said, as she placed Marble back in the box, "close it." So I did. "Seen Marble?" Mom asked, peaking in. We both shook our heads no. After she left, I started to open my mouth to cry or to call her or something, but Ginny covered my mouth with her hand. Then she stiffly tried to hug me, her straight arms bumping the outsides of my arms. She had never hugged me before and hasn't since.

That night, we held in our tears while Mom and Dad said goodnight, and after they left, we both cried ourselves to sleep.

The next day we buried Marble down by the creek. We dug a hole with our bare hands and thick sticks. We lined the hole with a layer of newspaper and then dropped Marble's hard, cold body out of the box and into the hole. More layers of newspaper, dirt, newspaper, dirt. "It's a ritual," Ginny said over and over. When we were done, I said the *God Is Great, God Is Good* prayer because it was the only prayer I knew and then Ginny pulled something out of her shirt pocket. Matches. The ones I had stolen from Betsy's room. She slowly slid the box open. I was scared. I was afraid she was going to set the grave on fire. But no. She pulled out a needle.

She sat there very solemnly, holding the needle up, and then she quickly pricked the top pad of her index finger. She flinched when the point hit the skin and then we both watched the bright red dot grow. She nodded to me to put my finger out. So I did. I cringed as she pricked it. She pushed her finger into mine, holding them hard together with her other hand. And then she leaned her face in very close to mine and whispered, "Blood Sisters." When she released, we both wiped our fingers in the grass.

"Oh, I just feel so sad about Marble," our mother said a few days later.

"She must have been hit by a car," said our father. "She still has nine lives," said Ginny. "Eight," I said. I already knew I was better at subtraction than she was. For the first time ever, I wondered if I knew many things better than Ginny did. "Dogs are better anyway," Betsy said. "Can we get one now?"

We never told anyone about what happened. Not Mom, not Dad, not Bets. Ginny didn't want to get in trouble and be sent to that special school, and I didn't want her to go there either. Also, I must confess, I was protecting myself. Because I had seen the flaps of the box start to sink. And even if my sister didn't think it was an emergency, maybe I should have said something. Maybe I should have run inside to tell Mom about it, even if dinner was on the table. It was a stupid thing we did and even at twelve and seven, we should have known better. Or at least, I was starting to realize, I should have known better.

Soon after that, Ginny sat on Mary Claire's head. I don't know what transpired between them, I just know that by the time I got off the bus, Mary Claire was on the ground over by the brick wall and Ginny was sitting on her head, which was turned to the side, and the other kids from the bus stop were watching. Mary Claire was crying out but I don't think the bus driver or the school patrol heard her. I didn't wait to see what would happen next, but ran straight home, ahead of Ginny, and straight into the kitchen to tell Mom. When Ginny appeared a few minutes later, she ran straight up the stairs and slammed our bedroom door behind her and Mom ran right up after her. I went to the bottom of the stairs, and from there, I could hear Ginny bawling.

Betsy came downstairs in her Friendly's ice cream shop uniform and asked me what was up. I told her all I knew and she said Mary Claire was a brat and was probably being mean to Ginny.

"Why?" I asked because I truly didn't understand. "Why are kids always being mean to Gin-Gin?"

Betsy bent down to meet me eye to eye. She was our biggest sister, about to educate me about something very important, something that apparently no one else had thought to do before that moment, a grave responsibility. "Our sister Virginia," she said, "she's different from everyone else. You see that, right? She wears those thick glasses and sometimes she picks her nose in public, that kind of thing."

"Oh . . . ," I said. I had noticed; it was kind of yucky.

"Something happened when she was born. Not enough oxygen to the brain." And here's where Betsy got really serious. "She's kind of retarded," she said.

I wondered about this. She didn't look like that girl in our town who had Down syndrome.

"Yeah," she said. She was looking in the living room mirror now, tying her hair back into a ponytail. "Not the cute kind."

At twelve years old, Ginny had a pot belly and big breasts and she wore those glasses and her hair was stringy and never looked neat. She combed it out when she got out of the shower but then she wouldn't touch it for days, and then by the time she took her next shower, it had usually grown a few knots and Mom would have to cut them out.

Betsy, on the other hand, was clean. She looked cool in her uniform, even when she put on the hairnet. She didn't need glasses but she put on sunglasses when she went outside. She had them on now, while she was folding up her uniform sleeves to show her upper arm muscles.

She explained that Ginny was slow, her brain worked super slow, sometimes it went backward it was so slow. I imagined the workings of a brain, like a clock, ticking time in sleepy reverse. But then I thought about how our father was always telling Ginny to sit still at dinnertime and stay put at church.

"Then how come she's always wiggling?" I asked.

"That's 'cause she's hyper," she said, "to make up for the slowness."

"Ooooh," I said. I pretended to understand even though I didn't, but I supposed that was the reason why some kids at school made fun of her.

"She'll probably die young, too," Betsy said. "They don't usually live past twenty."

They? I had so many questions. Did kids with slow brains die young? Does this mean she's sick? Is it catching? I never doubted that Betsy's word might not be true. She was the expert.

"Oh no," I said. Because even though I was starting to think that our middle sister was kind of weird, this was heavy news.

"Catch ya later, kid," my big sister said, and she was out the door. She'd be home later with a scoop of mint chip for me and a scoop of orange sherbet for Ginny.

The phone started ringing. Mom ran downstairs and patted my head on her way to answer it in the kitchen. I could hear her talking to someone about Ginny. Ginny opened our bedroom door and whispered loudly and viciously, "You're a squealer, Magpie!"

The very next week, she was moved to the special school.

⌯⌇⌯

"One mile to the exit, Gin-Gin," I say. "We're almost there."

She doesn't say anything.

"Gosh, I haven't done this drive in a hundred years. Not since Mom died anyway . . . With the house being gone and the boys being so busy. They really do get busier as they get older. I've flown down of course. To see you. And I think I took the train—oh, yeah, I did—that time I was worried about snow and it ended up being a whole lotta nothing. Remember that? When I took the train down? We went out to that steak place and you even got Rascal a steak to go because it was her birthday . . ."

"This drive takes me back, Gin-Gin . . ." Bill and the boys and I did it so many times. Gosh, those road trips were basically the soundtrack to our marriage. The first time I took him down there, to meet my parents and Ginny, we sang Beatles' songs the whole way. That's when he started slipping my name into lyrics. "Sexy Sadie" became "Sexy Maggie." "Baby,

You're a Rich Man" became "Maggie, You're a Great Girl," and "Love Me Do" became "Maggie-Do." That one stuck. Maggie-Do was what he called me in our happiest days. Also because he said I was a "do-er," which way back when, he meant without sarcasm.

When the boys were little, it was Woody Guthrie and Taj Mahal, and of course Bill's silly made-up tunes. The music filled the space that one time Bill and I didn't talk to each other the entire way down and back. We just talked to and through the boys and we all pretended that was normal. After that of course he became too "busy" to join us for those trips. Mom started wondering what was up but didn't really ask. No, she preferred that we worked these things out ourselves.

I prefer not to recall those times at the moment. I am determined to keep the spirit light. "We used to sing on our way down to see you guys, Gin." I sing, "*We're on our way to Granny and Papa's house, Granny and Papa's house, Granny and Papa's house* . . . And then we'd sing it again, *We're on our way to Ginny's house, to Ginny's house* . . ."

I am blabbing. I don't know why I'm blabbing. It's not as if I can't be quiet. I'm not one of those people that just can't stop. Bill told me I talk too much when I'm stressed. Am I stressed?

"What's Rascal doing?" I ask.

"She laid down."

"Oh good," I say.

"Ginny and Rascal's house," she says.

"Huh? Oh, yes! That is how we sang it." I remember that now . . . The boys would not let us forget to include Rascal, or Ginny's previous dog, Brownie.

I pull off 95 at Sandy Spring. This is going to be a long drive.

The wheelchair is fucking awkward. The wheelchair is fucking heavy. I am not savvy with the wheelchair. The guy at the medical store gave me a five-minute lesson before we hit the road. As it sits on top of our bags and her TV, I have to lift it up and then over and down, and it lands hard on my sneakered toes. "Mother," I say. I roll it around to her side and open her door. I reach over to unbuckle her. The buckle plays hide-and-seek under her large left thigh. I help her turn her knees toward me and I guide her feet out and down to the ground. "Ginny," I say, "can you stand yourself up?" She reaches for the door handle for support and the door starts to close on her so I grab it. She turns herself around and goes plop down into the chair, which starts to roll backward so I jump behind it, leaving my post at the door, which starts to shut.

"Shit," I say.

"You didn't put the brakes on," she says.

"Sorry," I say. "Where are the brakes again?" She shows me. I manage to turn her around, shut and lock the doors behind us, and we head into the gas station. "Do you want anything to eat?"

I'm praying she'll say no as I should have asked this question before I got her out of the car in the first place. If she'd wanted to eat I would have taken her to McDonald's or Starbucks.

"No," she says, and I feel a tiny leap of victory.

"Want me to come into the bathroom with you?"

"I can go to the bathroom by myself."

"But at Five Star Rehab didn't someone help you sit down and every-thing?" *Everything* means wipe.

"I'm not a baby," she says.

"Okay," I say. I really don't want to help her sit down and I especially don't want to help her wipe. Another tiny victory. When I say victory, by the way, I don't mean victory against my sister; it's not as if I am playing against her. No. I mean victory against life. Or something. I push her in and the heavy door slams behind her.

My phone rings. It's the high school, so I pick up. The school nurse is calling to say that Leo has not shown up. "Oh really?" I say, looking over the cash register at the clock to confirm that it's past noon. The nurse says, "He did not attend first, second, third, or fourth periods." "Darn," I say, "I'm usually there to wake him . . ." I explain that I'm away. I explain that I'm helping my sister. I may be neglecting Leo, but I am helping someone else. "He overslept," I say. "I'm sure of it."

"All we know is he's not in school," she says. "If you reach him, have him call me."

If? And now I am scared. I text him and he does not respond. I call him and leave a message, I FaceTime him. My heart is starting to race. I message him on Insta. I realize now why he is not responding. He is not responding because he is dead. I call Theresa next door and leave a message: "Please go check on Leo . . ." My other line starts ringing. Damn! I did not change the carbon monoxide alarm batteries, that's what happened. He forgot to turn off the gas after he made mac and cheese. His father kidnapped him to Tahiti. Most likely, though, it's because I did not change those batteries.

My other line is still ringing, I click over to see that it's Ginny Frederick who's calling. I answer and sure enough, she says, "I'm in the bathroom." I know this, I know she is in the bathroom, for goodness' sake. What this means is she needs help. I tell her I have to get someone to unlock the door for me and I'll be right there.

While waiting for the gas station attendant, a text from Leo: *Chill, Little Lady, I'm up. Got a headache.*

I thank my mother goddess. I send Theresa a quick text: *Nvm. My baby is alive.*

As I help Ginny pull up her sweatpants and get back in her chair, I realize that I am angry at Leo. I am angry that he is so damn irresponsible that he can't get himself up for school, I am angry that he was so unreachable that I was having scary imaginings, and I'm angry that he called me Little Lady. Also, I realize that I am angry that I haven't heard from my older baby, Graham, the college business major, in over a week. Sure, sure, he was so concerned when we all thought Ginny was dying. He told me to give Aunt Gin-Gin a hug from him. I said that I would, but that she wouldn't hug back. He said, "That's her brand." I remind myself that someone from Syracuse U would have called me by now to tell me if he's dead, so he's likely fine, so again I am angry.

As I push Ginny out, a big guy in a Harley jacket holds open the bathroom door. "Your mother's got a tail," he says.

I look down to see that Ginny does indeed have a long trail of toilet paper coming out of the top of her purple sweatpants. "Oh," I say. "Ginny, you have a tail."

"Like Rascal," she says.

I pull it out and say thanks to the man, who's on his way in.

"I'm not her mother, I'm her sister," Ginny says. "Blood."

He looks back at the two of us, back and forth between us, then closes the door behind him.

It's not the first time that someone has assumed she's my mother. I do look younger than my sis. Especially now.

I get Ginny back in the car, I get her wheelchair back in the car. I send off a quick text to Leo. I can't afford to have a tiff with him, he's the easiest one I've got right now. Keeping my cool, so he'll know I'm chill: *I'm so sorry, poor thing. I guess you missed your test in Global History ;-)*

I then suggest to Ginny that we let Rascal out to do her thing, too.

She says, "Rascal can hold it in forever."

I say, "Okay, well, I guess I'll go. It never hurts to try! Remember Mom used to say that?"

I used to say it to my own kids when they were little. Actually, I still say it to them. Once Bill and I got in a big fight when Leo told us he had to go only twenty minutes into a trip and Bill said to me, "Did you remind him to try?" Like it was my fault! That was just the beginning, though. Then he refused to stop the car because it was so early in the trip, so he told Leo to empty a perfectly good full bottle of water out the window and then he instructed him to pee in it. This did not please me. But it did please Graham, who thought it was so cool that he had to try it himself and then Bill asked me to empty a bottle for him and I said, "Absolutely not," and then he asked the boys to do it and Graham poured his pee out of the bottle and it hit the car behind us.

When I get back in the car, I tell Ginny this story. She asks if that's why we're getting divorced. "Not really," I say, "but kind of."

We're breezing up 95 now. I ask Ginny if she wants to keep listening to the Beach Boys and she says, "Is the pope Catholic?"

It's late April, and while still a bit breezy, spring is undoubtedly popping up. Trees are starting to show their green, even flowering. Redbuds. At the rest stops, cherry blossoms.

I look over at Ginny who is looking back at Rascal. "What's Rascal doing now?" I ask.

"Dreaming," she says.

"Oh, that's good," I say. "What do you think she's dreaming about?"

Ginny doesn't answer. She is just looking back at Rascal with profound longing.

"Maybe she's dreaming about playing outside with Coyote," I say. "Maybe she's dreaming about visiting you at Sunnyside."

I am putting all my eggs into a basket here, hoping and praying that Rascal will pass the test to be allowed to visit. They told me that she must meet approval with the Recreation Coordinator.

"First one to see the Empire State Building gets a quarter!" I say. I'm joking. This is a variation of something our dad used to say whenever we were driving home on the beltway from someplace. He always said, "First one to see the Mormon Temple gets a quarter!" Ginny and I were very competitive about that sighting. "You can't actually see the Empire State Building on the way to Croton," I say. "But if you want to, we can go visit it someday."

"Seen it already," Ginny says.

"I remember," I say.

Then Ginny volunteers, "That's where Dad went ballistic on me."

"What? Where?"

"Empire State Building. He went nuclear."

"Well . . . ," I say.

I look over at her and she's looking straight forward. She doesn't turn toward me when we're talking to each other in the car, the way anyone else would. She's looking straight ahead with a poker face.

"He was angry, Ginny, but I'm sure he didn't go nuclear," I say.

Yeah, that's because she got on the elevator and pressed the button and let the doors shut before we got on. She thought she was being clever, maybe? I remember looking up at my dad's face to see him shouting, "Virginia!" I remember him bending down to my level to ask me, "Did she go up or down, Margaret? Up or down?" The next thing I remember was being in the lobby of the Empire State Building and our father basically yelling at Ginny who was holding tight to our mother's hand. "What the hell were you thinking, Virginia? What the hell were you thinking?" he kept saying. I'm sure she scared the shit out of him.

"Dad was just scared, Ginny. He didn't know how to tell you that . . . How about the time you came to visit me and Bill? What did we do then? Do you remember?" I'm trying to divert.

"The taxi driver almost ran over a baby buggy," she says.

"That was a particularly scary taxi ride," I say.

"He was a fighter pilot or a hired assassin."

"Ha. Yeah, I remember. Bill said that." It's amazing the details that Ginny remembers. Bill was very sweet with Ginny on that trip. He really wanted to show her a good time. It was the first time I recall looking at him and thinking, Yeah, we could have kids . . . "Oh," I say, "and we took a horse and buggy ride through Central Park!"

"The horse was running away from the taxi driver," Ginny says.

I laugh. This is going to be great. I love Ginny and she loves me and she's coming to New York.

It's not long before Ginny announces her biological needs again. And this is good because I have a biological need for a very large, super large, unbelievably large latte. Rascal sleeps through the whole car to wheel-chair transfer and we head into Maryland House, the first of many official rest stops on I-95. Daffodils are up and tulips are on their way. They haven't bloomed yet, but on some, little bits of pink and orange peak out.

This time, we know what to do. I help Gin-Gin into the stall and I help her get out of the chair and turn herself around, etcetera, etcetera. Even though it's wheelchair accessible, it's tight in here. "How many clowns can you fit in a phone booth?" I say to my sister.

"Phone booths are history," she says as she plops down hard. "Everybody knows that."

I turn away to offer her privacy. My phone dings, I pull it out of my pocket and see that it's a text from Bets. *What about the evangelists?*

I let out a loud, "Ha!" Ginny grunts.

The evangelists are Ginny's neighbors, Ken and Karen, who are not evangelists, but retired conservative Christians. They have been very good neighbors to Ginny and for this I am extremely grateful. They are the ones who found Ginny on the floor of her bedroom, unconscious, cold to the touch, and in a "self-made mess." They are the ones who called 911 and they are the ones who called me. And they are the ones who told me the doctor said Ginny had sepsis, an infection of the blood, an open wound to the bone, and was close to death.

Funny that Bets would have this revelation now, funny that that's all she has to say, and even so, I know exactly what she means. She means: Can't the evangelists take care of our sister? As if the thought hadn't crossed my mind on Day One. And the answer is No, they cannot, they have already done too much. There is so much to say on this matter, and I begin a response, but then stop.

I check emails and see that my mortgage payment is overdue and Graham's account is overdrawn and my various political organizations tell me that the world is coming to an end and my three dollars might save it.

A voice mail. Strange, I didn't even hear it ring. My rep wants to know if I can start a job that'll last 'til Wednesday. They'll brief me around eight tonight. "It's a pitch," she says. Another pharmaceutical, a positive promise in the form of a doctor-prescribed pill. I call her back. "I'm in," I say as the toilet blasts. I help Ginny pull her pants up again and while she half-assed washes and dries her hands, I text Theresa: *Got gig. Fire ceremony tomorrow night?*

I order two grande lattes.

Ginny says, "I don't drink coffee."

I say, "The second one is for Rascal."

She doesn't smile, but I think she appreciates my humor.

I ask if she wants anything. She says she's not hungry. I remind her that I packed applesauce and yogurt and water and she says she's not hungry.

I buy a banana for two bucks. I get some salted almonds. I also get a Rice Krispies treat. Ginny and I used to make these together all the time. Once, I remember, after putting them in the fridge to chill, I opened it later to discover she'd eaten practically the entire pan of them, leaving me a corner piece. Once, I caught her eating a thick and sticky butter and marshmallow soup, directly from the pan. I said, "Ginny, aren't we gonna pour in the Rice Krispies?" And she said, "Why waste cereal?" I feel kind of guilty ordering this in front of her since she's on a strict no-sugar diet, but right now I really, really need a Rice Krispies treat. I tell her that I rarely eat sweets and since I am driving such a long drive by myself, I need certain foods to fuel me.

She reminds me to get gas. I get her back in the car and while we are waiting for our turn at the gas pump, I open my Rice Krispies treat and take my first bite.

"You better not get addicted," Ginny says, "or you'll get septic."

"I'm not diabetic," I remind her.

"Blood sisters," she says.

Ah, diabetes. Insulin, glucose, beta cells . . . I've tried to explain how it works, I've drawn pictures illustrating how it works. I've tried to explain

to her many, many times that exercise and diet can help her manage it.
"So many people have it, like millions." I told her this so she wouldn't
feel alone. "You should go lecture everybody else," my dear sister said.
I've tried to explain to her that I know it's hard for her to eat less sugar.
I know it's hard when you're busy to find time to work out. She says I
lucked out because skinny babies don't crave sweets.

According to Ginny's most recent doctor on the Intensive Care Unit,
diabetes is a "beast of a disease" that already affects one out of ten people
on the planet and is getting worse. He says ninety percent of those with
diabetes have type 2, what Ginny has, which is difficult and complicated
to manage in a world where we are constantly being bombarded with
images of fast foods, foods with high sugar content, foods that make us
crave. While he was explaining this, I appreciated his compassion and
frustration with the world we live in and I also noticed that his lips were
extremely plush and imagined myself kissing them.

After I get the gas, I get back in the car and quickly FaceTime Leo. I
want to make sure he actually went to school, though if he did, I'll be in-
terrupting him, so this move is counter-intuitive, as they say. He answers.
He's in his bedroom, on his bed. He answers with a long "Moooooom." No
smile. "Mooooooom," he says again. He's not looking at the phone, he's not
looking at me. I ask if he went to school and he rolls his eyes. I ask if he is
drunk, I ask if he is high. He denies both and asks if I am drunk or high. I
show him Rascal in the backseat and Ginny next to me. "Hi Aunt Ginny,"
he says. "Hey neighbor," she says, and he genuinely smiles.

I explain to him that I won't be home 'til later so I won't be able to
make dinner. Again. He does not seem devastated. He continues to seem
distracted. What on earth is he doing? I request that he has the house
cleared and cleaned before I arrive. "Will do," he says. I just made a funny
joke but he seems to have missed it. I try to catch his eyes. It's like trying
to get a goldfish to stand still.

"Leo," I say, "look at me. What are you doing?"

"Chill, Mom, I'm on the computer, actually doing some schoolwork," he says. "Isn't that what you want me to do? Turn my papers in on time?" How many screens does one teen need at any given moment? In the background I think I hear the TV.

Being frustrated by his lack of eye contact reminds me that I'm frustrated by his older brother's lack of contact. He hasn't returned my calls or texts in days. Suddenly, I say, "Where the hell is Graham?" catching us both off guard.

"He's in Switzerland," Leo says.

"What?!" I say.

"Sorry, I can't lie to you, Mom. He's skipping like three days of school. I told him if you asked me face-to-face, I would tell you the truth."

"What the hell is he doing in Switzerland? And who the hell is paying for it?" I will check my Visa bill the minute I get home.

"Getting laid? I'm kidding, Mom. He has a girlfriend, I think. One of his friends lives there or something. I dunno."

"Will you please tell him to contact his mother? Tell him if he doesn't, I'll contact his father." I can't believe I'm saying these words, so *Father Knows Best*, so ironic, too, because we all know that Bill is the chill one, Bill's the guy who says, "don't worry about it, let the kid have some fun." Still, Leo knows this is my way of saying I'm one step away from calling the police. I've done it before, I'm not ashamed slash kind of ashamed to admit it.

"I will, I will . . ."

"Thanks for telling me," I say. "That is really strange . . . but thanks . . . Love you."

"Love you," he says. He hangs up before I can say "See you soon."

"Well that's fricking weird," I say as I buckle myself in.

"You need to chill," Ginny says, which makes me roll my eyes. "You need to let the waves, wave," she says. She annoys me with her little bits of surfer wisdom.

I take a deep breath and then ask her permission to switch to my Mom playlist. Leo made it for my birthday. Alt and other stuff.

"It's a free country," Ginny says.

"You can take a nap if you want to . . ."

"Rascal's awake," she says.

"Oh," I say.

I see, she wants to spend every waking moment with Rascal. She's looking back at her again. Her eyes are wide behind her thick glasses. She's basically staring at her. When I look around to change lanes, I see that Rascal is staring back. It's funny, you always hear how you're not supposed to look a dog in the eyes, it freaks them out, they get aggressive. Most dogs will look away after a few moments, but not Rascal. I know that Ginny talks to her, but today she's not talking much. It's not necessary, I think. They seem to be communicating telepathically.

I asked Bill to take an intimacy workshop with me once. We were still having sex then, but I was starting to notice that something was missing. What was missing was the kissing. And the laughing and the tickling. And, it seemed, any desire to sit down and have coffee or a drink together, just check in, any semblance of fun. What was growing was impatience and frustration. At least on my side. I wanted to talk about it, I wanted to know what was going on with him. He said he would not pay money for a stranger to tell him how to be with his wife. I said, "Well maybe they know something we don't know, maybe they could make things . . ." "Make things, what?" he said. "More intimate," I said.

So, I bought their book. This married-couple-who-gave-these-workshops' book. Lesson One was How to Really Look at Each Other. The challenge was to try to meet each other's eyes for periods of ten seconds, thirty, a minute, five minutes. I asked Bill to try this with me. We made it to thirty and then he stopped, saying it felt forced.

"You and Rascal really love each other, don't you, Ginny?"

"Was Dennis Wilson the cutest Beach Boy?" she says.

The car fills with the scent of a hundred-year-old egg. It happens so fast that I start to gag. I put all four windows down without even asking Gin about it and the cool moist spring air helps the scent to evaporate.

"Rascal needs to go," Ginny says.

"Are you sure she didn't already?" I ask.

"That's how she tells me."

"Oh my," I say. The next stop isn't for twenty miles.

"She can hold it," Ginny says.

"Really?"

"Does it all the time," she says.

What does this mean? Does this mean that when Rascal has to go, she has been trained to keep it in, relieving the pressure in small but powerful gaseous increments until Ginny gets to the door?

"Are you sure? I mean, it's twenty minutes away."

"You can wait twenty minutes, right Rascal?" Ginny says this to Rascal in the rearview. She then looks straight forward. "She says yes."

I take a deep breath. I'm hoping and praying that Ginny is right as I really don't want to pull over to the side of the highway any more than I want to clean up a stinky mess in the backseat. "Okay, Mama knows best . . . ," I say.

I count the miles backward in my head, while Rascal lets out another and then another.

"Okay, Ginny," I say, "I think we need to pull over."

"She knows what she's doing," Ginny says. "S'only five miles," she says to Rascal.

So now if I pull over, it would demonstrate a complete lack of faith in both Rascal and Ginny's parenting skills. I must wait.

I pull in to the first space I can get to, I jump out of the car while it's still running, open Rascal's door, connect the leash on her collar and coax her to get out. She won't budge.

Another one. This one floats straight into my face as I am down there, trying to encourage her bottom to move. "Oh my God, Ginny," I say, "give me a treat! Quick, in the holder there, underneath the tissue, a treat!"

I have to reach around Rascal to retrieve the treat from Ginny. Rascal sees it and barks, directly into my ear. I say, "Come on, Rascal," as I wave the treat in front of her nose and put it down on the curb below. Rascal weightily plops out, lands on the ground on all fours, and while eating the treat, expels the largest poop I have ever seen. It's as if she was constipated until she got out of Maryland. "You go, girl," I say to Rascal. And then she just stands there as if we've reached our destination. "Rascal, do you want to take a walk? Rascal, do you want some water?" I offer some. Nope. "Okay, back into the car, Rascal," I say. She won't budge. I realize there is no way I can get her back in the car from this spot without one of us stepping in it. So I ask Ginny for more treats and then I make a path of them, around the car to the other side, and Rascal follows them. I have to push the stuff on the backseat over to the other side so that there is room for her to sit. Then place a treat on the top of that seat. She's interested but can't get up without my help. At the kennel, a big man helped me lift her. I risk my life lifting the front half of her, and as she growls, I lift her back side. Once she gets in, she eats the treat and lies down.

My second extra-large latte has gone lukewarm. I can't pound 'em like I used to. It's unsatisfying but serves its purpose. I am confident that I can get us to Sunnyside Nursing Home before six thirty p.m. and before I fall asleep. Ginny, unable to get a good look at Rascal, as Rascal is now directly behind her, reclines her seat with a bang and then closes her eyes.

Sigh. I glance over at my sister and see that her face, now facing me, is drooping. The deep pockets of her eyes have gotten darker. Her eyebrows are bushy and dark. Her skin tone is gray. Sometimes she puts tanning toner on her face to get that uneven, blotchy beach girl look, but not today.

I've drawn that face many times, sketched it, painted it, caricatured.

I've drawn her so many times, trying to capture her. *Hoooonk!* Yikes, I've swerved, the honk's directed at me. Keep your eyes on the road, Maggie! That's okay, I don't need to look at her, I've got her memorized.

When her eyes are open, they are a deep blue, dark gray in some light.

Her nose is prominent with its harsh slope and broad base. It has permanent dents on the top on both sides, a result of a lifetime wearing glasses.

Her lips are full and pale and dry.

A prominent mole sits in the middle of her right cheek. My sister is proud of this mole and we both call it her beauty mark.

There are wrinkles in all the usual places, but they aren't very deep. Her skin is mostly soft and appears pliable. I bet if I pressed my finger on her chin, it would leave a nice dimple.

Her chin has many chins. They are heavy and full, as if they carry the weight of all of the above.

The ICU doctor described my sister's state as anhedonic. After he left, I looked this up.

Anhedonic: from the noun anhedonia, meaning lack of pleasure or of the capacity to experience it. A core clinical feature of depression, schizophrenia, and some other mental illnesses. Derived from the Greek "a-" (without) "hedone" (pleasure, delight). Oh, these sexy doctors and their fancy words. Couldn't he simply have described my sister's state as *joyless*?

She wasn't always this way. Just a few months ago, right after she retired, she was low-key jolly. This latest episode has taken a toll. I look over at my sister, deeply sleeping now. I see a woman who is my responsibility.

Eyes back on the road. Leo's Mom playlist continues with Amy Winehouse:

They tried to make me go to Rehab
But I said no, no, no . . .

I laugh out loud remembering our oldest sister's latest text. If she only knew about the evangelicals. Oh, she'd get a kick out of that. "First off, Bets," I imagine I'd say, "just because people choose to go to church doesn't mean they're extremists." Then I'd tell her about how Ken and Karen had been bringing Ginny comfort food for who knows how long, how when I was cleaning out Gin's house I discovered ten—count 'em, ten!—plastic covered meals with sticky notes attached. *"Ginny, Enjoy the meatloaf. K & K" "Ginny, Chicken Parm. Enjoy. K & K"* "Untouched," I'd tell her. "Stinking and green!" "Ewwwww!" she'd say.

I'd tell her the whole story about how Ginny used to call me when she'd fallen in the street and I'd remind her I live five and a half hours away and she'd tell me she's okay, she's an independent woman, and then I'd call K & K and they'd go out and "find" her there, help her and Rascal back up the steep steps to her front door.

"Oh my," Bets would say.

"They don't drink," I'd tell her. "Every time they came over to Ginny's when she was in the hospital, I'd be sitting on the front deck with Rascal, drinking from Ginny's *Little Mermaid* mug, but my wine bottle was the giveaway. Every time they came over, to get the update on Gin's recovery, to share some new detail about her recent behavior, I'd offer them a glass, or a mug, and they'd turn me down. Finally, I dunno, the third time or so? Karen offered, "Oh, we're not drinkers, dear." "Like you," I could hear her thinking, "you Medieval Wench!"

Bets would get a kick out of that.

"Ultimately, though," I'd explain to her, "they fixed her stairs and her driveway and even her fence and I told them I was very grateful for all they'd been doing. Then Karen nodded at Ken encouragingly and he pulled out some folded papers from his back pocket. Bills, from various hardware stores. With an added item, circled, in his own pen: *Efforts made—$50 per hour.* "Well, damn, that Ken must take his sweet time," I'd say, "because his Efforts came to five hundred dollars!"

We would both laugh very hard at this.

ﻌﯟﻐ

My phone dings, which alerts me to the fact that I've been talking to my-self. Dings again, which reminds me that I'm worried about Graham. It's from him. Damn. I've gotta read this. Ginny's asleep, so she can't police me. I grab it and once I get myself behind the large Lucky Leprechaun tour bus, I read it: *I'm in Geneva, New York, NOT Switzerland. With a girl. Will call you when I get back to the 'Cuse.*

"Ahhhh," I say. And "Ha."

Two and a half more hours to go with I hope no interruptions. I feel my thoughts go into mellow-drive, under radar and outer space. My head feels clear in a way it hasn't in days, weeks, months. I don't feel worried about the past or the future and I'm not distracted with minu-tiae. My Mom playlist has ended and I am enjoying the quiet. I turn off my phone.

Passing Delaware House, the rest stop right before the Delaware Me-morial Bridge. We used to stop there every Christmas with the kids on our way to and from Granny and Papa's house. On the way down, we bought eggnog lattes and hot chocolates. It was tradition.

Our Christmas was quiet this past year. Just my boys, the creatures, and me. Bill went to Ohio to visit his parents. We tried to play board games and we tried to sing carols and we tried to read *A Christmas Carol* aloud, but it was all too strange without our fourth player, tenor, and read-aloud enthusiast. Let's face it, *A Christmas Carol* wasn't fun without Bill's bellowing Scrooge. The games weren't exciting without Bill's ridic-ulously competitive edge. And the songs weren't festive without Bill's improvised lyrics. It was sad as hell, actually. It made me wonder if Bill and I had done the right thing. Or the wrong thing. It filled me with re-gret and sorrow and shame. The boys voted we go see an action film and I went along. When we got home, they went upstairs to get high and I pretended I didn't realize they were doing that, just as the next morning they pretended they didn't realize that I had finished off the extremely strong eggnog by myself.

Over the DM Bridge. We're over halfway there. I'm over halfway through my life.

Ginny told me once that her brain was half there. I said, "Where's the other part?" She said, "You got it."

Passing the turnoff for Philly now. We're making pretty good time. Been there three times to see the Liberty Bell. Once as a kid, once with Graham's class when they went, and once with Leo's class. If Ginny were awake, I'd ask her if she wants to visit the Liberty Bell. That's another family joke. Our parents took us there when we were little. And then on another trip—probably the one to New York—my mom suggested we stop by and look at it again. "We've already seen it," Betsy said. "We're going straight home," said our father. And Ginny said, "Why would you want to see the Puberty Bell again?" And Bets and I laughed really hard. And then our mother said, "Well, I just love the Liberty Bell, and if it were solely up to me, I'd see it again!" So, from there on in, whenever we went on a trip or one of us was going somewhere, our dad would always dryly say, "And make sure you stop by the Liberty Bell."

It's not really funny. It's one of those jokes that lives with a family and just gets dumber with age. It's the kind of joke that you tell your kids about and they don't get it and then out of the blue, when you are driving from Lake George to Montreal, from the backseat one of them says to your then husband, "Hey Dad, let's stop by the Liberty Bell!" and everybody laughs.

I'll make sure to let Ginny know when she wakes up that we passed by the Liberty Bell.

Ah, the New Jersey Turnpike.

I sing, *"Everybody's got a hungry heart. Everybody's got a hungry heart . . ."*

Once, Bill and I went to Spring Lake. Mom and Dad came up to watch the boys so we could have a romantic getaway. It was very generous of them and I believe Mom sensed we were having trouble. When we returned, we thanked them profusely. We had gotten gifts for everyone. My mother looked at me earnestly and I told her it was great and Bill joked that we stopped by the Liberty Bell. We didn't tell them that while we were there, walking along the cold autumn beach, we talked about our likely someday divorce.

My heart aches. I thought I would have heard from Mr. X by now. I mean, it's been almost a year. And when I told him that Bill moved out, he seemed . . . moved . . . and then he moved to London. Well, that wasn't his choice. He was transferred to head the London office, which was an opportunity. He couldn't stay here, waiting for me to be ready. Maybe I should go on Match as Theresa keeps saying. I need Theresa to take some good pictures of me. I'll ask the boys for their opinions. No, that would be weird.

Bets has got a whole Insta following and posts selfies all the time. She still looks damn good in a swimsuit. My pics will be more modest than that. Frankly, I think Bets is pretty narcissistic. Maybe I should be narcissistic, too; look where my modesty has gotten me.

My parents would have thought our divorce was foolish. Well, it's still officially a separation. It'll go through in a few months.

And Bill wasn't a terrible father. He did change some diapers, sometimes.

Ginny really does love Bill. I'm sure it's confusing to her that we separated. It's not like he was beating me or anything. It's not like he was gay or I was gay or we had bad sex or anything. It's just, we didn't have it much. It didn't help when Ginny always said he was our "brother from a different mother." Yeah, that's right, he was the annoying, teasing brother who never had a job, not really, who didn't do his chores without being begged to first, who was always stoned, who sold weed to the neighbors, and on top of all that, was everybody's, especially the neighbors', favorite.

I remember him chatting them up outside after taking out the trash—the trash that I gathered and put by the front door and repeatedly reminded him to take out—while I was inside drawing storyboards while helping the boys with their homework. I could hear their laughter carry in through the front door, which he left open so that our indoor-living Crazy Cat could run outside, and so he could run in to tell me that I needed to stop everything to help him catch Crazy. So, yeah, I ran out there and had to yell at him to get the hell out of the way because his abrupt movements only made the cat run further, and he went back to chatting, while I slowly cornered Crazy Cat up against the compost and the fence. So the neighbors saw him as the happy helper. And me? I'm the angry cat herder.

Maybe he was less like a brother and more like a disappointing husband. All I know is, his behavior did not make me feel . . . amorous.

Anyway, apparently, he's been seen holding hands with an older woman. Oh, good, let him resolve his mother issues with her now. I haven't told Ginny about the older woman, but why would I?

She's snoring now. Rascal is snoring, too. They are both quite loud, so I am getting snoring in stereo.

Which is better than farting in stereo.

Where the hell did all this traffic come from?

Are these people all going to Sunnyside Nursing Home?

Goodness knows that old geezer I keep passing should go there.

Old geezer, I mean with affection.

I hope to be an old geezer someday.

I wonder where he's going? To visit his wife in hospice?

To meet a woman he met on Match.com? To meet a man he met on Match?

I need to do some art, that's what I need.

I need a vacation.

I need some sex.

I need affection.

I don't have time or money . . . But I have my health! Hahaha.

True, though. I do have that. Thank the lords and lordesses almighty.

Ginny has time and money, but she doesn't have health.

Thanks again to my parents who put money aside for Ginny's care. Shout out to you guys!

At this point, I imagine Mom and Dad in heaven, lounging on a cloud. Mom is in a long, beaded dress and Dad is in a tux. They are drinking champagne. No, Mom is more likely in a mint-green knee-length polyester dress, Dad in khakis and a maroon cardigan. More likely they are drinking an inexpensive Chablis. They look very beautiful.

Here's the turnoff to the Tappan Zee. Should I wake Ginny to show her the Hudson River? She asked me if I ever go on the river on a boat. I said, "Nope, not really." And then I said, "Maybe we can do that together, Gin-Gin." She said, "If Bets comes." I assume this meant if Betsy comes to visit. I have no idea if Bets will come to visit, and I'm not going to go there with Ginny. Right now, I prefer the image of just Ginny and me, on a kayak for two, even if Bets is the strongest rower. But "That would be fun," I said.

I was in an accident on this bridge once. With the boys when they were younger. Six and eleven, maybe. Five and ten? We were on our way down to Maryland. Bill missed that trip. He had an emergency gig at the local coffeehouse. A last-minute fill-in for a local band whose leader held the promise of bigger, better gigs. I told my dad it was a stomach bug that was keeping his only son-in-law away from his only eightieth birthday . . . The boys and I were cruising along and everything was okey-dokey when the car directly in front of me just stopped without warning. I slammed into it hard and we all screamed. Then we all screamed as we got hit from behind, again and again and again. I thought we all might die, I thought we might go over the rail and plunge headlights down into the Hudson, I thought my legs might get crushed, both of my babies were screaming. It was a six-car pile-up.

The car was totaled, but we all got out without a scratch. Only one person in the whole scene had to go to the hospital. I hope he or she is okay. We stood there on the side of the highest part of the Tappan Zee until a pickup came to deliver us to the far side of the bridge where we'd give a police report. Bill came down to meet us at the car graveyard, as Leo called it. He started to argue with the owner there—I don't remember about what. But I do remember him saying to the guy, "Could I have a little compassion? My car just got totaled!" He didn't say, "My family almost died!" That still really bothers me.

Ginny sent us flowers the next day. Mom and Dad were very concerned and offered to fly us down instead. Even Bets sent us a postcard. It said, *Glad you survived that gnarly wave!*

From the top of the Tappan Zee, you have a spectacular view of the river. You can see all the way down to Manhattan and all the way up to West Point. I remember pointing this out to my boys. "See? If that accident hadn't happened, we would never have had this chance, this chance to stand on the middle of the Tappan Zee over the middle of the Hudson, right here in the beginning of the Hudson River Valley."

We're over the bridge and I see that Ginny's eyes have opened. I say, "Twenty minutes to Sunnyside." At the red light before we turn right onto Route 9 in Tarrytown, I check myself out in the mirror and see that I have a frozen-looking smile on my face. I make my Liberty Bell joke but she doesn't respond. She's doing her best to turn around to see Rascal, but it's not easy as Rascal is still seated directly behind her and Ginny is not particularly flexible. I tell her about the exercise classes offered; I tell her about the craft days.

We arrive at Sunnyside just past dinnertime. I know this because they have given me the schedule. They told me they'd be able to serve her dinner upon her arrival. Nice. I pull up to the front of this lovely old building and ring the bell to announce that we are here. "Here we are, Ginny. Summer camp!" I hear myself, but I can't stop myself.

As I open up the back trunk, Roger and Marybeth come out to greet us. Roger is their very elegant receptionist. Marybeth is their teeny tiny admissions administrator. I met them both when I checked out the place. Roger struck me as out of place. He seems like he should be working in a high-end clothing store or salon. Marybeth sounded much younger on the phone. In real life I'm guessing that she's older than some of the residents, though she probably has more energy than all of them put together.

Sunnyside is one of the oldest nursing homes in Westchester, but their equipment is state-of-the-art. Because it is an old building, the residents' rooms are small. The shared living spaces, lovely with their dark wood fireplaces, oriental carpeting, and heavy drapery, feel like a step back in time. In the back of the building there is a large porch that has a nice high view of the Hudson and beyond. They use the porch for dining and recreation six months of the year. Overall, it has a feeling of safety and comfort, and because the staff is so kind, it feels familiar.

There are only three floors here. The bottom floor is for the more medically challenged patients. The second floor is for memory care. And the third floor, where my dear sister will stay, is for those needing nursing care but not on the verge of you-know-what. They have fewer than fifty residents and we were lucky that they have a room available for Ginny.

"Ginny," I say, as Roger helps her out of the car, "this is Roger who I told you about. And this is Marybeth."

They say, "We are so happy to meet you, Ms. Frederick. We've been looking forward to your arrival."

Ginny says nothing. She is following Roger's guidance, but all the while, she's got her eye on the backseat and whatever she can see of Rascal. I realize they need to say their goodbyes. I turn the car back on and put down the backseat window on Ginny's side. Rascal pops her wolf-y nose out.

I had told them about Ginny's connection with Rascal and they are sensitive to this. Ginny looks up at Rascal. She doesn't reach up to her or say anything.

"I'll see you soon, Ginny," I say, putting words in Rascal's mouth. And then, "It's going to be great, Gin-Gin. Everyone here is so nice. And they have great nurses, and they are going to help you get strong and get those wounds healed."

Roger and Marybeth nod in sympathy. Roger rolls Ginny in. I leave Rascal for a sec and follow. At this point, other residents are returning to their rooms from dinner. They either walk independently with walkers or are pushed in their wheelchairs. Some of them look ancient.

"It's rush hour at Sunnyside," Roger says. "Tonight, Ms. Frederick will get room service."

Nurses, aides, and some residents say hello and welcome Ginny as they pass by. A chipper fellow in a bright yellow sweater walks all by himself. He's humming a happy tune. I wonder why he's here. "He seems friendly," I say to Ginny. I notice that at least two women in wheelchairs are holding stuffed animals. Ginny and Binky Baby are going to fit right in.

❧

I pull into our driveway at precisely 7:17 p.m. This gives me forty-three minutes to bring Rascal into the house, hug Leo, enlist him to bring my bag into the house, pet Coyote and Crazy Cat, eat, and get settled before my 8:00 p.m. phone briefing.

It takes me forty-one minutes to get Rascal in the house.

Coyote and Crazy Cat are at the front door to greet me, and Rascal, who I am holding by the leash, goes into immediate attack mode. I drop my keys and what's left of my second latte, spilling its remains on the floor, and use both hands on the leash to hold Rascal back. Crazy Cat is howling in a way I've never heard before and he leaps over the leather armchair and tries to climb a sconce. Coyote, our sweet little old lady puppy, puts on her fighter suit and the two dogs go face-to-face with a most primal aggression.

I stand over them yelling, "Stop! Coyote! Rascal! Stop!" They don't obey. Meanwhile, Crazy Cat is running wild circles and every hair on his body stands tall. Leo comes running down the stairs, moves right between them and reaches down to grab both dogs by the collar. He holds them tight while directing me to grab Coyote, which I do. Rascal is still going nuts as Leo basically drags her to the bathroom and shuts the door.

My cell starts ringing.

"Holy shit!" we both say.

"Shit!" I look at my phone and see that it is the work call I was expecting and that my hand and phone are both wet with latte. "Shit!" I say again. I wipe them both on my shirt, answer the phone and go into work mode. Leo sees this and goes into soothe-the-creatures mode. I move toward my office, passing the kitchen that forgot I was coming home and the bathroom that is barking, and close the door. By the time I emerge I have completely switched hats. I forget to hug Leo, I have forgotten about my bag in the car and that the trunk is open, I barely remember that I have sisters. I need to make coffee, that's all I know. I'm going to be up all night. Fourteen frames with crowd scenes. The ad is for an antidepressant and this person feels so alone in all these crowds. Until he doesn't. By the end of the thirty-second spot, he's cheering, louder than anyone else in the stadium. "It's a remarkable comeback!" the announcer says.

Before I settle back down to work, I remember that I have two sons, one of whom is here, still petting Coyote. We share a big hug and I tell him I love him and he knows that I am Going Into Surgery now. That's what we call it. It means Mom is working hard to pay the bills, she will not be making dinner, do not ask her for anything. He understands.

But first, nature calls and I cannot ignore it. I open the door to the bathroom and Rascal comes barreling out, ready to destroy and devour any other four-legged creature that she can grab hold of.

Part Two

❧〰❧

Sunnyside Hell

Marybeth from Sunnyside calls to tell me that Ginny was up crying all night and she's refusing breakfast. Rascal was up crying all night, too. I know this because I was up all night, drawing. Leo put her bed down in the bathroom before he went up, and around 4:00 a.m., when I was making my third pot of coffee, she finally quieted down. Coyote and Crazy Cat slept upstairs and I am afraid they will never come downstairs again.

My art director told me she wants me to go back into the boards to brighten up the pills, make them "really pop." She also wants me to go into all the "happy" frames and lessen the lines on the face of the previously depressed man. So, not only does the pill help make you feel better, but it also provides some sort of Botox. I could use one of those pills right now. I've got the caffeine shakes, so I pour just a little bitta Baileys into my mug to steady the hand, then set an alarm to give myself time to brush my teeth before the high school full team support meeting. Screw showering, I'll put my cute cap on.

Marybeth had warned me that the first week or so could be rough. "There is an adjustment period," she said with a little laugh. "But after a while, they all settle in." Theresa told me that her mother was so angry when she moved her into her retirement home that she threatened to write her out of her will. "Then it was heaven on earth," Theresa said.

"She played bridge and got her hair done and flirted with the male residents!" I imagine Ginny flirting with bright yellow sweater man.

"Day one of Sunnyside Summer Camp," I say to Leo before he heads out to school.

"Number one, it's spring," he says. "Number two, you're delusional." He understands that I did what I had to do and he will visit her today after school. He's already out the door when I call back, "See you at the principal's office!"

Pulling into one of the visitor's spots at the high school, I note that the car next to mine looks exactly like our old Subaru, right down to the rear left bumper dent. It's actually about eight years old, our better car. I agreed that Bill could have that one as he supposedly needs it for interviews, and it makes a better impression than the truly old Honda Odyssey, which still has fruit rolls embedded into the backseats. Didn't seem fair considering he was the one that, against my approval, gave them the fruit rolls, but he allowed me to keep the house, the creatures, and the still-at-home kid so we're even, I guess. We're trying to be mature about the whole thing.

I have to wait at the sign-in window. A tall man in an ill-fitting suit is arguing with the receptionist lady. He's got a monk's bald spot. She's explaining to him that his son is not allowed to use his phone in class, which is probably why he hasn't responded to his father's texts. They have notified him now and he on his way. "Time is of the essence," the man says, "I've got a meeting to get to . . . a pretty important meeting . . ." He kind of chuckles as he does a little drumroll on the windowsill. Of course. The man is Bill.

"Bill?" I say.

He turns around, exasperated, and upon seeing me, looks caught.

"What are you doing here?" we say in unison.

The receptionist looks up at me in recognition and nods.

"I have an appointment," I say to her.

"Oh, I know," she says. "Come on in." And she buzzes the door for me to enter.

"Wait. What?" Bill says.

I'm standing there, holding the door open, looking back at him in that horrible suit. He's usually a jeans and T-shirt guy. "What's with the suit, Bill? Last time I saw you in that someone had died."

"A meeting. A business opportunity," he says. "Where are you going?"

"I have an appointment."

"Come on in!" the receptionist calls.

"With who? I'm taking the kid to lunch!"

"No, you're not," I say. Quite calmly, I might add.

Leo appears in the hallway and sees us there. "Shit," he says.

So, Bill didn't know about the meeting with the principal and Leo's whole team because neither Leo nor I had told him. He rarely went to parent-teacher conferences in all the years raising the boys, so why now? Leo had accepted a lunch date with Bill because let's face it, the kid still needs his father and he says yes when he gets an invitation, and apparently, he forgot that we had the meeting with the principal and the whole team. Until now.

Fifteen minutes later we are all sitting with the principal and the team and Bill is finally letting go of the fact that he wasn't invited. He's now nodding his head vigorously that Leo needs to finish his homework, he's shaking it hard that Leo was caught selling pot brownies in the school library. "Pot brownies?" I say in dismay. "Where on earth did you get the pot, Leo?" Leo looks uncomfortably over toward Bill and Bill looks intently at his cuticles. I continue, "I would like their name please. I mean, whoever it is, is selling or—I dunno—giving marijuana to an underage kid in a state that doesn't allow legal sale even to adults! What kind of a person would do that?" Now Bill sinks deeper into his chair and tries to go invisible.

The meeting ends with handshakes all around and a positive message that we all believe in Leo and will do all that we can to support him. His Intro to Poetry teacher tells me I smell like something warm and then lights up when she says, "Like Baileys!" Leo still wants to go to lunch with Bill but Bill has to get to that business meeting. Here's hoping it goes better than that school meeting just did. His pot belly is hanging out over his belt.

I try to imagine his résumé. How does one fluff up nothing? Did he include the ten straight years of bartending that he did over twenty years ago in downtown Manhattan? Because that's the steadiest gig he's ever had. After baby Graham came along and we moved out of the city, it was more . . . sporadic. Sure, he had some house contracting gigs. He's a good cabinet maker and lays a mean floor. He also did some one-on-one teaching at the local music school. That was off and on for three years but then he said it was sucking the musician out of him so he quit. A music gig here and there brought in a couple thousand a year, some occasional gigs at a friend's production studio. There was that time, back when the boys were small, when he decided to promote other musicians, he created his own website and went to several shows a week, seeking talent. And then his latest incarnation: substitute teacher. Initially he enjoyed going to school and "shooting the shit" with the kids, particularly high school ones, he especially enjoyed trying his hand at US History. But then he said that their apathy was so bad that he couldn't take it anymore. Maybe the apathy was his? Really, I think this was his convenient excuse when the schools stopped calling him after they discovered that he was offering the kids stuff that wasn't on the curriculum . . .

Ah, the suit. The dopey drumroll for the receptionist lady. He was nervous, that's why. He gets tense in situations that call for cool nerves. He used to say it made his performances more *authentic*. But honestly, it just made watching him uncomfortable. Which is why, I believe, he didn't get a lot of gigs. Even though he's really talented. He is. He had so wanted to make it as a musician, to go solo and have his own record label. I could see that he wasn't meant to be onstage. He was amazing in the studio, though, and a pretty great songwriter. I really wanted him to have success, but I felt his goals didn't match his talents. He sensed this of course and didn't appreciate what he saw as my lack of faith.

Honestly, seeing him in that suit makes me kind of sad, and not just because it takes me back to the funerals he wore it to and it accentuates his lack of a waist. He must have put on thirty pounds since my mom died just four years ago. But even then, he wasn't a suit guy. When we first met, when I went to check out the room for rent in his Lower East Side railroad apartment, he was wearing leather pants. He looked hot. I remember wondering if moving in with him would be playing with fire. He wore those same leather pants every day for years. When they started to stink, he sprayed them with Calvin Klein cologne and hung them out on the fire escape to dry. Some might have found that disgusting, but to me they smelled good. They looked good. I shiver at the thought of him wearing those things now.

≈

And tonight, the aforementioned ceremony at Theresa's, next door. We put it off one night due to the antidepressant gig. Theresa, the self-described "Irish lass with a butter cream ass," is my role model for getting in touch with my post-marriage passion and sexuality. She is getting me tipsy on Prosecco and popcorn and is now performing a fire-pit lit belly dance. Next, she pulls out sparklers and tells me to light mine on the fire and do my own fire dance, which I do. Soon, we are throwing unpopped corns into the fire and toasting marshmallows. Finally, she tells me to pull out my phone and she demands that I pull up the Match app.

"Really?" I say. "I'm not sure that now is the time for that."

"Are you kidding?" she says. "Now is especially the time!"

I tell her I'd rather have more Prosecco. I tell her I'd rather watch her belly roll. I tell her I'd rather watch my belly roll and I pull up my sweater and try rolling. I don't have that particular muscle group, I guess.

She starts filming me so I stop.

"Seriously," she says, "we could put this on your profile!"

"I'm not," I say. "It's just . . ."

"Don't tell me you're waiting to hear from Mr. X?" she says.

"I'm fine," I say. "I'm an independent woman," I say. I think about Ginny, laying there on the street.

"Well, that's good because I don't think the bloke is worth waiting for. And that's my pound's worth."

This is ouchy but I pretend it isn't. For whatever reason, Theresa has never been a fan of Mr. X. She never met him, she doesn't know what he's like with me. What I'm like with him. She pulls out her phone to show me her Match app. She shows me guys within a five-mile radius and I see at least three I know.

"No, thank you," I say. She expands to thirty miles. She shows me guys she's liked that haven't liked her back and guys who have liked her that she hasn't liked back. "Okay, seriously," I say, "that's enough." I'm laughing but I mean it. The whole thing makes me sick to the pit.

"You're no fun, Maggie," she says. "I mean, you, you are fun, but you are having no fun."

"They're just lonely guys," I say, "horny guys putting out their best faces and pecs . . ."

"And lonely ladies," she says. And she poses with her hand on her forehead tragically. "Actually, it's an ego boost. Gets your body parts flowing."

"Really? Those guys that didn't like you back. That doesn't hurt your feelings?"

"I've rejected many more, believe me."

I know for a fact that she's been on it for over a year and she's gone on many ridiculous dates and only one guy turned into an actual thing before it turned into nothing, so she's not really selling me on it.

"I'd rather meet someone organically," I say.

"Working from home?"

"I work in the city occasionally, I go places," I say.

"Like the nursing home? Oooo . . . an inheritance!"

"That's not the only place I go," I say in my own defense. "I go other places . . . like . . . the store."

Theresa lets out a guffaw.

Okay, so I don't go many places, and this is depressing. I would like to go to gallery openings, like Theresa, concerts, like Bill. I would like to go surfing, like my sister Bets. I will remain positive. "I'm sure some hot guys have feeble mothers," I say.

"Okay, well good luck with that. And meanwhile, I'll be meeting with Omar for coffee tomorrow . . . Richard for a drink tomorrow night . . ."

She's showing me their pictures. "Cute," I say.

"Look at this guy," she says, holding up the phone close enough for me to kiss it.

"Malick," I say.

She takes the phone back and reads. "Grad degree from Princeton, born in Senegal, lawyer for good causes . . ."

"It doesn't say that," I say, as I try to grab the phone.

"Loves to travel, hike with dog . . ."

"Sounds like a dream," I say. "And when are you having tea with Malick?"

"I'm not," Theresa says. She's pouring us each a refill. "He's intimidated by redheads. I remind him too much of Jessica Chastain, who he used to date."

"Jessica Chastain?" I say. "The actress? What is this guy doing on Match?"

"I'm kidding, you goof. He didn't like me back. But I'm sure he has his reasons. Anyway, he sounds like a good match for you. I'm telling you, you should get on Match right now and send him a wink! Maggie and Malick! Sounds cute, doesn't it?"

A wave washes over me—wouldn't it be refreshing to have a guy like that? A guy who really has his act together . . . Like. Mr. X . . . No, this Match thing is not my thing.

We've finished off the bottle and it's time for me to go home and to bed. "Sweet dreams," Theresa says suggestively.

"Please, Theresa," I say, "he's just a picture."

Though I do lie in bed trying to think about him.

And then my thoughts turn back to Mr. X. Mr. X is Xavier, the man with whom I had the most intense sex, the man I fucked up my marriage for. The man that I believe wanted me as strongly as I wanted him and did all he could to make it happen that work week at the Soho Grand. We'd had inappropriate exchanges. He told me that he liked the way I wore Converse with high-waisted pants, that a woman who knew how to wear Converse knew a thing or two. He told me that just because he wasn't interested in getting involved with a married woman didn't mean he wasn't interested in a married woman. He emphasized the "a." He started calling me Frederick, which is my last name, my maiden name. And I started calling him Mr. X.

He was a top exec of a trendy ad agency, and he had hired me for a couple of in-person ad pitches, the kind where I stand before the whole creative team and draw storyboards as they throw ideas at me. I'm good on my feet and I impressed him. He impressed me, too, in his classic, fitted suits, his tortoiseshell glasses. Honestly, before I met him, I had never imagined myself with a man in a suit. But then I started to imagine myself with that man in that suit. And then I started to imagine myself with him without the suit. He made drawing ads for a new bottled water seem vital and exciting. He had access to the penthouse suite of the Soho Grand where our work sessions were taking place. He liked that I had sons, he liked that I had a "real life" outside the city. He said it was "too bad" I was married, he wished I was "available" . . . I close my eyes. Oh, Xavier, Xavier . . . Mr. X . . . indeed . . . And now, I fall sadly to sleep.

ᐸᘿᐳ

Rascal and I are sitting in a cozy corner of the plush living room of Sunnyside. We're here for Rascal's interview and I am holding tight to the leash. It's a miracle I got her here. It took many, many treats. So far, the interview is going well. It needs to go well, because Ginny has refused to see me, speak to the nurses, or start physical therapy until she sees Rascal.

Paulina, the recreation coordinator, is doing most of the talking. She is extremely animated, and I am hoping that none of her animations will set off our currently subdued canine.

She tells me that she grew up in this neighborhood and dreamed to someday work in this building. "It's like a castle," she tells me, "and now I get to work here!" She makes a wide pose like a lady on a game show, presenting the prize. Rascal is keeping a close eye.

"I decorate for all the holidays, even not-so-famous ones like National Dog Day, International Rainbow Day . . . My most favorite thing is to sit in a circle with the residents and have them tell stories about their childhoods or when they had children and how they celebrated holidays." I imagine Ginny telling them all how we used to sneak under the Christmas tree to peek . . . "I put on music and we dance!" she says, and she does a little jig right there in her chair. Under Rascal's breath, I hear a low rumbling . . .

"Oh, and parties," she says. For every major holiday, they have a party for the residents and their families and the staff and their families. Everybody comes. Her own children would never miss it. Her grandchildren love to come.

"Grandchildren?" I say. I mean, she can't be over fifty.

"Oh, yes, I have five! Three children!" she says, clapping for each number. Rascal looks up at her hands, ears perked. "One husband," she says with a final clap, "a police officer." This Paulina is the proudest and happiest person I have ever met.

"And Rascal?" I say.

"Oh, she's a very gentle dog," Paulina says. "She reminds me of my most shy puppy."

"Oh?" I say. "And how many dogs do you have?"

"Seven!" she says, clapping it out. "All rescues."

Paulina and I take Rascal to Ginny's room. Or shall I say, Paulina does. She has taken her by the leash and Rascal just gallops along beside her. When we get to the door, Paulina says in a happy singsong, "Gin . . . ny . . . You have a visitorrr . . ." I open the door and Rascal trots right in.

Ginny is moved to tears as Rascal sniffs around. There are many new scents to smell, but the strongest one is antiseptic. I give Ginny a dog treat to give to Rascal and this puts the pup in close proximity to her dear love's face. She grabs the treat and plops down, right there in the middle of the small room. When I try to budge her gently with my foot so that Paulina and I can sit down, she growls. Paulina goes into stiff attention.

Ginny says, "She never does that."

I say, "No, that's very unusual."

Paulina relaxes her shoulders and says, "Oh, she is probably just excited to see you, Ms. Frederick."

"Ginny," I say, "Paulina has given us permission to let Rascal visit. Isn't that nice?"

Paulina nods angelically.

"Finally," Ginny says, "someone here I can trust."

After Paulina goes, I tell Ginny that Danielle, the social worker, is also very nice and she will be around to talk with her tomorrow. I tell her that everyone is very nice here and it's understandable that she is feeling all sorts of emotions but that soon, she will adjust, and everything will be okay. I suggest to her that she talk to the nurses as they are there to help her.

"They don't speak English," she says. "Not very . . ." She taps on her brain.

"Ginny, you know that's not true," I say. "Some of them have accents." When did my sister turn into such an ignorant, arrogant, high-maintenance diva?

"Vampires don't speak English." She calls them vampires because they come in to check her blood glucose levels in the middle of the night and this involves a prick to the finger. "It's cold as hell here," she continues. "My hands are ice cubes. Pretty soon they'll fall off."

"Pet Rascal, she'll warm them up," I say.

"Rascal, come here," Ginny says.

Rascal doesn't budge.

"Try it in a sweeter voice," I say.

"Rascal, come here," Ginny says in her usual monotone. Rascal doesn't move. "She doesn't listen," Ginny says.

I demonstrate. "Rascal, come here," I say in my lighter tone. I put out my hand to beckon her. Rascal pushes herself up to come to me. "See?" I say.

"She likes you better now," Ginny says.

"It's only been two days, Ginny. She understands that you are here until you get better and then she'll be with you again. She's so excited that she can come visit you."

"I have a plan," Ginny says. "Don't worry."

"You have a plan? What's your plan?" ... Ginny says stuff like this and leaves me hanging. I'm not going to beg. So, "They say you won't let them clean your private parts," I say.

"That's why they're called privates."

"You need to let them do that. You don't want to get another rash. They say your wound looks a little better, so that's good. And tomorrow you'll start working with Jorge, the physical therapist."

"Spelled with a 'J,'" Ginny says.

"Spanish spelling," I say, admiring my sister's expertise.

"They're in America," she says.

"I'm going to come watch you walk tomorrow, okay? I want to see you in action."

"They won't let me go to the bathroom without spying on me."

"They want to make sure you don't fall."

"When I close the door, they open it."

"I can ask them about that," I say. "Have you been watching TV?"

"It's acting weird and stopped speaking English. Just like everyone here."

Is my sister a fricking racist? "Where's the remote?" She hands it to me. It's sticky. "Let me try," I say. I point it to the TV and press various buttons. Something comes on but it's fuzzy in both picture and sound. "Must be the cable," I say. "I'll ask them." I add this to my list. "Ginny, you know you can ask them things yourself, right? You do have a voice."

Nothing, and then, "Bring Rascal." She reaches down and pats Rascal twice on the snout. "Tomorrow," she says. "With Jorge."

"Not tomorrow," I say. "I think she might be a distraction." And then I blurt out, "We have to hook Rascal up to the wall. She's been aggressive."

"It's New York," Ginny shrugs.

It's true. Rascal is now hooked up to a wall between the living room and the dining room. It was Leo's idea. I am not blaming Leo; I am thanking Leo. Previous to this, I was holding on to Rascal's leash while on the phone with the vet asking if she knew anyplace, anyone who could temporarily take a troubled dog. I was spending more time keeping Rascal away from Coyote and Crazy Cat than I was soothing them.

But then Leo ran into town to the hardware store and when he returned, he surprised me with a thick clip that screwed into the wall. And then he surprised Rascal by hooking her leash into the clip. Now Rascal's fast attacks are halted. She's learned she has a ten-foot radius in which to growl and rest. Coyote and Crazy Cat are learning the perimeters.

"Okay, we're going to go now. I need to make dinner. And then I have work."

"At night?"

"Yup." It's gonna be another late one. I'm too old for this.

"Dog food?"

I drew a dog food commercial once. Ginny is ever hopeful I'll do another. "I don't even know what the product is. They're briefing me in an hour."

"Get samples," Ginny says, as she always does.

"Okay," I say. "Do you want to say goodbye to Rascal?"

I bring Rascal over to Ginny's face, laying there sideways in the bed. Ginny is holding Binky Baby up to her face, so it's two faces looking out. "I've gotta plan, Rascal, don't worry. We're gonna get out of this hell hole."

As difficult as she is, I will be patient. I will give her the kind of love and attention that she so desperately needs. As if she were my own child. By the end of the summer, she'll be walking, and we'll be hanging at the park with our old pups. People will see us there and they will see that I am nurturing. The boys will appreciate my loyalty. They will admire my tenacity, my grace, my strength. They will both see a way to forgive me.

❧

At three o'clock in the morning I get an email from my rep who says they like what I'm doing, and in the morning, they will send more boards. This is nice but what the fuck? I still have at least two hours of drawing ahead before I can even consider going to bed. Also, since when are art directors looking at my work in the middle of the night? Art directors sleep like normal people.

Next, a text. From Mr. X. My insides somersault. Mr. X, the man with whom I had my frantic fling. *I told them you were good. Happy Anniversary.* I read it and then I read it again and then again. I don't have time for this shit or this elation or whatever it is.

Another text, which includes a screenshot from an email that he apparently received. It's from the Soho Grand Hotel: *Dear Mr. and Ms. . . . ,*

In honor of your anniversary, we at the Soho Grand are pleased to offer you a ten per-cent discount on your next stay. A bottle of champagne awaits your return.

Is he asking me to join him there again? Is he coming to New York? Is he acknowledging that what we shared and did was, in fact, meaningful and that he's sorry he moved to London so soon after I told him that Bill moved out?

I can't think about this. I have to draw this arm. This arm that is lifting this feather that is lifting a car. It's a high-concept commercial. But now I'm recalling his arm, when he reached past me so publicly while I was drawing those boards for his campaign pitch in the private meeting room of the Soho Grand. Yes, he reached past me to grab his coffee from the side table. Though he could have walked around. His jacket brushed the back of my sweater and I felt my pits immediately go hot.

I have to draw this flexed calf muscle, of the woman who is in the car, pushing the gas down hard. Because the car is weightless and she is taking off for space. Which is how I felt when he lifted me, swept me up really, off my feet, before carrying me into his penthouse suite, which I realize now was the honeymoon suite. Or something. He must have told them it was an anniversary before he checked in, before he and I had even kissed, before I had given him even a hint at Go. Because when he placed me down on the bed, he looked up to discover a bottle of cham-pagne that now, it seems, wasn't a surprise at all.

I wonder why he sent me this. At three a.m. Eastern Standard Time. Ah, he's in London, where it's eight a.m. Which is why he received this email from the Soho Grand. Because it was a year ago today, whatever day this is. So was he thinking of me and that night? Or had the email prompted him? He recommended me for this job. Oh, of course, he's the chief creative officer there. Yes, yes, the London office handles this light and fast-moving car. He probably drives one.

I'm no longer married. I want to write this back. *More available now*, I think to say. *I'm a sexy single lady*, I know not to write. *When you're back in town, let's celebrate*, I actually type. But no, I erase that fast. I simply write *Thank you*. Let him wonder what I'm thanking him for. Let him think about my ass and how it looked in that mirror on the opposite wall of that bed as I draw these wheels, slick with speed, wet with power.

ॐ

One week into Ginny's stay, I have come up with a plan to bring Ginny back to life. She wasn't into the paper and markers I brought her last week, so I decided she needed something more challenging, and oh my goodness, I discover a mini-surfboard design craft kit! I had no idea that something like this would even exist. Had it sent Express. Six-inch tall wooden pre-cut surfboards, a mini–paint set, four paint brushes, and colored yarn. The surfboards each have a hole at the wide end, so you just paint, let 'em dry, thread, and hang. Pretty soon there will be a mini-surfboard hanging around every resident's neck. They'll all be hangin' ten!

As I check in, I share my excitement with Marybeth and Roger at the front desk. I tell them that my goal is to help Ginny make a surfboard necklace for each of the residents. "Won't that be fun?" I say. Paulina passes by and says we cannot give them to the residents to wear as necklaces as they might accidentally hang themselves.

I present them to Ginny. "There'll be a surfboard hanging outside the door of every resident's room," I say. "They'll all be hangin' ten!"

Ginny will not even touch the box. When I open it to show her the pieces, she looks the other way. "Fine, Ginny," I say. "I'll leave this here for whenever you get inspiration."

She's mad at me because I didn't bring Rascal. I'm mad at her because she's refusing to walk to the dining room.

"Yellow legal pad," Ginny says.

"What about it?" I ask.

"Told them to get me one but nobody listens."

"You gonna practice your handwriting?"

"Letter to my lawyer," she says.

I am bored with this back and forth today, so I leave before it goes any further, purposefully forgetting to remind Roger in reception about the requested yellow legal pad.

Stop by Starbucks between Sunnyside and my place. I need a double strong whatever. As I reach for the door, I see Bill, sitting there by the window. Of course he is, always meeting a friend for coffee by day, beer by night. He's laughing. I don't care to see him right now but there he is, blocking my way to my latte. I walk in and ignore him. I go straight to the end of the line and start perusing the prepackaged snacks and the latest drink creations. I try to recall the last time I grabbed a chat and a drink with anyone in any public place. I easily recall the many times over the years that he'd call back over his shoulder on his way out the door, "Off for a brew, Maggie-Do!" That sweet nickname had seamlessly turned into a knife. Like actually doing things was so pedestrian, predictable.

I hear him laugh again. Did he really not see me enter? Who is this joker? After I place my order, I allow my eyes to wander over there, it is the window after all. His companion is not one of his middle-aged cronies, but a woman. A long-legged, long-silver-haired kind of woman. She must be the one Theresa told me about. She ran into them a couple of weeks ago at a gallery in Peekskill. Without staring, I assess that she is wearing a fitted green sweater, tan leather-looking jeans, bare feet. Her bare feet are crossed and resting on Bill's feet. Her empty sandals sit there on the floor between them.

I feel a sick sensation in my gut. Like maybe a small person punched me there. I look down to see my Converse-wearing feet. The barista calls my name and I look back toward Bill to see if he looks up. He doesn't. He's too engrossed. He's leaning back in his chair, looking at her intently. He laughs again.

I'm going to have to go by them. He's so captivated, if I move swiftly, it will work. I reach down to pick up my drink and my nosh and over my shoulder I see something tall and treelike passing me. She's gone to the end of the line. I turn to make my getaway and his eyes, which were following her, jump to me. I nod and head for the door. I don't need to stop at his table and chitchat, not now. He gets up to get the door for me.

"Not even hello?" he says.

"Hello," I say.

"How's Ginny?" he says.

"Ginny," I say. This is odd. I feel like we're on the basketball court and he's blocking me.

"How'd Leo do on his test?"

"Ask him," I say.

"Graham tells me he's coming this weekend."

"Cool," I say.

"Friday night?" he says.

"That's when he's coming?"

"Can I have them then? You get Saturday."

"Oh, yeah, sure. No problem," I say. He's still holding the door, letting other people go in and out around us. Why won't he just let me go? Does he want to make sure that I witness his happiness?

"Cool," he says. "Thanks, Maggie."

I need to get out of here. But first, as I've been in suspense, "Your 'business opportunity'?"

And just on cue, a vision in green appears, holding up a large cupcake. "Happy new job to you, happy new job to you," she sings. He kind of laughs and she says, "You can give up your doorman position now. You have a job!"

I let out a "ha!"

He says, "Yeah, I got it."

I don't say anything, I'm just kind of taking this in, the fact that he's got a job and a very beautiful woman is now sitting at the table behind him, unwrapping a frosted cupcake.

"The Griff Hunter thing, the insurance," he says. He looks sheepish when he says this and for good reason. Because Griff Hunter, his old college friend, former Punk Lite band member, and Best Man at our wedding, has been offering to hook him up with his agency for the past ten years and for the past ten years I have been encouraging Bill to follow up on this lead. He said that in terms of sexiness, insurance rep was up there with accountant and mortician, and I said that *entertainment* insurance was very sexy, especially as it came with a paycheck. They represent rock bands and concert venues. And now he has the job.

And behind him the simply stunning older woman is tracing the frosting of the cupcake with her tongue. I don't mean she's "pretty" or that "she's aged well," I mean she's stunning. Like, she was probably beautiful when she was younger and now, she's stunning. She's the kind of woman that I hope to look like someday, wonder what it's like to look like on any day.

"Yeah, I just got the email, the official offer," he says.

"Are you going to share this with me, or am I going to have to eat it all by myself?" the stunning woman says. Even her voice is sensuous. Perhaps she is a woodland nymph. She's not even looking at me, she thinks he's just being a good Samaritan, holding the door.

"Great," I say. "Congrats. You better go . . . eat . . . that."

He returns to the table and her dangly leaf earrings. She looks at me and smiles warmly, the way a stunning woman acknowledges a lesser one, and I hear him say, "This is Maggie."

"Maggie?" she says. "Oh, Maggie!" Like, Oh, That Maggie! as she smiles even wider.

I look down to see she has put out her hand for me to shake, take, kiss? I don't. I simply say, "What nice teeth you have," and try to smile my lesser smile back. As I bolt, I realize that that is exactly what Little

Red Riding Hood says to the wolf in Grandmother's clothing and this makes me laugh.

Just half a mile down the road, on the ten-minute drive home, I get pulled over for speeding.

❧

Graham does come home for the weekend and I do get them Saturday night. He's down. Leo told me his girlfriend broke up with him. Girlfriend? Is she the one whose family lives in Geneva? Is she the one he was FaceTiming all New Year's Eve? Graham's dated—if that's the word—lots of girls. He never tells me their names. He's always said that he would when he met one that was worthy of meeting me. And now he tells me that he thought she was the one. I guess she didn't agree. When I ask her name, he says, "History."

I make tarragon pepper lamb chops because this is my college boy's favorite. I make chocolate coconut cake because this is everyone's favorite—it was my go-to for almost every single birthday party. I am savoring them. My boys. I am taking in every little word they say, every thoughtful gesture, every silly quirk. Every burp, every fart joke, every fart.

I've painted my boys. I've done a whole bunch of drawings and sketches, some of which are studies for paintings that I intend to paint someday. In the one painting I've completed, they are small boys, wearing shorts and T-shirts, meeting at their crisscrossed knobby knees. They are facing one another in a cozy red cave. Graham, in his famous baseball cap, Leo, in his safari hat. The cave is my heart.

When I was younger, in college, then for a few years in the city, I was an artist. I produced. I stayed up all night getting messy and filling canvases. I had promise. I was even featured in a funky indie mag as an artist to watch. Those were the days when Bill and I met and mated like bonobos, as he liked to say. To Bono. U2, Roxy Music, the Pretenders.

I didn't know then what I know now. That sitting across from my fully grown sons would be so thrilling. That sitting here with Coyote at our feet and Crazy Cat on my lap, I'd feel almost complete. Nor could I have known that when they'd finished their last bites of cake, the moment after they've both kissed me on the forehead goodnight, off to a late-night concert in Tarrytown with their father—who am I to say no? it's an opportunity—I would feel such utter remorse for all of my awful deeds, that I would feel responsible for the breaking up of what was once my family, that I would feel a deep inconsolable loneliness.

The next morning, they are raving about Bill's new car. They say it came with his new job. I highly doubt this. Oh? Like the time he said he got a great deal on a Montauk beach time-share and then I discovered ten grand less in our savings account? Or the time he decided to collect vintage motorcycles as an "investment"? I highly doubt that Rock Insurance Performance Coverage provided him with a bright blue Camaro to make his rounds. But I do not tell them this. I must tread lightly. They tell me his girlfriend is a triathlete. They're not being mean, they're simply sharing.

I recall that dark night when we told them we were going to divorce. I thought telling them would be a relief. I thought they were grown enough to understand. Graham was twenty and Leo was sixteen. For sure they'd seen all the years I put up with Bill's malaise, his bitterness, lack of employment. I thought they'd celebrate my release. He let it slip that I'd cheated. So remiss. "A slip of passion," he told me later. "Though nothing near your slip," he also said. This worked in his favor of course. They were outraged, enraged. Graham didn't talk to me for a month and Leo threatened to move out with his dad.

I learned a hard lesson that night. My boys can ignore so very many things—curfews, dirty dishes, even Mom and Dad's fights—but betrayal? Oh no. Betrayal is hard to dismiss.

ॐ

Three months have passed, and summer has finally come to Summer Camp. Ginny's wounds have healed, but she does the bare minimum of walking. We've learned that the reason she's always cold and her hands feel like icebergs is because of her poor circulation, a symptom of her diabetes, so I bought her extra blankets, which I wash weekly.

I haven't heard from Mr. X, nor have I gone on Match, and I ask the boys about their father's girlfriend only very rarely. Because Ginny's TV continues to be ornery, I have just purchased her a smaller, handheld device for watching movies. I have purchased it with her money, and I will tell her this. I have also bought her several pairs of purple gloves. The gloves have pro-text technology.

"I don't even have an iPad," Leo says.

"Neither do I," I respond.

Graham is back home for the summer. He got an internship in the city. And now he's setting up the iPad for Easy-as-123 use.

"I thought they were designed to be easy," Leo says.

"This is Ginny we're talking about," Graham says.

"Be nice," I say.

"You think I'm not being nice?" Graham says, looking up at me.

"Oh, right, of course you're nice. You're very nice, Graham-y Pants."

He shoots me the appropriate look for a twenty-one-year-old to his mother—or anyone for that matter—for calling him that.

He comes with Rascal and me to visit Ginny. He thinks Sunnyside has Horror Movie Potential. "The elevator's locked unless you have the code? An alarm goes off if the door to the staircase opens? And that guy who comes in to lead them in karaoke? He's e-vil . . ."

I ask him to stop and tell him it is a very nice place.

Ginny is thrilled to see him, and she puts on a pair of purples right away. "How's college?" she asks.

"It's good," Graham says. "Halfway through."

"What's your job?"

"I'm interning at one of the top financial firms in New York and I expect to get a job offer for after I graduate by the end of the summer." Cocky, I think.

Ginny asks him if he has a girlfriend and I try not to lean in too far for his answer.

"A few," he says. Which is interesting.

"Use protection," Ginny says. The expert.

Graham smiles and says, "I do! We all do!" How many of them are there, I wonder? Maybe that's why the girlfriend named History broke up with him?

Ginny told me to use protection once. Protection for my period. "You should start wearing pads now," Ginny said to me. "You don't want to get your minstrel period and leave a big red puddle on the chair." I was only ten! She was getting teased again even in her special school for walking around with a big stain on her crotch. Betsy, who was home from college, pulled us both into her bedroom. "Gin-Gin," she advised, "you've gotta start wearing tampons, pads are so yesterday." "I'm a virgin!" Ginny protested. "That's disgusting!" "Yeah," Bets said, "but think about what it's like for everyone looking at your bloody patch. It's about protection—our protection."

Graham gives her a lesson on the iPad, shows her how to access Amazon Prime and how to order a movie and make a list of movies she wants to watch. He gives her a quick lesson in googling and searching. We don't know how much of this Ginny has taken in, but she is very appreciative. She is extremely proud of her nephews, she really loves them.

"Thank you," she says to Graham.

And "My pleasure, Aunt Ginny," Graham says.

"Let me know when you make your first million," Ginny says.

On the way out, Graham and I hug Ginny and she doesn't hug back, and I tell Rascal it's time to go and Graham tells Ginny to "hang ten."

Then, he pops his head back in and says, "Use protection." If Ginny were one to laugh, I believe she might have laughed at that.

When I get home, I get to googling our big sister, who hasn't been in touch. According to Instagram and Twitter, she's alive and well. Yep, there she is, flexing comically in front of some crazy waves. There she is, riding high on top of one. There she is, smoking a doob and exposing one boob. Tweets about freeing nipples, saving whales, legalizing mushrooms. I do know that she talks to Ginny, as Ginny likes to report.

I miss Betsy. That's the crazy thing. I miss her even while she ignores me. I don't know when that started happening. I mean, I know when her latest cold shoulder went up, but before that, I wonder, when did she start avoiding me? As a kid, I so admired her. Bets likes to be admired. In time, my admiration turned into a combination of exasperation and envy. How could she choose to be so far away from our aging parents? Didn't she want to spend more time with them? Gin-Gin? Her nephews? And what about me, Magpie? How could she have such trouble committing to anything but the waves? I'm sure she thought my choices were boring and maybe she was right and that gnawed at me, too. Oh, how wonderful to be so careless and carefree! I wished, still wish, that I could be more like that.

I dare to call her once more, to remind her that I, too, exist. I leave a stupidly friendly message.

ᥱᥴᠣᢣᥱ

A few days later, Ginny tells me she's a child predator. Not fully alarmed, I say, "What do you mean?" She says, "I put in my name and it's on the internet." I google her to see what it reveals. Her full name. Her age. Her address in Maryland. Then there's some scam where it says you can pay money to find out if a person has a criminal record and it lists all the crimes that person may have committed, and the boxes are checked next to the crimes. The boxes are checked because if you pay the money you will find out about each of these specific things. Not because Ginny is a child predator.

In the process, I see that Ginny has a significant internet presence. She has become a movie reviewer for Amazon. Yes, there is her full name and a list of many, many movies that she has watched, rated with anywhere between zero to five stars and often with comments.

Big, five stars, "Tom han so kuit."

Trainwreck, zero stars, "to sluty."

The Little Mermaid, five stars, "the best."

Love & Mercy, about Brian Wilson's (of the Beach Boys) struggle with addiction, two stars, "weerd."

Baywatch, four stars, "Zak Fron. is H.O.T."

And now her old cell phone is having trouble. Her theory is that it's because of New York. "When you bring electronics to New York," she says, "something in the wires makes them break so that you have to buy new ones and this way the state gets the sales taxes."

"Okay," I say, "well if we're going to get you a new phone in New York, I'm taking you to the Apple Store to pick it out. It's very modern, you'll feel like you're entering the future."

"With Michael J. Fox," she says.

"Right," I say. "But he won't be there."

"He has Parkinson's," Ginny says. "Everybody knows that." She asks if we can bring the dogs and I say no, we can't leave them alone in the car and she says, "No thank you."

I order her the latest model in Rose Gold. I buy her a sparkly pink cover. And now I am teaching my sister how to text. "It's a little hard at first," I explain to her, "because the letters are so small. But you'll get the hang of it." I plug in my number so she has a direct line. "Sometimes when I'm working I don't have time to answer the phone, but if you text me, I can usually answer pretty fast."

I also show her how to take pictures. I take a picture of her and send it to her. Then she takes a picture of me and sends it. I'm amazed at how I look in the picture. Like a middle-aged lady wearing glasses.

She asks me to plug in other numbers. Graham's. Leo's. I hesitate when she asks for Bill's, but I plug him in, too. I consider entering one digit off for Bets's, but I don't.

As I am making dinner, I hear a ding. It's from Ginny. A photo of a little white-haired lady with accompanying text: *nu.kit.In.Twon.* New kid in town.

Leo and I sit down to eat. This is my five minutes of quality time with him before he's out the door again. *Ding. Ding.* Another pic. This one of cute old Abraham from down the hall. Ginny told me earlier that the ambulance has come for him several times. He wears a messenger cap and vest: *he Gon. krok.enee. Minit.* He's going to croak any minute.

ع입ره

Today is Ginny's fifty-seventh birthday. I invited Bets to come celebrate and she actually called me back. There's a big event at Newport Beach this weekend for which she's the Master of Ceremonies. "So sorry," she said, but she'll be sure to call. Anyway, I have planned another surprise for Ginny. With the dietician's permission, I am allowed to bring in lunch from McDonald's and even get her a small Coke. With Paulina's permission, I can also bring Coyote. It's been four months since Rascal moved in with us and I am finally somewhat confident that I can put the dogs in the backseat together without a murder taking place. An adventure.

I let the dogs lead the way into her room. We are greeted by a *Little Mermaid* Happy Birthday balloon, a gift from the staff of Sunnyside, and the dogs go crazy. Paulina comes running to check on the scene and the quiet lady in the next room starts to scream. Paulina takes the balloon out and closes the door behind her.

Ginny is very happy. How does one know when Ginny is happy? Does she smile? Does she laugh? Does she make public declaration? Answer:

She talks a lot. She talks to the dogs and she talks to me and she even talks to the nurses and aides animatedly. She declares the dogs Best Friends Forever. "Course they are," she says. "They're cousins."

"Which kind of burger do you want?" I ask.

She picks.

Then she gives one to each of the pups who enthusiastically accept. "Party favors," she says.

I ask if she wants to take off her gloves before we eat, and she ignores me. I comment on how good she is looking now that she's eating healthily. How great it is that she's now doing steps with Jorge. "Minimal effort" is actually what he told me but it's a celebration.

The dogs have both demolished their burgers. Ginny and I have each had a few bites. Now we move on to fries. Ginny is hand-feeding them to the pups. It's all very messy. Her gloves are getting greasy. Crumbs are everywhere, including in Ginny's hair.

"Ginny," I offer, "would you like for me to take you to my hairdresser? She could give you a fresh dye job."

"I'll just do it when I get home," she says. "It's August. Summer Camp is almost over." I get busy wiping up the floor in my effort to ignore.

"Your ex sent me roses," she adds oh so casually. "Purple for passion."

"Bill?" I say. "Bill sent you . . . ?" I look over to the window where she is looking and sure enough, a beautiful bouquet. Wow. Really, Bill? I'm trying to remember the last time he gave me flowers, let alone had them delivered.

"Paulina says he's trying to make you jealous."

It was nice of him to remember her birthday and I do feel jealous.

Jorge arrives and he tells Ginny he wants to take her for a spin in her wheelchair. "Naptime," she says.

He says, "I promise you don't have to walk. The dogs want to come, too, it's a birthday parade." This guy's got Gin's number. We all go down in the elevator and he starts rolling her toward the living room.

"Where are you taking me?" she says. She thinks he's heading to the PT room, tricking her into therapy.

And then, around the corner and, Tada! Leo and Graham are there! They stand up and applaud her. Ginny is surprised. She smiles! As they bend down to hug her, I notice that their smiles are strangely strange. On the table are a couple dozen cupcakes.

And in walks Bets. She was hiding in the next room. Surprise! Ginny and I are both caught off guard and now I understand the strangeness of my sons' smiles. They were apparently caught off guard, too. Betsy fills the room with her energy, she's wearing patterned and fluorescent things, her hair is now short and hot pink.

"Happy Birthday, Gin-Gin!" she says, throwing her arms possessively around my sister, our sister.

It takes Ginny a minute, but then she says, "A surprise party."

Victory! Bets feels great that she pulled it off. Paulina and Roger are impressed. The boys are kind of sunk into the large sofa, legs spread wide, taking her in. Their grins are growing. Let's face it, Bets is a star. There's something about her that just lights up a room. Even before the hot pink hair, even before she was a surfing queen, she had it. Other Sunnyside folks weave in and out of the room, not just for cupcakes and to wish Ginny a happy one, but to catch a glimpse of the celebrity sister they didn't know she had.

"How old are you today, Ginny?" asks Bets. Does she really not know that?

"I lost count," Ginny says.

"She's fifty-seven," I say. "Fifty-seven years young."

"Oh, you are young!" the nurse says. "That's almost fifty years younger than Miss Romano!"

I wish she wouldn't point this out. I'd just assumed Ginny feels like one of the pack.

We give her gifts. I got her purple furry slippers that won't slip. Leo, a sweatshirt with a picture of Rascal on it. Graham got her a poster of a surfer in the center of a giant wave. The text says: *Live it.* And then Bets retreats into the next room and returns with a purple surfboard. It's a Moon Board of course, her latest model, complete with LED lights for surfing under the stars. Rascal growls at it, Coyote starts whining with fear, and Ginny looks pleased.

"I'm gonna put that in the Surfing Museum," she says.

"Awesome," Bets says. "Does this mean you're finally going home?" She winks at me. I don't know what the hell she is doing. When I spoke to her last week I was very clear that Ginny is not anywhere near ready to go back to Maryland. She's still in a freaking wheelchair, my sister can see that.

"She won't let me," Ginny says, nodding her head in my direction. I decide that it is Ginny's naptime and direct the boys to take her back to her room.

"Happy Birthday, big sister," I say to Ginny's frosting-covered face.

"Bets is my big sister. You're the baby," Ginny says. Binky Baby stares up at me.

"Go ahead," I say to my boys, "the dogs and I will meet you at home."

"Aunt Bets?" Leo says.

"Oh, I'd love to come," Betsy says, "but I need to fly back on the red-eye. I've got a big event this weekend for which I am the Guest of Honor. Love you, Gin-Gin," she says as she goes in for another hug. Then she turns to look up at my tall sons. "Wow, you boys are so handsome and grown-up."

"Juniors this year," Ginny says.

"Juniors? Both of you? Wowza! That's pretty crazy." Does she even re-call that Graham goes to Syracuse? Then she punches him in the arm and says, "Gooooo Orange!" Oh, I guess she does. "How's the team this year?"

"Not on the team anymore," Graham says. This is a sore spot for him and he's sorry to disappoint Bets who's so athletic. "Still shooting hoops!" he says, and mimes doing so.

"Cool, cool. And you, Leo Lion? Thinking 'bout college yet?"

I can't believe she's getting away with this, charming them so.

"Yeah, I dunno . . . still a couple years away. I might not even go . . ."

Not go? First I've heard. Probably because he's having his own doubts that he'll get in . . . I need to talk with him.

"I have one word of advice for you, my man," dear Bets says. "Cal-i-fornia."

Is she kidding me? They're enamored with her for Christ's sake, and I can see they're disappointed that she's not hanging around longer. Yup, Aunt Bets is the best. "Place your bets on Bets!" they used to say. She taught them to say it. She's the one who chucked their bedtime books in favor of pajama dance parties, until, so tired, they begged to go to sleep. She's the hero who took them to Universal and Hard Rock Cafe a few years ago over spring break. Paid for by me, of course, I flew them out there. They share big hugs and I sneak a second cupcake.

"The surfboard," Ginny says as Leo rolls her out of the room. Graham grabs it and follows behind.

After they've gone, I start to pick up the party trash. Bets sits down on the floor with her legs on either side of the dogs. She's practically in the splits. She pets them and they receive gratefully.

"Graham's going back to school next week. He was here for the summer, working downtown. We'll miss him."

"I bet, Mama," my big sis says. "I bet . . ."

It was a good day, a real surprise party, I tell myself. I should just be happy that Bets came around, how cool that she brought Gin that thing . . . But instead of expressing this, I say,

"Her room is small, there's no place for the board."

"Oh, come on," she says. "They just took it up, it'll be fine."

Her room is really small. I told her that. That board will sit in the corner until the next time I visit and then it's going to have to live at my place. What's going on with me? Why am I so . . . ? I think it's just. Well, she just drops in. None of us have seen her and we weren't prepared and . . . And it's disappointing, that's what. "So you can't even spend the night, not even just one night?"

"Wish I could," she says.

"I don't get it," I dare to say. "I thought you were the Master of Ceremonies. That's what you said on the phone."

"Yea, I am," my big sister says. She's looking at me all innocently.

"Oh, okay, well you just said you were the Guest of Honor . . ." I can't believe I'm saying this. Our sister shows up and I'm being really rude.

"Well, can't I be both, MC and . . . ?" No, I think, you can't be. It doesn't make sense. But at least I don't say this out loud. And then Bets stands up and she looks right at me. "Look," she says. "I see that you're stressed out, but don't put that on me, Magpie. You chose to bring her here, against my advice."

"What?" I say. "It was the only choice. How would she possibly have made it in Maryland with me all the way up here and you, all the way . . . out there?" Out There, I want to say again, because I am starting to realize that maybe Bets lives on another planet.

We stand there facing each other for a minute and I'm thinking about how good she looks. Bets is the picture of health! Bets looks like she'd more likely hang with college kids than the likes of me. Well, she probably does.

She goes on her phone while I'm throwing stuff away and thanking Marybeth for allowing the party. When I return, I see she has retrieved her surf-themed rollaway suitcase from the other room. It's got a dinosaur riding on a board and simply says RIDE. Really? You just flew in for this party, Big Sis?

After I put the dogs in the car, I wait with her by the entrance for her Lyft. I tell her she looks great and I congratulate her on the honoring. She tells me the boys look great and I should be really, really proud of that and to say hey to Bill. "If you talk to him," she cringe-smiles.

"I do," I say. "I will."

And then, "Look," she says, "I see it's been a lot of work. Ginny's not easy. Believe me, I know." She kind of rolls her eyes and I'm thinking, Really? How do you know? You went out west when she was thirteen, so how do you know? "But really, you've gotta get her out of that place." She's putting her thumb out toward it like she's hitching a ride. "That place smells like death."

"Only two people have died since she's been here," I say, "maybe three . . . She's getting great care here. It's a lovely place." How could she not see this?

She checks her phone. Her Lyft has turned onto the property. "She thinks she's going home," Bets says. "She told me on the phone last week. She said summer camp was over and your next road trip would be back to Maryland."

She's not ready yet, I'm thinking. She can't even walk. Can't you see that? She can't take care of herself! "She's not walking," I say. "I think she's depressed."

"Well, no wonder," she laughs.

"I wish she would take meds, but she refuses. That might help. Motivate. Maybe you could try . . . talking with her . . ."

"Look," my sister says, "it's all gonna be great. Truly. I can feel it." She's looking deep in my eyes now in the way I imagine she does to her surfers before they go out.

"Yeah," I say. "Maybe . . . I'll talk to the nursing crew here and see what they think." Because really, maybe I've completely lost perspective. It wouldn't be the first time. My biggest sister seems so sure. She's such a winner! God, she's clearly doing something right. Maybe she really does know best. Shit. I feel like such a fuckup.

The driver gets out of the car and opens the trunk. It's hitting me now that she's leaving. Why can't she just stay for one night? We could drink wine and talk about it all, there's so much to tell her and I have so many questions. I really wish she could stay.

We hug, we kiss. Bets picks up her bag and throws it in the backseat. The driver shrugs, closes the trunk, and Bets gets in the front passenger seat. So like her. The driver asks if she wants to drive, and she laughs.

"I'll let you know how that goes," I say, referring to the professional feedback.

"How what goes?" she says. "Hey," she puts her hand out the window to take mine, "she's got the surfboard now. Maybe she'll ride it back. Straight down the Hudson to the Atlantic and then just cruise down the coast!" She laughs again and I try to laugh, too.

ॐ

A week later, Roger from Sunnyside calls. "We received three boxes addressed to your sister today," he says.

"Oh? Interesting . . . ," I say. Is Bets sending her stuff?

"They're from Amazon," he says. "We received boxes for her yesterday as well."

"From Amazon?"

"Yes."

"Huh," I say. I'm in the middle of drawing a rather difficult storyboard that involves a set of dominos turning into butterflies.

"I'm sorry to bother you," says Roger. He asks if he can put me on hold for a moment as Marybeth would like to speak with me. I guess the problem is bigger than it appears?

Marybeth gets on the phone and tells me, "She is ordering food. We know this because the nurses have found wrappers and things. Residents aren't allowed to have food in their rooms unless it has been approved by the nutritionist."

"Oh, dear. We put her on Amazon Prime so she can order movies. I didn't realize she could order food, too."

"Apparently," Marybeth says.

"What has she ordered, Marybeth?" I am afraid to find out.

"Several boxes of Lorna Doone shortbread cookies, which is strange, because we give them those."

Ah yes, I recall the picture Ginny sent of two lonely cookies on a plate. *You Kall tis a SNAK???* she wrote.

". . . and Hawaiian Punch . . . and Twizzlers. At least that's what came yesterday."

"Oh dear," I say. I'm shaking my head and rolling my eyes but she can't see this.

"Dahlia, the head nurse, says her blood sugar has gone up. Your sister denies eating these things, but she can't deny the six empty cans by her bedside and the evidence in her diapers."

"Ugh," I say.

"She denies it," Marybeth says. I can hear Roger telling her something in the background. "Yes," Marybeth continues, "she says that she is not eating or drinking these things, but she has Twizzlers sticking out of her mouth as she is saying it."

"Oh dear," I say.

"It's against the rules," Marybeth says. "And when we tell her this must stop, she becomes extremely rude."

My doorbell rings and I tell her I have to go.

"Please talk with her about it," she says, sounding annoyed. With me.

I look outside to see the UPS guy jumping into his brown van. Open the door and look down to see a bright orange Shutterfly box sitting on my doorstep. I didn't order anything from Shutterfly. Are they connected to Amazon and is it possible Ginny sent me something? Curious and confused, I pull it open. Within the box is paper packaging that protects . . . a small photo album. Hm. Hmm? I did not order an album and I highly doubt that Ginny had the wherewithal to put one together herself—that Shutterfly site is very challenging. I look at the box again, for the address, and I see that it is indeed addressed to this house, but the person it is addressed to is Bill. He ordered something and accidentally had it shipped to this address, his old address, the address linked to our account.

A love album to his new girlfriend? I can't look at it. I shove it back in the box. The open box is sitting there on the kitchen counter, staring at me, tempting me while I feed Coyote and Crazy Cat. Once the creatures are eating, I text Bill to let him know I'll leave it on the porch for pickup, an understandable mix-up. He responds quickly: *Oh my God. I'm sorry. I didn't expect. I can explain.*

Wait. What? I'm now afraid the contents of this album will reveal something terribly wrong. Or maybe the album will explain something that justifies the failing of our marriage? Or maybe it's a bunch of nudies of his paramour. I will not look. I reward myself with a shot of Baileys in my coffee and determine that if I can get through these last few frames, in which the final falling domino starts to sprout wings, without peeking, I will reward myself with a straight shot.

I can't help it—I have to peek. I pull the album out of its sleeve. The photo on the cover is a picture of Bill and the boys when they were little. Graham is holding an apple up close to his face. Wilkens Fruit farm. Innocent enough. In fact, strangely sweet. Slowly, I open it to see a full-page photo of our house. This house. Our home, where we raised the boys together. Let's face it; he helped a little. The house is in its springtime splendor, complete with blooming azaleas and lilacs, and oh—there's Crazy Cat in the window.

The next photo is of him and the boys and Coyote and . . . me. It's from two summers ago. Our last family trip to the Cape. My heart is pounding. I start flipping through it now. I'm shaking as I turn the pages.

Here, the four of us standing in the grand entrance of El Convento in San Juan.

Here, Bill and the boys at Mount Rainier. I took that shot.

Ha, there they are in those silly pig hats.

That Yankees game on Easter Sunday when it snowed.

It's an album of our greatest hits.

I have to call him.

Is this some kind of torture? But I say, "Is this some kind of joke?"

"What? No," Bill quietly says. "I meant to send it to me. Here. At my new address."

I don't understand what's happening to my body right now, but suddenly I have to sit down. I feel the whole of me get hot, followed by a full-blown swell in the region that can only be identified as the heart. I put my hand over it, just like the man in that heart disease prevention commercial that I drew. "I don't get it," I finally say.

"I made it for me. That's all. You weren't meant to see it. It's not that strange," he says, confirming that it is indeed strange, his creating for himself a photo album of a life he chose to leave. He might argue that he did not choose to leave, he might argue that I left first. I might argue that he left before me and so on and so on. We always argued that way. Back and forth, with neither one of us taking responsibility. "It's been a year now since we separated. I just wanted something. Something."

Something. Well, he got many things, didn't he? He got the better car, he got the record collection, he got the majority of our friends, he got the boys to look at me in a negative light. "Something," I ask. "Something, what?"

"Something to remind me . . . of that chapter of my life."

"Chapter?" I'm feeling strange now, like we're talking in a dream. Like my body is floating out to sea, while my heart is swelling on the beach.

"That chapter when I had a family," he says.

I sit down. Maybe I'm having a hot flash? I thought I was over those. I'm not sure why this is making me so upset, they're just photos, and I've seen them all before. I thought I was over him. I get quiet and I sense that he senses I am taking this in.

"Don't get all sentimental," he says, which is really just plain mean.

"I just wanted documentation before you cut me from the family photo stream."

Oh. And Ow. I know he's being reactive. I know he's playing this mean card in an attempt to exorcise his own pain. I was married to the guy for twenty-plus years—I know his tricks. And even though I know all this, it hurts. Yes, my heart is now reconnected to the rest of me, and my brain has registered that it all hurts.

"Well, thanks for the memories, Bill," I say before I hang up.

And now I can review another album of our top hits. This album I call *Bill's Asshole Review*. Yes, here he is, telling me once when I was crying about my failed career as an artist, "It's not like you were Van Gogh." And here he is asking me, on our way out for a date, in front of the sitter and the boys, "You're wearing that?" Here, shaking his head at me before I call Graham's friend's mom to apologize for the nits she was now picking out of her son's hair. Why couldn't Bill have played the loyal husband and stood by my decision to send Graham to school? It was really such a little bit of lice.

Actually, this little review is bringing on a sense of relief. I stuff the photo album back into its sleeve and paper and shove it into the box. I consider tossing it out the front door, but no, I will not do that to pictures of my babies. I gently place it on the ledge outside the door for him to pick up.

Damn, I have to get back to those butterflies with domino dots on their wings. Shit, I'm way behind schedule now. I practically forgot that I'm a woman with an actual deadline. Another cup of coffee, another shot of Baileys. "To all of it," I toast, and I'm back at the table, head down, drawing.

⟿⟾

Sunnyside calls me in for an intervention. I tell Ginny we've been called in to the principal's office. All the principals are gathering. Ginny, me,

Nurse Dahlia, Marybeth, Danielle, Jorge, Paulina, and Rascal. We're meeting in the small library for privacy. Before it's even officially begun, Ginny says, "Summer Camp is over. Take me home."

I say, "You're not ready yet. Since you've been ordering in, your blood sugar is up again. I need to have faith that you will give up sugar and take care of yourself. You still aren't walking. How would you let Rascal out?"

She says, "The nanny will."

The Sunnyside staff is just kind of listening, taking it in.

"I told you, an aide won't work in that house. And you don't even have a ramp."

"You just want to keep Rascal. You want to keep my car."

Oh yeah, the ancient Honda Odyssey is kind of a driveway car now, her CR-V so much more reliable . . . "When you can walk Rascal and drive your car, you can go back," I say.

Everyone nods encouragingly.

When Graham was little, maybe four, he begged to go swimming by himself. He begged to go in without a parent. I said, "No, Graham, you have to wait 'til Mommy is ready to come with you." Bill said, "This is how a kid learns to swim." He picked him up and threw him in. "What the hell!" I screamed. We were at a friend's pool party. People turned. Though Graham was light, he sank quite deep. Bill went into rescue mode, jumped in there in shorts and tee and pulled Graham up. Graham gasped for breath and as soon as he caught it, he screamed, "Why'd you do that?!" "Because you wanted to go swimming by yourself," Bill said. A couple people applauded, and one even shouted, "Way to go, Bill!" They didn't know that he threw Graham in. Graham cried and started hitting Bill and he said he never wanted to go swimming again. Bill looked at me and said, "See? That worked." I grabbed Graham and left Bill alone at the party, without a ride home.

Bill could be a real dick. But it did solve the problem sometimes.

Graham always waited for me to be ready to join him for a swim after that episode.

I say, "Ginny, remember when you went surfing in Malibu?" I'm thinking she might need to be reminded of the time she swallowed half the Pacific Ocean.

"Malibu was a dream come true," she says.

Marybeth clears her throat and begins the meeting. "Ginny," she says, "we are concerned about you. You are sneaking sugar, you are refusing to walk, you are refusing to take your pills."

"Not motivated," she says.

"Ginny," I say, "I think you're depressed. I wish you would try antidepressants."

"Try for a month," Nurse Dahlia says. "The doctor will prescribe something that will make you feel better."

"I don't do drugs," she says.

"Ginny," Danielle says, "do you understand that the better you take care of yourself now, the sooner you will get better and be able to be reunited with Rascal?"

"Do it for little Rascal!" Paulina cheers.

"Miss Ginny," Jorge says, "God gave you legs so you can walk! You just need to try!"

"I'll walk when I feel like it," Ginny says. "I don't need to run in a marathon. You want me to run in a marathon."

Sighs all around. I reach down to pet Rascal who growls. Ginny snickers.

Next order of business, her phone. Ginny has learned to make various sounds on it. Her favorites are the dog bark and the cat meow. She enjoys setting these off in the dining room to see how many old people turn around to look for the animal. The staff of Sunnyside told her that this was not appropriate. They explained to her that phones are not allowed in the dining room and that in order to live here, she must follow the rules. Ginny said she didn't see a sign. They explained that this is because other residents do not have phones.

They put up a sign, right over Ginny's regular table: *Cell phones are NOT permitted in the dining room.* And Ginny set off the animal sounds again, chuckling as she did it. And then they gave her "an official warning" and of course, here we are, discussing it.

"And finally, Ginny," Marybeth says, "one more thing." This is the main event. She's disguising it as an afterthought, though it's really what we came for. "We will no longer bring your Amazon boxes to your room. It is not responsible for us to allow such sugar consumption when you are here under our care to get your blood sugar under control. I have spoken with your sister and from here on, she will need to come here and open the boxes before they can be delivered to your room." We look to each other for mutual support.

Ginny takes this in and then firmly says, "I have rights."

I take a deep breath. "Of course you do, Ginny, but Sunnyside has to follow the rules. If they knowingly give you things that aren't good for your health, they are knowingly breaking the law, isn't that right, Marybeth? Aren't you under contract to take good care of your residents?"

Marybeth is looking at me as I babble on, searching for her next defense, when Ginny yells. "I want to speak to the Head Honcho!"

Everyone's eyebrows go up.

"Virginia," I say in my sternest mom voice.

"I know you don't want to scare the other residents," Marybeth says.

"Head. Honcho," she fumes.

We reason and explain and some of us plead.

"I'm used to it," she says. "Everybody lectures all the time. I just ignore it." She takes off her glasses, picks up her phone and starts tapping the way she does, with her face really close to it, her fingertips hitting it hard. "You and your dog can go now," she dismisses me with a wave to the air.

"Calling your lawyer, Ginny?" I say, trying to make light of it all, trying to dismiss her dissing me.

"I'm calling my sister Bets."

"Oh really?" I say. "Good." I stand up, throw my bag over my shoulder, and give Rascal a tug. Ginny stops tapping and looks up at me. "Go ahead. Do it. Give Bets a call. I'm sure she'll agree with you. I've treated you like shit. We've all treated you like shit. I bet she'd be more than happy to take care of you."

Ginny is blank faced. The Sunnyside team is stunned.

From the door of the Sunnyside library, I look back and say, "Rascal and I are not taking you back to your room. You'll have to politely ask one of these lovely people to help you. Or of course, you could wheel yourself there. That would be a first." And then I look at Marybeth who is looking at me wide-eyed. I look at each individual member of Team Ginny, and say, "Thank you all very much. Please do let me know when our sister Betsy makes arrangements to fly Ginny out to California."

In the parking lot, I lift Rascal into the backseat. I'm not afraid of her anymore. I turn around to see that Marybeth has followed me. She reports that Bets did indeed pick up the call, told Ginny she was busy and would have to call her back. Jorge is taking her back to her room. "This is a difficult situation," she says. "The staff appreciates that it is difficult for you, too." She offers me a hug, and I accept.

"You probably think I was lying," I say to her as we break away, "when I told you she was so sweet. But really, I was telling the truth . . ." The truth as I then believed it, I don't need to say. The harder truth is, I have fallen out of love with my sister.

She says goodbye and I get in the car and look back at Rascal. "Your mother, child, and best friend is a royal pain in the ass. Wouldn't it be nice if I could just ship her ass off to California?" Rascal just stares at me. "Of course, we'd have to ship you, too." Ahhh, I'm feeling better just thinking about it . . . And wouldn't it be nice if I could ship my ass to London and Mr. X? I feel a song coming on and I sing it on the way home.

Wouldn't it be nice if Ginny flew west?

And wouldn't it be nice if I flew east?

Wouldn't it be nice if Betsy took her?

And wouldn't it be nice if he took me?

Apparently my *Wouldn't It Be's* are powerful because once home, I get a text. Mr. X is coming to town and he wants to meet me for . . . a drink.

⌒⌒

I can't believe I'm standing here, at the downstairs bar of the Soho Grand. I'm wearing heels and a pencil dress that is flattering. I'm wearing my light leather jacket. I feel like an actual human being. I've shaved my legs. They still look pretty damn good. Got my hair cut for the first time in six months and the light layers frame my face. Theresa did my makeup despite her lack of enthusiasm for Mr. X. She penciled in my eyebrows and even accentuated a mole on my upper right cheekbone.

He's not here at seven o'clock. A barstool opens up and I sit down, order a glass of water. I don't know if he hopes to have a drink here first or just go straight to dinner, which I assume will be someplace chic in the neighborhood. Knowing him, he made reservations. He's not here at seven fifteen, so I order a white wine. Just the house stuff is fine, I say, and Yes, start a tab. First round on me.

At seven twenty-seven, I check our text stream again and then the date again and reapply my lipstick. The wine is nice and I am confident that he is being held back by some late meeting, traffic, something mundane. I'm guessing that he is as anxious as I am, having waited all this time. I'm sure he's dying to know if I am really still separated, if I'm actually free.

At seven thirty-five, I see him coming through the revolving door. I know it's seven thirty-five, because I've started texting him. I close the text exchange and shove the phone in my bag, take another sip and look over toward a younger couple sitting next to me and compliment the man's bag. In other words, I haven't been waiting and wondering this whole time. I'm not that kind of girl.

The man with the nice bag looks up and above my shoulder and I turn to be kissed by a large stem of hot pink orchids. I turn to discover Xavier, signaling "two" to the bartender. He places the orchid plant on the bar and then turns to kiss me. Not on the cheek, but on the lips. A warm and wet one. The man with the bag says, "Well, nice to see you, too!" laughs and turns back to his partner. Let's face it, the entrance, while late, is impressive. He's wearing those tortoiseshell glasses and a suit, which really isn't the norm in the ad biz these days. Most men show up to advertising pitches in baggy jeans and Star Wars T-shirts. He meets me eye to eye and says, "You look great."

Two Kir Royales later, he's procured the barstool next to me and we're facing each other, both crossing our legs. He tells me he loves London and I should come visit him there. He shares agency gossip and spills the beans that he's in town to win over a new, very exclusive client. I don't really want to tell him about the National Psoriasis Awareness campaign I've been working on, nor the adult I am caring for who has diaper rash, so I just tell him funny stories about my boys and joke about the current political climate. I'm actually racking my brain to find something interesting I might have done since I last saw him, and I can't even think of a museum exhibit to refer to. I'm trying hard to think of a good book. I turn it on him and ask what he's been reading, and it seems he's been reading a lot. He says he'll text me the titles.

We've almost finished our third bowl of bar nuts and pretzels when he asks if I'm hungry. "I am," I say, looking forward to wherever he's taking me. He asks the bartender for the menu. Wait. What . . . ? "Don't you want to go someplace?" I say.

He smiles and says, "I do, but I thought you said you were hungry."

"Oh," I say. "I just thought. We'd go out."

"I had a late lunch but am happy to accompany you wherever you would like to dine," he says.

Oh. Oh this is silly. I set expectations unrealistically high as usual. He had invited me to meet for a drink, for goodness' sake. The guy doesn't even know if I'm divorced! He hasn't asked, which is respectful. So I decide to just spit it out, to cut to the chase. "It's official," I say, bending my head to the side.

He reaches over, playing with my freshly cut face-framing layers. "Oh?" he says.

"We separated," I say. And then with a little flip of the hair, "I'm a single lady."

"Wow," he says. "Cool. I guess?"

"Yeah," I say, trying to keep it light, "it's pretty cool."

I pick a noodle shop around the corner from the Soho Grand. I'm a modern woman and do not presume he will pay. The potted orchid works well as our centerpiece. Over ramen he asks if I've been seeing other men and I tell him I've been busy. "You still like men?" he asks.

"Well, yes." Like, isn't it obvious?

"I was just wondering, 'cause I know a girl who used to like men and then she only liked women and now she likes men again."

Oh. Is this girl actually a woman? I'm wondering if he is the man she likes now.

He refills my little Saki glass and then raises his whiskey to me. "That's a big deal," he says to me. "It can't have been easy."

"Thanks," I say. His toast makes me brave so, "You know our whatever-we-want-to-call-it thing that happened . . . last year?"

He takes my right hand and traces where my wedding ring used to be. "Yeah." He smiles coyly. "I know that thing. Why do you think I wanted to meet you at the Soho Grand?" he says with puppy eyes.

I'm single now. I can do what I want. I don't have to feel guilt or shame or any of it. And the fact that we are reunited now only confirms that what we had was real, that my big self-indulgence was actually worth it. My sons will like this guy when they meet him. He said he's always wanted a son or two but he hasn't been so fortunate. Leo is at his father's tonight and Theresa said she'd pick up Coyote if I text her by eleven.

Back in the honeymoon suite at the Soho Grand, Xavier unzips my dress. He pushes the caps over my shoulders and asks me to let it drop. I do. I'm standing there in my high heels while he opens the champagne that was waiting for us. Which is romantic. I feel embarrassed about my belly flab, so I sit down on the edge of the bed and put a pillow there. In a moment I will allow him to put the pillow aside while he gently pushes me down. He pulls my panties down and he kisses me there. I pull him up to taste myself and then flip him over onto his back. "Wow," he says, "even better now." I'm not sure what he means but I tell him I am ready for him. "Not yet," he says, "I want to see you first." And he gets to pleasing me and pleasing me he does, and he says, "Nice to see you," and I say, "Nice . . . to . . . see you . . . too . . ."

This is what I've been waiting for, right? I'm not sure why, I feel strangely . . . shy? No. Not shy, it's more a self-consciousness. Like I'm watching myself from that mirror there, not totally on this side of it. He enters me then, and I realize now that it's just been . . . so . . . long and . . . maybe that's why I don't feel fully present, the way I imagined I would. Still, we reach an appropriate mutual conclusion. Afterward, I acknowledge, "It's been a long time," and he says, "Too long," and we do it all over again.

I wake at six a.m. without an alarm or the pets to wake me. It's an uneasy feeling that wakes me, not the feeling of calm or elation I might have expected. Still, it's good that I'm up as I need to catch an early train home for my nine o'clock phone briefing. It feels ridiculous putting heels on before coffee. "Wait," he whispers, "we can order up."

"No," I say, walking over to him, still reclined. "I've gotta go."

"Tonight?" he says as he reaches out again for my hand.

As if, I think. I have work. And did he forget that I commute? I have a life up the river that's a train ride away? "Can't," I say, wishing that I could, that I could find a way to make my life more flexible, to make these heels more comfortable this morning after.

He pulls me toward him and now I'm sitting on the bed, next to him. His head on the pillow, he says, "I need to see you again. Soon."

I sigh, longingly. He gets up to use the restroom. I watch his nakedness pass by. I sit there on this king-size bed and look at myself in the mirror on the opposite wall. This is what success looks like, I think. Even the morning after, I look svelte in this pencil dress, light leather jacket, heels. I look like a woman in a commercial for the Soho Grand, a place where sexy and sophisticated humans pass through on their way to other more exotic adventures.

Xavier comes out of the bathroom wearing a white plush robe. He's holding another. "Shower?"

"Oh," I say. "I wish I could, Xavier . . ." This could be the beginning of my new life, the one I've been waiting for. He sees that I'm thinking about it. He calls room service and orders up coffee for two, fresh fruit . . . He's looking at me to add to the order, he's looking for confirmation. I laugh and mouth "Gotta go . . ."

"Okay," he resigns. "I understand. Next time I'm in town I'll give you more heads-up."

"That would be nice," I say. Though I'm thinking next time, perhaps someplace more intimate. Perhaps an Airbnb?

So now he's standing next to me at the doorway. He kisses me hard and I kiss him gently back. I could get used to this kissing thing. I could throw him down right now and he would happily meet me.

"I know we live on opposite sides of the pond," he says, "but . . . now that you're single . . ."

"Yes?" I say.

"You're more available, right? Seriously, you should come to London."

"Okay," I jump. "When? You name it."

He chuckles. "I do appreciate enthusiasm," he says. "I see that in you when you're drawing. In front of the crowd. Taking in ideas being thrown at you from all sides. You really are one of the best storyboard artists I know, Maggie."

Thanks?

He's tilting his head and doing some sort of calculations. I imagine he's running through his calendar in his mind and quickly moving things about to get me to London ASAP. Finally, he looks directly at me and says, "October is a busy month. Lots of birthdays. November's pretty open until Thanksgiving when all the gang comes home. How about November? Tenth or so? A few days midweek? You can come into the office—we'll write it off as business. I know a lovely country estate not far out of town."

I'm a little confused. "Birthdays? Gang?" I'm shaking my head and smiling.

And then he cups his hand around his mouth and goes into stage whispers, "The twin girlies, the wife, even the nanny. Libras, every one of them. And then my older girls come visit for a bit." He makes exaggerated eyebrows and rolls his eyes at the same time.

"You're married?" I hear myself say. I'm really, really having a hard time understanding what he just said. He'd told me he was married and divorced, never mentioned a second wife, never mentioned girlies. I'm having a really hard time balancing on these heelies, my vision feels blurry, like I can't really make him out.

He steps back casually. "Maggie, I thought you knew that."

"No." I say this very calm-and-coolly.

"Everybody knows it. It's no secret. I've got their pictures in my office, on my phone." He walks over to the side table and picks up his phone as if he is going to show them to me.

"No," I say, "that's okay. I believe you." How is this possible?

He puts up his hands like he's not guilty or something and says, "I swear I just assumed you knew . . . You were married, I was married. Just grown-ups doing what grown-ups do."

"Wow," I say. "Yeah, totally. Of course." But no. It's not what I do. I did it once, that's all. Just those several times over a three-day period over a year ago with you.

"I'm sorry," he says, "if you misunderstood." He moves into me, his pelvis into me. "But still, it's a reeeally lovely country estate. Think about it? Me?"

I pull back, his pressing maleness suddenly disgusting to me. His face registers this and I don't want him to, to see whatever it is I'm feeling now, as I try to identify what exactly it is. "I'll think about it," I force a giggle. I mean, I work with the guy, right? I can't just run out and slam a door behind me. I've gotta keep it light. It is light, right? Just grown-ups doing what grown-ups do? "A lot to think about," I say.

"Or not," he says. And he winks.

"Good luck wooing the client," I say.

"Oh, I'll let you know how it goes. I'm hoping you'll be drawing the boards," he says.

"Of course," I say. But I don't want to draw his boards. I don't care how much I could use the money. I have to detach, and fast.

"Oh," he says, "your orchid." He reaches for the pot.

"No thanks," I say. "Give it to your wife." I feel naked and want to cover myself with a pillow.

"Frederick," he says so sincerely. "Doesn't mean what we have isn't . . ."

"One ice cube, once a week," I say to him. "That's all it needs. Tell her I said so." And then I wink at him before I turn to proudly stride down the hallway to the elevator. As I step onto it, I stumble in my too-tall heels. I look back to see if he's watching and of course he isn't.

c‹›ɔ

Summer Camp has turned into Fall Retreat. And like me, the staff at Sunnyside are trying to come to terms with the fact that Ginny might become a permanent resident. They've asked my permission to hire an outside psychiatrist to give her an intelligence test, which would be covered by her insurance. Basically, I believe that they are trying to determine if my sister really is intellectually disabled or if she is simply evil. I think, can't a person be both?

The need for a label, to put a name on it, is very strong. I'm not judging. They want to know who they're dealing with. Her whole life, people had been trying to figure out what it is that makes Ginny, Ginny. I tell them I am fine with it, so long as Ginny is. Ginny shrugs her shoulders and says, "That's fine." She's matter-of-fact about it. As if she's used to people giving her IQ tests. She does not appear to be offended or threatened by it.

"Are you sure, Ginny?" I ask. "You don't have to say yes."

"It's fine," she says. "I just go with the flow, like Bets."

I insist I be present for the test and Ginny does not argue with this either. It's as if she's a reclusive movie star, giving approval for an interview.

She allowed one of the nurses to braid her hair and she wears a purple headband and of course her purple gloves. Her lipstick, she tells us, is Revlon's Summer Dreams.

"I've done this several times before," she tells the doctor. "I'm used to it."

I wonder if this is true. Maybe when she was young our parents had her tested? She was in special ed, so I suppose there was some testing, though I never heard a diagnosis.

The doctor sits in a large leather chair on one side of the large dark desk. Ginny and I, in the medium-size leather chairs on the other.

The doctor addresses her respectfully. "Ms. Frederick, how are you today?"

"You can call me Ginny," Ginny says. "Ms. Frederick is my mother."

He smiles. "Okay. Ginny it is."

"If you call me that maybe her ghost would show up."

"Our parents have both passed away," I say.

"And do you see your mother's ghost?" the doctor says.

Oh please, I think.

"Not really," Ginny says. She's already bored. "Our dad died and a year later, our mom died."

"I'm sorry for your losses," he says.

"My sister put me here. Took away my dog, my car, my minis."

"Minis?"

Oh yes, she was ordering in mini marshmallows, too. Bags of them. "I believe my sister is depressed," I say.

The doctor pretty much cuts me off and says, "Okay Ginny, shall we talk privately?" She shrugs. "Perhaps you could wait outside," he says to me. "Okay with you, Ginny?" Ginny nods. I pick up my bag and depart. From a stiff chair in the hallway, I try to listen, but he's put that white noise machine on so I can only hear the back and forth murmur.

Ginny knows she has disabilities, it's no secret. I recall the first time I learned that she knew this. I was in bed drawing Pippi Longstocking on a pirate ship. My bed was against the wall to our parents' bedroom. And I heard Ginny cry my name. "Why not Magpie?!" I stopped my pencil so I could really listen. "Why not her? Why am I the one who is handicapped? Why me, out of three girls? Why not Magpie?" I'm sure then that they told her that everyone, even Magpie, has problems, because then I heard Ginny yell, "Magpie doesn't have any problems!"

By the time she came back to the bedroom, I'd put my drawing down and was pretending to be asleep. I heard her sniffling in her bed 'til she started snoring. I lay awake for hours wondering what my own problems were. Was there a dark secret that had yet to be revealed?

Years later, I remember going into our mom's room as she was waking from a nap, a prime time for private inquiries. I wasn't really doing well in school, was having trouble remembering the names and the dates in World History, for example. All my friends were moving into AP classes, but not me. I dared to ask her, "Mom, is it possible for more than one child in a family to have learning disabilities?" I really thought I was onto something, I thought this was it. She laughed as she shook her head and she said, "You know, Maggie, sometimes I think you're just a little bit lazy."

Lazy? Was that it? Not a learning problem? Not a "maybe we should get you extra help" problem? Not a "Honey, you're an artist, not an academic and that's not a problem," problem? In truth, I think I've spent my entire life trying to prove to myself and the world that I'm not lazy.

The results of the test are not groundbreaking. Ginny knows a lot. She has her bearings about who she is, where she is. She knows who the president is and expresses an opinion about this ("zero stars") and she knows that New York is famous for both cheesecake and apples ("five stars"). She knows that two plus two equals four. Beyond that, she doesn't care so much. "That's what calculators are for," I imagine she said.

Her biggest area of weakness? Self-knowledge and self-care. "In conclusion," the psychiatrist's notes say, "it is recommended that she have regular assistance to monitor and encourage a healthy lifestyle." He prescribes antidepressants, which we all know my sister will refuse. The bottom line: Ginny is so complex that a social worker, a psychologist, and even a psychiatrist can't figure her out.

⸎

The very next day, while I am at my desk drawing a coral reef out of lemons and limes because the client thinks this is a good idea, I get a call from Marybeth. Ginny told Paulina that if she has to stay at Sunnyside the rest of her life, she'll kill herself. Now they've put her on suicide watch.

This means they have taken away her pens and her hairbrush. This means she is not allowed to shut her door, not even at bedtime. This means that a staff attendant must sit and watch her while she eats. No forks, no knives. Only spoons.

I tell Marybeth that I find this hard to believe, I'm sure she wouldn't consider such a thing. I'm sure it was a figure of speech. Leave it to sweet Paulina to take an off-the-cuff comment seriously.

She says, "You can never be sure. This is policy. Right now, she is yelling at Danielle."

This can't be happening, I think, as I turn up the green on the lime blowfish. "I'll be right there," I say. I'm in the middle of a huge job, but we must take these things seriously.

I get there fast and Ginny tells me to go away. "Did you mean it, Ginny? Are you serious?"

She turns away from me. "Of course not, I would never do that. I have Rascal."

"That's what I thought," I say. "Good. Very glad to hear that." Sweet relief.

"Leave," she says.

Back at home, I pass by Leo who is still watching *The Simpsons*. I say, "Haven't you watched this episode before, and don't you have that big project to do?"

He says, "No and no."

I do not believe him on either count. I tell him I'm back and I'm Going Back Into Surgery.

He says, "Oh," which I think means that he didn't even know I was gone.

I tell Leo about Ginny's threat.

"Really?" Leo says, putting Homer on mute. "Do you think she really means it?"

"No," I say, "of course not." And quietly I wonder if she really does want to kill herself, if she would if she had the means to, if this is all my fault.

"No," my sweet son says, "of course not."

Rascal growls at Crazy Cat. Rascal growls at Coyote. I growl at Rascal. And then I'm back in my office at the drawing board.

I had such high hopes! I had such vision! I believed that I could brighten up Ginny's dark life! I believed that I could open up her small world! I saw her losing weight and rocking her PT and really getting her mojo back! Actually, getting mojo that she never had before! What is mojo? I don't know, but I know it's good and it's something I wished for both of us!

Did I say *both* of us?

Well, yes, it's true. I envisioned that we'd be known as Those Crazy Two. We'd make a name for ourselves as The Frederick Sisters! People at the local coffee shop and ice-cream shop and all along our little main street would see us and they'd say, "Look who's coming!"

I envisioned that I would give my sister a makeover. Keeping her individual style, her sparkly purple and pink palette, her surfing vibe, while shining up her unique individual essence. I could give a makeover worthy of any Queer Eye. She would learn to comb her hair and would do it several times a day. Or she would let me do it. Or one of the Sunnyside staff. We'd all say, "Ginny, what lovely locks you have!"

I envisioned that in the process, I, too, would become more fully myself. A sexy, stylin' middle-aged babe with maximum appeal and minimal makeup. People would see me for who I truly am: a loving, devoted, patient-to-the-point-of-saintlike woman. "Oh," I'd say modestly, "but saints are so boring!" and they'd laugh and say, "You, Maggie, are a fascinating saint." They would realize that I am not the coldhearted bitch that cheated on her husband, who kind-of kicked him out of the house, who atom-bombed her family of four.

Ginny and I would both start dating. I'd get her involved in a social group for adults with special needs. I'd meet a brother of one of these adults and he would fulfill my special needs. Fuck Mr. X—he'd be a nice guy. We'd go on double dates! We'd drive down Main Street in his convertible, laughing and singing *I wish they all could be Croton-on-Hudson girls*. The boys would really like him—my new guy. They'd suddenly understand where their own father was lacking. Not as a father and a human being—he will still be a role model for them—but they will see what he lacked for me. Bill would be supportive, likely humbled by my new matching, and this would inspire him to grow up, though not so much that I have regrets. Ginny and her boyfriend and me and my boyfriend would probably take a double-date trip to Disney World, where we would ride "It's a Small World" ten consecutive times, because it would still be Ginny's favorite.

Well. "That's not gonna happen," I can hear Ginny say.

Nor is she going to commit suicide at Sunnyside. Nor will she die there due to her various medical conditions. In fact, I now understand, my sister will live. Because life is like that. The college kid who is a do-gooder health nut falls off a cliff while hiking. And Ginny, our not-so-secret Twizzler-swindler, overgrown child without the wonder, self-declared lazy hero, will live forever.

And now, the big questions: Will she stay miserable at Sunnyside? Or will I arrange for something else long-term and nearby? And will she be miserable there?

If I had just let Ginny go home, she'd be dead by now.

And this is when I realize the full truth. Ginny will never return to Maryland. My middle sister, my largest, stickiest, and secret blood sister, will be attached to me forever.

I receive a long text from Bill:

I can get us a v good comprehensive family health insurance plan that will cover us and my sons until they are each 26. More cost efficient than the freelance which is bleeding my balls. We'd have to put off official divorce until then but makes sense financially. Kapeesh? Lmkasap. Bill.

"My" sons? Since when did his balls start bleeding? When I asked him last month to pay that bill for the first time in almost twenty years? Put off the divorce for a few more years? Kapeesh? Lmkasap? Bill?

He wants us to stay married in order to save money. This seems cheap, doesn't it? Where was this cheapness when he purchased that flash new vehicle? Where was it when he blew the cost of a family vacation on the tables of Atlantic City? But still. Saving money is a good thing and better late than never, I guess. And if it's good for the boys it's good for me. "His sons," I say to Crazy Cat who is sitting on the table staring at me. Also, as of now, it seems my need to get officially divorced is not on deadline. I just read in the trades that Mr. X's top-secret ad campaign did very well even without my drawing the boards.

I have a citrus coral reef to draw. I have dogs to walk. I text Bill back: *ok*

I get a call back from our parents' scraggly lawyer. I put the phone on speaker as he says, "Confirmed, the money is in your sister's name, and fortunately there is a healthy sum."

"Yes, but do I really need to get her permission to do anything with it?"

"Once she signs the documents, you'll have access."

"Ha," I say. "I'll have to catch her on a day that she trusts me."

Leo comes through my office door and gives me the wind-it-up sign followed by the at-the-steering-wheel sign. I told him I'd take him out for another spin toward his required driving hours. I give him a shoot-myself-in-the-head sign. He laughs and I love him for it. Leave it to Leo to keep it light.

He bends down to give each of the dogs a treat, which he does every time he passes between them. Part of his Plan for Peace Among the Pets.

The ancient lawyer continues, "Your parents took good care of her, Maggie, and in that way, they've taken good care of you."

"Yes," I say, grateful that I don't have to send my sister back to the rat's nest for inevitable death by strawberry Jell-O. Also grateful that I don't have to move her here, to live in my own home office, which likely would have inspired a new season of *American Horror Story*. Still, I do not say, Wouldn't it have been better if they put the money in my name? If they had some sort of monthly allowance for efforts made? I receive an email from my art director with a long list of required changes, so "Shit" is what I say.

"Sorry, I'm a bit hard of hearing," he says.

After I hang up, Leo shakes the car keys.

"I'm sorry, sweets," I have to say. "I can't take you driving. I'm way behind. And now changes."

As usual, he sings his little Bowie tribute, "*Ch-ch-ch-changes.*"

"I have to make all the white people Black, all the Black people Latino and all the Latino people white," I say.

"Really?" he says.

I sigh. "Not everybody but a lot. I have to change some skin tones and change one person's sexuality to more ambiguous."

"But that's cool, though," he says. "Diversity."

"Diversity rocks, diversity is awesome."

"You get paid for the changes, right?"

"Up to a point. I'm all for diversity. I just wish it had occurred to them before I drew all this stuff," I say. I'm getting a headache. "Try your dad?"

"He's in Chicago."

"Oh right." He just texted me from there. Said he was "between meetings."

Bill had a hard time keeping a job when we were married. Now he seems to be doing just fine. Not only does he have an actual job, but he gets to travel. I understand now that that trip to Nashville last month was basically an audition for him to impress a big client: Dollywood. His agency handles all forms of insurance coverage for major players in the music and entertainment industry. He wooed the client with his knowledge of electric dulcimers. Prince's estate Paisley Park in Minnesota is another client. Not sure who he's wooing in Chicago. He's been providing our sons weekly cash, he got us a better health insurance plan, and he seems happier and more engaged with his work than he's been in the thirty years that I've known him. I know I should be happy about this, but I am actually deeply hurt.

"Mom?" Leo says.

"Yes?" My head is down as I turn a blowfish into a pineapple.

"Twenty?"

Bucks, that is. "Sure," I say.

"Mom?"

"Yes?" I look up at him and am stunned by his height, his light.

"Dad said it's okay for me to apply wherever. He says we'll figure it out."

"Huh." This is news. Previously Bill had insisted on a state school for Leo. Said a private one wasn't "worth the investment."

"I just. Didn't know if he told you that."

"Well, good," I say cheerfully. "I'm glad he and I are finally on the same page." "Finally" is meant as a dig to Bill and I'm not sure if I want Leo to pick up on that or not.

"He says Chicago is really cool. Said he could take me there, look at campuses, over break."

"That's great, sweetie," I say. Though really, I'm jealous. Why does Bill get to take our son to Chicago? Who is he to just throw that offer out? Here I am, nagging Leo to do his homework, reminding him to take his meds, lining up tutors and accommodations meetings, and Bill gets to just fly him to Chicago? Could Leo even get into those schools? I have a vision of the two of them getting high together in their hotel room and laughing their asses off.

I'm all over the place today. I so desperately need a massage. Back in the day, Bill would rub my back. Sometimes in the middle of the night. He had magic hands . . . I will make an appointment for one. I'm going to ask Ginny to pay for it.

Ding. It's Ginny: *Thank.u. for putt me in this hell. If. I. Die today. U. Fault.*
And then: *Tell. Rascul. I. Lovet. Him. Tell him. You did it.*

Torture by text. This is Ginny's new power. I text back: *Okay. See you tomorrow.*

When I visit her tomorrow, I will listen to her complaints. I will tell her I am sorry for the situation. I will try to imagine if she could live there the rest of her life. I will try to imagine if I could live with myself if she lived there the rest of her life. She will be angry. She will be belligerent and pale and childish. I will tell her that I love her and she will not tell me that she loves me back. That's okay. She never does. She can't. I will love her even more because of that.

⸎

The autumnal wreath on the door of Sunnyside Nursing Home and Rehabilitation Center has taken on a spooky edge. Paulina has covered it with cobwebs and plastic white spiders and on the top of it perches a black cat in classic curved back position. Frightening or frightened? Hard to tell. A friendly pumpkin hangs next to the sign. I'm sure Paulina is very proud of her work here, and she should be.

Roger greets me warmly and I imagine him in a long cape with plastic vampire teeth. The place is old, so it doesn't take much to give it that haunted house kind of feeling.

I look around and this is what I see: An extremely frail-looking man being pushed in his chair by a bored aide. A woman with tubes up her nose taking steps with a walker while a nurse, pushing oxygen alongside, cheers her on. And here comes bright yellow sweater man. Just a few months ago he looked so cheerful, humming his happy tunes. Now, he has a long face. His sweater has a dark stain on the chest, I'm guessing from dribbling prune juice.

When I first toured the place, I asked Marybeth if the residents made friends with one another. "Not really," she said. I see now that this is true.

Their job here at Sunnyside is to keep the residents safe and comfortable. So they are not allowed to go to the bathroom independently even if they want to, even with the use of a walker or a wheelchair, for fear that they might fall or, I don't know, crash? And when the residents use the toilet, the nurse or aide must stand there, back to them, just three feet away, for fear that they might topple off. Also, I suppose, to keep track of the status of their bowel movements, because if they were to simply ask them, some might lie, and some may not recall. I imagine sometimes a resident may fall asleep there, on the toilet, or the nurse, late at night, might nod off while leaning against the wall.

I, for one, can't go to the bathroom with another person in the room, not even in the next room. An empty house is ideal.

I bring Ginny downstairs to the living room where they have set up a table for the two of us for lunch. My sis has been sending me pictures of the food with accompanying text saying things like: *u.cal.thid.FUD??????* and *wood.nt.gv to Razacl.* So I am determined to eat this food and enjoy it. The food looks like something that comes out of you rather than something that should go in. It is soft, I'll give it that. I smile as I swallow and tell Ginny it's not bad.

Ginny looks bad. She's washed-out and her long, bleached hair is now half-gray so it looks particularly ghostly. She's lost twenty-five pounds since she's been here, which is going on six months. Now that we've put the kibosh on her sneaky binge-fest, she's back to her healthier diet and the nutritionist is thrilled. I want to agree with her of course, but really, I think my sister looks like someone who is being slowly starved to death. And even with her hot-pink *California Dreamin'* sweatshirt, or maybe because of it, my sister looks particularly frightening. Ghosts aren't generally scary but for the angry ones, and she would definitely be one of those. If this were a haunted house, Ginny would be the lady in the wheelchair in the open closet that you have to pass slowly while taking a tight corner. Through her thick wire-rims, her eyes would pierce and follow. In her deep and vacant voice, she'd say, "You can check out but you can never leave." She'd freak the shit out of people.

A man plays Debussy on the grand piano of the living area. His father is there, in a rather fancy reclining wheelchair. The father is asleep most of the time. Right now the aide is spoon-feeding him. I compliment the man playing Debussy. "Very nice," I say. "I'm off-key," he says. "I'm not very good, but I enjoy playing. My father was very critical of my playing when I was younger. If he were here right now, he'd hate it." He nods in his father's general direction and we both kind of chuckle. His father is here, and some might say he's alive and I can't tell if he has any opinion whatsoever of his son's Debussy.

Another woman whom I like very much comes every single day to visit her mother, who is one hundred and four. Every time I come here, she's here. She comes over to Ginny's and my table to say hello, leaving her mother alone and scowling at their table about ten feet away.

"She won't die," she says to us in a stage whisper. "I'm the only one that visits, she yells at me for putting her here. My brother spent all her money, so I am paying for it and he won't visit. There's no money for me after she dies. Just funeral expenses." This woman is a hoot, just like her one-hundred-and-four-year-old mother. "Wait a minute," I say. "If your mother is one hundred and four, how old are you?" "Eighty-four!" she says. "And my mother won't do what she is supposed to do and just die and let me be!" I laugh uncomfortably as I'm not sure if her mother can hear us. Ginny's single chuckle has a sardonic edge.

When I look back at her one-hundred-and-four-year-old mother, she smiles at me and nods wildly. Usually, I see her as a harmless and ancient inspiration, but right now, she seems to be saying, "Damn right I'll stay alive, long enough to see my daughter go mad!"

I try one more bite of my pureed some-kind-of-meat and mashed bland potato. I can't fake it anymore. I look right at Ginny and whisper, "This tastes like shit."

She kind of smiles and says, "I told you so" in a teasing tone.

"Too bad Rascal's not here," I say, insinuating that I'd give my portion to her.

"Told you, she wouldn't eat it either," Ginny says. She's balancing a line between validation and fury.

Another look over at the mostly-sleeping father and I have this image of him sitting up abruptly and screaming at his piano-playing son to "Shut the hell up!" The zombie critiques.

If they weren't here, getting this kind attention and medical care, many of these humans would not be alive. Yes, some will be rehabilitated and able to go home, but in most cases they won't be. Sunnyside is in the business of keeping people comfortable and postponing the inevitable. And humans are in the habit of avoiding death at all costs. I get it. It is the natural instinct to preserve the life of a loved one, no matter how dark the diagnosis. Very few would put a cat with incurable cancer outside in the cold. They would opt instead to spoon feed it tuna juice for three weeks until it meets its inescapable fate. This makes perfect sense. Of course, with the sickly kitty there's another option . . .

I wave goodbye to Marybeth, who is talking with someone on the phone. I hear her say, "We might have a bed available next week." Creepy.

⦅⦆

As soon as I'm home, I make a pot of coffee, set myself up to draw, and call Bets. "I'm drawing storyboards for a new feminine hygiene product," I tell her. "Made me think of you," I say. She starred in that Tampax commercial way back when, in which they showed her surfing. That one went national and played for years.

This seems to lighten her. When she answered she sounded heavy, or strange, like she didn't want to answer the phone? "I wouldn't mind one of those ads now," she says, "but I've passed that peak." Menopause.

"Ha," I say. I'm sure there was good money in it. We go back and forth with the weather, the boys, and when we get to our dear middle sister, I work myself up to say, "You're right, Bets. We need to get her out of there."

"Thata girl," she says. Big sister is approving and it feels good.

"Ugh." I humbly tell her about my observations and revelations, how miserable our Ginny has been, in both mood and behavior.

"That's really great," she says, "the revelation part, that is—ha. So . . . what's the moving date? I'll try to swing out. Would be nice to see the old place, maybe I'll look up some pals . . ."

Um. "Well, I don't know the moving date yet," I say. She's thinking about Maryland, she thinks I'm sending our sister back to Maryland.

"Let me know when you have one. I'd like to be there for that."

This is throwing me a curve ball, or what do they say in the surf world—a loop? I need to draw Olympic uniforms on this gymnast while I attempt a reboot. So, "What are you up to these days, anyway, Bets? The birthday surprise was too fast."

I can tell she's surprised I'm asking. Frankly, I'm surprised I caught her at all. It's noon California time, I figured she'd be out catching waves.

"I'm cool. All well. You know, surfin', teachin', chillin'," she laughs.

"That's great," I say. Really, I'm happy she's doing well. Truth is, she always seems to be doing well. I guess she drew the My Life Rocks card among the Frederick sisters. And then I'm surprised when I hear myself say, "Why don't you come for another visit and stay? We'd all love to see you more. You must know that."

"Really?" she says. "That's nice . . . You know, it's hard for me to get away these days, so . . . I kinda have to pick and choose . . . Gin's move would be good, though, that, I'd like to do." She always sounds like she's laughing, even when she isn't.

"Betsy," I finally say, "I'm sorry if I wasn't clear. But. She can't go back there. I mean, Maryland. It won't work."

She's quiet for a while. "So what are you going to do, Maggie?"

You mean "we," I want to say, she's our sister. "I thought we could buy her a small house. Something here in Croton, where she could be with Rascal and have a twenty-four seven aide," I say.

She doesn't say anything for a long time. I'm getting texts from my rep that I need to address. "That sounds expensive," she says.

"Mom and Dad left her some money. You know that. We could just buy her something here and then sell her house there . . ."

"It doesn't make any sense," she says.

"Well, yeah, it kinda does. I'm sorry you couldn't stay longer but, if you had, you'd have seen . . . she really can't walk anymore, she needs help with so many things."

"She could have an aide in Maryland."

"Her house isn't set up for it, she's rude to aides, she plays the TV really loud, and she's a slob."

"So then why buy her a new house with an aide? It doesn't make sense, Magpie."

She's talking to me like I'm ten years old and suddenly I'm second-guessing my whole plan, suddenly I'm seeing the sides of the box cave in and I don't know what to do about it.

"Look," my big sister says to me, "why don't you just let the girl go home and let life play out the way it's meant to play out? Just let the girl be!"

Let the girl be? I say, "Just let the girl be?"

"That's what I said," Bets says.

"First off, she's not a girl. She's a full-grown woman. That's kind of . . . I dunno . . . patronizing, don't you think? Also, do you even know what that means? To just let Ginny be?" I'm trying to figure out what detail in the picture I haven't illustrated clearly. How can she not see? "She can't walk," I say for the hundredth time. "She's not independent like she used to be." Was she ever independent? Mom and Dad used to help her with so many things. "She wears diapers. She needs help. Even with an aide, she needs someone to manage it."

"Manage what?"

"Everything!"

"What about her neighbors, the evangelists? What about them?"

"They're not evang—No! I mean, I won't ask that of them, they've already done too much."

"Let the queen go back to her castle." She says this like she's bored with this conversation, like the answer is so very obvious to everyone but me.

"So basically, what you are saying, Betsy, is that we should just let Ginny suffer and die."

"She's suffering now, isn't she?"

Whoa. I don't know what to say to that so I don't say anything.

"Kinda seems like you're playing God, is all I'm saying. Why don't you let her decide when it's her time? That's what I would do, if it were up to me. Take her home."

"Well, isn't that playing God, too?" I say. Now she's the quiet one. And then I have a revelation, which I say out loud as it comes to me. "Maybe her time was thirty-five years ago, when she practically died right there on the beach. Maybe I should have told your friends not to bother . . . pushed that braided guy away when he started mouth-to-mouth." Oh, that's right, I think but do not say, You weren't there. You weren't there to see her go blue in the face.

"What does Bill say?" she asks. She sounds exasperated.

"Why the hell does it matter?" I'm the one that knows what's going on. I'm the one that's here on the front line, facing the enemy. I'm showing my anger when I really don't want to. We need to be a team. Why would she say this but to hurt me? She doesn't say anything. Maybe she didn't mean it that way, that Bill's opinion is more valid than mine. Maybe she's not trying to dig that I'm over a year separated from my once husband. Maybe I'm overreacting. "How 'bout you?" I finally say. "Are you seeing anyone these days?"

"I've got a friend," she says. "You know."

"That's cool," I say.

"It was never that easy for me," she says. "I never knew how you did that commitment thing, that I'm yours and you're mine thing, never mastered it."

"Well, obviously, I didn't either," I say.

"Oooh, I get it," she says like she's got it all figured out, like she's always had it figured out. "And now you have Gin-Gin. It works out."

Something in me goes totally hot and I am having trouble believing what I'm hearing.

"You guys were always close. Private clubs and forts. I wasn't part of that, but that's cool."

"What are you talking about, Betsy? We were kids and you were never around. We were just . . . playing."

"I've got a board to ride," she finally says. "A class."

"I've got a board to draw," I say. "A commercial."

"Look, you do whatever you want to do with her money. Make it work, you always do. You two always had fun together."

"Look," I say, "I don't know which part I haven't drawn clearly enough for you, but this is the picture. We're not having lots of fun. While you are out there on the West Coast, riding gnarly waves, Ginny and I are here, on the East Coast, riding sugar waves."

She's quiet for a minute and finally says, "Cute, real cute."

"I wanted to do this together, you and me," I say. "I mean, it's you and me, looking out for our middle sister. Together."

"Yeah, well . . ." She pauses. "Whatever I say, you'll do the opposite, so you just do what you do."

"This is our sister," I say. "Our sister."

"I don't approve," Big Sister says. "I don't know why you call if you don't want to listen." She's sounding really upset, she actually sounds like she's crying. "Like I said," she says, "maybe it's more about your needs . . ."

How is my helping our sister in need about my needs?

"You were always the favorite, always the good one . . ." she drifts off.

What the fuck is she talking about? Is she stoned? She now says a few muffled words to someone else, someone else in the room, she's covered the receiver. It dawns on me that I don't even know where she's living. All this time I was just envisioning her in her beachside rent-a-surf hut, but maybe she's actually in her spacious, modern mansion. Maybe she's looking out at the ocean as she lounges in a white leather chair, all her medals and awards on display behind her. Maybe the person that entered the room is her extremely toned, extremely tan girlfriend. Or boyfriend. Either way, they're toned and tan . . . We say goodbyes without any agreement or closure.

I respond to my rep and turn up Lizzo. My drawing hand is shaking. Oh. The rest of me is shaking, too. A bitta Baileys in my coffee to steady the hand.

⊷⊶

I am up all night, composing this letter to Ginny:

> *Dear Ginny,*
>   *I have GOOD NEWS:*
>   *Your family loves you.*
>   *We want you to stay healthy and safe.*
>   *We want to help you feel happy.*
>   *We will always be here for you.*
>   *We would like to help you reunite with Rascal.*
>   *You don't have to stay at Sunnyside if you don't want to.*
>   *Now the BAD NEWS:*
>   *You are no longer physically able to live in your house in Maryland.*
>   *That part of your life is over.*

*I UNDERSTAND that this news will bring up all kinds of
feelings for you. I know it is HARD news.*

*Now MORE GOOD NEWS: I will help you find an apartment
or a house near me in Croton-on-Hudson. There, you will live with
Rascal and a full-time aide. Your new home will be handicapped-
accessible and OF COURSE you will need to get along with the
aide. You CANNOT FIRE the aide. We will have a CONTRACT.*

*Ginny, you have family that loves you and will always take care
of you. You are lucky that Mom and Dad were able to help you save
money to help hire good caregivers.*

WE ARE LUCKY to know and love you!

*Many people move when they retire. Now that you are retired
from your janitor job, you can move to Croton-on-Hudson! Yay!*

I love you, Ginny,

Maggie

To this letter, I attach three printouts of small houses for sale in
Croton-on-Hudson.

And tonight, I have a dream that Ginny and I are attached at the hip.
We're in Mom's womb. We're hitting each other and there's no escape.
When I wake, I am happy to discover it was only a dream and in analyz-
ing it, I try to find humor. Strangely, though, I have a pain in my left hip. I
look down to see if it's bruised and it's not, which is good, I guess.

I bring Rascal to help with the visualization. Danielle, the social
worker, joins us for the presentation. This way it feels like we're a team,
like it's not all my idea, I'm not the bad guy. We go into Ginny's small
and stinky room and close the door behind. We don't want to frighten
the other residents when she starts to yell and cry. But she doesn't do either of those things. Instead, as I read the letter to her, she is very quiet.
When I am done reading all of it, I hand it to her, open to the listings.
She looks at each one and then oh so clumsily pulls the papers back so

she can see the first page, the letter. She stares at this a moment and Danielle nods to me for courage.

"*You*," Ginny says.

"'I' what?" I say.

"*You*." She points to me. "All that stuff. In the letter. Not *We*."

"Oh, yes, *We*," I say. "Graham and Leo and me. And Bill," I add. "We all want you to be healthy. We all care about you."

"He's not family anymore. You're divorced." She points her finger up and makes a circle with it like the wind-up sign. "Separated," she says.

"He was your brother-in-law for over twenty years. He cares about you. He's visited you a few times now, right? He cares about you, too," I say again. "And . . . Bets," I say, "she cares about you, too." Saying this isn't easy.

She is quiet for a minute.

"Ginny, you are not alone. Your family is always here for you."

I had anticipated tears and anger, sarcasm or the silent treatment. What she exudes is something else completely. She seems . . . relieved?

"The yellow house has a fence," Ginny says.

"Yes," I say. "Yes, it does."

"Beach Street," she says.

"Ah, yes, Beach!" It's actually Beech, like the tree, but I do not tell her that.

"That's a sign," Ginny says.

～

It's March now. One year since Ginny almost died. I'm back in Maryland at 25 Montgomery Street. I'm here to clear and clean out Ginny's Castle to put it on the market. Our closing date for Beech Street is May first. The boys are in school so I dared to ask Bill if he could help. If he could send Ginny flowers, he could certainly do some of the dirty work. He said, "Really wish I could, but I'm heading outta town." "Where this time?" I asked. "The Villa Nellcôte?" The Nellcôte is the mansion in the Côte d'Azur where the Rolling Stones recorded *Exile on Main St.* I am demonstrating for him that I still have a hip sense of humor. "Not business," he says, without offering where he is going or with whom. It's okay, I don't want to know and I already know.

I rented a large dumpster and now will fill it to the brim with half the contents of her home and most of her garage. I had no idea she collected lawn mowers. These are things she won't see again. Decided by me.

The greasy broken blinds have fingerprints, proving her a spy, on an outside that she was afraid of. I hope she'll feel safer in the new house. I throw the blinds in the dumpster.

The door in the floor that opens to the crawl space is nailed down and covered by a ratty rug. Ha. Rats. I throw that in the dumpster, too.

I will have the house painted, white, white, white. The floors will be sanded and stripped.

The doorknobs, sanitized, many fixtures replaced.

A few things she told me to save, things I might not have placed value on. Like the unopened bag of Doritos Mom last gave her, the first checkbook Dad helped her with.

I put those in a box on the passenger seat.

I find secrets. That pack of cards that I found decades ago on the bathroom sink at Mom and Dad's. Of soft-porn scenarios. At the time, Ginny denied that they were hers. Well, here they are.

Also, copies of *Playgirl* and *Penthouse*. Dog-eared.

An 8x10 glossy of a Chippendales dancer, signed: *Ginny, great to be your neighbor. Rodney.* On the back in Ginny's handwriting: I lik sexxx wih Rodny. Really? Did she? Or did she just imagine it? Oh, wow.

A typed-up story that she wrote, single-spaced, about farm animals in their own little town and a party they were getting ready for. The animals are all named after us. Ginny is a dog. I am a cat. Mom is a cow and Dad, a horse. Bets is a dolphin with legs, which is an amusing image.

And so on. I did not know that Ginny ever wrote. Or typed. But it's in her voice and I have no doubt that she is the author of this work.

I put these in the box.

I rented a U-Haul, and in that, I pack all the practical things, like sheets and towels, all beach-themed, lamps, dishes, her winter clothes. I'm not bringing her large bed, as we've already ordered a king-size hospital-style one. With the larger pieces, I need help. I've hired Ken of K & K fame for fifty bucks an hour. He helps me load Mom and Dad's old table, a couple of shelves. With the bureau and the recliner, though, we need more help. He suggests that I hire Rodney, the exotic dancer.

Rodney. He's a very built guy with a crew cut and a baby face. His youth didn't show in the picture. He acts like he's never been inside her place, but who knows if this is true. Did he and my sister have relations? I'm wondering this as he lifts the huge chair by himself. Says he hopes she gets better soon. When I flip him a twenty, I'm tempted to tuck it into his pocket.

All this stuff will be unpacked into my basement until move-in day.

Ginny did not know when she passed out that she'd had her last glimpse of all this, her comforts and most precious things. She did not care that her treasures were coated in dust, dirt, grime. To her, they were fine. She won't see this place again, won't drive to Wheaton Plaza again, or to Petco in Rockville. She won't drive by the new houses where once stood our old house. I never went by there and I won't. She won't drive again, but she doesn't know that yet. She won't return to this place, these places.

There's a map of Maryland on her wall. It's ripped in several places. I throw that in the dumpster, too.

Part Three

❧

59 Beech Street

*P*hilomena is interview number four. Rascal and I are hanging curbside on the outside of the large hedge that surrounds Sunnyside when we see her coming. She's short and she's wide, dressed completely in white. She looks intimidatingly cool with her headphones and golden braids and mirrored Gucci glasses, all shining. I know it's her because she told me she'd get dropped at the corner and would walk from there. I don't know if a bus or a friend or a limousine dropped her off. She said her car was in the shop. It's a bright late May day and I wish I was wearing my sunglasses, too. When I say her name, she smiles. Her teeth shine bright, too.

When we step into the foyer of the dark old building, she does not take the sunglasses off. This strikes me as strange, especially as she's here for an interview. But then our favorite one-hundred-four-year-old resident and her eighty-four-year-old daughter get off the elevator and there are exclamations of recognition and joy. Apparently, Philomena cared for a neighbor of theirs for several years until he died. At the remembrance of his death, Philomena appears visibly moved. She puts her hand over her heart and hugs them each again, even though the mother now doesn't seem to have any idea who she is.

Philomena is the first potential caregiver that Ginny has even acknowledged because she is the first to pet Rascal. While the other contenders had said they liked dogs, they all seemed afraid of Rascal.

Philomena is five feet tall, so therefore lower to the floor, making the hand-to-dog-head distance shorter than most. Often, the move of a hand coming down to pet Rascal inspires a growl. But then again, maybe Philomena doesn't see Rascal's growly face and so is not afraid. She's still wearing those sunglasses.

Ginny does not seem to be alarmed by the sunglasses. Her eyes are focused on Philomena's hand on Rascal's head. I wonder for a moment if Philomena is blind. Perhaps she left her white cane on the bus? But then Ginny starts talking about how Rascal is her everything and Rascal is a good dog and Philomena says, "Oh yes! I can see that!"

I tell her that twice a day she will need to give Ginny her pills and help her check her blood sugar. Legally, Philomena can't stick her with the needle herself as she is not an RN, but she can prepare the prick and monitor her levels.

Ginny tells her about Joey Stiles, the childhood neighbor who told the Black girl to go back to Africa, and Ginny tells her that she is not prejudiced of people who are different. Philomena actually laughs. "Well, that's good," she says, "because everyone is different!" Philomena tells her that she will make her good foods from her native Ghana and she will keep her and her house clean, and most importantly, she will take good care of Rascal. Finally, Ginny declares that Rascal likes Philomena because she likes the way she smells—she does have a nice warm patchouli scent about her—and we declare her hired.

When I call the care agency, I do not ask about her sunglasses for fear that she is indeed sight impaired. I don't want to sound doubtful of a person with a disability's abilities.

One week later, we say our goodbyes to the staff of Sunnyside and there are even some tears. Mine. Ginny says, "Sorry I was a pain in the ass," and nobody denies it. They all wish us luck, but we know they are really wishing me luck. We all know that this is a gamble, a big one. We all now know how impossible and spoiled dear Ginny can be and we all know there is a very good chance that Ginny could try to fire Philomena, or worse, Philomena could quit. I did indeed give Ginny a contract and Rule Number One was that she's not allowed to fire the caregiver. She refused to sign. I asked the staff at Sunnyside if they would take Ginny back if it doesn't work out. They all looked around at each other and finally Marybeth responded with a fuzzy and non-reassuring, "It really depends on if a room is available."

So, basically, we are putting all our money on Philomena.

It's June. A year and three months since Rascal saved Ginny's life. Rascal has finally adjusted to life at our house. We are able to let her walk freely, she understands that Coyote and Crazy Cat are not her dinner, and Coyote and Crazy Cat have come to terms with the fact that some relatives must simply be tolerated. "No animals have been killed in the making of this commercial," Leo likes to say. Graham is home for another summer internship in the city, the same company as last summer.

When Ginny and I pull up to the little yellow house, we see the U-Haul is parked in the driveway, doors open. The boys are bringing in boxes. Bill is in the back of the truck, pushing the recliner forward. Yes, Bill has signed on to help. He looks up at us and says, "Welcome home, Gin-Gin." It's almost two years since he moved out. For Ginny, I suppose, we can do this family-oriented thing. We'll get furniture and boxes in place this morning, Rascal and Philomena will join this afternoon.

When Graham asks if she is excited, she simply shrugs. "Doesn't matter," she says, "I'm going to California very soon."

"Oh really, Aunt Gin?" he says. "What are you going to do there?"

"Get a place near Bets," she says. "Chill."

To Ginny, Bets is the Holy Sibling to Trust. She knows this irks me. She knows that Bets and I had a disagreement about the purchase of this house. She knows that Bets thought I should have just let her and Rascal go home. She knows that Bets and I haven't talked for several months.

"Surf's up!" Leo says as he enters with the surfboard Old Yeller upon his head.

"I hand it to you, Maggie," Bill says, "this was a big job."

It was, but I don't want to play hero, so I say, "Thanks to my parents."

He nods. We've been separated two years and were married twenty-three years before that. He knew my parents well. He grieved their deaths as I did. But I was strangely empowered by their absence, and when they were gone, I started to become extra critical of him. The truth is, it was easier to see a life without him without my mother's "Oh, but he's such a nice guy," or my father's, "He's a good father and a loyal husband. Now be a good girl and make it work." Maybe I wanted more than a good guy, a nice guy. Maybe I wanted a great guy, an exciting guy. Sometimes I just get so tired of being the good girl that makes everything work. So I started pushing back, giving in to my frustration.

Leo, Graham, Bill, and I are moving this way and that with various-size boxes and Ginny's old familiar furniture. She's parked in the middle of the now-empty dining room watching things go by. She's not talking. It's hard to know if she is angry or overwhelmed or what. If one of us asks where to put something, she points. It's not as if she's incapable of doing simple jobs. I ask her if she would like to arrange her toiletries in the low cabinet in her wheelchair-friendly bathroom and she simply grunts.

"This is your house, Ginny. It's really up to you where things go."

"Doesn't matter," she says. "Nobody listens to me."

"What are you talking about?" I say. "It's your constant complaining that got you here."

She goes back into silent mode.

Once the Ikea sofa has been built and both the beds made, Bill goes out to get pizza for lunch. Graham pulls a cooler from the front of the U-Haul. Beer. I watched him open his first before noon and kept my mouth shut. He's twenty-one, has completed his junior year of college with flying colors, and well, he's still managing to be helpful. He hands Leo a beer and Leo looks to me. He is underage, but it's not as if he never drinks, I certainly know that. Leo is also my baby, and he knows how to work his earnest look. He's finishing his junior year in high school, he's waited until after the hard work is done. I give him an appropriate look of disapproval but approval. Graham hands me a cold one and I am grateful.

Here we are. Me, my two tall and handsome sons, and my large and half-bleached-blond sister, sitting around the dining room table that used to live in our parents' house. The boys and I toast Ginny and Rascal and their new house. Ginny downs her milk before adjusting Binky Baby in her high chair.

She lets out a large belch, and says, "What's your ex doing hanging around, anyway?"

I have to laugh. "Do you mean Bill," I say, "who you've known for twenty-five years, Ginny? I think you know his name by now . . . He's helping, not hanging. He's been helping us move you into your new house, that's what he's doing."

"In hell they think he's your husband." She's referring to Sunnyside and his occasional visits. His apartment is also in Ossining, so he was able to walk there. Graham and Leo have now started a belching competition. They are trying to divert. "You dumped him and he doesn't get the hint," she says.

"No, Ginny, that's not how it is and you know that. Bill is still your nephews' father, right?"

"Not to me."

"Not to you, what?"

"Not my family. He's my ex."

At this point, I decide to sigh and take another long swig of my nice and cool beer. Both the boys are looking at their phones. There are other places they would rather be.

"Dad says he's on his way," says Leo.

"Excellent," I say. "I'm stah-ving."

"I'm stah-ving, too," Graham says in an equally refined English accent.

"I am as well," says Leo, oh so British-ly.

"He doesn't get the hint," Ginny says as she gives Binky Baby her bottle.

"It must be so nice for Binky Baby to have her chair and her bottle back," I say.

"You need to spell it out."

I stand up to seek shelter in the kitchen.

I hear Graham ask, "Ginny, do you watch relationship shows? Like *Doctor Phil*?"

"You know I do," she says. "And *Sally Jessy* and *Oprah*."

"Sounds like you have a lot of relationship advice," he says. "You could have your own show."

"I know but I don't want to," she says.

Graham chuckles. Sometimes I wonder if Graham is making fun of Ginny, and then I remind myself that of course he isn't, because my first son is not an asshole.

Bill arrives with pizza and salad. The boys are outta here as soon as they've consumed an entire large pizza all by themselves. They're off to return the U-Haul and then who knows what. I have cut Ginny's pizza into small bite-size pieces and she plops them in her mouth. Bill and I eat in a civilized manner at a civilized pace, chatting, reminding Ginny to chew because we don't want her to choke. We are the parents, and she is the daughter that we never had. Ginny has managed to get a bit of tomato sauce on her chin and Bill reaches over with his napkin to gently wipe it off. "Thank you, Da-da," Ginny says in a funny baby voice, and Bill and I both chuckle quietly. We're caught off guard, all of us; we're in uncharted territory.

Ginny oh so casually mentions that her baby crib has not yet been reassembled. Her baby crib is where all her baby dolls sleep. She doesn't ask Bill to assemble it, but this is her way. I tell Bill to go, I'll figure it out, though certainly not today. Instead, he goes to her bedroom to put it together, while I finish putting things away in the kitchen. He's put this crib together before, of course. It was our sons'.

We did a pretty efficient job, I think. Just a few boxes to go, and then the hanging of Ginny's art and The Official Surfing Museum of Maryland. She hasn't decided yet if she will change it to The Official Surfing Museum of New York. I asked her where she wants that to go and she pointed to the wall opposite her recliner and her TV. "Good spot," I said, and directed the boys to put her long low shelves there.

I'm handwashing her pots and pans now, looking out the window as I do. Ginny's new house is on a corner, just a couple of blocks from the middle school. She'll be able to see kids pass by on their way to school and neighbors walk their dogs. It's a good neighborhood for riding a bike around, whereas mine is across the little bridge and all curvy, hilly roads. In my neck of the woods, biking is a sport.

We used to bike around our neighborhood growing up, Ginny and I. We would ride to 7-Eleven and get Slurpees. We both liked penny candies and we both spit when we passed by Joey Stile's house. Most older girls wouldn't want to hang around with their baby sisters the way Ginny did, and I appreciated this. Also, she had all kinds of information about things that I found interesting. She'd point to houses as we rode by and tell me, "That family's Greek mafia" and "That one's Russian mafia." This added intrigue to the neighborhood, but it also scared me enough that I mentioned it to our mother. "Oh, Maggie, your sister does have an imagination, but her imaginings aren't usually true," she said.

I wonder, as I dry the final frying pan, what intrigue Ginny will imagine here, on her corner of Beech and Maple. A woman I vaguely know walks by with two pint-size poodles. French mafia?

Ginny has nodded off in her old familiar recliner. I ask Bill if he'd mind if I run out to get Rascal. "Philomena will be here in an hour," I say.

He says no worries, he's still putting finishing touches on the crib. I have a moment of déjà vu. He's said those words to me before. He seems to feel it, too, and he looks at me and shakes his head somberly.

When Rascal and I return, I look down at her before we enter and say, "Home again, home again, Rascal. The adventure continues." I pet behind her ear, she growls, and I push open the door.

Ginny opens her eyes and looks at us. "It's about time you give my dog back," she says. Groggy, but not off her game.

Still, the moment is significant. Without direction, Rascal walks right over to Ginny and Ginny reaches into her fanny pack and holds out a biscuit. Rascal grabs it and, again, without either of us leading her, goes directly to her bed and plops down. Ginny makes a hiccup kind of sound, which I believe is a gasp for air through her silent tears.

Bill comes out of her bedroom to see this. He goes to Rascal for a pet and she barks at him. The old girl hasn't seen him in a while.

"She's in the home zone, chillin' like a villain," Ginny says.

Bill backs off and announces that the crib is ready for move-in.

"Thanks, Bill," I say. "You didn't have to do that."

"I need to put my babies asleep," Ginny says.

I ask him if he could help me get her from the recliner back to the wheelchair and he obliges. In the process, we both catch a whiff of her and our eyes meet.

"Okay, Frederick sisters, I'm heading home . . . " he says.

He doesn't usually refer to his apartment as Home. He usually says My Apartment. I suppose it is time for his apartment to feel like a home. Still, I wonder what it is that suddenly makes it this way. A goldfish or plant or some other living presence? Is he letting us go?

"Ginny," I say, as I start to turn her toward her new bedroom, "is there anything you would like to say to Bill?"

Bill patiently waits.

"Thank you, ex-brother," she finally says.

"Thanks for all your help, Bill. We really appreciate it," I say, and he's off.

In Ginny's room, she starts to dig through the boxes of baby dolls and put them down in the crib. Bill left the side rail down, which is helpful. I peek out the window hoping to see Philomena pull up, but instead I see Bill, leaning against his car, talking on his phone.

From this distance, from inside Ginny's new house, I confirm that he does indeed look good. Inside, when he and the boys were passing by me with boxes, I thought I noticed that his biceps had gotten bigger. In the reflection of the window, I see that my hair is out of control, even in a ponytail. I see the bags under my eyes are heavy . . . He's texting someone. Is he communicating with his sensuous, sage lover? Making plans for a hot date? Am I the biggest fool on this side of the Hudson River? Possibly. Am I the loneliest one?

My phone dings and I check to see if it's Mr. X, texting me with regret. No. It's from Ginny. She has sent me a picture: twenty-one baby dolls, lying down, head-to-head, toe to toe, some perpendicular. I look over and she flashes one of her blank-faced smiles.

From her bed in the living room, Rascal begins to howl. I run to the front door and open it to see two suitcases and some bags of groceries on the wheelchair ramp. Rascal's howling simmers down, she's too comfortable to get further involved. And there's Philomena shutting the trunk of a sporty white Camry. She wears a soft yellow blouse, white pants, and sneakers. The Gucci sunglasses. A Gucci purse. She holds a Crockpot. She has driven herself, so she's definitely not blind.

"Hello Philomena!" I call.

We bring her things in and Ginny rolls herself to the door. Binky Baby is in her lap. "Well, hello Ginny," Philomena says, "and how are you and Binky Baby today?"

Ginny starts to tear up and says, "We're back with Rascal." She nods to Rascal growling there.

"Oh, hello Rascal!" Philomena says.

We give Philomena the house tour, move her things into her bedroom. I take her down to the basement where the washer and dryer live. It's pretty dark down there, and she is still wearing the sunglasses. I show her the dials on the washer and dryer and explain to her that I need to wear my reading glasses to read them, but she says she sees just fine. While we're down there, Rascal stands at the top of the stairs, whining.

I woo Rascal with treats to get her to lay back down in her bed, there against the wall between Ginny's recliner and the TV. We help Ginny back into the recliner. Ginny is talking to Binky Baby, saying, "See? Now we're a family again." I tell Ginny I am running out to pick up Rascal's food from my house. I tell her that Philomena is getting herself settled and then she'll prepare dinner. "I'll be back in about an hour or so," I say.

I don't really have to get Rascal's food. I'm just breaking in the new sitter. As I get into the car, I hear that Doctor Phil has moved in, too.

When I return, everything is lovely. *Dr. Phil* is now background noise. Ginny and Binky Baby are asleep in their chair and Rascal is resting on her bed. The table is set for two. I wake Ginny, and she and I sit down to her favorite meal: fish sticks, french fries, applesauce, and milk. Philomena has remembered to put a jar of mayonnaise by Ginny's place mat, as Ginny had told her of her addiction to the stuff. I ask Philomena to sit down and join us and she says, "No thank you. I will eat my African food later."

I say to Ginny, "Aren't we lucky to have Philomena here to help?"

She shrugs.

"Well, I know I am thankful. Thank you, Philomena, thank you so much, and welcome."

"You are very welcome, Ginny and Maggie," she says, smiling and nodding her head.

In Theresa's cozy kitchen, I toast Philomena and I thank the lords and lordesses for bringing her to me. I mean Ginny. "She is the gold and white angel ornament that tops the Christmas tree," I say.

Theresa pours me a refill and tells me I'm a good person.

"Good person? Me?" I say. That's something I'm not sure I believe.

"Well, you've been taking care of your sister, haven't you?"

"Not really," I say. "Sunnyside, Philomena . . . Not me."

Theresa says, "Lots of people wouldn't take care of a sibling in need, lots would leave their care to the state or let them go back to a rat-infested house or let them become homeless and just not give a bollocks."

I say, "Really? But do you actually know anyone like that?"

"They're out there," she says confidently, as Theresa says everything. "They're out there and you know it. Think of that man in Japan. Went into a hospital for those with long-term mental and physical disability and went on a knife wielding rampage. He said he did it for their parents and for the state as these people were a burden to them all."

"That's awful!" I say.

"See?" she says. "You wouldn't do that!"

"Setting the bar low there, Theresa." But true, I have never considered mass murder, not even on my worst days. Tell that to the neighbors, and anyone else who's judged me poorly.

Most of our friends sided with Bill. The word was that I dumped him. No one ever bothered to ask if this was true. No one asked if maybe he dumped me, in less obvious ways, if he neglected certain commitments and responsibilities.

Theresa puts down her empty wineglass and goes into Irish limerick mode. She sings, "There once was a woman from Croton . . . Whose heart was so good, even broken . . . da da da da da da, da da da da da . . . about this I'm really not jokin'!"

I applaud her and down the last of my wine. "Lovely," I say. "But really. I'm simply doing what I do. Caring. My day begins with feeding animals and ends with folding Leo's clothes. I fall asleep and Graham starts texting me. I'm not complaining."

"Maybe a tiny little bit?" Theresa says.

"I'm just saying, caring is what I do."

"Ya, just one more human whose well-being is your responsibility," she says in her excellent exaggerated brogue. "Throw another one on the pile."

"Someday . . . I'll have more . . . time." Theresa knows what *someday* is. Someday Ginny will be dead.

"Hard to imagine the freedom, isn't it?" Theresa has been without husband or live-at-home daughter for four years, but still, the anchor of a dying father. "Ah, yes, we'll be living the dream," she says, "not giving two bollocks about anyone! Should we open another bottle?" She holds one up. "Farzana gave this to me after I helped her move Roland's clothes out of the house today."

Other neighbors. He died of lung cancer a few months ago.

"Mother have mercy, it's not a twist off. I've got to move my sweet ass to get the bottle opener."

"You do have a nice ass," I say as she goes to get one.

"The finest in the town," she says.

Theresa thrives in her singledom. She doesn't give a hoot about who thinks what. In the past few years she's hiked each of New York's highest peaks, got her scuba diving certification, and jumped out of a plane. She returns and opens and pours and sinks back into the chair, her cat Mr. Pogue back on her breasts.

"Malick is back," she says casually. The guy from Match that she showed me last year.

"I figured he'd be married by now," I say.

"Tweaked his profile. He put travel before hiking and he added museums."

"Too good to be true," I say. "Did he happen to add rich?"

"He still doesn't like me," she says. "Boo hoo. Some sexy Senegal boys aren't into hot Irish girls . . . It's okay. He's not my type, I'm realizing . . . I'm just not attracted to . . . fancy chefs these days."

"Chef? Since when is he a chef?" I ask. Taking her bait, I know.

"Studied at Le Cordon Bleu . . . I told you, he updated his profile. Maybe, Maggie, he's waiting for you . . ."

"The Big Bad Wolf moved out today," I say to my now empty glass.

Theresa says, "To be with her proper mommy."

"Yes." I'm getting a bit teary eyed. Because I do love Rascal. And my sister does not pet.

Theresa says, "Now I will amuse you with tales of my unamusing dates. Which one would you like to hear first? Passionate Garden–Man or Passive Activist–Man?"

She does amuse me. We finish the bottle and I wobble home. Graham's car is gone, which means he and Leo are still out. Crazy Cat and Coyote greet me at the door. Oh dear, Coyote hasn't been out for hours. When my head meets the pillow, the room spins.

"Theresa says I'm a good person," I say aloud. Then, to the ceiling fan, "Fuck off, Mr. X," and then, "I'm sorry, Bill. I'm really, really sorry. I should have just told you how bad it was. Before I did a bad thing."

I pick up my phone and, oh my, that screen is bright. I find my way to the app store and I buy myself that app. I post the most attractive pic I can find of myself. It's from two years ago, pre–a whole lotta stuff. I answer the basic intake questions and create the most minimal profile: my name, commercial artist, lover of dogs and cats. Next thing I know I'm strolling down the hot guy street. I bump into Malick there and send him a wink, as Theresa says. Which means I "like" his profile.

⁂

In the morning I call the care agency. I thank them again and again. They inform me that Philomena has a medical condition that requires her to wear dark glasses all the time. She can see fine, but her eyes are very sensitive to light. They say she's been wearing the glasses for years and probably forgets to mention them. I'm doodling as we speak. A short and wide goddess, with many braids, graceful wings and halo, and extremely large sunglasses.

Now Graham returns with me to Ginny's to change a couple of lightbulbs. He does not want to come, he wants to head to the beach with his friends, but I tell him he'll have more fun in the sun if he does this good deed first. "Wasn't moving her in a good deed?" he says. "You'll have more fun with an extra forty bucks in your pocket," I say. And he agrees.

As we pull up, we are surprised to see a blue van parked behind Philomena's car in the driveway. On the side it says *Larry the Locksmith*.

"Oh God," I say, shaking my head.

"What'd she do this time?" he says.

"He's the guy who advertises on TV."

"Knows how to reach his customers," my business major says. "You've gotta give him that."

"And he shows up," I say. Unlike the 1-800 lawyer guy Ginny called from Sunnyside, or the various Realtors in California.

Ugh. There she is sitting in her wheelchair inside the front door, bent over the guy. Her huge breasts are practically falling out of her *Aloha* T-shirt. He's just minding his own business, changing the lock. I suppose he's been in stranger situations.

"Virginia, what are you doing?" I say to her as we reach the door. Larry the Locksmith makes way for us to squeeze in.

Ginny doesn't answer.

Philomena has set the table again. Isn't she amazing? Graham goes straight to the kitchen to change the bulbs and meet Philomena. I hear him telling her how good something smells. Meanwhile, Larry the Locksmith is handing Ginny her new keys and explaining to her which works for which lock and I'm doubting that Ginny follows, but what do I know?

I find myself thanking Larry to fill the void where my sister didn't, and Ginny hands him her credit card. Yes, Ginny still has her credit card, despite the fact that the staff at Sunnyside strongly recommended I take it away. Larry gives her the receipt and leaves.

"What did he charge you?" I ask.

"Not your concern," she says as she stuffs the keys in her fanny pack.

"The locks were brand-new," I say. "We just had new doors and locks put in, Ginny. You know that."

"You did," she says.

"Yes, I did." I'll take ownership of the fact that I have done all the work, damnit.

Dead silence.

"Lunch is ready, Mom," Graham says, and he and Philomena are both standing there by the table. Of course she is wearing sunglasses, though this time, Chanel.

"Okay, Ginny," I say. "Just give me two keys. One for me and one for Philomena."

She ignores me as she tries the different keys out. I wait until she is done and she wheels herself over to the table.

"Okay, Ginny, please just give me two keys and then we can give hugs to Graham and have this nice lunch that Philomena made for us."

She puts Binky Baby in her high chair and then she reaches for her milk.

"Remember the contract?" My sister says nothing. "That was a big waste of money . . ."

She picks up a fish stick and offers some to Binky Baby. Rascal is now at her feet.

"Ginny," I say, "just give me two keys." I feel myself breaking into an all-body sweat. I feel my patience being incinerated by my anger and resentment. We've come this far. Really, Ginny, can't today be easy? Can't today be a celebration of the beginning of your new life? I know move-in day was long and tiring and stressful, but can't today be the day you express gratitude? And maybe excitement—that we're neighbors now? We're going to grow old together here in Croton-on-Hudson! We're going to have so much fun! Am I the most naïve, ignorant Pollyanna that I ever thought for a moment that this might actually go well?

Graham is now waving me into the kitchen, so I go. He can see that I am struggling. He whispers, "You had a deal, right? That you and the aide would each have a key?"

"Well, not exactly," I stutter. "I mean, that wasn't specifically on the contract . . . Just that she'd behave . . ."

"Well, she's not behaving."

"She didn't sign the contract," I tell him.

"Fuck contracts," my dear son says. "Take Rascal."

Wait. What?

"She breaks a rule, you take Rascal. As simple as that," he says.

"Really?" I say.

"Really."

My son is giving me good, standard parenting advice. Actions have consequences, right? And I'm in charge here, right?

I close my eyes and take an extremely deep breath before reaching for Rascal's leash. Rascal has lived with me for over a year and trusts me now. Ginny is sitting there, stuffing fries into her mouth. *Oprah* is booming. I take the hook and connect it to Rascal's collar, and I say, "Come on, Rascal," and Rascal gets up. "Goodbye, Ginny," I say. "I'll bring Rascal back when you are ready to give me two keys—one for me, one for Philomena. Text me when you are ready to make the exchange."

I nod solemnly to Philomena and quickly manage to get Rascal out of the house, down the ramp, and into the backseat of my car. Let's face it, Rascal is more used to being with me now than with Ginny. I close the backseat passenger door, walk around to the driver's side, and get in. Graham is coming out with Philomena. He must have told her what was transpiring.

Suddenly, at the front door of the sweet little yellow house, appears a standing Ginny. This is a strange and surprising picture. I haven't seen Ginny stand, but for wheelchair transfers and forced physical therapy, since pre-sepsis. Her wheelchair is behind her and she is standing. Binky Baby is with her of course, but she is hanging down as an extension of Ginny's left arm, as Ginny is holding her by the ankles.

Ginny comes barreling down the ramp, using the railings as bumpers. This is after I have been pushing her up and down the halls of Sunnyside, to doctor's appointments, to pick out furniture for this new house that I bought for her, renovated for her, and so on, for the past twelve-plus months. I have watched her in rehab, cheered her on as she made her first steps. I have encouraged her to walk to the dining room for meals, but she refused. Either a member of the staff or I, when I was there, would have to push her. I even took her to a Brian Wilson Christmas concert, and I pushed her down the aisle to our seats and then back up the aisle, as in, uphill, when it was finished. And now Ginny is barreling toward me.

She stops at the car. Or the car stops her. She slams into it. She puts her sticky gloved hands on the front window and uses the car to support her as she steps back to the closed rear window where Rascal is.

"Goodbye, Rascal," she says, her voice trembling. "I'll never see you again. Goodbye, Rascal. Have a good life, Rascal." She's crying.

I am just sitting here in the driver's seat and my heart is jumping out of my tank top. I'm not sure how I got myself here. I really don't like that I got myself here. I wish I could go back in time five minutes and erase that this ever happened. But here we are and maybe this is exactly what I needed to do to make sure Ginny behaves in the future. Who knows what else she might do? Who knows what a mess she could make of all of this? I had to do this, right? Set things straight from the start? I'm really, really trying to believe this while the seconds are spinning.

Ginny puts her face right down to the window to meet Rascal's and she says, "I'll get you, Rascal, don't worry." I see that Graham is reaching for Ginny's arm. When Graham makes contact, she throws him off hard and then she turns into something else completely. An animal or a monster, but a kind that I've never seen before. Now she's looking directly at me and she's screaming loud enough so that I can hear her clearly through the car's windshield. The whole neighborhood can hear her.

"FUCK YOU!" she screams at me, and then, "GIVE ME BACK MY DOG OR I'LL CALL THE POLICE!" She raises Binky Baby high and slams her down hard to hit the rooftop. Then she swings back and begins hitting the windows of the car, which is of course her car, her Honda CR-V, with Binky Baby's head. "I'll break the FUCKING WINDOWS!" She slams again and again. Her glasses look like they're going to fall off. Rascal jumps down to hide, and again, Graham tries unsuccessfully to grab her by the arms. "BITCH!" she screams at me.

That's what she looks like. A bitch. An actual feral bitch defending her pups. Her pup.

I am scared. I have never before been scared of my sister. One of the nurses told me that some of the residents at Sunnyside were scared of her. "She wouldn't hurt a fly," I assured him. "I'm not sure she's even capable of hurting a fly." He begged to differ. And now, my sister is spitting and sweating and red and purple and raging and screaming, "FUCK YOU, MAGPIE!"

Graham leans toward me in the car and says, "I can pick her up, Mom. Should I pick her up?" As in, he could pick up Ginny. I have no doubts that he could take control even if she fought back. He was a football player in high school and he regularly goes to the gym. His voice sounds fuzzy and filtered, and I feel as if I am hearing it through a deep dream, as if this is just a nightmare I may soon jolt awake from. "MOM?" he asks.

And then Ginny, exhausted, with her arms spread wide on the front and side of the car, the weight of her fallen into the car, her face, distraught, staring hard at me through the windshield, screams one final defiant, "FUCK YOU, BABY SISTER!"

Ginny is large, but Graham is strong. I am ready to tell him to go ahead, tuck her under one arm and run her kicking and screaming back up the ramp into her new house. But in the time that I consider this, Philomena has appeared at Ginny's other side. She's wearing the sunglasses so I can't see her eyes. She shakes her head. She looks like a cop. She looks like a cop who is about to pull me over. Ginny lifts up Binky Baby, poised to strike the car again.

I get out of the car. "Okay," I say to Ginny. "Stop," I say. "I'll give you back your dog. Just stop."

We all wait for Ginny to lower her arm. She pushes her glasses back up. Ginny is staring at me and I wonder if she is considering hitting me and I hate myself for thinking this.

"I do not need key," Philomena says.

"Really, Philomena? I mean . . ." I don't even know what I'm trying to say.

"It is fine," she says. And I believe she means it.

I sigh and Ginny sighs and I look at Graham and I can't tell what the hell he's thinking. With some determination, I pull Rascal out and walk her around the back of the car toward my sister. Purposefully I come around to the side that is not holding Binky Baby, but still, I am afraid she may hit me.

"Come, Ginny," Philomena says. "I will help you." And with confidence, she takes Rascal's leash from me and then she takes Ginny's arm and helps to turn her around. "Come, Rascal," she says. And she and Ginny and Rascal move slowly up the ramp together.

Graham and I both get in the car and close the doors. I'm closing my eyes, afraid to open them and realize that we are actually here. When I open them, I see that Graham is indeed sitting in the passenger's seat and we are indeed parked in front of my sister's new house and that my older son is disappointed in me. "You let her win, Mom," he says.

"Yes," I say. I want to cry but I do not want my son to see. So instead, I say, "I'll be right back," and I head back up the ramp myself.

Philomena has already returned Ginny to her wheelchair and parked her back at her place at the table. Rascal is still on her leash, hooked to the handle on the chair next to her. Binky Baby is back in her high chair and she looks like hell, with a deep dent on the side of her head, dirt—or maybe scratches—on the side of her face.

As calmly as I can muster, I say to my sister, Ginny, "Why are you doing this? I've worked so hard to make this nice for you . . . Why are you being like this?"

And Ginny looks at me more coldly than I have ever seen her in our whole lives. "Where is the deed?" she says. "I want to see the deed."

"It's your house," I say. "You signed all the papers, remember?"

"Show me the deed!" She picks up her spoon and throws it at the wall, which leaves a mark.

I look at Philomena. I had told her that my sister could be difficult, but I hadn't told her like this. I hadn't told her that she gets violent and throws things. I plead with her as best I can without words. Please do not leave us today, I beg. Philomena removes her glasses and she looks right at me with what I see now are lovely and warm brown eyes. She nods her head with compassion. Ginny is looking up at her, so presumably she sees Philomena's lovely eyes as well. Philomena puts the glasses back on.

"Goodbye, Ginny," I say. "I hope you and Rascal and Binky Baby and Philomena have a good second night here in your very nice new home. I will talk to you when you are ready to be civil again."

The drive home with Graham is only six minutes but feels longer. He tells me I'm a saint and that Ginny doesn't appreciate me. He tells me not to give in or I'll set a bad precedent. Once we're back, I pack him some snacks and we give each other hugs and he's off to join his friends on the Jersey shore. I am glad he'll be gone for the weekend.

Leo is at his lifeguard training 'til at least six. And even then, there's no guessing as to when he'll be home. I'd call Theresa but she's back with her dad who's now in hospice. I'd call Bill but he's not my husband. I need someone to tell me what to do. Someone who's not Graham. Definitely someone who's not Bets. I can't call Sunnyside. It's too soon.

When did Graham become such a dick? Telling me to take Rascal. Is this what business school teaches?

When did I become such a prick? Following his stupid suggestion. Such a spineless mindless follower!

Ding. From Leo: *Ginny says you tried to steal Rascal?*

Ding. From Graham: *Don't cave.*

Ding. Bill: *Did you take Rascal away?*

And then my phone rings. It's Bets who hasn't returned my calls or texts in over six months. I do not answer, though she does leave a message, in which her mellow-yellow voice says, "Ginny told me that you took Rascal. I can't think of one good reason why you'd do that. You should take her dog back. That's the least you could do. I told her if you don't return Rascal by end of day, I'll get involved."

It's only two o'clock and I want nothing more than to sleep. I should put on my sneakers to take Coyote for a walk. She would like that. A call. Oh no. Oh good. My weekend storyboards for the new erectile dysfunction pill are moved to Monday. It's Friday, which means I have an actual weekend. But with whom? Anyway, I can't get off the sofa.

I take the other end of Coyote's toy and wrestle with her.

I want to cry, but I won't.

Instead, I text Ginny: *I am sorry I took Rascal. Rascal is your dog and you need each other. I will never take Rascal again. I was angry and I didn't know what to do. I am angry that you switched the locks and did not give me or Philomena a key. I understand that you are angry about things, too. I love you, Ginny, but I am still angry. I will see you in a few days.*

Then I text Philomena: *I am sorry, Philomena. I texted Ginny and told her I was sorry for taking her dog. That was wrong of me but I was angry that she changed the locks. Thank you for being there. If you don't mind, I will not come over for a few days. Please call me if you need anything.*

She texts back: *Everything fine. Do not worry.*

I check Match to see if Malick has liked me back. Theresa said we'd be good together. But he hasn't liked me, so maybe he doesn't agree. Or maybe, like me, he's been busy. I look at him again. He seems to have nice eyes. I won't really know until they meet mine. He's handsome in a warm wide smile kind of way. Not show-stopping. Nose to nose with his . . . Shih Tzu? She's wearing a bow in her hair, which is amusing. Holding up a beautiful loaf of bread. On the top of a mountain with a bike. He says he's of average height, which is fine. I don't need someone towering over me. I would like to meet him and I hope I like him and I hope that he would like the likes of me. But right now, I do not like myself. No wonder he hasn't liked me. I go to sleep.

❦

It's Saturday and I am going to visit my sister. Graham's not back so he's not here to shake his head. I bake a quiche because I know Ginny likes quiche. She has very few teeth. I took her to my dentist a few months ago on Sunnyside's dentist's recommendation, and my dentist was able to get Ginny to trust her enough to get a good look into her mouth. Five teeth, she counted. She asked Ginny if she was in pain and Ginny said no. She supposed that she needed some root canals but suggested instead to just have the teeth pulled and use dentures. Ginny said she'd think about it, which of course meant No. The quiche is an apology.

I also want Philomena to know that even though I'm not taking my sister under my own roof and I royally screwed up yesterday, I am actually nurturing.

I bring Coyote, too. I know this is important to Ginny, for the cousins to continue their beautiful bond, and if need be, if I'm not up for completely swallowing my pride, I can blame the visit on Coyote's needs and not my own.

And I bring something else. Something that Ginny has requested. The deed to 59 Beech Street with her name on it.

I ring, I knock, I ring. I hear the locks unlocking. Philomena lets us in. She wears rubber gloves and an apron. She says she doesn't need an apology. Coyote runs in enthusiastically and Rascal growls at her like a bitch.

"I thought you weren't coming," Ginny says over the screaming TV.

"Coyote wanted to come," I say. My sister and her dog do not deserve us.

At exactly twelve thirty, Philomena serves lunch. Again, a place for me. Take two. Frozen fish sticks and french fries, applesauce, a half a gallon of milk.

"This is delicious, Philomena, thank you so much. It sure is nice to have your own private cook, isn't it, Ginny?" I say these things so that Philomena can hear and in an attempt to turn my sister into a person with manners.

The fish sticks are dry and the fries, greasy. This is not Philomena's fault, this is the way they are. Ginny dips them both into her bowl of mayonnaise. She pours herself another tall glass of milk. She chews slowly and with her mouth open so I can see her gums gnawing at her food.

Finally, I get my purse and pull an envelope out of it. The envelope says *Ginny*. "Here," I say as I hand it to her.

Ginny takes her mayonnaise-covered knife and uses it as a letter opener. She pulls the paper out of the envelope and unfolds it. She takes her glasses off and brings it close to her face so she can read it. Her eyes slowly scan the text, left to right and left to right again. She moves the paper accordingly, squinting.

Yes, I have taken her to an eye doctor and Yes, she has cataracts and is legally blind in her right eye and No, she does not want "needles in her eyes" so she refuses that surgery, too.

Ginny puts the paper down and pours another tall milk.

"You stole Rascal," she says.

"No, I did not steal Rascal. You broke a rule, and I was angry, so I took her until you kept your end of the promise. But as you can see, I gave her back to you without your keeping your end of the promise. I'm sorry that I took Rascal. I was angry and was trying to make my point."

"I would have called the police."

"Okay," I say as I stand up. From dear Danielle at Sunnyside I have learned that when I can't take it anymore I can just politely excuse myself. There is no required time allotment for a visit. Sometimes five minutes is the difference between sanity and suicide. I go to Ginny's bedroom, where Philomena is now remaking the bed, and I thank her again and remind her that I am only a phone call away.

"Come on, Coyote," I say, and Coyote gets up, only to be blocked by Rascal. "I made you a quiche," I say to Ginny. "You can have that for dinner."

"Does Crazy Cat miss Rascal?"

"Yes," I say, though the answer is a definitive No.

"It's my house."

"That's what the paper says . . ."

"I keep the keys in my fanny pack."

"Good," I say. I kiss her sweaty head even though I don't want to and I pat Rascal's growly head even though I'm still a bit scared to.

"You better never take Rascal away. Or Binky Baby."

I stand there over my sister with her mayonnaise hands and her mayonnaise glasses giving Binky Baby her mayonnaise milk bottle. I look over at Rascal, who is out of sorts for good reason. I say, "You were mad at me yesterday, but I was angry at you, too. Be polite to Philomena, you are lucky to have her here taking care of you. Nobody is cooking or cleaning for me at my house."

"It's my house and my keys," Ginny says, licking her mayonnaise fingers. "I don't have to give you a key if I don't feel like it."

And at this moment I am done with Ginny. At this moment I see my sister for what she is: a lazy, spoiled, stubborn, selfish, and stupid—yes, just because she has learning disabilities doesn't mean she's not stupid—sloth. At this moment I feel all good doings and hopeful thoughts turn inside out. At this moment I feel some internal flame turn on and light my innards into a fury-filled inferno.

I bend down close to my sister's ear so that she and only she can hear me, and I whisper fiercely, "I don't want your key. In fact, dear sister, I don't give a *shit* about your key."

I say "shit" hard and sharp. I want to make sure that Ginny hears it. I want to be sure that Ginny understands that I am washing my hands of that responsibility. If they get locked out, Ginny can call Larry the Locksmith. If they don't respond to my calls or texts for three days due to death by carbon monoxide poisoning, I will not check on them and I will not feel guilty. I've pulled my end of the wagon and will now happily drop it.

Ginny's face registers that she did hear it. Her eyes open wide and she blinks hard.

"See you soon, Philomena!" I call. She pops out of the bedroom and says, "Bye-bye!"

Ginny watches as both of the dogs follow me to the door. "No, Rascal," I say as I push her back with my foot to allow Coyote to pass. I close the locked door behind me.

Back the next day, Sunday. To hang pictures, go over her meds with Philomena, check a problem with the brand-new washing machine, deliver a list of important phone numbers—neighbors, sanitation, the library . . . I also give them a list titled, *Fun Things to Do!* We all get in the car, including Rascal, which means that Philomena dares to sit with her in the backseat, and I give them a tour of the town. I show them the library, the parks, the local coffee joint, our town beach, which is actually a small river front. I say, "Hey Gin-Gin, since Philomena drives, she can take you places."

Philomena nods. "This is true! Ginny, I am your friend and I will take you any place you want to go. To Africa, if you like!"

"Go to the beach," I say, "and I'll meet you there!"

"I ordered a one-piece on Amazon," Ginny announces without a smile. "Like the American flag. Red, white, and blue." With her purple gloved hand, she indicates where the stripes will go across her belly.

⌘

Our parents took us to Bethany Beach, Delaware, every summer for a week. One year Ginny brought a cheap CB radio. Mom and Dad knew we were using the CB and they said it was okay to talk so long as we didn't tell anyone our real names or address. My handle was Sugar Plum and I was three days into a vacation romance with a guy named Honey Bear who said he was seventeen. I was fourteen.

He'd call me, *Breaker one nine, this is the Honey Bear seeking his Sugar Plum. Are you there, Sugar Plum?*

I'd answer, "Sugar Plum here. Hi, Honey Bear."

He'd tell me he'd been calling me all morning and I'd tell him I was at the beach. "Probably got a nice tan," he'd say. "Pretty nice," I'd say back, as I lifted my string bikini away from my hip to see the distinct mark. I had coated myself in baby oil and put lemon juice in my hair for highlights. Now Honey Bear wanted to meet.

There was a pool hall that had pinball machines off the main highway and Ginny knew where it was. Ginny could drive now, and she was going to be a senior in high school. She went to a different high school than the one I was entering in the fall. Ginny was in a special education class and this was going to be her second time as a senior. But still, she could drive, and she also had a job at the local Dairy Queen. She didn't serve people because her people skills weren't the best, but she was very helpful with bringing in deliveries, stocking the shelves, and taking out the trash. Ginny said her boss was a Bitch from Hell because she went ballistic on her after Ginny dropped a whole box of ice-cream cones and they all broke.

We decided I should meet Honey Bear and we decided not to tell our mom and dad. Ginny would drive to the pool hall and she promised to protect me. Ginny was strong, and when inspired, stronger. Once she accidentally backed up onto the neighbors' dog and she got right out of the car and lifted it and I reached under the wheel and pulled the thing out. The dog limped away, whining. Ginny didn't want me to tell anyone, but I ran inside and told our parents who of course called the neighbors to apologize and paid the veterinarian's bills. "I saved the dog's life!" Ginny had said. "That's one way of looking at it," our father said.

Honey Bear said he'd be wearing a red T-shirt and I said I'd be wearing a light blue one. I was planning to wear my terry cloth. But then at the last minute I changed my mind and changed into my green-and-white-checkered halter top that I had made in Home Economics. Not because I looked prettier in it, though maybe I did, but because this way he would not know I was Sugar Plum when we walked into the pool hall.

It took a minute for our eyes to adjust. It was bright outside and so dark inside. Why would anyone choose to come here on a nice sunny day? I guessed that if you lived here in this beach town you might get sick of the beach, just like how where we lived, we sometimes got sick of the mall.

Ginny and I stood by the front door and nobody looked our way. The red T-shirt popped out like a cherry on top of a sundae. Yep, curly brown hair. That was Honey Bear. He was at the pool table, in the process of shooting. He looked seventeen like he said.

Ginny whispered loudly, "That's him."

"Shhh, I know," I whispered back.

We walked over to the Pac-Man machine. I snuck another glance. Yup, he was holding the pool cue and laughing, the laugh I'd heard before on the CB. Here, it sounded like a snorty kind of laugh. But also. His face was puffy and he had acne blotches and his arms were pale. We slowly walked the perimeter of the room. Ginny liked pinball and her shorts pockets were full of quarters. Honey Bear did not even look up once.

I was glad I didn't wear my light blue terry cloth shirt.

He was so pale and puffy and he had that weird laugh. I was used to boys noticing me at school and at the mall. But Honey Bear and even his friends did not notice me. Not even in my very cute green halter top. People usually looked at Ginny, too, but for different reasons. Maybe it was too dark and they just couldn't see us or maybe they liked pool and pinball games better than girls. I decided I didn't want to meet Honey Bear and I whispered this to my sister. Ginny, who had just put her coins in the machine, nodded and followed me out of there. I told her I was sorry to waste her money and I'd pay her back when I got my next allowance and she said, "Some things are worth more than Pac-Man," which meant a lot because I knew how much she loved that game.

We went to Dairy Queen on the way back to the beach house. Ginny was proud to pull out her employee identification card and we both got free sprinkles. The guy who handed us our ice cream smiled at me.

When we got back to the beach house Ginny put on the CB until finally we heard Honey Bear calling out for me: *Sugar Plum, where were you? Why didn't you come, Sugar Plum? This is the Honey Bear looking for his Sugar Plum. Sugar Plum, Sugar Plum, are you there? You're just a big tease, Sugar Plum, that's what you are. Don't ever come round here again.*

This scared me so I asked Ginny not to use the CB anymore and she didn't.

That week at the beach with Ginny stayed with me, and in college, I made it the subject of my first large painting. I'd built the frame and stretched the canvas myself:

It's humid. And the sun and shade are strong. Two teenage girls, one older and bigger than the other, her beach towel wrapped around her and tucked under her arms; the younger, skinny, in a crocheted bikini, her towel draped over her shoulders. Flip-flops, both of them, hair sticking to their faces. They are each holding soft ice-cream cones. With sprinkles on the ice cream. The scene is from the ice-cream server's point of view. His hand is returning an ID card to the bigger girl, whose eyes are all about her ice cream and her tongue is all about the sprinkles. The younger girl looks up to him with a trying-it-out kind of smile and one of her shoulders is higher than the other as she's got her hand on that hip. They are both smiling, the girls. The older one's teeth are crooked; the younger one wears braces.

Beach Boys was the title.

My teacher said it was my best work yet and I should continue to explore this theme. At the time I wasn't sure what the theme was. When I showed it to Ginny, she said she didn't get why the name had *Boys* when it was two girls. Nor did she know anyone who would hang it in their house. She said I shouldn't put it in a museum because I might get sued by the Beach Boys.

❦

I receive an onslaught of troublesome texts.

Ginny: *I no why Filomena is name. that. She is MEEN.*

Philomena: *Ginny will not take her pills or test blood sugar. Don't worry. I will keep trying.*

Ginny: *She. nice Wen.you here. ware sunglssis cuz she want by the LAW.*

Philomena: *Ginny told me she don't like African food but I made her Macaroni and Cheese with no spices.*

Ginny: *If die of poy.sun MEENA did it.*

Ginny: *MEENa try to kill me*

Ginny: *I wil fyre MeenA*

Ginny: *MeenA lyes . my beech boy blankt GON*

Ginny: *MEENA. steeeeelZ!*

Ginny: *I dnt need Nani*

Ginny: *AfKan food give me runnnnns*

I tell Ginny it will be an adjustment. I explain that I can't answer all of her texts because I am working and have sons and there are just so very many texts. I explain once again that Philomena's eyes are very sensitive to light and so she is protecting them. I suggest she write things down that are bothering her and we can talk about them when I see her.

The next time I go to her house, she presents her Official Complaints. In her glasses, with her pen and legal pad on the table, she looks strangely professional. There, on the top line, in childlike handwriting with childlike spelling, it says: Ofishil Complayns.

"I did what you told me to," she says. "Wrote it down."

"I see," I say. "Wow. Long list."

"I already have another one but I didn't have time."

"Another thing to add?"

"Nother list."

"You can just tell me now."

Ginny shrugs. "Doesn't matter," she says.

I read:

You tuk way my hose.
You tuk way my car.
You kidnapd my dog.
You tuk way stat ov Marland.

Yu put my baybes in a box so thy cud dii.
Yu highd meen nanni.
Meena iz tryg to kill me nd Razkle.
Meena shrt sheettid my bed.
Food frum Afrika is gong to kill me.
Meena iz big fat lieer.
Meena want me and Rascul ded.

Meanwhile, Ginny lectures Rascal. "I don't want you being mean to Coyote. See, your Aunt Maggie didn't bring her this time? Coyote is your cousin and you should be nice to your cousin cause if you can't trust family, who can you trust?" Binky Baby just sits there, her mouth covered in syrup and Eggo crumbs, the dent on her head now covered by a Band-Aid.

∾⟨∿⟩∾

Two weeks into it, we have all learned Ginny's schedule:

Wake around 8:30.

From bed, turn on the TV, volume very loud.

Go to the bathroom by herself because she will not allow Philomena to help her.

Take off dirty diaper and pajamas and leave them on the floor.

Climb into the handicap accessible shower and sit on the chair and take a shower.

Get dressed.

Sit in wheelchair. Watch TV.

Text me: I.am.fine.and.clean. (One of the rules is that she has to stay in touch with me and can't just shut herself in like she did with Mom. This is the only rule that Ginny is actually following. She texts me every morning, some variation of the above.)

9:30–10—Grab Binky Baby from her crib, throw her on her lap. Wheel their way to dining table, where a beautiful breakfast awaits them.

Say hello to Rascal. Ignore Philomena. Refuse to check her blood sugar.

Watch a Disney movie from her phone while eating every bit of waffles, pie, and applesauce and drinking half a gallon of milk.

On way to recliner, stop and look up at the thermostat to see if Philomena turned down the heat. Yes, it is warm outside, but Ginny requires it be hot inside because Ginny is always cold.

Go to recliner. Watch TV.

Take morning nap, while TV is on at full volume.

Wake to alarm, set to Island Tunes.

1:00—Light lunch due to late breakfast. Grilled cheese dipped in mayonnaise, perhaps.

Watch more TV.

2:40—Watch neighborhood kids walk by while returning from school. Weather permitting, she does this from the front porch.

3:30—Nap in bed, which has been made with fresh, clean linens.

5:00—Wake to alarm of Island Tunes.

Watch TV, text.

6:30—Go to dining room table for dinner, which is waiting for her.

Watch movie on phone while eating fish and chips and mayonnaise very slowly.

Go to recliner to watch whatever is on TV.

10:00—Say goodnight to Rascal, say nothing to Philomena, roll herself and Binky Baby into bedroom.

⸙

I have taken to praying for Philomena. Each night before I get into bed, I look out my bedroom window, to the silhouettes of the tall tulip poplars, and say, "Peace to Philomena."

Philomena came here all the way from Ghana after her husband didn't return from his business trip. He was in the visa business, or so he said, but when police came to her house, they said all the visas were fake. Even her own visa was fake. She learned this when she took her young daughters, Effy and Farida, to Accra Airport. They wouldn't let them on the plane.

So she applied for a new visa, a real visa. And waited for many years for it to come through. Every year on Christmas day she watched *Home Alone* with her girls and said, "Someday, we will go to New York. We will live with Nana." Nana is Philomena's mother, her daughters' grandmother, who they had never met.

And when her girls were thirteen and eleven, she brought them here. They live in a four-story walk-up in the Bronx. She says the drivers are crazy there, but the rent is good. Her girls come straight home after school. Farida is a serious girl. A good student. Effy is interested in cartoons and American Girl dolls.

Philomena loves her church and she loves her God and she has many friends and family nearby. She wears sunglasses in many shades, though she never throws it. She always looks so beautiful, with her hair and gold hoops and chains. From one hangs a crucifix. She says Jesus died for our pains. And she cares for my sister on Beech Street while her mother cares for her two in the Bronx.

She never complains, often laughs, always carries herself with elegance. I admire Philomena. And while my God is the trees, and hers is her own, I pray for her and her family. I hope she gets help with her eyes. I hope she completes her online courses, so she can become a nurse aide and live with her children and mother full-time. And until then, I pray that my childish sister doesn't drive her away.

❧

It's dinnertime. When my cell rings, I ignore it. These are my few precious minutes of Leo time before he runs off to play basketball with his dad. But then the home phone starts so now I am compelled to check. It's Philomena. Philomena doesn't call in the evening. My sister died, she will tell me, a heart attack while watching a rerun of *Starsky & Hutch*.

"She fell today," she says. "Moving from her chair to her wheelchair. As she sat down, it move behind her and she slide off the wheelchair onto the floor."

"Oh dear," I say, while Leo watches and listens intently. I mouth to him that his aunt is okay and he gets up from the table without clearing a single dish and disappears upstairs.

"She okay, she say she fine. She does not want me to tell you."

"Are you telling me that Ginny spoke to you?" I say.

Philomena laughs. "Yea, she did!"

"Why, Philomena, this is a breakthrough!"

"Yes," she says, "but I could not get her up. She very heavy, your sister."

I know this. And I know that my sister lacks the strength to help in such an endeavor. Once at Sunnyside, I watched Jorge work with her on how to get herself up off the floor. She struggled to turn her own body sideways and to lift herself to her hands and knees. She couldn't do it. Afterward Ginny told me that Jorge was into torture and probably S 'n' N.

Philomena described how they were lucky because it was close to the time that the mailman usually came by, so she brought Ginny a pillow and told her to wait a few minutes and then when he came, Philomena asked him to come in and help her get Ginny back into her wheelchair. "I told her not to eat so much sugar so she can get stronger and she say she gave up sugar and something is wrong with the wheelchair," she says.

Oh yes, shortly after move-in day, the packages started coming. While challenged in many ways, my sister had no trouble changing her delivery address on Amazon. And at 59 Beech Street, there's no baby sister to steal her packages. Sigh.

"You know she will not let me help her with her blood sugar test,"

Philomena says. When Philomena speaks, her delivery is calm, every word, deliberate.

"Yes," I say. I know.

"She say she do it herself but no needles, no test strips in her trash can."

"Sigh," I say.

"Now she won't talk to me again," laughs Philomena.

"Did she thank you at least?"

"I see your sister as my sister and I care for her as I care for my sister."

I thank Philomena again and tell her she is an angel and that I don't know how she does it, putting up with my sister's rudeness. I tell her she should take the weekend off to go see her family. We'll get a replacement through the agency. It's been three weeks since her only weekend off in two months' time.

⚬⚬⚬

Bets has gone viral. Overnight, over ten thousand hits. This is news I get piecemeal in a group text that Graham started. He included a link. Leo writes *She's famous!* and Ginny writes *allredy famus.* I watch the link and sure enough, there she is, dancing on Venice Beach boardwalk in disco wear. She's dancing with a firefighter. A hose and a burning hoop are involved. And then when they bow, the firefighter whips off his firefighter hat and long willowy hair falls down to reveal that he is a she. Another link from Graham. A local news story. It's a FUNdraiser to promote awareness about wildfires. The newscaster makes a predictable joke about how the heat between them could start a fire and it's good they are here on the beach and far away from kindling.

My sister, now with bright yellow spiky short hair, is shimmying while this gal rubs up all around her. I'm uncomfortable watching it and not because they are two women but because one of them is my sister. I'm uncomfortable because my sister Bets is so very comfortable showing off her stuff to the whole entire world. There's nothing modest about it, nothing private. *Look at me! I'm in your face with my awesomeness. And you believe I'm awesome. I'm barely there for my sisters back east, but here, on the West Coast, I'm fricking awesome.* I do not comment on the text thread but I do give the video a thumbs-up because I want my sons to see that I appreciate that my sister is raising awareness for obvious causes.

Oops, Graham texts me separately. *Sorry Mom. Wasn't meant for you.* Which means he wanted to keep me out of the loop about his cool aunt, my coolest sister, and this makes me uncomfortable, too.

She didn't always make me uncomfortable. I used to think she was cool, too. Bill and I both looked forward to our nights out with Bets every time we all went back home for the holidays. Christmas was cozy at our parents' house, with Mom welcoming us with an enormous variety of fresh baked cookies, Dad, with eggnogs, and Gin-Gin showing up in her Santa hat, her pup wearing reindeer bells. In addition to our usual traditions of listening to Dad read "The Night Before Christmas" on Christmas Eve and then a walk along the creek, we had our annual Pizza Party at Ginny's and our once-a-year Fete with Bets. My parents would babysit. We invited Ginny, but she had already established herself as a homebody and also the kind of parent who would never leave her child just to go out and party. Still, she always told us to "Party hardy."

We'd head down to a bar in Adams Morgan. Bets usually started us out with something wild like tequila followed by pickle juice chasers. Then Bill kept things festive, with peppermint schnapps and grenadine. My shot was usually something sweet. The first round was always on Bets, the rest on Bill and me. Eventually she and Bill would step out and smoke and then return with a good case of the munchies, meaning hot chicken wings and fries.

One year I threw up and another time Bill did. Once, Bets actually passed out right there at the table. She's petite. She was awakened by the sound of tap shoes. The bartender had promised us entertainment and sure enough, they had a professional dancer come in. Bill and I watched as he literally jumped from the floor up onto the bar. He slid across it and then started tapping. Bets woke with a jolt and looked up at him and by the end of the night we had all taken turns, faux-tapping with the tapper.

Bets was my holiday sister. She left home when I was still so little. Eight, nine? And she came home for holidays, my wedding, sometimes she'd just show up and surprise us. I never saw her doing homework when she was a teen, I never saw her seated at a desk even. Hard to imagine actually. If I painted that image it would have to be an abstract.

When Dad and then Mom died, she flew east. She helped me put together their services and at both, she held on to me tight. Bill and the boys held each other, and Ginny cried hard with Binky Baby. After Mom's service, in the driveway before Bill drove her to the airport, Bets confided in me that she had decided to quit drinking in Mom and Dad's honor. I said, "Okay. We'll find another way to Fete with Bets." She said, "No, I'm done with that altogether. No more fetes. From here on in, I'm going to be fully sober and present. No more running away." After we sold their old house, we divided the money evenly. It was enough to "keep us all afloat" as Bets said, "but not enough to send us sailing."

I've watched the boardwalk dancing thing at least ten times now and I've got to stop. Who knew my sister could dance like that? Well, I did. She danced like that at our wedding, Bill's and mine. We all danced like wild things to the sound of Bill's mix-tape. I remember Griff lifting her above his head. Her waist was teeny-tiny. Her waist is still teeny-tiny. When the firefighter brings her up from the deep dip, she smiles a dazzling smile.

Graham calls me to tell me something serious. He says he doesn't want me to hear it from Ginny first. "*Dancing with the Stars* reached out to her," he says. They want her on their next season. "Well, of course!" I say, enthusiastically. It makes such sense. Former surfing star Bets Frederick. I say, "Maybe this will be her big break!" Though I have no idea what she'll be breaking into.

⋙⋘

Ah, another day, another onslaught of texts. Sometimes I have two text streams going at once with both Ginny and Philomena, neither knowing I'm communicating with the other.

Ginny: *Filo meana pat logkil lire* (Philomena pathological liar.)

Philomena: *Today I pray for Farida*

Me to Ginny: *Philomena is a good woman and you are lucky to have her helping you*

Me to Philomena: *Is Farida okay?*

Philomena: *LOL yes! She take special test for college so I make special prayer*

Me to Ginny: *Fantastic! SAT?*

Ginny: *NO*

Me to Ginny: *NO what?*

Ginny: *NO FANtasik*

Ginny: *fell wen sat she killn me*

Oops—that Fantastic SAT text was meant for Philomena.

Me to Philomena: *Oh good! SAT?*

Ginny: *skweelr*

Philomena: *Her school tell her to take test. Ginny sat down and chair slipped.*

Philomena: *for college*

Me to Philomena: *Oh, Wow! That's exciting!*

Me to Philomena: *Be grateful. You are very lucky to have her.*

Oops—that was meant for Ginny. I imagine them there: Philomena in the laundry room, Ginny lounging in front of the TV.

Philomena: *I very great full. Thank my god every day for her. And my mother and Effy.*

Me to Philomena: *Of course!*

Philomena: *thanks to God every day.*

Me to Philomena: *I do!* In my own way. *Sending good thoughts!*

Ginny: *fire Filo meena*

Philomena: a photo of the trees across the street from Ginny's house, *colors of our Ghana Flag,* Ghana flag emoji, red, yellow, green

Ah, so Philomena is on the deck!

Me to Philomena: *So pretty!* And then I send a photo of the trees that I see from my deck.

Me to Ginny: *Be grateful!*

Ginny: *Im gun fire Filo meen*

Ginny: a photo of her pink Crocs with Rascal asleep on her pillow next to her, confirming that Ginny is indeed lounging in her chair.

ᏩᏳᎦ

I tell Bill it's not going well. I hadn't meant to do that. I had meant to project that I had everything under control, that I was succeeding in giving Ginny a better life in the process of saving her life. I hadn't meant to tell him, but he caught me off guard, calling me while deep in a board. That's the one good thing about my job. While drawing, I can listen to kick-ass playlists and I can also converse. And Bill may be my ex, but we have things to talk about, so many things. Like what the heck is going on with Graham's girlfriends and what the hay is happening with Leo's grades and he wants permission to take Coyote on a walk with his stunning and sensuous girlfriend. I say yes, but he'll need to spend the same amount of time with Crazy Cat and I don't want Stunning Sensuous Girlfriend in the house. He says it's still partly his house and I say fine then come sometime when I'm not here. Like when I'm at Ginny's house. Because let's face it, that's the only other place I go. Shit. I've revealed too much.

I tell him that she wants to fire Philomena and I'm wondering now if I made a mistake. I tell him I can't call my other sister because she will surely give me shit. He tells me her jump through the fire hoop has now become a viral gif. I hadn't meant to tell Bill. I should have just saved it for Theresa, but I needed to talk to someone, another adult who knows Ginny, and truth is, he's the only other adult in the vicinity who even knows her really, one of the few lucky ones who actually has affection for her.

"Hang in there," he says. "Just give her time."

I take a deep breath, grateful for the lack of bitterness and the appearance of actual support. "Thank you," I say. "Do you think she'll come around?"

"Hey, like the song says," and he sings now, "*Don't give up, you know it's never been easy.*"

He's singing the Peter Gabriel song, the one he sings with Kate Bush, the song he knows makes me melt every time I hear it.

"Thanks, Bill," I say. "I appreciate the faith." I'm not being sarcastic or sharp or any of those things.

"Course," he says. And I think he means it.

After we hang up, I just have to sit for a minute. I haven't heard Bill sing in a very long time.

૯✦૭

It's one of those spectacular October days that you see pictured in the *I Love New York* commercials. It's been more than two months since the big move and my sister is still having trouble adjusting—not accepting Philomena, not behaving like her best self, the self I imagine, the self I'm still hoping she'll evolve to. It's my fault, I suspect, as I always accept responsibility for other's deficiencies. What she needs is some fun. What she needs is some unadulterated sister-and-dog time and my full attention. She needs to know how happy I am to have her here, in my little Hudson River neck of the woods. I show up at her house unannounced, with both Coyote and pumpkin bread, her favorite.

"We're going on a road trip," I say.

"I'm done with doctors," Ginny says.

"No doctors. Just sisters and dogs."

"Where?"

I shrug. "Wherever," I say.

I expect resistance, but Ginny is in. She rolls herself to her bedroom to use the bathroom and get her wallet. I inform Philomena that she has the next four hours off and she is elated.

"Four hours?" she says. "Really?" She actually takes off her sunglasses to look me straight in the eyes, which makes me wonder if she's usually not really seeing me.

"Four hours?" Ginny says.

"Yes, Philomena, really. Ginny, we're gonna go have some fun and when we come back you can take your nap," I say.

"Four hours?" Philomena is now dabbing her eyes, which are back hidden under her sunglasses. I think she's crying. "I will go see my daughters and my mother. I be back in time to make dinner."

"I think that's a great idea," I say. "Ginny, don't you agree?" I can see that Philomena has already done the math. An hour to drive to and park in the Bronx, two hours with her precious family, an hour back. I can see that Ginny is doing some sort of math that has to do with Philomena getting paid for time off.

Whatever. We've got a plan!

Five hundred dog biscuits woo Rascal into the car. Coyote shrinks into the floor behind the driver's seat, hoping Rascal will not see her there. They haven't been together in this small a space in a long time, so I say a medium-size prayer. I have to dig under Ginny's large thigh to find the safety belt buckle—she's definitely put that weight back on. Philomena is in her car now, too, and I can see that she is praying. I honk and we wave to one another before we both take off.

"Leaves!" I say as we turn off Beech Street. "Isn't it beautiful, Gin-Gin?" She doesn't say anything. She's wearing her *Life's a Beach* sweatshirt and a baseball cap that says *Malibu*. Binky Baby is on her lap. She's looking to the backseat to the pups.

"Are they okay back there, Gin-Gin? No blood yet?"

"There is blood."

I panic and try to grab a look back. "Wait. What?"

"Cousins," Ginny grins.

We're on Maple Street now and headed north to 129. My goal is to take her on the back roads and maybe up to a local farm where we can get out and get donuts and cider.

"Pretty, huh?" I say.

"The leaves turn earlier than in Maryland. In Maryland they turn on Halloween."

"Huh," I say.

"You would go to sleep the night before and all the leaves would be green and then when you woke up on Halloween they'd be different colors."

"I guess the trees wear costumes, too," I say. "You know, for Halloween?"

Ginny is still watching the dogs as we approach the bridge that crosses over the reservoir.

"Ginny, look," I say. And she does. It couldn't be more beautiful. Really. The water is a mirror image of the bright autumn hills. "This is where we live!"

"Elephants," my sister says.

Ah, she's still thinking about Halloween. "A heard of elephants," I say. Ah, yes, I went as a herd of elephants. I wore gray panty hose and Dad's big gray sweater with pictures of elephants safety-pinned all over it. Pics I cut from *National Geographic*, pics I drew . . . On my head I wore ears and a trunk that I made out of construction paper. One of my finer costumes, I believe. "Yup," I say. "What was your favorite costume that you ever wore?"

"Malibu Barbie."

"But you always look like Malibu Barbie, with your tan and your blond hair."

"There's always a first time," Ginny says. "Bets went as Elvis."

"Yea," I say. I can still see her in that wig and that crazy jumpsuit. I thought she was so super cool back then. She hasn't reached out to me even once since the big move, since the kidnapping of Rascal, and I haven't reached out to her either. It's going on three months and look at me and Ginny now, bitches! I don't really think she's a bitch. I don't know what to think of her really. I just know I'm mad. "Elvis has left the building," I say, and Ginny doesn't say anything. "Talk to her lately?" I dare to ask.

"Not lately," Ginny says. "She's busy with reality. She's gonna save the coral reef she said when it goes on TV." Yeah. She used to be a spokesperson for that cause, now I guess she'll dance for it?

I can't help myself. I have to ask. "Does it ever bother you, Ginny, that our big sister is never here? That she's not around to help? Like, ever?"

"She's got her own life," she says.

"Yea," I say, "but shouldn't she sometimes be here? Shouldn't she take time away from her fricking coral reef to be here?" Helping you. Helping me help you.

She's looking back at the dogs again. Perhaps I'm making her upset, which isn't what I meant to do . . . Or maybe it is what I meant to do.

"A sister is still a sister even if she's weird," Ginny says.

"Yea," I say. I guess . . .

"And anyway, she's got—what do you call it? Si-col . . . Si-col . . . With her head?"

"Psychology?" I say. "Psychological?"

"Yeah," Ginny says. "Fear of being tied down. That's why she doesn't have a dog. Fear of leashes, anything with rope."

"Did she tell you that?"

"Doesn't haf to. I know what I know," Ginny says.

The truth of it is, it would be so fun if Bets was here with us now, taking a fall foliage road trip. "You don't get leaves like these in California!" I say. Bets would be driving, of course, so I'd be relegated to the backseat. But she'd be joking, laughing, she'd probably put the windows down to catch the fresh crisp air and start a round of "Row, Row, Row Your Boat" and I would join in. We'd try to get Ginny to sing, but she'd refuse, so this would make us laugh even harder. Maybe we'd even pull over by the reservoir and take selfies!

I turn on the radio and the news comes on, which is the last thing we need to hear, so I quickly plug in my jazz station. Ahhh, it's Ella, singing "Autumn in New York."

"Oh my goodness, Ginny," I say as I turn up the volume. "It doesn't get any better than this!"

We pass a dead raccoon. We pass a tree so orange it looks inflamed. A bunch of bikers pass by on the other side of the road. I wonder if Ginny listens to the words of the song, if they go straight to her heart the way they do to my own: *the gleaming rooftops at sundown . . . it lifts you up when you run down . . .*

"In Maryland you have to pile 'em up on the street," she says. "Here you've gotta bag 'em." The leaves. I hired my lawn guys to do her yard. I'm sure she watched their every move.

"Huh, that's right."

"The wind just blew 'em everywhere again," she says, as she takes her finger to draw the wind as a cyclone.

"*Autumn in New York,*" I sing.

When we reach the farm, she doesn't want to get out of the car. She says it's because she's been to farms and she doesn't eat apples anyway. She says it's not because they are too hard to chew and she only has five teeth. I suggest we could buy some and make applesauce with cinnamon. She says she'd feel like she's cheating on Maryland because New York is famous for apples.

The bathroom? Nope. So I leave her there with the pups and I get out to buy each of us a donut, even donuts for dogs. Ginny will share hers with Binky Baby and by the time we get back to her place I know they will both be covered in crumbs.

On the drive back, she observes that people in New York really go all out for Halloween and she's never seen so many skeletons. I tell her about a great corn maze where I used to take the boys. It's just a bit up the Taconic, and if she wants, I can take her there right now. I say this knowing that she doesn't and I won't.

"Gin-Gin," I say, "you are in the best neighborhood for Halloween, lots of kids are going to come by."

"You told me that already."

"I know, but I thought you might be excited."

"Got my candy a month ago."

"You did? Wow."

"Don't worry. It's safe."

"I'm not worried."

"It's in the safe," she says. One of her purchases from Amazon was a heavy portable safe. Philomena needed my help carrying the box into her bedroom. Ginny told us she was using it for important documents. "I don't eat candy anymore," she says. "Gave it up."

This is not true and I know it. Philomena has reported regular Amazon deliveries, candy wrappers and cookie packages in her room, and the sound of crunch and crinkles from there in the morning before she comes out. Ginny used to emerge around nine thirty for breakfast. Now it's more like eleven thirty for brunch. Apparently, every day is Halloween at Ginny's house.

"Cool," I say.

"Just one a day. That's all."

Um hmmm . . . "Cool," I say again. "You're checking your blood sugar every day, right?" Slipping this in oh so casually and of course she ignores me.

"Don't know where my decorations are. If I even have decorations anymore unless you threw them out. Nobody tells me anything."

"They're in your basement, remember? Remember I told you there's a room with all your holiday stuff and all the boxes are marked and all you have to do is ask Philomena to go down and get them?"

"She doesn't speak English."

"She does. She has an accent."

"Not politically."

"Correct? It's politically correct if it's her own accent."

She pulls some crumbled dog biscuits out of her sparkly purple fanny pack and throws them to the backseat for the dogs.

Okay, so I'm ready for this good deed to be over. Does that negate the good deed completely? Was it supposed to be a good deed? Or just a good time? I'm kicking myself again because I think it was just supposed to be a good time. But guess what? It has been a good time! So there!

By the time we get back and get her out of the car and into her wheelchair and Rascal and Coyote out of the car to finally pee, I am ready for her to go immediately to her room for a nap so that I can go immediately home for a nap.

And now here we are—ha ha—here I am, hanging up plastic ghosts, paper skeletons, a dancing scarecrow, and a *Happy Halloween* flag on the front porch. I put a tiny witch hat on Rascal and Rascal growls and Ginny and I both laugh. Then, "That's for Binky Baby," Ginny says, and I make the correction.

৽৵৻

I pour myself a shot of bourbon because I'm a grown-up and I can do that. I eat my locally grown apple with Spanish cheese and I feel like I could be anywhere, sitting outside here on my deck at my house in the woods. These could be Spanish woods. Or Alaskan. Costa Rican. Do they have trees this tall in Japan? Then why not, maybe Japanese woods. It doesn't matter. The point is that I could be anywhere, and this could be anytime and it's a bit chilly to be outside so I go inside to draw a bath. I mean turn on the hot water to fill the tub, not actual drawing!

I remember the time that Graham didn't want a bath and I was pregnant with Leo and I was so big and he was so dirty and Bill said, "Hey Graham-y Pants, maybe if you get in the bath, your mama could draw a picture of you." And I said, "Sure, I could draw you and bubbles and frogs and all sorts of things." And Graham looked right at my belly and said, "A whale?"

It's nice in the tub. My bourbon is warm. My body is warm. My heart is warm, I swear it is. I try to play with myself down there, but it's difficult with no lubrication. I would like to invent a lubricant that works under water. I'd make a zillion dollars and could quit drawing storyboards and who knows what I'd do then?

My toes do a little dance on the other end of the tub. My huge boobs pop out of the water like twin islands. They've gotten bigger since menopause. I'm sure people think I had a boob job. But seriously, I want to say to them, if I was to get plastic surgery, is that really what you think I'd get done?

I get a notification from Match that somebody has liked me back. Liked me back? I haven't been on Match in months! Who could it be? It's Malick. Oh, Malick! Well, hello! Yes, I remember you! I figured you just weren't into me . . . Thought by now you'd have been scooped up! Huh, I click on his images again. He does have a nice and warm smile . . . He does have a silly Shih Tzu . . . I suppose it's time to get out of this tub and check my calendar for a date.

♈

Tomorrow is Leo's driving test. We're all sitting on Ginny's porch. I have bribed him to come here to get Ginny's permission to drive her car for the test. Philomena is leaning against the doorway. She never sits down with us even when invited. She is too busy to sit, but also, she knows that Ginny does not want her to sit down with us.

"What car are you gonna drive?" Ginny asks Leo.

"I was hoping I could drive your car, Aunt Ginny. Would that be okay?"

"Your name is on my insurance."

"Thanks, Ginny," Leo says. He's giving me the eye, done deal.

"Ginny," I say, "you know I'd be happy to buy your car from you. All you have to do is name your price."

"Not ready yet. Might drive again next year," Ginny says.

Ginny hasn't driven since Maryland, almost a year and a half ago. When I drove her and Rascal up here in Ginny's car, I promised to take good care of both of them—the pup and the car, that is. Now of course Ginny has Rascal back, but she's had no luck with the car. I won't give it to her, not even to park it in her driveway. I don't trust that Ginny won't get the urge to get behind the wheel and start it up, and I can't wipe out the image of Ginny accelerating backward into a neighborhood cat or dog or kid. That's the last thing we need. Ginny was pissed about this until I explained that it's the car insurance company's fault. Their policy is that you can't have a car in your driveway unless you are physically able to drive it. This is a lie.

"Don't be scared of your instructor," Ginny advises. "Just think of them naked."

"Yikes, not sure I'd want to do that," Leo says.

"Depends on the instructor," I say.

"Yeah, but even then . . ."

I laugh and Ginny half laughs. I see Leo struggle between desire to bolt and the concept that perhaps he's actually enjoying himself.

"When did you get your driving license, Philomena?"

"Oh, I didn't need to drive in Accra," she says. "There are many buses and taxis. But here, in New Jersey, I did." Ginny resumes watching *The Little Mermaid* on her phone.

"Did you take Driver's Ed?" Leo asks.

Philomena says, "I had just moved here and was living with my sister for a couple months. My sister's husband is very successful dentist and she had just had her baby, so our mother was there, too, taking care of the little ones. I applied for a job at McDonald's and they called and told me I could work there if I started the next day. My first job in the United States."

"Oh wow," I say. "Ginny, are you listening? This is so interesting!"

Philomena doesn't care that she is not listening, she knows she has a captivated audience in Leo and me. And the dogs. The dogs are looking up at her adoringly. Does she have biscuits in her pocket?

"The problem was," she continues, "I had to take a bus there and the bus was always late and it was spring and sometimes it would rain and there was no shelter at that bus stop, the one near my sister's house. But I took an umbrella and I went there by bus at five o'clock in the morning and it took me hour and fifteen minutes to get there from door to door even though the McDonald's was only about ten minutes away by car. It was on the other side of the highway, couple miles away."

I swear to myself that I will never complain about my job, my finances, or anything else ever again. I say, "That's a long commute for only ten minutes away, isn't it Ginny?"

"That would drive me crazy," Leo says.

"Um hmmm," Philomena says.

"So . . . don't keep us in suspense!"

"My brother-in-law had an old car in his garage—a Jaguar."

"A Jaguar?" Leo pipes in.

"He was going to fix up and sell but he said it good enough for me to drive to work and he gave me permission to drive it. But you see, I didn't know how to drive it and neither did my mother or my sister!"

"He was going to let you drive his Jaguar?" Leo is appropriately impressed.

"He is very busy man because he is successful dentist but he only had one afternoon to show me how to do it and he took me out in the neighborhood and first he drove and then he told me to drive."

"Say what?" says Leo. "But you never drove before!"

"I was very nervous!" Now Philomena is laughing. As she laughs the falling leaves dance in her mirrored frames. "Then he went to work and said I could practice by myself. All afternoon, I went around the block and parked in his driveway and then I went around again. And then it was time for dinner and to give my children their showers and then to bed and I went around some more at night! But I didn't know where the lights were because he did not show me so I only had the street lights and it was very dark and somebody honked at me!"

Leo and I are completely captivated and Ginny just bends down over her phone, turning the volume up on the songs.

"The next morning, I wake up at four thirty in the morning because I want to practice some more and I know there would not be too much traffic. And then I drive to work and I made it there in one piece and I was so proud of myself! But it was only then five o'clock in the morning so I went back to the house and parked the car and I tried to take a little nap but I was nervous I would fall asleep and be late to my job at McDonald's and then I turn around and I drove to work and I just waited in my car from five twenty to six o'clock."

"That is a crazy story!"

"Really crazy," says Leo.

"Then when my papers come from my own country, my brother-in-law drove me to the Department of Motor Vehicles and I take the test and I pass on the first try. My sister was jealous, so I taught her!"

"You are amazing, Philomena. When there's a will, there's a way, right Gin-Gin?"

Ginny is still looking at her phone and feigning complete disinterest.

"I will go move the laundry," Philomena says. "Good luck, Leo," and she goes inside.

"I better pass tomorrow or I will be extremely embarrassed," Leo says, standing up to go.

Later, Ginny texts me: *Fill o meena drive against the law.*

Ginny was so proud when she got her driver's license. I was eleven then and I still remember when Ginny and our mother got home. They had gone to Friendly's on the way back to get sundaes to celebrate. I was mad that they did this without me. I wrote on the dry erase board on the refrigerator "Mommy is a Green Bean Fart." I would have written Ginny was a green bean fart, too, but I knew that Ginny got called this already because she came home from school crying once after someone had written it on her spiral.

Our father got very angry with me and hit my bottom and sent me to my room. Later my mother told me that this was Ginny's accomplishment, and it was a special celebration just for Ginny. Ginny kept her license in her wallet, which she carried in her little purse that she wore across her shoulder. She wore it at breakfast, lunch, and dinner and to school, even on days that she didn't have use of the car. She said she wanted to be prepared.

Our parents said she was a very good driver. After a couple of years, they even let her drive me to my dance classes and sometimes Ginny and I would go to the mall or to Friendly's.

The first time I took the test, I failed. It was the parallel parking. The tester stopped me after I'd gone back and forth about four or five times and he said, "What are you gonna do? See-saw back and forth like this in traffic?" I had to take the test two more times and Ginny was rather condescending with her sympathy. "Some people aren't natural drivers," she said. "Some people are born to drive, some people are not. Driving is a very big responsibility and maybe you aren't ready," etcetera.

Graham passed the first time. He was cocky and he picked up three friends and they went down to the river and got drunk and he got pulled over on his way home and lost his license that very night.

Leo, he's been taking his time. No rush to get his license. He has plenty of friends who've been driving him around for months. He has what Ginny calls the Chill and Laid-Back way of life. Even during the test, he took his time. The lady warned him he was almost under the speed limit, but she said that slowness served him during the parallel parking part. He drove by Ginny's tonight with his windows down and honked the horn until he saw her look out.

Ding from Ginny: with fireworks, *LEO. is born.To drive.*

⁂

"Did you know that one in nine human beings on this planet are supported by a relative who is a migrant?" I'm sitting across from Malick. We're on an actual date at a nice sushi restaurant in White Plains, halfway between where he lives in Greenwich, Connecticut, and where I live in COH. He has a very light and appealing French accent. And while he is indeed the same height as me, his build is strong and sinewy.

"No," I say, "that really is amazing."

"It's what makes the world go 'round," he says. This is after he's told me that he sends money to Senegal to his ex-wife and children.

Yes, he studied baking in France, and he's also lived in Tokyo and Miami. He practices international real estate law and does pro bono work for immigrants and refugees. And this is funny, before this first date, I asked him if he is really and actually divorced, and he sent me a photo of his official papers. It also turned out that we have a mutual friend in the city, an old art school friend of mine who runs a nonprofit for immigration services. On Match his updated profile says he is looking for "something real." He feels real.

He convinces me to share the Exotic Sushi Platter, which is enough to feed a family. He says I need to get more daring than tuna and salmon rolls. I can't believe I am actually having an actual date with an actual human being. An adult. A man who doesn't cheat or skirt responsibility. I'm amazed at his ability to consume sushi!

"Check this out," he says. "Roe on the outside, crabmeat and jalapeño peppers on the in." He tosses it up in the air with his chopsticks and actually catches it in his mouth.

"Impressive!" I applaud.

"Now you try one," he says.

"No," I tell him, "I'm sure to miss."

"Then come up with another trick," he says.

I put a full and salty edamame pod in my mouth and one by one, pop out and eat the beans before pushing the shell out with my tongue. We actually laugh and the conversation feels easy. "I have to tell you," I say, "you won me over with the bow." I'm referring to his pup of course.

"The bow?" He chuckles. "Oh, yes, her hair falls in her eyes and we can't have that!"

He says that Coyote looks like a nice dog. "A big dog, a furry one, yes?"

"Oh yes, she does shed," I say. "Sometimes pillows!"

He says that we should take them on a walk together and I say yes, but does his little toy dog really walk? He admits that he carries her. "I can't help it," he says. "She's my baby!"

And then the conversation takes a more serious tone. I tell him I sympathize. I can't imagine having my children on the other side of the world. He tells me he couldn't take them from his ex-wife. It would devastate her. I appreciate his kindness. He says that soon they may choose to go to college here, for which he would pay. So complicated.

He is sympathetic about my Ginny tale, too. He says it's "commendable" that I've done what I've done for her. Again, I feel awkward because I really haven't done that much, have I? I thank him anyway.

We joke about baggage, the emotional kind, how we all carry it, especially as we get older. I say mine is small and not too shabby. He says he threw his off a moving train years ago, travels light, carries with him a pair of boxers in his back pocket and a toothbrush in his front. He actually shows me the toothbrush, which I say is presumptuous. He laughs. "Not really, about the boxers," he says, "but I do like to have fresh breath!"

His mother is back in Senegal, too. In a home. "That must be hard," I say, and "Yes," he agrees. "What kind of home?" "You know," he says, sadly, "dementia." He visits them all regularly.

"We should go for a hike," he says. "Before it gets too cold."

"With the dogs," I say.

"Of course," he says. "Kitsu has a variety of bows that match my hiking gear."

After dinner, he walks me out to my car. I trip a little bit as we step down into the parking lot. "You good to drive?" he asks with what seems true concern.

"I'm good, just klutzy," I say. We only had two bottles of Saki between the two of us, right?

I stop behind Ginny's Honda CR-V and he says, "Yours?" I explain. "Good to keep it running. I'd write Wash Me here, but I don't want to get my hands dirty." He's funny. And a gentleman, he opens my door for me.

"I like your accent, Malick," I say to him.

"And I like yours, Maggie," he says back.

Which makes me laugh. And then we kiss. Just once. And this is very nice.

⸎

Another late call from Philomena. Nine thirty, not good. Could be: Your sister fell out of her bed and hit her head. Your sister fell asleep in the chair and won't wake up. Rascal broke out and ate the old man across the street for dessert. But no, it's about her daughter.

"My Effy," she says, Effy is her younger girl, now fifteen, "got hit by a car. She in the hospital."

I can hear the panic underneath the calm. "Oh my God, Philomena," I say.

"She okay," she says, and then reports a likely broken left leg and wrist. Oh my, I think, they live in a walk-up building. "My mother is there. I have called the agency and will send someone soon. Your sister has already gone to bed . . ."

"Oh, please Philomena," I say, "go. Go to your daughter. Oh my gosh, Philomena, I am so sorry. I'll be right there, you just go."

"She is scared, is the main thing, she did not see the car coming, she did not see it leave."

Some son of a bitch had hit and run. The Bronx. Philomena has always told us that the drivers there were crazy. She also told me once that she understood why there are so many hit and runs. It is not because they are bad people, she had said, it is because they are illegal citizens and therefore illegal drivers.

I go to Ginny's and sleep in Philomena's bed. The replacement will come tomorrow at noon.

In the morning I feed my sister Eggos with fake maple syrup and milk and a large slice of pumpkin pie. I set up a card table so I can work in the back room, where I try to block out the extremely high volume of *Love Boat*. Once I send off my initial drawings, I go toward my sister's bedroom to change the sheets and clean the bathroom.

"No," she says loud and firm. "That is Philomena's job."

"But Philomena is not here."

"It can wait."

My sister does not want me to see the state of her bedroom or her bathroom.

"But if it's dirty," I say, "it must be cleaned."

"NO."

"Gin-Gin, you can't nap on dirty sheets . . . I don't mind doing it, I've washed a lot of sheets in my time."

"No," she says. "You can go home now."

"No, I will wait until the replacement comes."

I stand there for a minute at Ginny's bedroom doorway. I understand that she is ashamed. This is why she hid her diapers in her own home when she lived alone. This is why she doesn't thank Philomena, because she does not want to acknowledge the truth.

I watch Ginny throw scraps to Rascal and smoosh Eggos into Binky Baby's mouth. I wish I had my sketchbook, but then remember I have to get back to my boards for orthopedics.

The doorbell rings, followed by several enthusiastic knocks. Rascal starts howling and I step over her on my way to the door. When I open it, there stands a tall, blond, and skinny middle-aged woman. Her hair is wild as if she was just caught in the eye of a tornado.

"I am Lika Dadeshkeliani!" she announces. In and past me she whisks. She goes directly to Rascal and bends down to meet her. Rascal growls viciously. "What an adorable doggy!" She says. Her accent is thick. She is from the Republic of Georgia, formerly part of Russia, not Georgia the state, I have explained to Ginny. I am about to say you should move away from the dog's face and give her space or she might bite off your nose, when Lika Dadeshkeliani puts hers right up to Rascal's and they both growl.

Ginny finds this amusing.

I put my hand out to introduce myself and she pulls me in for a kiss. She kisses Ginny, too, right on the cheek. Ginny shakes it off and wipes it with her sleeve.

"I cook for you," she says, "very good Georgian food. Do you like barbecue? I give some to dog, too! Do you mind if my husband comes by late at night after Ginny goes to sleep? He is ancient, like me, good man, you can trust him. He can fix things and he will leave before midnight, if this okay. Do you mind if we drink a little bit? We don't get drunk, just a beer or two to relax at nighttime, sometime whiskey, that is all."

Ginny shrugs and says, "I don't care."

"Sure," I say. Whatever you say. You want a million dollars a night? No problem. To roast a pig on the front lawn? Absolutely. On my drive home I thank the lordesses for Lika Dadeshkeliani. From here on, Lika will work the weekends, the holidays.

⁓

It's early December and Malick has invited me on a "holiday hike." "Let's keep the mood jolly, in keeping with the season," he said on the phone. "Oh, wow, that sounds refreshing," I said. He told me his name means King. "Only cheerful subjects," he decreed. I happily agreed.

I pull into the lot at Teatown nature preserve and see that he has already arrived. He's leaning against his silver BMW—ah, I didn't see his car on our sushi date. He's wearing a hot-pink baby carrier. Out the top pops a furry white head. "There they are, Coyote. See the nice man and his cute little dog?" I make a wish that my dog and his get along. Coyote is generally easy going, but sometimes little yappers annoy her.

"Hello!" Malick calls. He puts the flap down in the front of the carrier so we can see his little Shih Tzu's face. "Say hello, Kitsu," he says, and he makes her little paw wave. She wears a red bow and he wears red shoe laces. This is a move Ginny would appreciate.

"Do you always dress to match?" I tease.

"I just did it to see if you pay attention," he smiles. "And now, you have passed the test."

His quirkiness cracks me up. I help Coyote out of the car and the introduction goes well. Malick gives her a treat, which is very nice. He tells me funny stories about growing up in Senegal. I tell him how I'd love to travel there. I mention my summer sighting of a black bear here. He looks alarmed but then says Kitsu's bark is frightening.

I let Coyote off leash as there's no one else here. She runs down to the lake to get a drink.

"Are you going to let Kitsu down?" I ask. He does carry a leash.

He hooks her up and puts her down and she goes over to a tree to do her thing. "Good job, my dear," he says as he picks her up and places her back in the carrier.

"Really?" I say. "I thought this was a holiday hike!"

"A princess must be treated royally," he says. "And anyway, I don't want her to hurt the bear." Her hair is long and silky. He says he brushes it every night.

"Lucky girl," I say.

He makes an exaggerated gesture of bowing down to her and we giggle heartily.

After the hike, we are chilly. I take him to a local tap room that allows canine friends. It's late afternoon on a Sunday. We order mulled wine and artisanal pizzas. Coyote is at my feet, Kitsu, on Malick's lap. He pets her the entire time. I imagine him brushing my hair, petting my back. He knows how to treat a princess. Imagine how he'd treat his queen.

He's off to Africa soon to see his family. Malick is a good man, with excellent priorities. He says he will call me upon his return in January. He would like to see my house, meet my boys. "Our pups do get along," he says. He gives them each a bit of crust and both of their tails wag.

⁂

Philomena is with her mother and daughters for a few days and Lika has signed on for the holiday. She is now commonly referred to as Georgian Woman, and I invite her for Christmas. Ginny says she can't pronounce Lika's name, even though we both tell her all she has to say is Lika, not Lika Dadeshkeliani.

"Just say Lika," I say. "Like *like*, but with an A at the end."

"Say Lika," Lika instructs.

Ginny refuses.

"Lika!" Lika says. "Everybody Like Lika!"

Even so, Ginny finds it easier to say Georgian Woman and Lika approves, adding, "Gorgeous Georgian Woman!"

I had considered just inviting Ginny. Just family, I thought, Ginny, the boys, and me. But Lika had told a tragic tale of how her parents are old and suffering back in the Republic and her own daughter is too busy with her own children in Iowa and her husband is not a holiday person. She said Christmas brought back too much pain about his younger days when everything was so beautiful in their old country. So I invited her and now I'm glad that I did.

After she and Graham manage to get Ginny and her wheelchair into the house, after Crazy Cat and Coyote go to greet them, Georgian Woman goes back out to the car and pulls out pot after pot after pot. "Here," she says, as she places each one on the counter, "Georgian barbecue. Here, Georgian dumplings. Here Georgian honey cake, here, Georgian grape pudding. Now we have Georgian Christmas!"

I am glad that Leo is here to add some green to the mix. He makes Santa's Spinach, a dish he invented that he swears is the fuel that keeps the guy going. Graham picked out the beer and wine and keeps it flowing freely as he tends to the fire. Bill had the boys for Christmas Eve. I called to wish him a merry one this morning and dared to ask what he was doing. "A quiet day with a friend," was all he said. I did not ask him which one and he didn't offer.

I had told Ginny I was sorry but Rascal could not come for Christmas. She had created too much havoc at Thanksgiving when she reverted to her earlier terrorizing tactics. Ginny didn't mind because she was still pissed at Rascal for growling at and otherwise ignoring her that day. "She was just kind of overwhelmed being back in our house and with the other animals," I had said. "It wasn't personal, Gin-Gin." "I know when I'm being blown off," she replied. She seemed to think that Rascal's lack of invitation was fair payback.

So here is Georgian Woman, laughing and throwing some sort of pancakes in the air, taking vodka shots with Graham. He gets a kick out of her and this is good because he's been seeming kind of down.

"We had big house in my country," she says. "The biggest on the street. People stop to look at our house at Christmastime because all of the candles and lights! My husband decorate the tree in the front yard with colored ornaments and he dress like Saint Nick, and I bake for weeks and hand out cookies to all of the children!"

"Cool," Graham says.

"But that is not the all! He hired a reindeer! A real reindeer! And he put bells around his neck and he would stand next to him and sing Christmas songs!"

"That sounds really cool."

"So now he depressed."

"He didn't want to come to the U.S.?"

"He never want to leave. He owned the most—cele-brity?—famous? Yes, the most famous butcher shop and everybody loved him. Our life was everyone's dream. And better! But then the new regime came and went to everybody, anybody who owned business, they said, 'You have to sell this to me.'"

"But it was his shop," Leo says.

I'm basting the duck, and now we're all gathered in the kitchen, even Ginny, even Coyote and Crazy Cat.

"He had no choice. They had guns. They said, 'We know where you live.' They said, 'We know where your daughter goes to school. But no worries,' they said, 'this is business transaction, we buy it very good price.' Do you know how much they bought it for?"

Ginny jumps in and says, "One dollar."

And Georgian woman looks at her and says, "That is amazing! How did you know? That is exactly how much they gave my husband for his very beautiful butcher shop!"

"Wow, that's terrible," we all say. "How did you cope? And, Ginny, how on earth did you know? Did you hear this story before?"

"No," Ginny says. "I have a head for business."

Georgian Woman finds this very, very funny and she toasts Ginny with her next shot. Graham offers Ginny a shot and she says, "I always say no to alcohol."

"Smart girl," Georgian Woman says, and she pats her on the head. Pats Ginny on the head! She continues, "So my parents are old now. You can imagine—look at me! I'm grandmother! My parents are great-grandmother and great-grandfather! They have no income. The government sends them checks, but very small checks. This is why I work for you, Ginny. So I can send some money to my parents back in my country. They tell me not to, they say my husband and I should buy nice car but they do not know how expensive nice car costs here!" Again, she finds this very funny, and surprisingly, so does Ginny.

There are presents exchanged under the Christmas tree. And too many desserts. Leo and Coyote fall asleep on the floor in front of the fireplace, and Graham gets a call that makes him disappear for the rest of the night.

"You sit down, Miss Maggie. I will do the dishes and Ginny will dry them," Lika says.

Ginny gives her a look that means No Way.

"Fine, Ginny," she says. "You rest, too." She wheels her over to the living room and helps her into the leather chair. I try not to worry about my sister having an accident there.

"I will dry," I announce, as I push myself up off the sofa.

While drying, I listen to Georgia Woman's tale of her first hunt, her introduction to her ancient husband, their early somewhat perverted carnal connection . . . I wonder if Bill is having Christmas sex. Sex with Malick would be . . . sweet . . . Now she's talking about how she taught herself to do plumbing and carpentry when she first moved to this country, and her husband's special diet, which includes two raw eggs and a shot of vodka for breakfast.

We have to wake Ginny up from a deep snoozle. I wake Leo and call to Graham upstairs. We'll need their help getting Ginny from our front door to the car. Our path to the driveway is not wheelchair friendly, so Ginny will have to walk, which means she'll have to be supported by two while one of us spots and the other cheers on.

Graham comes downstairs and meets us at the front door, where Ginny, still seated in her wheelchair, is focused on the unzipping of her gold sparkly fanny pack. There she is. Bundled up in her purple plush coat, *Little Mermaid* hat, and matching gloves, my sister is a sight to see. A Christmas fairy. A sugar plum. A sugar plump! Her eyes light with victory as she pulls something out. Then, my sister opens up her hand to reveal a single key. "It's for you," she says.

"Oh?" I say.

"I don't use 'em anyway," she says.

"Oh," I say. "Thanks." I pick it up from her purple-gloved palm. My periphery vision shows me that Graham is grinning. I understand the significance of it, it being Christmas and all. I get that she sees this as a generous act, an olive branch, a special surprise. She's been waiting all night to spring this on me. And guess what? It is generous. And it is a special surprise. This is Ginny's way of saying thank you.

"Don't lock the door," she says, shrugging it off. "It's a safe neighborhood."

I smile. This is huge, said by the self-proclaimed paranoid. I realize this, too. "That's great, Ginny," I say. "I'll keep it in my key drawer, but I know I won't need to use it." I put it in my jeans pocket and look up to see Ginny, looking sweeter and more vulnerable than ever. "Ginny?" I say. "Do you mind if I hug you?"

"I'm not gonna call the cops," she says.

I bend down and hug her tight. She doesn't hug back. She smells like whipped cream. And then, "One, two, three," everybody says. The boys lift Ginny to her feet and I open the door.

∽∂∾

Up until the moment of telling our boys of the divorce, had anyone ever asked me what the saddest moment of my life was, I would have told them it was the night my sister Ginny had a party. She'd been working at Roy Rogers for two years and she wanted to have a party to celebrate. I was in high school then.

Our parents gave her permission and they even arranged to go out for the night so that she could play hostess. The plan was that I could invite one friend over and we would stay upstairs in my bedroom. Ginny told us that we weren't invited to the party, but if we wanted, we could crash it once the dancing started. She knew I loved to dance.

For weeks, she made lists. Guest list (she wrote down the names of everyone who worked at Roy Rogers the entire time she had worked there), shopping list (a variety of chips, Hostess cupcakes, Ho Hos, three extra-large everything pizzas from Continental Pizza, Hawaiian Punch), music list (Beach Boys). Yes, our parents said she was old enough to buy and drink beer, so long as nobody got drunk. She bought a six-pack of Pabst Blue Ribbon for her guests.

As our parents headed out, our mom pulled me aside and said, "Keep an eye on the party, okay? Just pass by every once in a while, make sure that Ginny and her friends don't get carried away." So while Ginny felt that our parents were putting trust in her, I knew that I was the one they trusted.

My friend Lissa and I hung out upstairs listening to the Bee Gees and Fleetwood Mac. We talked about the boys in school and who was edible versus who was bitable, which basically meant who was kissable and who was more than kissable. We took turns describing our perfect dream houses, including pets. Mine was round with a large indoor garden complete with waterfall, pet tiger, and monkeys.

Around nine o'clock we heard the doorbell. We hadn't been paying attention. We were reminded that there was a party going on that I was supposed to keep an eye on. "Let's just go down there and grab some Cokes and chips," I said. "Act casual."

"Okay, but I don't drink Coke," Lissa said.

"Doesn't matter, just grab one."

"Okay."

As we went down the staircase, we could hear Jimmy Buffett singing "Margaritaville." Ginny had been broadening her music horizons. It was a little loud, but hey—it was a party. Before I pushed open the door into the family room, I looked at Lissa and whispered, "I hope she's not making out with someone," and we both cringed.

The door opened to reveal the family room table where we ate most of our meals, draped with a red-and-white checkered tablecloth, and many, many bowls of chips. At the closer end were the pizza boxes, the top of which was opened to reveal a pizza with two slices missing. At the end of the table was Ginny, sitting in our father's usual chair, drinking a Hawaiian Punch. Next to her was a young Black man wearing a brown suit and plaid tie. He was drinking a beer. Ginny looked up to see us enter, but she did not acknowledge us. The guest smiled uncomfortably. A quick perusal of the room confirmed that the man in the suit was her only guest.

"Hi Gin-Gin," I said. Ginny slightly shrugged. The music was really loud. I looked back to Lissa to see if she was still in and she nodded. "Do you mind if we join the party?"

"So long as you don't drink beer," Ginny said.

Lissa and I sat down at the table with them. Next to Ginny were several cupcake wrappers and empty cans of Hawaiian Punch. The twenty-four cupcakes were now sixteen. Next to her guest was a plate with two slices of pizza and an open beer can. Now he was opening another. He only just arrived five minutes ago, didn't he?

"He's my boss, Mr. Williams," Ginny said. "That's Magpie," Ginny said. "And Melissa." She didn't say that I was her sister.

"Hello girls," he said politely.

Lissa and I each got some chips and cupcakes. I took two Cokes out of the cooler and handed one to Lissa who opened it but wouldn't take a sip.

"This is good pizza, Virginia," Mr. Williams said.

"Continental," she said.

"I'll have to go there."

Lissa said she was going to get some water and she did and came back. When she came back, she sat back down and I noticed that the record had stopped playing and must have gotten stuck because I could hear the quiet *thump, thump* of the needle. I got up to turn it off and Ginny said, "'Bout time that was over. 'Cheeseburger in Paradise' is the only good song."

Her boss nodded respectfully. He finished eating his pizza and drinking his second beer. He belched quietly into his fist. "You girls in high school?" he said to Lissa and me.

"Yea," we both said.

He nodded knowingly.

Popping Cheetos into her mouth, Ginny said, "Wouldn't want to go back."

Mr. Williams chuckled. Then he excused himself to use the restroom and he left us alone at the large table covered in full bowls of every kind of chip. When he returned, he excused himself to go home.

"That's fine," Ginny said.

He shook hands with all three of us and walked out without accompaniment.

Our parents got home a little after ten. "How was the party?" our father asked. "Was it fun?" asked our mother.

"Not too crazy," Ginny said.

"Well, that's good!" said our mother cheerfully. Aside from the two open beer cans, the evidence proved that it was not crazy at all, but our mother did not mention this.

"Mr. Williams came," I volunteered.

"Oh, Ginny, your boss? Well, isn't that nice!" she cheered.

I said I'd help Ginny clean up and we sent our parents to bed. Ginny offered Lissa some chips and cupcakes to take home. "That's okay," she said, "we don't really eat that stuff." After her parents picked her up, Ginny and I turned off all the lights but the one in the front window.

"Mr. Williams is nice," I said.

"He's a loser," Ginny said. "Don't ever get a job at Roy Rogers, bunch of losers."

⁌⟷⟿

Tonight, it's New Year's Eve and I am going to Ginny's. I bring Prosecco and sparkling apple cider. Ginny has bought chips and cookies and special treats for the dogs, glittery New Year's Eve glasses for the humans. I put mine on and Philomena puts hers on over her sunglasses. While opening the bottles, I ask, "Philomena, you'll join us, won't you?"

"Thank you," she says, "but I do not drink alcohol when I am working."

"Just a little bit? It's New Year's Eve!"

Ginny tells me not to be a pusher. She looks so cute in her glittery glasses. Part of what makes her cute is that she doesn't know she's cute. She doesn't get that they are campy. She's wearing them in all seriousness.

I convince Philomena to have half a glass of Prosecco and Ginny gives each of the pups a treat. Rascal growls at Coyote and tries to take hers, but Philomena puts her foot in the way and says, "Rascal, be good." The dogs settle in opposite corners of the kitchen while Philomena and I lean against the counters and Ginny sits in her wheelchair. "To Peace Among Pups," I say.

This is where we usually gather because Philomena is still not comfortable sitting down at the table with us because Ginny never invites her to. I have told Ginny since the beginning that she should let Philomena sit down with her and how nice that would be for them to have meals together, but she says Philomena has to do the dishes and make her own African food.

We don't sit down in the living room together either because Ginny banished the Ikea sofa. Ginny hated it and complained that it got in the way of her museum. She kept telling me to take it, but I said every living room needs a sofa. One day Philomena came out of the bathroom to discover that Ginny had managed to get herself up and was leaning against it, pushing it toward the entryway. That is where it sits now, and this is where her babies sit now. The crib was difficult to move around in the bedroom with the wheelchair. I suggested she put the crib in the entryway and leave the sofa in the living room for guests to sit on, but these suggestions were nixed. "Ginny, don't you want to make your guests comfortable?" No response.

Still, the mood is festive in Ginny's kitchen at 59 Beech Street at seven thirty on New Year's Eve.

"I used to give my dogs champagne," Ginny says, "but it was too expensive."

"You gave your dogs champagne?!" Philomena says.

"Brownie got so drunk she walked around in circles and Peanuts was an alcoholic."

"I don't know about that, Gin-Gin," I say.

"Oh my goodness!" says Philomena, laughing.

"I was addicted to JD and Crush. Yea, we both had to break the habit," Ginny says. "Had to quit cold turkey."

I'm shaking my head. "Ginny, you never drank that much, and I'm sure you didn't give Peanuts all that alcohol."

"That's when I was in Maryland and you were here so you don't know about it. Had to join Triple A," she says. "Just look in my wallet you don't believe me." I believe she is getting Triple A mixed up with AA.

I am mouthing the word *No* to Philomena who is good-naturedly shaking her head. "You had some wild times back in Maryland," I say.

"Changed my ways after the septic," she says.

Now Philomena and I are both sitting on the floor, each petting a dog. Philomena has never sat on the floor in all the times that I have visited. Must be the cheap champagne.

"Philomena, what are your mother and daughters doing tonight? Will they stay up to watch the ball drop in Times Square?"

"They will go to midnight mass and then tomorrow to morning mass."

I think about how Philomena must wish she were home with her family getting ready for church right now. But I also understand that she gets paid double for both New Year's Eve and New Year's Day. Georgian Woman had offered to work these days but Philomena said no.

Ginny starts yawning her big bear yawns.

"And now I will tell you both," Philomena says.

I'm thinking, Please Philomena, don't quit, not tonight!

"I am engaged," she says. And the hugest smile takes over her face.

"You're what?!" I say. "Philomena!! I didn't even know you had a boyfriend! Ginny, did you? Did you know that Philomena had a boyfriend?"

He is also from Ghana, a widower, and goes to her church. She knew his family back in Accra. He has a cleaning business here and a sanitation business there. His name is Amandzeba, but everyone calls him Nat.

"I wanted to wait until it official. Our goal is to get married in Ghana very soon."

"What?! That's amazing!" Oh, I am so happy for you and please say you will return."

"We will go for two weeks and then return," she says.

"Oh my goodness, that's amazing, that's fantastic! Ginny, don't you think?"

"Cowabunga," she says with a straight face.

Philomena looks at her inquisitively, I tell her this is a good thing. Ginny half smiles.

Philomena is laughing with the reveal of her secret. "Cowbunga!" she says.

"What are your goals for the New Year, Gin-Gin?" I ask my sister as I put on my coat and gloves.

"Keep riding the waves," she says.

"That's awesome," I say. I haven't heard her say that since way back when, before she almost died. Ginny doesn't ask what my goals are, so I volunteer. "I'm going to keep enjoying life, too," I say. "And maybe enjoy it even more."

Philomena takes off her sunglasses and we share a hug. "You have beautiful eyes, Philomena," I say. She puts the glasses back on before I can see her take in the compliment. I pat Rascal's growly head, I kiss my sister's sweaty head.

Ginny doesn't say anything. She never says goodbye. She just gets quiet.

"Great party, Ginny," I say. "Thank you for the cookies. Coyote had fun, too. Come on, Coyote!"

During my six-minute drive home, I hear my phone go *Ding, Ding, Ding*. In the driveway I check the texts. They're all from Ginny:

R U going.

To watch ball drop?

Rascl miss Coyotie alredy.

I text back: *See you next year!* ♥ 🎉 🐶 ♥

When I get inside, I pet the creatures, let Coyote out and in, pour myself a sherry and toast Philomena and Nat and their engagement. Here's to love!

And so I decide to call Bets. I feel my heart palpitating at the first ring. By the third ring I feel my underarms in full sweat and of course she's out, it's New Year's Eve, what the hell was I thinking? I was thinking of extending an olive branch, that's what. Because it's New Year's Fucking Eve and fresh starts and all that and she answers.

"Hello," Bets says. She sounds clear, she sounds young, it's early there. Heck, it's not even midnight here yet, I left Ginny's at nine, so. "Is Ginny okay?" she says.

"She's fine," I say. "She's just fine."

"Just?"

"No," I say, "I mean, she's really fine. That's why I called. Partly. Happy New Year, big sister Bets!" I say very cheerfully. She doesn't say anything. I pull back from the phone to make sure I called Bets and not Ginny herself. It's Bets.

"So?" she says.

"So, I thought you'd like to know. That she's settled in and everything is really fine and we've kind of come to a . . . good place. So you don't have to worry."

She laughs strangely and sounds like she's rolling over in bed next to her toned, tan girlfriend and she says, "I wasn't worried. I figured if there was a problem, you'd call. You always do."

This is a very strange thing to say, very strange indeed, because there have been many problems, many, many problems that I have not called her about for good reason. Has she imagined that it's been an easy-peasy breeze since the last time we spoke over a year ago?

"Also," I say, "I wanted to congratulate you on your new star turn. That's really cool. I look forward to watching."

"Star turn?" she says.

"*Dancing with the Stars*?"

"It's not a done deal yet, they're trying to woo me."

"Oh. Well, cool. To be wooed."

"And let me guess," Bets says. "You're calling to apologize."

At this point I down my sherry. "Apologize for what?" I imagine her girlfriend is rolling her eyes about me and Bets is tickling her flab-free waist.

"Oh, gosh, I dunno, stealing Ginny from the state of Maryland, not listening to me, writing me out of her will, probably." She snorts.

"I would never do that," I say. It's crossed my mind that she doesn't deserve it, but I would never. Ever. Can she read my mind? Does she see all the awfulness in me?

"Well you sure did some of it."

"Why are you being like this, Betsy? I don't understand. I really just called to say—"

"Yeah, I know," she says, cutting me off.

Wait, what? I'm having déjà vu and wondering if we're replaying that last phone call from fourteen months ago. How is this possible? When so much has really changed? So much time has passed. So many, so many visits to Ginny's house! And while I've been doing that, she's been surfing! And skiing! And dancing now! How could she still be so . . . angry?

I wonder if something is wrong with Bets. Maybe a board hit her in the head. It's the first time that I've ever thought that maybe something is seriously wrong with my oldest sister, the one that I so looked up to. Also, I wonder if something is seriously wrong with me. Because Bets is very smart and if she perceives this, it must be true. She's still there, on the other end of the phone, on the other side of the country. She hasn't hung up, she's waiting there. "Bets?" I say, just to be sure.

"Hm," she says, and nothing else.

And I muster up my most earnest strength and say, "Betsy, I don't know what you are talking about but I am sorry for whatever it is that I did. I am sorry for anything I ever did to offend you in any way. I never meant to hurt you and I would never mean to. I miss our annual Fete with Bets. I called to wish you a happy new year. I really just thought you'd be happy to hear that Ginny's okay and I really did want to congratulate you. That's all. I love you, Bets," I say, even though I hadn't meant to say that. I can still hear her breath. But nothing, so I hang up.

I pour myself another sherry. I give Coyote a hug and lay down on the sofa with a blanket and invite Crazy Cat to join me, which he does. I'm not crying. Honestly, I don't even feel like crying, which surprises me.

Perhaps I moved Gin here for my own sanity. Maybe I should have flown out to California to see Bets a year ago, when she'd mentioned she'd felt left out. I should have taken Ginny. I have reveled in my role as Ginny's savior, it's true. Maybe that's partly why I called Bets. Not all, but partly . . .

"I will never talk to Betsy again," I tell Coyote and Crazy Cat.

My phone rings and they are looking at me to see if I'm going to answer it, to see if I am good for my word. But it's not Bets, it's Bill. I lay there holding the phone for two rings.

"Hello?" I say, as if I don't know it's him.

"Hello?" Bill says. "I'm returning your call."

What? I am confused. Did I call him by accident when dialing my sister?

"From Christmas," he saves me. "You called me on Christmas, so I'm now calling you back."

"But we spoke on Christmas?" I say, sinking deeper into confusion.

"Oh, we did? Yeah, well, I guess I didn't owe you a call after all. Oh well."

"Are you high?" I ask.

"Kind of low, actually," Bill says. "Going to bed but I guess it felt weird entering a new year without . . ."

"Without?" I ask. I'm aware at this point that he is indeed alone and he is aware that I am, too. I imagine he is also reclined on his sofa, has not yet made it to his unmade bed. I wonder if he's dressed, if he is dressed up from having gone out, or if he's in his pajama bottoms and T-shirt, and if so, which one? Probably Debbie Harry.

"Without calling you back."

"Oh, I see," I say. "Well, thank you. You've been very efficient, very . . . reliable. About getting back to me."

"What are you wearing?" he says, in a drunk, prank call kind of way.

"Where is your girlfriend?" I say, my first time verbally acknowledging that she exists.

"Sleeping," he says.

Like, right there? Like, you're calling me while she's sleeping on New Year's Eve?

"Goes to bed at ten, wakes up at five to swim."

"Cool," I say, trying to imagine any one of those things being possible in my life. "Like, Polar Bear Club?"

"Nah. She has access to an indoor pool . . ."

I've been holding the phone in my right hand while petting Coyote on the floor to my left. I do a switcharoo to pet Crazy now, who has sunk deep into my chest.

"She doesn't have kids. Never did." His words are starting to slur together. "Has a lot of birds! An intense garden. Terr . . . aniam? Big glass thing, structure, you know, for plants?"

I don't answer him, just let him spin his wheels for a bit.

"She's got an assistant!"

"Huh," I say. I know from the boys that she was in the music industry. She's now into holistic branding or something, that's what Graham said.

"Seeing anyone?" he surprises me.

"Um, I dunno. Kind of. Yea," I say.

"Oh," he says. "Oh wow. This . . . is . . . news . . ." And then, "Serious?"

"I dunno," I say. I hope so?

He's quiet for a bit and then says, "She's . . . fun." He says *fun* like it's a word that surprises him, a concept he didn't believe was possible. "And that is all," he says. And then I'm pretty sure he hangs up. I say his name a few more times and am answered by a dial tone.

I stay up wondering about so many things until Leo comes in around two. "You don't have to wait up for me, Mom," he says, in a chill, annoyed sort of way. "Happy New Year," I say, and he grunts in my general direction on his way upstairs. I mean to stay up for Graham, but I fall asleep.

I wake to the sound of someone shuffling around in the kitchen and soon I smell coffee. I see that Ginny has sent her usual morning texts:

I.Am. fine . And. clean.

And: *wlcum To. the FYUCHER*

⸜♡⸝

A few weeks, a few sketches:

Ginny gives me dating advice.

Ginny tells me to get out more, meet someone, go on Meet Me, a dating service that advertises on her phone, she says. I tell her it's a trashy dating service for hookups. She says she trusts the internet more than people but less than dogs. She says I should make up with Bill. She says, "Even ten isn't perfect, like Dennis Wilson." Is she calling Bill a ten? I say, "He has a girlfriend, remember?" "Maybe he'll dump the old lady," she says. Which makes me laugh. I say, "Who says I need a man?" She says, "You come around here too much." "Ouch," I say. "And what about you? Would you like to meet someone?" She says she has Rascal. Doesn't need someone nagging her, telling her what to do.

Ginny is sticky.

The fact that Ginny is always a little bit sticky is not because her aides are neglectful. No, no, no. They would much rather have her be clean and her hair be combed, and the hair on the mole on her cheek, tweezed. But Ginny won't let them help her. She won't let them help her get out of bed. She won't let them help her to the bathroom or in the shower. Ginny really does take a shower every day, but we do not know how well she cleans. She seems to have a rash because she is always ordering Johnson's Baby Powder and her bathroom floor is often covered with it. She won't let her aides wash her hands and face after she gets all covered in mayonnaise. Her toothbrush is always dry and her toothpaste tube appears to be untouched, so I supremely doubt that she brushes her five teeth. And the sweat. She is often sweaty. This is because she is big and she is salty and her house is eighty-five degrees.

Ginny sends selfies.

Sometimes I think Ginny sends them to me to show me that she's alive. But she doesn't look so alive. She looks quite desolate in her self-ies. She does not smile. She does not make duck-face or any other kind of sexy or serious or funny face. She simply shows her face. If you didn't know her and you received her picture you might think she was a crazy person or a mentally ill person or a deranged person. I like her selfies because they are so devoid of vanity. But also, they make me sad. Be-cause she so clearly doesn't know how to play the game and she looks so vulnerable.

Ginny is thoughtful.

Today would have been Bill's and my twenty-sixth anniversary. Ginny gives me a card for the occasion that she says I need to share with Bill. It has a picture of a hot couple in the shower together. They are facing each other so we can't see their fronts. We just see their wet hair, their kiss-ing tongues, and their suds-y backs, asses, and thighs. Inside the card, it says, *Happy Anniversary, let's have some good clean fun.* And then, in Ginny's handwriting, *You shood get back togethr, Gin-Gin*

Ginny is falling again.

Lika calls. "Our sister is too heavy for me to lift," she says. She put her head on a pillow and will wait for me. I am there in ten minutes. From the floor, Ginny tells me she wants to fire both nannies. From the floor, Ginny tells me that her phone is broken.

"Broken broken?" I say.

"It texts," she says. "But everything else is slow as molasses." Lika and I determine that she is too heavy for both of us to lift. Really. She's just dead weight. Doesn't help one iota. I recruit a neighbor. It's embarrassing because Ginny smells.

"I am sure her blood sugar is very high," says Lika. "She is very weak. She eats too much of the candy. She must go to the doctor."

Ginny is a high-powered lawyer.

I tell her I will take her phone to the Apple Store if she first comes with me to the doctor. I explain that both Philomena and Lika think something's not right. She says she's not going to sign anything. I say, "I'm not asking you to sign anything, I just want you to understand the terms of agreement." She says, "I'm slow but I'm not stupid. And if the nannies are wrong, I'll sue 'em." Charming. "For what?" I say. "Motional rest," says she.

⟋⟍⟍

At Doctor Finkelstein's office. I fill out the forms and Ginny gets her insurance card from her wallet, which is in her fanny pack. When the nurse calls for her, she asks if I am her daughter. Ah, she has lifted my sinking spirits. Ginny tells her we are blood sisters.

The nurse and I help Ginny up on the examination table and I make myself comfortable in the chair next to it. I look at my sister and her feet hanging there.

"Nice sneaks," I say. They're hot pink and make my sister's large feet look even larger.

"I'm an Amazon junkie," she says. "I can't help it."

"Velcro. Very nice."

"Don't have time for ties."

"Who does?"

In comes the doctor. She asks Ginny all the usual questions. "How is your diet? Are you taking your meds? How often do you urinate?" Ginny gives her usual answers. "Gave up sugar. Down to one pill, the other ones give me Mont-zuma's revenge. I dunno."

The doctor asks Ginny when the last time was that she had a mammogram and Ginny says she doesn't believe in torture. The doctor asks if she checked her own breasts and Ginny says, "That's personal." The doctor asks if perhaps she could check her breasts and Ginny says, "Not unless you want a lawsuit."

They take blood samples and conclude that her blood sugar levels are indeed very high. Dangerously high. The doctor tells us to go to the ER immediately.

On the way to the ER, Ginny complains about the doctor and complains about her phone, but she doesn't put up a big stink about going to the hospital, which surprises me. She must know that something is not right with her body.

They hook her up to an IV, a strong antibiotic, and tell us we got here just in time. They tell us she'll need to stay the night.

Little do I know that Graham has come down for a surprise visit. Surprise! He meets us in the Emergency Room. Ginny was in on the surprise. While I was filling out forms, she texted him that we were here, the sneak. He's at the coffee station getting himself and me a refill, when I receive a text from my art director: *Love it, great stuff. One more frame needed: a mirrored reflection in front store window with lively parking lot and customers beyond.* This is a commercial storyboard artist's nightmare. Anything that requires both translucence and clarity, a complete reversal of perspective and a "lively" scene behind, topped off by the casualness of the request, is a combination of tortures.

"Should I tell her my sister is in the hospital?" I wonder to my son.

"She won't get it. It's not like she's your child," he says.

"Oh really?" I say.

"She won't get it."

"Can I tell her my older son is home from college for a surprise weekend?"

"Tell her I say Bite Me," Graham says.

"And you are going into business?"

"In my business, we'll take weekends off."

"Ha, good luck with that." I get to texting.

"So what are you saying?" he asks.

"That if she pays me fifty thousand dollars, I'm in."

"Good to know what I'm worth."

"That's you plus your aunt," I say. I put the phone down. "I told her I'll have it for her by eight a.m." Because let's be real.

I kiss Ginny's sweaty head and she suppresses tears of fear as she says, "My nephews will take care of me."

"Course we will," Graham says as he texts Leo to join them. It's already eight o'clock on a Friday. So much for the brothers' wild night out.

On the way out, I wonder if I should let the other sister know about this sister being in the hospital and I decide that I should not. Why upset her? According to Gin-Gin, she's having some sort of launch event for her new Moon Boards where she's doing another dance, the dancing stars people will be there, and I don't want to throw off her cha-cha. I laugh a rather maniacal laugh while driving home.

An hour later I am deep into drawing when I hear a horn honk. *Honk, honk.* Leo comes lumbering down the stairs. *Honk.* How annoying. It's a quiet country lane, fuckers! Don't his friends know to text? He's out the door with "Later!" He wrangled a ride to the hospital, which I appreciate. I stand up to catch a peek at which friend is the honker. It's Bill's bright blue Camaro. *Honk, honk, honk.* He's given Leo a turn at the wheel.

I return to the hospital Saturday at nine a.m. Ginny's been transferred to a room but will be released later today. My eyes are blurry, the boys' eyes are furry. Ginny says, "See, I told you not to worry." I remind them all that Philomena is getting married in Ghana today so we should send good vibes. Ginny says, "If she's even getting married." Oh yes, Ginny has come up with some conspiracy theory that the whole fiancé and wedding away is some sort of fib that Philomena made up so she can take a vacation. I try to understand the machinations of my sister's mind. Is she afraid that Philomena won't return? Is she jealous that she has a life beyond Beech Street? Doesn't matter. The boys and I share fist bumps and I send them home.

When the doctor finally comes by, I ask him to tell my sister like it is. "Tell her what will happen if she doesn't change her ways, Doctor Carver," I say. "No pussyfooting." These are the things the doctor says could happen:

Neuropathy

Diabetic coma

Stroke

Gangrene

Amputation

Heart Attack

Blindness

Kidney Damage

Liver Failure

Prolonged and uncomfortable death

"Did you hear that, Ginny?" I say. "Ginny, what did Doctor Carver say?"

Ginny shrugs. "Doctor Carver," she says and she kind of chuckles.

"Yes?" says Doctor Carver.

"That why you became a doctor?" This is a Ginny joke. Connecting the word *carver* with doctor. A connection that has likely been referenced a thousand times since he applied to medical school.

"What's going on here?" the doctor asks. "Mental illness?"

"Special needs," I say.

"Since birth?"

He's saying this right in front of Ginny, talking about her as if she isn't here. After all the nice people who have helped us in the past twenty-four hours, this so-called smarty-pants so-called doctor can't assess that Ginny is a child in a motorcycle mama's body?

"Yes," I say. I cut to the chase and direct myself back to Ginny. "So, Ginny, you could die fast, but more likely, you could die slowly, with a whole lot of suffering, that's the bottom line. Right, Doc?" I've decided to call him Doc from now on.

"Yes," says Doc Carver.

"Thanks, Doc," I say. "We really appreciate your honesty. We have a wonderful caregiver lined up. Two, actually. And there is no question of stairs, as we already have a very nice ramp. Can she go home now?"

"He probably thinks you're mental," Ginny says to me as soon as the doctor has left.

"He'd be right! I was up all night! Did you hear everything the doctor said, Ginny?"

"Everyone dies sometimes," she says.

I'M SO TIRED OF TRYING TO KEEP YOU ALIVE! I yell. But not out loud.

It takes three more hours to get her out of there with the waiting and the papers and the various well-meaning and thorough folks. Ginny watches *The Little Mermaid* on her iPad while hugging tight to Binky Baby.

I badly want to go home to my sons. I could call Georgian Woman in for the checkout, couldn't I? Isn't that why I hired her? To deal with the bullshit? But Georgian Woman is back at Ginny's house doing the laundry, scooping Rascal's poop, FaceTiming her frail husband. And goodness knows things are going to be rough with Ginny for a while as we all try to get her back to the low sugar diet she was on at Sunnyside.

The thing is, I also know that my sister needs for me to be here. Ginny needs a sensitive and trusted interpreter. Ginny is scared of hospitals. She says that they are where people go to die. Ginny doesn't have a parent or a spouse or even children to care for her. I am it for Ginny.

A text from Bill: *Took sons to lunch. Want relief?*

This is very nice. I tell Ginny about the lunch part.

"You should go," Ginny says. "See your college son."

"That's okay, I'll spend time with him tonight."

Also, I think, I want to be here. Not just because my sister needs me, not just because her need seems stronger than my son's, but because it's what I need. I need to be needed.

I text Bill back: *I'm good but thanx*

I mean it. I'm starting to think that maybe I am good. At least, maybe I'm better than I thought I was. And I am also grateful for his offering.

❧

The front door is unlocked, as it always is, and big fat Rascal comes to greet us on her tiny stick legs. We are all happy to see each other. The house is filled with the aroma of spices . . . and cologne? In the kitchen, there is a guy with his back toward us, working under the sink. I recall that they were having trouble with the disposal, but I don't recall calling in a plumber yet. Leave it to Lika to take charge of this, too.

Our favorite Georgian whirlwind emerges from the basement holding a full laundry basket. "Welcome home!" she shouts warmly. "I see you have met my husband!" she says.

The guy pulls out from under the sink, stands, and turns around to reveal that he is the sexiest seventy-five-year-old man alive. He has thick dark hair with just a speck of silver, large brown eyes, and strong features. He nods warmly and holds up a piece of hardware, presumably the defective piece that he just replaced.

"Give kiss!" she says as she passes to carry the laundry into Ginny's room.

I offer to shake his hand and he indicates he will wash first. As he dries, I introduce myself and Ginny. He takes Ginny's hands in his and he kisses them. He then takes my hands in his and kisses them. He raises his head to present a shy and radiant smile.

Lika returns to stir a large pot on the stovetop. "My poor husband," she says, "he brings me here and he fixes sink and dryer while I make the healthy soup!" She bends down to my sister's level, "Ginny, Lika will make you healthy again. Healthier than you ever been!"

Ginny is of course sitting in her wheelchair and I am leaning against the counter and Rascal has joined us, too. We all watch as Lika's most handsome husband reaches into his back pocket and pulls out a dog treat. He nods to Rascal who then sits without command. If he had offered one to the human ladies, I likely would have sat, too, and I believe Ginny might have rolled over.

"He loves dogs more than life!" Georgian Woman says.

When it is time for him to leave, they kiss most passionately at the door and we fangirls pretend not to notice.

When I finally return home, I see that it is empty of sons, the dog and cat dishes are empty of food, and the sink is full. Coyote looks at me and then her dish. Crazy Cat meows.

Ding. From Graham: A selfie of him and Leo on their bikes, who knows where.

Ding: Home for dinner. Your famous lasagna, Mama? Pretty please!

⚜

Ah, the Apple Store . . . How could a place be so shiny and clean and welcoming with all that is going on in the world? A place devoid of problems, illness, conflict, dirt, or dust. The girl who greets me as I enter the store is so lovely that I want to adopt her. Perhaps I can connect with her later on Facebook and then connect her with one of my sons on Insta or TikTok or whatever. How old is she? And why is she here in the middle of the day on a Monday? Must be a high school graduate, taking a gap year. A girl who did not have everything handed to her and values working for a dollar. A girl who is so tech savvy that she is perhaps skipping college altogether to work her way from the bottom up to a managing position and then on to start her own shiny and clean conglomerate.

"Yes," I say, of course I am happy to wait here. I am happy to sit on this tall stool at this tall table with this tall warm latte in hand.

Then a young man comes around. "Ginny?" he says.

"That's me," I say. "Well, I'm her sister, Maggie. I told them that when I made the appointment. You need to see my ID?"

"No, that's okay, we're good," he says. "I'm Muhammed and I'll be helping you today." His wears a green turban, a gold nose ring, his eyebrows are thick and well coifed. He does not have an accent, though I imagine his parents do. I imagine I would like them very much.

I pull a Ziploc bag out of my shoulder bag and say, "Oops. Sorry. I meant to clean this before I got here. Do you have any wipes?"

Of course he does, right there in his back pocket, and he gives the shiny pink thing a professional shine.

"Sorry," I say. "My sister uses her phone with sticky hands. Syrup, mostly. She puts syrup on everything. And mayonnaise."

"No worries," he says. This guy is very Zen. "So what's going on with your phone, Ginny?"

"Maggie," I correct. "Like I said, it's my sister's . . . she says it's slow. Takes the weekends off. She's a character."

"Hm. Let me look at the settings . . ."

"I've looked at her settings. I think sometimes she forgets to charge it or she overcharges it . . . I dunno. Figured it was time to call in the professionals . . ."

He just starts doing things, bringing new settings and screens up. Finally he says, "Looks like a lot of open pages, number one. Number two, a whole lot of videos."

"Videos? But if they're on Prime they don't actually go on her phone, right?"

"Check it out," he says. He demonstrates how to open up pages and click them closed one at a time. I know how to do this; I'm not an idiot. Though I suppose I'm kind of an idiot for not thinking to do this with Ginny's phone before schlepping here. Yup. Disney World's website, next, another Realtor in Southern California, Amazon, Amazon, Amazon, the Beach Boys tour dates, A Big Wet Dick.

"Wait—what?" I grab the phone. "Sorry, I don't know what that was."

"I've seen it all," he says.

"This is my sister's phone," I say. "Who knows what clickbait she hit . . ." I continue to flip open pages to discover a dating site for adults "who like to play," another one for "quick tricks," some guys in cummerbunds and nothing else. "This is really weird," I say.

"So why don't you just delete those pages and I'll be right back," Muhammed says.

My handsome helper fellow leaves me here looking at one male porn site after another with Amazon orders thrown in. "Hot chocolate," a site strictly for Black guys. Extra-large feminine diapers for Ginny. "Firemen for hire." 1-800-Flowers. Oh, that was sweet, when Ginny sent me flowers for Valentine's Day. But wait—how far back do these go? Another site called "Clit bait" offering "self-fulfillment at your own discretion."

Holy shit. I didn't even know she still had it in her. Does she still masturbate? Can she still— Another huge dick. And then the notion of my sister's hands on this phone makes me suddenly drop it. It lands hard on the floor.

"Don't worry about it, that's a good cover," Muhammed says, as he reaches down to pick it up.

"This is so crazy," I say. "I had no idea."

Muhammed is very nonchalant about the whole thing. This must be part of their training. Do not judge the customer or her sister. He asks me if I have closed the open pages and I explain I have scrolled through and there look to be hundreds more. He demonstrates how to close every single page with two moves.

"Good, that's good," I say.

He then goes back to settings and pulls up the page that shows how much of the space is occupied by video. I am starting to sweat. "Do you mind if I . . . ?"

I nod. "Go for it, Muhammed," I say. Let's have a good time, shall we? I'm trying to keep it light.

"Oh, I see . . . It's this app," he says. He turns the phone to me again. Meet Me.

Oh my God. How is it possible that my sister had the wherewithal to download that app, but can't get it together to go to the bathroom when she has to do number two?

"And this one." Hook Ups.

"Hook Ups?" I say. "Seriously? I didn't even know that existed."

"Everything you can imagine exists. And everything you imagine does not."

Suddenly this guy is a philosopher.

"We can delete the apps. That should pretty much solve the problem."

Yea, um. Of course. I click on Hook Ups and it seems a video is trying to upload. Yup, it's slow. And then, it starts—a hairy chested guy talks to the camera, "Hi Ginny, I'm Gary. You watch me and then I'll watch you." The guy pushes down his sweatpants to reveal. "Holy shit," I say. "Yes, delete it. Delete them both. Oh my God."

Do these guys KNOW WHERE SHE LIVES?

"Excuse me," he says, and he disappears to consult a colleague. They call over another and as I reach the bottom of my latte, I look up to see them all looking at me. He returns.

"If I delete them, they'll be gone," he says. "You'll have to download and pay for them again if you want them back."

"I don't! She doesn't! This is my sister Ginny's phone. Trust me. I had no idea she was doing this stuff."

"Okay," Muhammed says. Calm and warm. These Buddha-techno guys and gals really know the art of playing it down. But couldn't he at least join me in my shock, couldn't he make a joke for levity?

"My sister has special needs," I ejaculate.

He smiles.

"I mean, she's a little . . ."

"Okay," Mohammed says. "Look." He demonstrates what to do.

"Wait a minute," I say. "Are there possibly videos of her on there?"

"I have no idea how the apps work, Ginny," Mohammed says. And then he reboots her phone and I reset her password.

When I walk out of there, the apps and pages are deleted. I walk around the long tables to avoid making eye contact with my no-longer-future-daughter-in-law. Every one of those open-faced employees is watching me. *Dirty old lady,* I hear them thinking. And, *Ginny, Ginny, Ginny,* I hear them chant, the name echoing off the bright ceilings and bouncing off the floors and the walls.

When I get to my sister's, I try the door and for whatever reason, it is locked. I knock and ring and wait. When no one appears, I text Lika to let her know that I'm here. The TV is so loud I can hear it from outside. I wait. It's certainly possible that Lika is in the laundry room and therefore can't hear the knock or the ring or even receive my text. It is possible that my sister is deep in one of her slothlike snoozles. Is it possible that that gross guy Gary showed up at her house, walked right in, locking the door behind him, tied up and gagged Lika and Rascal, and is now doing things I don't even want to think about to my sister?

The sound of the lock being unlocked. Slowly the door opens a bit. The front of a bright pink sneaker appears, then, a wheel from her chair. Ah, thank God, I let out a huge exhale. Finally, Ginny's sticky face peaks out. She's looking down toward the ground. "Where's your little buddy?" she asks.

"She's not with me because I just went to the Apple Store," I say.

Ginny rolls back a bit in order to allow me to enter. Lika is in the background, coming toward the door. "Sorry, I did not hear," she says.

"Hi Lika. I'm not coming in today. I just need to give Ginny her phone back."

I am allowing Lika to see my seriousness. Even Rascal senses my intensity and moves away. Lika nods and returns to the laundry room. I hand Ginny her phone. I bend down so that only Ginny can hear me and I say, "It's clean." She accepts it with sticky hands. "Clean," I repeat, "on the inside and out."

"Thank you," Ginny says. She can tell that I'm upset.

"Get it? Clean on the inside and out? We erased all your porn sites and those . . . apps."

She is already poking at her phone.

"Are you hearing me, Ginny?" I ask.

"I can't hear anything because Lika talks so loud on the phone."

"What are you doing, Ginny? I am talking to you."

"Trying to order ear plugs."

"Ginny, I'm very disturbed by what you've been doing. Do you hear me? Do these guys know where you live?" I look at her there, struggling with something on her phone.

"Still broken," she says.

"Virginia, are you hearing me? Who is that Gary guy? Do you make videos for him? Does he actually . . . ?" I don't want to finish that sentence. "How many guys are there, Ginny? Do you give these guys your full name? Do they know where you live?"

She looks up at me.

"You need to stop, Ginny. Right now. Immediately. It's not safe."

Ginny shrugs. "I have needs," she says.

Oh. Oh wow. This pauses me. Needs. Needs. Needs? I know about needs. I have needs. But do I know about Ginny's needs? I knew she had needs way back then in Maryland, but I did not know she has needs now. I did not know she had it in her to have those needs and the fact that she still has them is surprising . . . and . . . a sign of life, I guess? But to fulfill those needs in such a way—with those sleazeballs, those losers—I mean, I don't even care about them or their disgustingness. I just . . . I need my sister to be safe. And now she's telling me she's got needs.

"Ginny," I say, "I need to know if any of those guys know your name and address. Do they, Ginny?"

"Course not," she says.

"Really? You sure? What information do they have? Please Virginia, be honest with me."

"Just first names."

Thank the lords and lordesses almighty. I can breathe again. Okay, okay, that's good.

"That's the fun of it," she says.

Oh. Okay. Big sigh. "Okay," I say. I start racking my brain to think of ways that I can help her fulfill her needs in a more . . . pedestrian way. "Look, I can buy you magazines—whatever you want . . . I can subscribe you to an adults-only channel . . . I can introduce you to people! Nice guys! I can take you places. Seriously. I can do that." Seriously, why didn't I take her to a local church or help her join a social club months ago? I'm kicking myself.

"Nah, this is easier," she says, back to touching her sticky fingers to the screen.

"It's highly dangerous what you are doing, do you hear me? Ginny, I really need you to stop!" She's ignoring me. "Okay, okay . . . well then fine. I'm not going to help you with your phone anymore. I'm not going to touch it. I'm not going to enable . . . Ginny, next time you fill it with creepy guys showing you their schlongs, you can let Philomena or Lika take you to the Apple Store, okay?" I put my hand on top of hers to stop her. "Okay?"

She puts on one of her evil smiles and says, "You said you wouldn't touch my phone."

I pull my hand away. "Ha ha," I say. "Got me on that one." I feel helpless. I feel like something has started that I can't stop. I'm recalling the time I discovered that Graham had googled "Boobs" on the family computer and so many other images popped up. I'm recalling the first time I found a joint in Leo's coat pocket. I'm recalling a time that I, too, couldn't be stopped, even when I told myself I should. "I am very concerned if you can't tell," I say and turn to go.

Before the door closes, I hear her say, "I can't help it if I have a love life."

I turn back and she shrugs. My sister thinks I'm jealous. "That's not love, Big Sister," I say, shaking my head. She thinks I'm a prude, she thinks I'm a puritan. "I'll see you next week, Virginia. I need a break," I say, and close the door behind me.

By the time I arrive home, my phone has dinged twice.

It's Lika: *Ginny cannot get into her phone. The code doesn't work. Locked.*

"Oh my God," I say to myself.

I go back to get Ginny's phone. She's down for a nap so Lika greets me at the door to hand it to me. From the doorway, I call Apple and am put on hold. Lika asks if she can get me some tea. She looks like she needs company. She's been covering for Philomena since she's been in Ghana for almost two weeks, only one night with her handsome husband while Ginny was in the hospital. I say yes. She beckons me inside, to sit at the table.

She goes to the kitchen while I sit there, listening to Apple Store's pop playlist and Rascal's snores, watching kids pass by the bay window, returning home from school.

Ah, the scent of warm mint tea. Lika places it down in front of me. She pulls out a chair and places down another. She disappears and returns with one, two shot glasses. And a bottle of vodka. "Lika listen," she says, as she starts to unscrew.

It's four o'clock in the afternoon, I've got no work lined up ahead of me. I tell her the whole sticky story. She listens with great intensity.

She pours two shots and lifts her glass, "To most passionate lady."

I laugh. "Salute!" I say, and we knock 'em down.

At 4:10, Apple answers. I change Ginny's code to four, rather than six digits. It's S-U-R-F, not S-U-R-F-E-R, silly me. "I swear," I say, "after this, I will never touch my sister's phone again."

A shot to that.

By 4:20, Lika has begun her litany and I have become the listener. Like Ginny, she is angry about Philomena's wedding, but not because she doesn't believe it. She is angry because she wasn't invited. Not invited? It's in West Africa, for goodness' sake! And you don't even like Philomena! And someone needs to stay here to take care of Ginny! "When there is wedding," Lika says, "I go to wedding. Doesn't matter where is. I find my way. Like love. Even when seems impossible, even when husband old with hanging skin, I make love!"

Oh my, I think. His skin didn't look so hanging to me. His skin looked soft and tan. And why am I even thinking this? Rascal has risen and snorts her way to Ginny's door. It's Twizzler time.

"When no invitation to love, to wedding, there is war!" Lika declares. "And to this, I do not drink."

Okay . . . So that's probably a good thing, because now Lika needs to get herself up to serve my sister and I need to escape before sister emerges.

"But you do! You drink!" she says. She pours me another shot. "Drink to it! Drink to war! Drink for all the people who die because not invitation!"

"Lika," I say, "I am sorry that your feelings are hurt, but I can't drink to that."

"Fine," she says, and she slides the shot over to herself. "I drink to all the stupid fools who have love and then reject it." She drinks it down, pushes out her chair, and goes to the kitchen to slam Rascal's food bowl down on the counter. Lika seems out of sorts. An angry drunk, apparently.

I follow her in there and quietly say, "Lika, are you . . . okay?"

She stops her flurried movements and looks to me with tears in her eyes. "A little bit of sexy movie is a little bit okay, you think? . . . With ancient husband?" she says. "Sometimes make sexy movie?"

"Of course, Lika, of course," I say, rubbing her back.

Oh my God, way too much information in one day. And when will Malick be back?

⁓

It's Thursday night and I'm in Manhattan with Theresa who has treated me to *Hamilton* on Broadway and now dinner at Sardis. Last minute her pre-med daughter couldn't come. Theresa knows I'm broke and we both need a good time, so we're drinking martinis.

It's been eleven days since Ginny was released from the hospital, since both she and her phone were cleaned up. It's been rough. Poor Philomena, who had returned from her beautiful Ghanaian wedding to Ginny's world, called me crying on the first night. "She yelled at me for no pie at breakfast. She yelled at me for no Hawaiian Punch!" She understood fully what we were trying to do, but still, back from the ball and into the ashes! I gave in. I said, "Give her the pie, but hold the whipped cream. Give her the pancakes but withhold the fake syrup." Ginny rolled herself to the refrigerator and sprayed whipped cream and poured syrup directly into her own snout. I mean mouth. Philomena and I both cried that night and I told her I was so happy to have her back. I said, "Give my sister what she wants then," and she said, "I don't have to, Maggie, I can do whatever you want, whatever is best for Ginny."

I called Lika and asked her advice and she cried, too, and she said, "Give the lady what she wants! We cannot deprive our dear sister a moment longer!" So we did. Or Philomena did. And now Ginny's officially back to her old sugar spins. Philomena found empty sugar packets in the trash can next to Ginny's bed this morning. Sugar packets! I assume my sister's back to her porn habits, too. I pray for her safety and I cringe at the thought of Gary. But at least she's returned to nodding in Philomena's general direction again. This afternoon she texted me that it was *gud to hav my life bk.* Good to have her life back.

"I have dark thoughts," I say. "I'm afraid of them. I'm ashamed of them."

"Um hmm," Theresa says. She always knows what to say. She orders us another round.

"I mean, it's not like she's my mother who raised me, it's not like she's my child. There's no sibling or sister or fricking blood sister law that says I need to do this! Maybe I just should have let her go home . . ."

"Blood sister?" Theresa says.

"You know," I say, demonstrating by putting the tips of my index fingers together. Which isn't easy due to the martini.

"You did that?"

"Well, yes. As kids."

"Oh dear."

"What?"

"That's a pact."

"Are you serious?"

Theresa laughs, which I think is just a cover because she was serious. And then, "Maybe you should just pack 'er up and send her to big sis on the West Coast." Thank you, thank you, Theresa for releasing me. "She's such a winner . . . let her have a go for a bit."

"She'd probably have her up on her feet and on a board in three months' time," I say. I really think this. I really fear that this might be true. Bets would have her surfing. I'm in over my head.

My phone dings. I sigh and close my eyes before I turn it over. It's a notification. A notification from Apple telling me this: Ginny is sharing her location with me. Which is funny. Which is sweet. Theresa and I check it out and sure enough, Ginny is at 59 Beech Street.

Here's a true thing: Sometimes I drive by Ginny's house at night. I park across the street and I don't get out of the car. I just want to see her, see what others might see when they pass. There she is, at her dining table, slowly eating and talking to Binky Baby. Or there she is, reclining, the lights of the TV illuminating her face. I don't want to go in and chat with Philomena and Lika, I don't want to wake Rascal or interrupt her routine. I just want to see her and make sure she's okay. I just need to confirm that I've done the right thing and she really is okay. I think I'm trying to assess if she's happy.

It's eleven fifteen p.m. so my sister Ginny is up late. When I go to the city she gets a little bit nervous, even though I tell her I will be fine and I will be home late and I will text her in the morning.

Another notification asks if I would like to share my location with Ginny. I would, I do. We then take a selfie with our martinis and I text her: *Cheers from NYC! We love you, Ginny!*

She texts back: *PATY hrd on* (Party hard on)—I believe she is getting Party Hearty mixed up with Party On.

And then: *j.can. You ggt me.jIHERT NEW York. Shrt* (Can you get me an I Heart New York shirt?)

"OMG Maggie," Theresa says, "this is amazing, this is huge!"

I feel a smile come up to my ears. We toast to Ginny. We toast to Ginny's accepting her new home. We toast to Ginny's embracing her inner New Yorker.

We look in three cheesy little tourist shops on the way to Grand Central until we find an I Heart NY tee in extra-extra-large. We also buy a couple of those foam Statue of Liberty crowns and wear them home on the train. Tomorrow I will give them to Ginny and Rascal.

⚜

We're expecting two feet of heavy snow, high winds, likely power outages. Leo was a gem and went to the store to buy batteries, peanut butter, basic survival stuff. I got my work done and sent it off before the storm, as living in the woods, we are prone to outages. Now, we have a nice fire going and Leo is up in his room and Theresa is here and it feels cozy and safe knowing that we can get tipped here on the sofa without worrying about having to go anywhere. A big scary storm is coming, but here, we are protected, hibernated.

The setting is intimate and confessional. Theresa tells me of the last moments of her father's life and her own part in it. She and her daughter quietly pulled the plug. The nursing staff politely looked the other way.

I tell her of my fear that I am enabling my sister to kill herself. Assisted Suicide by Sugar. Theresa understands my pain.

"MOM!"

I am jolted. Did a tree fall on Leo's room and I didn't hear it?

Then, "MOM!" No. The tone is more I'm in my room and am too lazy to open the door or come down the stairs.

"WHAT?!" I shoot back, straight up the stairs, down the hall, and to hit his shut door.

"GINNY KEEPS TEXTING ME!"

"SO WHAT?!"

Theresa pours herself more merlot and offers me another chocolate from the box that Farzana gifted her with condolences.

"SO SHE SAYS PHILOMENA IS TRYING TO CALL YOU!"

I had turned down the volume on my phone earlier when I was on deadline. Now, it's plugged into the wall in the kitchen charging, in preparation.

I get up and my light head drains down to my feet, which are suddenly prickly with sleep. "THANKS, KID!" I scream super loud just because.

I turn over my phone to see it is full of messages. Turn up the volume to hear Philomena's sweet voice inform me of what I already know because I'm reading it in Ginny's texts over and over and over.

From Ginny: *Powr out. Loss pow er. Tree?? Fell????? Hope u ok. Still no powr. Ras.cul don no wat go on.* A picture of Rascal, lit by flashlight, looking as relaxed as ever. *Did u loose pow. Er? Gary say hi.* Then she posted a picture of short and hairy Gary with his hand in his pants.

"LEO!" I yell, "WE NEED TO GO GET THEM! I NEED YOUR HELP!"

Leo comes barreling down, God bless him.

"No. Wait. No," I say. I look over to the fire. "You need to stay here. With the fire. The house. Damn." I'm imagining how Philomena and I are going to get Ginny and Rascal into the car.

"You sure?" he says. He looks worried.

"Ginny's car has four-wheel drive," I say.

"I dunno, Mom."

"I'll bring them back," I nod. "And anyway, don't you have a college essay to write?"

"Really?" he says.

He's applying to an almost guaranteed safety. Late. Do I really expect him to work on this during a snowstorm? I dunno. I'm programmed to encourage. Or, perchance, to dream? "Kidding," I say. "Keep an eye on the fire."

Outside, the wind is ferocious. Coyote won't even consider going out to do her biz. It's the kind of wind that forces you to take wide steps while leaning into it and holding on to your hat. Insane gusts. From inside the house by the fireplace it just looked like a lot of whooshing white; outside, it feels like pushing through frozen waves. I'll drop Theresa at her house, which is only next door, some five hundred feet away, then Ginny's.

Theresa is in the passenger seat. Her house suddenly seems much further away. "Seriously," she says, "I'll walk home. You can't drive in this."

I turn on the engine. We have no choice. What are we going to do? Let my sister and her dog and her caregiver freeze to death? With Gary?

"Neighbors?" Theresa says hopefully.

"I'm sure the whole neighborhood is out."

"Yeah, but some of them might have generators?"

I imagine Philomena going out in this insanity to knock on a neighbor's door and then the moving of the three of them, including the killer dog. It's just too awful. Why the hell didn't I get my sister's house a generator?

I start to move forward. Slowly. Inch by inch, like the way one does when blindfolded, praying there's no step or cliff in the path ahead. Another inch.

"Maggie," my dear friend says, "I'm not sure this is a good idea."

A loud crack. Followed by a longer crack followed by a boom. The front of the car jumps and we both jump and scream. A tree or a branch just fell on the front of the car. Theresa's flashlight indicates that it is indeed a large branch. We guess that the rest of the tree fell with it and we thank the lord that it didn't fall on us. Together we wonder if it would be better or worse for us to stay in the car than attempt to get back in the house. Dropping Theresa at her house is no longer an option, let alone, driving to Ginny's. We consider staying in the car, but no, Leo. We need to get back to Leo. We conclude that we will each pray in our own way before getting out. The plan: to hold hands, and if we hear another loud crack we will hunker down and cover our heads.

Back safe inside, I discover that Ginny has sent a selfie. From the bottom of her nose up, her face is white, her eyes, remote, expressionless. I can see her nose is running. The text: *Nice.been.On/ Afntartk.a*

I text Ginny and Philomena: *I am sorry we can't come to get you. A tree just fell on the car and street and we can't get out. Please cover yourselves and Rascal with blankets and in the morning, we will try to come get you. Don't go out, Philomena, it is not safe.*

Separately, I text Ginny: *I love you, Big Sister. I am sorry I can't help you more. We will come get you in the morning.*

Neither text goes through. So now they've lost cell power, too.

"Oh my gosh," I say, "what are we going to do?" I call 911 and they ask if it's a life or death emergency. "God, I hope not!" I say. "Yes, maybe! Definitely! She's got health issues . . ." "IV?" he asks. "No," I say. "Wheelchair." The guy takes down her address and says she's on the list.

"Mom, she keeps her place at a hundred degrees. It'll probably just hit the eighties by sunrise," Leo says.

I decide I am going to fall asleep in front of the fireplace, so I offer Theresa my bed. She refuses it and says I am crazy not to sleep there myself. I explain that by being here in the living room I feel somehow closer to my sister and Graham, who has texted me that his apartment building four hours north of here lost power but is on an automatic generator. Theresa sleeps on the sofa and I, on the floor. I am up every hour or so adding another log to the fire. I don't have to keep the fire going. We still have power, which is a miracle indeed. But for whatever reason, I feel compelled.

I go to sleep in little deep intervals, in and out of dreams, memories, and shames. My first shame is that I did not even think to set up my sister's house with a generator in the first place. How stupid was I? Ginny is fat, but as feeble as a skinny little old lady and could die as the night goes on and the temperature drops. My only comfort is the thought that maybe the heavy snow will create a thick blanket for the house, therefore keeping it above freezing temperatures.

Then, I am ashamed of my impatience with Ginny. Ginny is different, for God's sake. She doesn't have the capacity to understand some things. Ginny sometimes says, "My brain's a bit slow." My sister has special needs, sure. But what she really is? Special. Just special.

I am ashamed of being short with her when she is doing the best she can in her personal capacity. I don't want my sister to think she is a burden to me and I am ashamed that sometimes I feel that she is. My sister is a project, that's for damn sure. My sister requires assistance with so many things. My sister has enough pride that she doesn't come right out and ask for assistance, so she'll drop hints about whatever it is she needs to have fixed. My sister doesn't want to be a burden.

I put another log on the fire and stir it a bit and then I lie down and remember another cold night. A night when I was in high school, and our parents went away for the weekend. It was probably their annual Honeymoon Weekend. I guess they considered me old enough to hold the fort with Ginny. I was a senior.

It was snowing lightly that night, the Christmas tree lights were on. And my two best friends were there when the boys showed up. Three of them. One was my sort-of boyfriend. The boys found the liquor shelf, the boys did shots. All this while Ginny was upstairs in her room. She saw the boys arrive and she said she was giving us privacy in case we were going to make out. She said this as if it was something she knew all about. She also didn't know that my sort-of boyfriend and I had already attempted sex, if one considered sex his putting his thing into mine on his single bed during lunch break.

So he got a little drunk and maybe the other boys did, too. Looking back, I wonder if my girlfriends and I even drank a little bit, but no, I don't think so. And I'm ashamed of that, too! It was more like we were watching to see what the boys would do. Well instead of heavy kissing or silly dancing, the sort-of boyfriend got all daring. Daring to punch his fist through one of the windows that framed the front door. "Don't do that," I remember his friends saying. "Don't do that," I remember myself saying. So he did it. Punched it right through. He was dripping with blood and Ginny came lumbering down the stairs to see what the commotion was and his friends said they were going to take him to the hospital and the snow had stopped.

Ginny went to get the broom and dustpan. My friends and I started to pick up the pieces of bloody glass. Ginny swept. I got some wet rags and wiped up what was left. Then Ginny went down to the basement and got a box and she tore a section of it off and taped it to the window.

The next day Ginny replaced the window. I didn't have to beg her to not tell our parents. I already knew that she wouldn't. Ever.

Looking into the embers of the fire, I now wonder, how on earth did my sister know how to do that? It's hard to imagine her repairing anything now. Hard to remember the days when she used her own two feet to walk and ride a bike and drive a car. Hard to recall that she used to go to stores all by herself, pick out things and pay for them, measure things, and without reading the instructions, take things apart and put them together. Ginny used to be able to do things!

My big sister helped me. And all these years she's kept the secret! I will thank her for that tomorrow. If I can get to her house. If she is still alive.

The snow falls throughout the night and into the morning. Just when we think we've come through it unscathed, the transformers start to pop. We can hear them exploding like fireworks, one off in the direction of the dam, the other down the hill toward the bridge. Yes, from my bedroom window, we can see a small fire through the woods. The light on the coffeepot goes out.

Even after the neighbors have rallied and cut up the trunks of the two fallen trees on our little country lane and rolled the huge logs to the side of the road, the roads into town are impassable. Also, with its front hood slammed, Ginny's car is not drivable. Our own car is okay, but it is old and not good in snow. The loss of power is something we are strangely used to, living out of town in the woods, so the five homes are all prepared with wood-burning stoves or various-size generators and extra refills of gas. I have a small generator that is currently broken. Two of the neighbors have plows. One of those is Theresa. Farzana comes out with fresh baked scones for all—she's got one of those fail-proof generators. One neighbor's son is with the local police. He usually shows up with a plow and news from town, but so far, he hasn't.

I can't shake the image of my dear sister shaking to death; of Philomena, who has come so far, meeting her own end just a few miles north of her own family and new husband. And even poor Rascal, quaking beneath her thick layer of fur and fat. I should have prepared for the worst. If I was going to go to the trouble of completely displacing my sister from her own home in Maryland, shouldn't I have made sure that we had every single safety measure in order? How could I have allowed this to happen on my watch?

I will walk to her. I would recruit Leo to come with me, but after the neighborhood logging adventure, he has suddenly come down with a fever and a cough, so he is going nowhere. Anyway, I need him to stay home to keep the fire in the fireplace going, the animals warm.

With three layers on every part of my body, a duffel stuffed with blankets on my back, and a backpack stuffed with a down comforter on my front, I head out. I'll be back to my sick baby before sundown.

On a clear spring day, this walk would take thirty minutes, but I rarely take it because it involves crossing the Quaker Bridge which, with its iron grating, is not built for dog paws. The road to the bridge is windy and hilly and has no sidewalks. Once over the bridge, there is a rather steep path into the woods that leads to a half-mile trail before reaching the road. Today, it is thick with slippery snow. Today, just getting down the road to the bridge, I have to sit on my ski-pants-covered bottom to slide down small sections and hold on to the guardrail on others. I walk around what are probably live wires—the electric company trucks haven't appeared yet to mark them off. And I keep my eyes and ears open for the sound of falling branches. Along the way I hear the humming of generators near and far. The Croton River is rushing fast and furious.

The path up into the woods is an obstacle course that I can only manage by grabbing one tree trunk after another. Even so, with my bags, it is especially awkward, and I slip and fall a couple of times. I stop and grab a handful of thick snow and bite into it. I am Laura Ingalls Wilder off to save my sister on the other side of the prairie! Oh, but my sister! Quivering and dripping and pale and cold to touch! I shake off the thought as I plan my next steps.

Once I get to roads, I find that very few of them had been plowed. Trees and broken branches everywhere. I can hear the familiar humming again and also the distinct sound of a busy shovel. There are a few adults out clearing their cars and throwing down salt, a few kids, braving the elements. This is perfect snowman-making snow. Heavy, packable. The sidewalks are hit or miss, so I opt for the center of the road. My snow boots are my saviors. My snow pants are my hero. Truly, I can negotiate snow drifts as deep as two feet. I can step up and into the snow without losing a boot or my footing. My feet are still warm.

Whole blocks are cordoned off due to downed wires. ConEd or someone with caution tape has been around. It takes well over an hour to finally reach my sister's little beach retreat. The wooden pole that holds her various flags has broken. A tree limb impales the ground right beneath. The Aloha sign that hangs on the front door remains fully intact. The house is dark, of course.

The door is locked. The doorbell does not ring, so I knock like crazy before reaching for my keys. As I reach into my zippered snow pants pocket I see that there are many footprints on the small deck, and they aren't all mine. Boot prints of various sizes. Paw prints. A neighbor calls out, "A firetruck came!"

"What? When?!" I call.

"Middle of the night!"

On impulse, I open the mailbox that hangs to the right of the door, and sure enough, there is a note. In handwriting unfamiliar to me, it says:

Maggie, the fire men take us to get warm at town hall. Rascal, too. Thankful to God almighty, Philomena.

Oh, my goodness. Oh my goodness oh my goodness oh my goodness. I am off, to the center of town and my sister. On my way I see that the whole town is dark. They must have a massive generator at the municipal building.

There must be some scientific name for the phenomenon that happens when a person walks into a crowded room and their eyes go immediately to the eyes of their loved one. Because how could I have possibly known that in the far-right corner of that large high-ceilinged room where I go once a year to vote, would be my big sister, sitting in her wheelchair, covered by a blue blanket, accompanied by her faithful companion, Rascal. And how in the world would Ginny have known that I, her little sister, dressed like an arctic explorer, would enter the warming center at that exact moment? Our eyes meet and we are home.

There's Philomena, standing behind a long table, ladling soup. I run to Ginny and as I do, Rascal looks up and starts wagging. Ginny's face is pale, and she is wearing her *I'd rather be in Hawaii* ski cap. She clutches Binky Baby in her lap. I drop my heavy bags and throw my arms around my sister, knowing full well that her arms will not move to meet me. "I am so happy to see you!" I say. "Oh, Ginny, I was so worried, I am so sorry you had to go through that, it must have been so scary. You must have been so cold!"

Ginny looks up to me and says, "Thanks for calling the firemen." Her eyes are wet.

"Oh, Ginny, I'm so grateful that they came! When did they? Are you all okay?"

"We're fine," she says. She's wiping her eyes with her sleeve. "Rascal thought she was gonna freeze to death, but now she's okay."

I wave to Philomena who waves back. I take Ginny to the restroom, bringing Rascal along. I take Rascal outside to do her thing. Then I deliver them to their original resting place, the perfect spot from which Ginny has a full view of the goings-on. There are many people here, mostly elderly. There is a young couple with two babies, a couple of other dogs, and a cat in a carrier. There are cots set up and lots of blue blankets. I am surprised by the number of volunteers who managed to get here, including a lot of the same folks I see on voting day and a woman my own age who previous to this moment I strongly disliked.

I thank the firemen when they bring someone else in. "Just doing our job," they say humbly. It's like a commercial for the fire department. But better. I scan the room to take in the details just in case I should ever have to draw it. Ah, at least two people have oxygen tanks and a teenager is hooked up to an IV. A young woman comes over to pour Rascal more water. Oh my, someone is handing out cupcakes. Nothing fancy, just those little ones you buy by the dozen at the grocery store, but still.

ConEd says they'll have power back up at Ginny's by eight tonight. My house could take days. It then dawns on me that my own teenager is home, sick on the sofa, and I need to get back before dark. I tell the ladies I hate to leave them, I ask if they'll be okay.

"We're fine," Ginny says again. Really, she seems to be enjoying the whole thing. "Biggest blizzard of the century," she keeps saying. "So far." Then she asks me if the Croton Firefighters have a calendar. "It's no wonder they're firemen. They're hot," she says.

Philomena hasn't been in touch with her family yet, but she has faith that her new husband is making sure that her mother and daughters are fine.

"How is Binky Baby doing?" I ask.

"She's better now," Ginny says. "She likes the cake." Like Ginny's, her lips are dotted with frosting. "You need to go home to Leo and Coyote and Crazy Cat," Ginny says to me.

The walk back is just as difficult, though I feel light. This time I guide myself between shadows and shimmering bright white. The only humming I hear now is my own humming, as I catch myself humming that tune that I sometimes hum. Not a real song, just a happy tune. I laugh at myself. And I say, "Ho, ho, ho!" And I remember Ginny, as a kid, dressed up in a Santa suit. I have a December birthday, and more than once, she made an appearance, carrying a pillowcase and handing out small party gifts. One of my friends asked, "Is that really Santa?" And another one said, "That's not Santa, that's her sister!" I could see that underneath that white beard and red hat was Ginny, but still, part of me knew that she was Santa, too.

I arrive to my country lane happily exhausted and strangely satisfied. I check out the cars parked up on the street and assess the damage to Ginny's car. Our dear street gang has removed the tree branch from the hood. It's got an ugly dent and the windshield's been smashed, but it looks repairable. I turn to walk down the hill to the house and am greeted by not one, but two snowmen. One has a head, the other does not. They are on the front lawn, facing out. Well, the one wearing hat, scarf, radishes for eyes and mouth, and a carrot nose is facing out. Did a feverish Leo go snow crazy? What magical creature built these? I scan around for evidence. Nothin'.

Inside the house is a sickly boy on the sofa and a cozy cat in front of a fire in the fireplace. The place isn't freezing. Leo smiles at me vaguely. At the top of the basement stairs appears an excitable Coyote dog. Then Bill. He's holding a few more pieces from our old dress-up trunk. The Court Jester hat, a pink feather boa. Coyote comes running to greet me and I swear, if Bill were a dog, his tail would be wagging, too.

"He got the generator going," Leo says, his half smile turning into a full one.

"I had to park down by the bridge. Couldn't get up the hill," Bill says.

"Oh," I say, "I must have walked right by the car without noticing."

It took some effort for Bill to get here. It took some determination. I realize now that it might have been his large boot prints that provided my footing as I climbed up the hill. Bill. Is here. Checking on us. Which means he was worried about us. Which means, like I do for Ginny, he feels some responsibility. And maybe other things.

"How's Ginny?" they both ask in unison.

I tell them both that Ginny is okay. That Rascal is, too, and so is Philomena.

"I assume Graham's okay," I hopefully say.

"Of course he is," Bill says, picking up his cue perfectly.

"Graham's always okay," Leo says, sinking down comfortably under his extra covers. Bill makes me and Leo some tea and then he and Coyote go back outside. He calls us out when he's done. "It's a snowman and a snow lady," he says. "Or. I dunno. Two snow ladies. They're a couple. Or. You know. Friends, hanging out." He's blushing. Or his cheeks are just red from the cold and the wet. Leo smiles and goes back inside. I just stand there, taking in what Bill has built, how surprisingly handsome he looks, the unabashed joy Coyote feels in his presence.

He smiles at me. A true, genuine smile. "Well," he says, "there you go, Maggie-do."

He hasn't called me that in a really long time. He used to call me that all the time. Not just because I am a "doer," which he always said I was, but because he popped it into "Love Me Do" and it stuck. He used to sing to me a lot. He used to pop my name into a million song lyrics. We used to make snowmen together, too. With the boys. Before the boys.

Looking at Bill standing there now, I realize that I don't want him to go. He looks so familiar there in his Timberland boots, his ridiculous plaid hunter's hat. I always hated that hat, those ear flaps, I made fun of it. Now, I find it kind of . . . cute.

"How's the job?" I say, breaking whatever this is.

"The job? Oh. It's good. Challenging. A fire at Dolly's headquarters cost us some cash. A new client: Graceland."

"Wow," I say.

"It's not as exotic as it sounds," he says. "You know. Insurance."

"I drew an ad for Mountain Dew last week. Ryan Reynolds. I doubt he'll do it . . ."

"Wow," he says, still smiling. "I've cut back my smoking," he announces. "Though I do enjoy my cannabis tea. It's organic, so."

"Cool," I say.

"Less smoking, more meditating." He says this almost sheepishly, like he expects I'll make fun.

"Cool," I say again. It's hard to imagine him doing that, sitting still without a joint, but great, good for him. I guess his leggy leafy lady inspires him or something. Oh yes. She has a greenhouse. Holistic marketing. I'm starting to get the picture.

"Well. I'll be on my way. I just wanted to make sure you guys were okay." He indicates that the sun is starting to set, and like a good pioneer, he's got a ways to go.

"Sure," I say. "Of course. And thanks for the heat . . . and stuff."

"Course," he says. He's looking at me now like he's not sure if he knows me but like maybe he would like to know me.

Coyote jumps up on the snowman and takes a bite of the pink feather boa, in the process knocking off the snowman's head. "Coyote, you goof!" he yells as he goes chasing her. She runs over to me and I throw a snowball in the air for her to catch and Bill wipes out on his ass, right there in front of me.

I gasp. "You okay?" I say, because let's face it, at our age, a little wipeout like that can be damaging. He looks up at me and laughs. Coyote is all over him now, a wet, sloppy mess. I want to say, "You okay, Billy Boy?" but I don't.

"Give me a hand, will you?" he says.

And I do. And he fakes that he's going to pull me down, too, but he doesn't. And part of me is sorry that he doesn't. Once he's standing again, we let go of each other's hands and just kind of look at each other. I notice he has a pink feather stuck to his left earflap and without thinking, I reach over and remove it. He tilts his head and I show it to him. "A feather," I say. "That's good luck, I think. When a pink feather gets stuck to your hunting hat." We both look down to see that he has more pink feathers stuck to his jeans, which are very wet. "Oh wow," I say. "Your jeans are soaked. You want to borrow some of Leo's?"

"That's okay," he says. "I should really get back. I'll crank the heat in the car."

"Oh, okay," I say. "Well, be careful going down the hill. It's slippery."

He smiles at me kind of funny. "Okay, Maggie. I'll be careful."

"Thanks for stopping by, Bill," I say.

He's giving Coyote a vigorous body hug now. "Course," he says. He's just a few feet away from me and I can see him debating if he should come closer. He shakes the snow and the feathers off. And then bows to me.

It's weird. I bow back. "Got power at your apartment?"

"Nah," Bill says, "but she does." "She" is his girlfriend whose name we never use.

⸙

It's my third date with Malick. We meet at the Met. I've been patient, I've been good, I've packed panties and a toothbrush. It feels so good to stroll through these wide, light spaces, among sculptures that have survived centuries. It's been two months since our last date, Senegal and storms have slowed us, and perhaps this is a good thing. We've done some texting and even talked a few times on the phone, and being with him now feels surprisingly comfortable.

He appreciates art and is knowledgeable about works that even I, an art school graduate, am not familiar with. For example, did I know that Carpeaux's *Ugolino and His Sons* was inspiration for Rodin's *Ugolino and His Children*, which is even more desperate and on display at the Musée Rodin? I did not!

We visit Art of Native America and Dutch Masterpieces and the American Wing. I tell him I can skip the medieval armor. I've seen that gallery with my boys so many countless times. He says his children love it, too, and he forces me to go there to show him which armor I find the most attractive and or frightening. I lead him directly to it and he laughs and says that's exactly the one he would like to wear.

At lunch I start to order a glass of wine and he suggests I wait 'til later. "We don't want to get sleepy," he says, "do we? Don't want to be stumbling down the marble stairs!"

"Perhaps you're right," I say, and I show him my travel toothbrush.

"Oh my!" he says, quite pleased.

Afterward, I tell him I will lead him to my favorite, secret room in the entire Metropolitan Museum. I take his hand and say, "Come with me." And he does. We hold hands all the way to the Far East. We stop at a door that leads to the secret room and I tell him to close his eyes. I lead him into another world, Astor Chinese Garden Court, complete with rock garden and bonsai and even a small waterfall. It's the quietest room in the Met, people come here to meditate. He opens his eyes and says, "Ahhhh . . ." Yes, he agrees that it is very nice. We sit on one of the stone benches.

"Well, aren't we lucky?" he says. He's still holding my hand and his hand is warm. Even his nails, I notice, gleam. "I would love to travel to China. Spectacular landscape, fascinating architecture."

"Really?" I say. "You really do like to see the world, don't you?"

He pauses for a moment and says, "I am interested in progress. I am interested in innovation and beauty. Like this garden here." He looks around. "The latticed windows project shadows and light. It is a garden, yes, but no dirt, no weeds. Just peace."

Again, I have to laugh. As I look around this room, this room that I've loved since I moved to the city over thirty years ago, I notice that while it is indeed a garden, there is no grass. I see a couple of art students with their drawing pads try to sit down on a step and the security guard gives them the evil eye.

"Huh," I say. "I never saw it that way. But yes, I suppose this is the ideal garden for the reluctant gardener!"

"Shhh," the guard says.

Malick silently and jokingly scolds me.

As we walk down Fifth Avenue along the park, I say, "Next time your kids come to visit, you can take them there."

He says, "What? Where?"

I say, "The Chinese garden, silly."

He nods his head but he is quiet.

"It must be so hard to be so far away. I can only imagine," I say.

"Let's not talk about family and messy things. I prefer the smooth lines of Michelangelo."

"It's our third date, Malick. I want to know more about them than just their names."

"He's a challenge and she's a spoiled girl."

"Oh, come on," I say. "I know they are more than that. Much more." It's hard for me to understand this resistance to talking about one's own children and all I can fathom is the deep swelling pain.

"He is smart and she is ambitious," he says.

"Um hmm . . ." I say.

"He is a very good cook! She wins trophies for her athletics!"

"Ah," I say. "Tell me more!"

We're standing now in front of the Central Park Zoo. From this spot on this side of the fence, we are able to see the polar bears.

"They like to come here," he says. "New York City."

"I see! And what are their favorite things to do? What do you always do with them when they come to visit you?"

"Oh, you know. Get spa treatments. Go shopping on Madison Avenue."

"Really?" I say. "That's what you do with them when they come all the way to New York from western Africa?"

"I take them for nice dinners. Now they are older I allow them alcohol. Their mother doesn't need to come anymore."

"Well, they must love Kitsu, I am sure of that!"

"Oh, yes, of course they do. I often bring her."

Bring? "Do you cook with them, bake them bread? Stay up late watching movies?"

And now Malick looks at me like I'm foreign. And finally, he says, "Well, they don't stay with me. I put them up at the Ritz-Carlton in White Plains."

"The Ritz-Carlton? What's the matter? Are they allergic . . . ?"

"Well, no, she is a hypo-allergenic dog! I told you, my princess is perfect!"

I'm noticing now how well-coifed Malick is. His face without a scratch, his coat without a smudge, his boots without a scuff. He's noticing that I don't fully understand what he is saying.

He looks at me and speaks slowly, "Of course they could stay with me. But it is better this way. This way we all have our space. Kids are messy, you know that."

I do, I think, but I'm not allergic to them.

"Like you and your sister," Malick spells it out. "You are responsible for her, but you don't want her in your house!"

I feel a sudden bout with nausea. Don't want her in my house? Why, I just had her in my house for Christmas! I have her at my house often! It's not easy, but even with her wheelchair and her growly dog and her sometimes wet diapers, my sister is always welcome.

"What's the matter?" he says. "You're looking at me like I'm a monster!" He laughs nervously.

Well, maybe that's what you are. Maybe that's just exactly what you are. A pressed and perfect monster. "Oh no," I say. "No, it's just. I need to go home."

"I thought you were coming home with me? You packed your tooth-brush." He flutters his eyelashes.

No, I'm not, I think. I might accidentally leave a strand of hair on the sink. Sometimes I fart between the sheets. My sister is revolting, that's what you'd think. We're just ten blocks from Grand Central. I catch the next train home, holding tight to my beleaguered baggage. He said he loves his children dearly, and I believe in his way he does, though I sus-pect his dearly is a pat on the back, a peck on the cheek. His love is ster-ile and neat and I will never be that clean.

⤜⟿⤛

Today is the day that Leo will hear from colleges. All six that he applied to will send him an acceptance or rejection, electronically. Many of his friends have received acceptances already. Ideally, he would have heard good news earlier this week, but alas, this is the day he should hear either way. He came straight home from school, assuming he went to school, ran past me and up the stairs to his room, slamming his bed-room door behind him. I called up, "Standing by to celebrate!" Please College Goddesses and Gods, be good to him. Please, at least his safety?

By seven, I haven't heard a peep. I call up to him that it's dinnertime. *Not hungry,* he texts me.

I knock on his door. "Room Service," I say.

"Not hungry," he says.

"I'll just leave it on the floor, okay?"

. . .

"Any news?"

. . .

"Okay. I'll be downstairs," I say.

Three hours later, a bloodcurdling scream. Coyote starts barking and Crazy Cat's hair goes up. Another scream. It's Leo, of course. I trip over the creatures and take the stairs by threes. A retching sound. Another. I run to the boys' bathroom and there he is, on his knees, facing the toilet. Has he been drinking? He looks up at me and throws up again.

"Oh my God, Leo, are you okay?" I say. "What's going on? Are you okay?"

He's still retching. I look over to the trash can to see if there is any evidence. Once he left an Absolut bottle there, twice I've found beer bottles. He gags a few times and then lifts up his upper body, using both his forearms on the toilet rim for support, and howls at the ceiling light fixture, which is flashing. The bulb needs to be changed. I've asked him to do this several times.

"Leo," I say. "What is going on? Are you sick?"

He's now wiping his mouth with a towel that was already on the floor, one of many wet and stinky towels that have been growing there. He's looking at me with dazed eyes. He starts to gag again and then screams. Crazy Cat is running up and down the hallway meowing and Coyote is whining at the bottom of the stairs. "Leo, do we need to go to the hospital?"

"I didn't get in!" he starts to cry.

Okay. Oh shit.

"I didn't get into any of them!" His phone is sitting there on the bathtub edge, he grabs it and starts using it and then shoves it in my face. "Look. Rejection five. Rejection six. I didn't even get into my safeties!" He reeks of vomit and booze.

We knew Northeastern was a reach, I knew it was an extremely far one, but we did make a point to apply to at least three that his guidance counselor said were practically guarantees.

"Leo," I say. "It's okay. It's okay . . . We'll figure something out. There are plenty of colleges."

He's just a blubbering mess now on the floor. I see there is no cup on the sink, so I run to my bathroom to get one and return to fill it up and offer it. He knocks it out of my hand, sending water flying to the ceiling, the plastic cup bouncing on the floor. He pulls himself up and then reaches for the cup and fills it himself and drinks the whole cup's worth, fills it up and then drinks again.

"Have you been drinking?" I ask.

"I played a game," he says.

"Oh yeah? What game?" Is there some new college acceptance game I don't know about?

"Where I take a shot with every rejection I got. And then before I opened each new one, I took another one."

"Why would you do that, sweetie?"

He kneels down again to the toilet and starts to gag again. "For good luck," he says.

That's a lot of shots. I am glad he's throwing up. I reach down to wipe his mouth and he hits my hand away. He stands up to get more water. It's crowded in his bathroom. I think this is the first time I've been in here with him since his early shower days, when I'd sit on the toilet and wait. He's two heads taller than me. I lean against the sink.

"I'm like Ginny!" he cries. And then he climbs into the bathtub and sits down in there. "I always knew I was stupid and now it's confirmed! Nobody wants me! I suck at school, I'm the student that teachers give up on, that's who I am!" He pulls the curtain closed on himself. He's quietly crying behind it.

"Leo, you know that's not true!" I say. "Your teachers love you!" That's not true. "I'm sure many of them do!" His teachers start out loving him because, well, he's so light. He's likeable, that's what. He's funny and loyal and a good friend to boot. We all know he has ADHD, he was diagnosed really early. And so everyone—well, some of them—tries hard to reach him . . . They try, he tries. Sometimes he tries, it's just really hard . . .

"Look, Leo," I say. "It's been a couple of years, you know? I mean, you've, we've had a lot going on. It hasn't been easy . . . And you have been amazing! So strong! And sweet! You make amazing ramen!" He does. And many times he has made some for me. "It's been a challenge, and you have risen to it! You have an amazing positive attitude! And I, Leo, your mother, truly believe in you! You can do anything! Do you hear me in there?" He's so quiet now I'm wondering if he just curled up and fell asleep. "There are other schools. Schools that don't ask for those stupid tests. There are probably even schools that don't ask for grades! I'm pretty sure! All they have to do is meet you. You're so great! I've never met a person that didn't love you, Leo." Except his chemistry teacher, who said he practically lit the room on fire, and his algebra teacher who said he was dismissive, his boss at the local pet store who called him lazy to his face . . . "Leo? You okay?"

I hear metal scratching metal. I look up to see the shower curtain rings are tightening. The curtain is now pulling and with one swift move, the entire bar slams down with a crash. Leo is now standing up and he is looking down at me.

"It's all because of you," he says. "You fucked it up. Fucked me up. Fucked up Dad. Why the fuck did you do that, Mom? Why the fuck did you cheat? You always told me not to cheat. Well guess what, you cheated. You cheated on your whole entire family."

I feel weak all of a sudden and pretty much collapse onto the toilet seat. "Leo, there's more to it than that." I'm stumbling for words now. "You know that. I would never . . ."

"Yeah, and Dad fucked up, too, didn't he? Isn't that what you're going to say? He did fuck up! He didn't even want kids, you think I don't know that?"

What is he talking about? This is true, or at least way back then before we had them, it was, but we've never told them that, never. He must have overheard us. It was part of my arsenal, I pulled that out a couple of times.

"We have you. And Graham. And we both love you. Both. Very much," I say.

He just stands there, holding on to the shower curtain, staring at me.

"Leo, it's all going to be okay," I say. And then, making my best effort not to cry, I say, "And I am so sorry that we, I, have hurt you."

Nothing. His eyes are holding me. Honestly, I'd wondered if he'd lost that ability.

"Can I make you a cup 'a tea?" I say, oh so Britishly, trying to alleviate.

"NO!" he says. "I don't want any stupid tea!" He steps out of the bathtub and trips on the shower rod, gets his foot stuck between the plastic curtain and the base. I offer my hand for support, but he refuses it. He's holding on to the wall for support, and once untangled, barrels past me, out the door and into his bedroom and slams the door.

"Leo," I say, holding myself back from saying Leo Lion, "please, can we talk this out? Leo, please."

Nothing.

I stand there staring at the door until he screams, "Leave me the fuck alone!" I still can't bring myself to leave, and he must sense this because he surprises me with a slight opening of the door. Peeks his face out to see me and says, "Please, Mom, please. Just . . . leave."

⁓

Another antidepressant board. In this one, the woman is a singer who can't sing until the end when she is singing loud and clear from a small stage at a coffeehouse. The board was given to me an hour ago and is due yesterday.

A text from Leo, with an important announcement. He tells us to mark our calendars. *Dancing with the Stars* starring Bets premieres in three weeks. He even sends us a promo video. Yup. There's Former Surf Champion Bets Frederick twerking while holding a surfboard. Ginny invites us to her place for a Pizza and Watch Party. The text stream goes wild. Yes, we'll all be there. Even Bill. I wonder if he'll bring his woodland witch. And hey, it's great that Leo is excited about something.

I can see it now. We'll bring the chairs in from the dining room; Ginny can't force us to stand. We'll turn up the volume to her satisfaction as we watch an extremely suave guy spin my other sparkly sister. She will win the first round or whatever it is and when they interview her at the end she'll be breathing deeply and shiny with sweat and success. She'll say, "I would like to dedicate this win to my dear sister Ginny who lives back on the East Coast!" She'll look at the camera and say, "Gin-Gin, you know I love you! This is for all the adult people with intellectual disabilities!" And the judges will love this and the live audience will stand and the fans will love her and our family will applaud so heartily. This is how it will go, I think. I can handle this.

I watch the promo many times. I tell the gang I'll bring the cupcakes and I've gotta leave the group chat as I'm in the middle of working, not twerking. Back to my comfort zone with the antidepressant campaign.

❧

She's eating her latest favorite. Black and whites, cookies the size of pancakes, frosted half chocolate and half vanilla. She picks them up in the store bakery, ignoring Philomena's shaking head. Philomena tells me she says, "No, no, no," and Ginny nods and says, "Yes, yes, yes." They come by the dozen, in a plastic container that holds them individually, so they don't break. I tell her I am concerned about her sugar intake. She says I worry too much; she only has one a day.

I know, because the ladies report, that she buys this container of twelve every week, and finishes them in three days. I've done the math. And this is in addition to the stuff we don't see. I don't tell her that I know this because then she calls them tattletales and we can't afford to lose the bit of trust that's been built.

I say, "What if your blood sugar goes too high again and we have to take you to the hospital?"

She says, "I won't go."

I say, "Why not?"

She says, "I'll miss Rascal too much."

I say, "But what if you might die? Like last time?"

She says, "I'm not going."

I say, "So you'd rather stay at home to die?"

She says, "If I die, I die sweet."

I take this in as it's kind of poetic, like all truly true things, I suppose. I say, "What about Rascal then? Won't you miss her if you die? Won't she miss you?"

She says, "She'll meet me there, two months later."

Before I leave, she hands me a book she ordered on Amazon. *No More Pricks*, it's called, *Alternative Ways to Beat Type 2 Diabetes*. It's a self-published book and I commend the author for the title.

"I bet it's going to say to change your diet," I say.

She says nothing.

I say, "Have you read it yet?"

She says, "I'm a bit slow."

I say, "How about if I read it and get back to you with a report?"

"Okay," she says.

"Are you feeling okay, do you want to change your ways? Should we go see the doctor?"

She says, "If it's not broken . . . Like Dad said."

"I miss Dad," I say. And soon, I'll miss you, I think.

She has little brown frosting pieces and little white frosting pieces stuck in her hair. She doesn't care, she'll just leave them there.

⸎

Today I will try a different approach to persuade her to change her ways. It will involve two steps. First, a sister adventure and activity that will show that her future is bright; second, a cautionary tale. I will fit the tale in when appropriate. I take her to Westchester Surgical and Medical Supplies for a new wheelchair. Hers is dirty due to . . . well . . . accidents. But today, I will propose a Motorized Chair. Wow! Pow! Wham! She'll be feeling like a superhero as she drives herself out of here.

Today my sister is wearing her bright blue and yellow Hawaiian shirt, pastel pink shorts, yellow-striped knee-high athletic socks, and purple Crocs. She's wearing her pink canvas fanny pack and new eyeglasses that are Transitions, meaning they turn into sunglasses when she is outside. They take a long time to transition back to regular glasses so as the salesgirl is showing us her wares, it looks like my sister is wearing sunglasses.

I tell her she looks mysterious, like Philomena. She says people have been wearing sunglasses inside for a long time and Philomena didn't start that.

Oh, her baseball cap says *Peace, Love, Waves.*

I help her stand up and the salesgirl holds the latest model in place as Ginny plops down into it. By the way, I'm not saying "salesgirl" to be disrespectful. She really is a girl, like, under eighteen. She's the owner's granddaughter and she's sexy in her short little sweater dress and I wonder how many heart attacks she has inspired working here.

Before she's done showing us the controls, Ginny takes off. She's riding down the aisle, past other, lesser wheelchairs, walkers, raised toilets. She's doing her best to stay on track, but the salesgirl keeps having to catch up and redirect her.

I say, "Gin-Gin, you're doing great!"

Ginny doesn't say anything. She's focused. In the zone.

I pull out my phone because this is a moment to capture. Ginny on video. I'll title it *Here Comes Trouble* when I send it to the boys. But my phone has died, completely out of juice. I could kick myself for this.

I look up and Ginny is kicking at some boxes, trying to get herself unstuck. The salesgirl is leaning over her, showing her the Reverse button. Ginny backs up really fast and into a stack of plastic-covered mattresses. She flips to forward again and she's movin' and groovin'. If I made that video, I would surely give it a soundtrack. Something R&B with a good horn section and some syntho-phonic beat. Tower of Power's "What Is Hip" comes to mind. Or perhaps "Brick House." Leo would have to show me how to lay down the track.

"She's on fire!" I say.

The salesgirl calls, "Remember the brake!"

Ginny is working on turning a corner. It's a complicated maneuver because it's tight and she's got to get the angle just right if she doesn't want to bump into the sales desk. The older guy sitting there looks up over his glasses with concern. She makes it! God, I wish my stupid phone was charged.

Down the other side now, back toward where she started. It's an oval, a racetrack, an obstacle course. Ginny's face is totally straight. No expression at all. It's all concentration. I see her mind working, I imagine the freedom she is imagining.

Soon, she'll be able to go out her front door, down that ramp and to the end of the block. She'll practice going back and forth on the sidewalk there while from the top of the ramp Philomena talks to her new husband, mother, and daughters on the phone or Lika cheers loudly. She'll know when the sidewalk dips or cracks and she'll master each and every challenge. And then, who knows what? She'll be able to go to Dunkin' herself! She can pick up her own prescriptions! She can walk Rascal!

She smashes into the back of an elderly woman's manual wheelchair. Fortunately, it's a light smash, though the woman is frightened. She tries to wheel herself away as fast as she can. Ginny backs up, turns herself, and then passes the woman on the right.

"Brake!" the salesgirl yells as she runs toward her.

"Ginny," I say, once I've caught up with them, "you were really baking. Just think how good you'll be with some practice."

I see now that Ginny has broken out into a full sweat. She's dripping from her eyebrows, from her nose, her underarms are soaked.

"No, thank you," Ginny says.

"Not today?" I say.

"You can think about it and call my grandpa," the salesgirl says.

Ginny is lifting up her shirt collar to try to dry her face. "I just wanna get one like my old one," she says.

We leave there with an exact replacement. In the car, Ginny says, "Probly next year I'll be ready to drive again. I'm not gonna waste my money."

I ask if she wants to go to McDonald's or pick up some shrimp shumai, a recent favorite that I turned her on to.

"No, thank you," my sister says.

"Ginny, are you feeling okay?"

"I'm fine," she says.

"I'm sorry. I thought you'd like being able to go a little faster, but maybe it was too fast," I say.

"Fast things are overrated."

"Yeah." And then I start to sing, an old Beach Boy lyric that just pops into my head. "*First gear, it's all right. Second gear, I'll lean right . . .*" She doesn't say anything, though I'm sure she knows what I'm singing. It's the Honda song that inspired her choice of this car. I start it up and we head for home.

Here's a strange thing. I've found myself reading about the Beach Boys. I was looking for a new shower curtain for Ginny and one thing led to another and there I was reading a story about Dennis Wilson's death. It was powerful and upsetting, partly because it was told from the point of view of his friend who witnessed the event. I knew I wanted to talk to Ginny about it and thought I would today and now after the driving drama I'm not so sure it's the time. But then, maybe now is the perfect time.

"I've been reading about Dennis Wilson," I say. "Do you know how he died?"

"Too young," she says.

"Yep. Thirty-nine," I say, "Crazy."

"He was a sex fiend."

"Is that why you like him?"

"One of the reasons," she says.

Yeah. I should leave it right here but now that I've started, I can't stop myself.

"He was a big drinker," I continue. "He got drunk a lot. He'd have a drink for breakfast and then he'd drink throughout the day."

My sister doesn't say anything.

"His friends worried about him. Sometimes they worried that the next time they'd see him would be at his funeral . . ." No comment. She's on to me. "Did you know all this about Dennis Wilson?" I ask.

"He was hot."

True. And let's keep it light and drop the whole thing. "I liked him better with the beard and wild hair," I say. "When he was young, he looked too preppy."

"I liked him all the ways. I probly would of liked him old and bald."

"You're a true fan," I say. "Did you know he was married and divorced four times? And then married and separated again? At thirty-nine?"

Ginny shrugs.

We get back to her house and Rascal greets us at the door and Lika greets us from the floor. She's cleaning up throw up, apparently. Rascal's. Ginny rolls herself to the bathroom and I tell Lika about the motorized chair and Ginny comes back, moves herself to her recliner, and grabs the remote.

"Rascal, come," she says, as she throws a rather large beef jerky on the floor. Rascal trots over.

"Ginny, I tell you, that not good for her!" Lika throws up her hands.

I sink down to the floor, leaning against the large television console, as I often do because as we all know Ginny has no sofa or chairs for guests. After Rascal has gobbled up her treat, I put my hand out for her and she comes to crash down next to me. I continue my story, because now that I've started, I feel the impulse to complete.

"Anyway," I say, petting Rascal behind the ears, "one day, well, it was kind of a regular day for him probably—"

"For who?" Ginny asks.

"Dennis Wilson," I say.

"You're obsessed with him, too."

"Maybe," I say. "So he got up and had a drink and then he hung out with some friends and drank more and then he went on a friend's boat and he drank some more and they all told him to stop and so he did—he passed out for a while. But then when he woke up, he drank more!"

Ginny's just staring at Rascal. Who knows if she's listening.

"And he got off the boat. Oh, at this point they were docked—and he wobbled over to another boat and asked if they had any liquor and they gave him some and he just kept drinking, even though his friends and his new girlfriend kept telling him to stop. Isn't that crazy?" I ask this to see if my sister is paying attention.

"You see this on TV?" she says.

"Nah, an article online. *Rolling Stone* magazine."

"That's been around forever," she says.

"Yeah," I say. "Well, he jumped into the water—Dennis—and he kept going down to the bottom—I guess it wasn't too deep because they were at the dock, but still, deep enough for boats. And he kept pulling up things from the bottom. Including his old wedding picture! Years before, he had gotten drunk and threw it overboard, and now, here it was!"

I can see that Ginny is getting sleepy. When she yawns she looks like a bear.

"I don't know what the picture was like, but apparently the frame was intact."

She yawns again so I know I have to get to my moral.

"So Dennis kept on diving in deep and his friends kept telling him to stop and rest and his one friend, the one that was hanging with him at that particular moment—he heard him on the other side of some docked boat. He called out to him and then he heard him go down. He thought Dennis was playing hide-and-seek. Dennis popped up again and his friend laughed and said something like, 'Buddy, you're crazy, why don't you come up for air?' And the next time he went down, he didn't come up."

My sister yawns another bear yawn. And I do, too. Even Rascal does. I seem to have lost track of my point. My point being that she eats too much sugar, like he drank too much alcohol. But right now, it just feels like I was retelling a sad but true tale for entertainment. That wasn't my mission, not at all.

"Naptime," my sister says.

I do not tell her that I also looked up Brian Wilson, Dennis's oldest brother, the true leader of the Beach Boys, and much-beloved genius. He had a hard time, too, he had his struggles, but he got through. He has soulful eyes. He's still making music and performing. I have a fantasy. About contacting his manager and telling him about my sugar-addicted sister and arranging for him to show up at her door to share his good vibes. Maybe that's the inspiration Ginny needs. Maybe I'll do this and surprise her. Or hey, maybe Bets knows him personally? Now this is something Bets can do!

"Yeah, I need to get back to my boards," I say. "And coffee." I give her and Rascal goodbye pats. "See you next weekend, Lika!" I call.

She pops her head out of the kitchen and says, "Live your life with Lust!"

꘎꘎꘎

A text from Gin-Gin: *yor sSISR ER HER*

    I text back: *Ha ha. I see that. I can see your location.*

    From Ginny: *oher one*

    Other one. Oh. Oh no. Bets. Bets has come to take Ginny away.

    Ginny's complaints and grievances finally piled up high enough to warrant that Bets drive across country in her aquamarine converted school bus. Perhaps Ginny resorted to begging her, perhaps Bets just plain offered, "Magpie had her try, now I'll show you a good time." Our big sis is here with a few of her pals—Malibu Barbie and Ken and the tall drink of margarita that is her "friend." They're going to help carry all Gin's stuff to the bus, they'll even carry her there in her wheelchair.

    I'm sweating in places I didn't know I could sweat. My fingers, for instance. They slip when I try to unscrew the cap of the Baileys. I grab a kitchen towel and that does the job, and then I use it to wipe my hands, my neck, my eyebrows. As I pull out of our narrow driveway, I hit the stone wall. When I get to the street, I see that I've given Ginny's SUV a nice racing stripe. That'll cost five hundred dollars to fix. I'll park on the other side of the street, so she won't see it.

    As I pull in across from Ginny's house, I see that she, Rascal, Philomena, and Bets are all out on the deck together. It's late spring, but today's cool and gray. All the ladies are wearing sweatshirts and sunglasses. Ginny's are purple and mirrored. Another great gift from Bets. A quick scan of Ginny's driveway and up and down the block and no sight of a converted school bus, minivan, or convertible. Did she take a Lyft from California? They see me. I take a breath. I also take a breath refresher because of the Baileys. I'm scared. I put my sunglasses on, too.

    I get out and walk toward them, remembering that Ginny, Rascal, and Philomena all actually like me. I'm pretty sure of it. I don't say hi like

I usually do from the car when one of them is out there waiting for me. I don't say anything.

"Hey," Philomena says. She's never met Bets, but she's certainly heard about her. She knows this is some strange reunion.

"Hey," I say. "How'd the move go?" She and her family just moved into a larger apartment with her new husband. But of course, she is mostly here.

"Good, good," she says. She smiles reassuringly and steps inside. I go up the steps to the deck and then lean against the banister.

"Sit down," Ginny says. So, we three Frederick sisters and Rascal are all sitting here now, on Ginny's deck in this small Hudson River town on a gray spring day.

Bets doesn't look so great. I don't know what it is. Is it possible for someone to be tan and pale at the same time? Because that's what she is. Her bright yellow spiky hair is now a strange green and she looks like some sort of amphibian. You'd think for TV, they'd be jazzing her up, not frogging her down. Maybe it's the jet lag.

"Ginny told me she's dying," Bets says, all matter-of-fact.

What? I look to Ginny. "But you're not. I mean. What do you mean?"

"You're always saying I am," Ginny says.

"Not now," I say. Neither one of them are looking at me now. They share a secret. My sweat is starting to fade, so I'm feeling the cool. "I don't get it," I say to my biggest sister. "Aren't you supposed to be in Hollywood?"

"Well, thanks for putting out the welcome mat!" Bets says, though not accompanied by her usual laugh. Her legs are crossed oh so casually, but I notice that her hanging foot is bouncing, shaking.

"There is a mat," Ginny says, indicating the one right in front of the door there. It says *Wipe Your Paws*.

"She told me that she's dying and that this is her dying wish," Bets says.

"What is?" I say to Bets. "What is, Ginny?" She's playing mute. "Are you taking her to California, Betsy? Is that why you're here? Ginny, is that your dying wish?" I'm saying words I can't even believe I'm saying because they are just too awful and too hard but the only way to get them out of me is apparently to get them out.

"What?" Bets says. She looks stunned, like she's been duped or something.

"She's in Rockabye," Ginny says.

"Rock-a-way," Bets says. "Beach, on Long Island."

"I know where Rockaway Beach is," I say.

"It's a surf thing," she says. "The original teacher got hurt, so they flew me out. It's just a couple of weeks, an East Coast spring break thing."

"Oh," I say. I don't get it. "What about your dancing thing?"

Bets flinches her chin toward me like I just said a bad word.

"Okay," I say. "So you came out here for work." So you just kinda tagged us on, I don't say. You're not stealing my Ginny.

"I told Gin-Gin I was coming," she says, looking at Ginny, kind of scared in a way I've never seen her before.

"Well, she didn't tell me," I say, looking at Ginny, scary in a way I've never felt before.

I look at my oldest sister and I do not say a word. She doesn't like the nice girl, I will not be the nice girl. She looks uncomfortable, in her bright blue leggings, her big white sneakers, her big white jacket, and guacamole hair. Her giant sunglasses look like she's trying too hard. Jesus, it's not even sunny. I take mine off. Rascal has sunk down under the table, not a clue what's going on.

"Gin-Gin's house is really nice," Bets says. "Meena is really nice."

"Her name is Philomena," I say.

"Oh," she says. "I did not know that . . ."

"I couldn't have done this without Philomena," I say. "Or Lika. They are real-life angels, aren't they Gin?"

Ginny shrugs. She's watching a neighbor go by with her little bulldog.

"Mom and Dad would be . . ." Bets is looking at the house, the fenced-in yard, ". . . Wow."

"Yeah," I say. "They would. They would be 'Wow.'"

"You two should get along," Ginny says. Then she says she has to go to the bathroom, so I help push her wheelchair inside and call to Philomena. "I can go by myself," Ginny says. "Rascal," she says, and the big girl pushes herself up to follow her in. It feels like a setup. I'm not sitting back down.

"She told me she was dying and this was her dying wish," Bets says again.

"Everything's fine," I say. "She's fine. Relatively. But let's be real, you didn't come for that. You came for Rockaway."

"I told her about Rockaway, I said I'd stop by, and then she said that."

"Ha," I say. "Gotcha!" I say it like it's some sort of surfing lingo and I don't even know if it is.

"Okay," Bets says, "well after she's done, I'll just head back . . ."

"How did you even get here from Rockaway? Did your limousine drop you off?"

"Oh, you're funny," she says. "I took the train. Three trains, actually. Walked from the station, that's how. I need to get back cuz we have an event tonight."

"Yeah, I bet," I say. Ginny is taking her sweet time and Bets is putting her hands in her pockets. It's colder here than she expected, I guess. "Here's the big question," I say, as the celebrity seems to have gone quiet, "was Elvis ever in the building?"

"What?"

"I'm just wondering . . . You said you know how hard it is, how challenging Ginny is, you've been there, done that. I just wonder if you were ever actually in the building."

Bets gets up and stares at me there. She takes off her sunglasses so I can really see her pale eyebrows and bloodshot eyes. "I love Ginny," she finally says. "I've always loved Ginny. And believe it or not, you, too, Magpie." She doesn't put the sunglasses back on, which surprises me. "For many years, it was my job to look after Ginny. For many years I was told not to go out and play unless I brought Ginny with me. When my friends came over, Ginny would embarrass me. Mom didn't want me to go to California, did you know? She wanted me to be a secretary or a nurse, something helpful. Did you know that? Did you know any of that?"

"No," I say. I mean, I'm not really buying this. Bets left when she was eighteen. How much time did she spend babysitting Ginny? Ginny was always playing with me. Mom didn't make her take care of me. And Mom was always there. In the kitchen. In the laundry room. She worked part-time as a receptionist but was always there when we got home. So, "No," I say. "I guess I don't remember that."

"I had to get out. I could never live here. On the crowded East Coast? Claustrophobic. Ivy Leagues. It's not me."

"It's not me either," I say. "Art school. Remember?"

"Yeah, well. You adapted."

Let's be real, Biggest Sister. "It's not the East Coast you ran away from."

"I don't know what you mean," she says, knowing quite clearly what I mean.

"You came out once since Ginny almost died in Maryland. Once. And you stayed for less than an hour." I want to tell her to leave, I want to tell her to stay. I'm so scared and upset all at once.

"I've been getting therapy," she says. She starts kind of pacing, back and forth on Ginny's little deck. "It's an intense intervention. It's been suggested that maybe all those years of my having to protect our special needy sister, like my entire childhood, fucked me up."

What? Is this some sort of bullshit therapy? Are you fucking kidding me?

"Look," she says, and she's meaning this sincerely, "I've had memories, okay? Guilt. Like. Seriously screwed me up. My girlfriend broke up with me. Dumped me."

"Oh," I say.

"I'm broke."

I feel guilty that I'm even doubting her a tiny bit. "Well, what about your *Dancing* gig? That must be paying pretty well."

"Dancing gig?" she lets out a hard "Ha."

"What?" I say, shaking my head.

"I dropped out! After two weeks of lessons, rehearsals. Couldn't follow basic choreography. Didn't want to humiliate myself on national TV."

This is not the Betsy I know. Who was she to ever be embarrassed or humiliated about anything? And wait, has she told Ginny?

"I haven't told her yet," she says, reading my mind. "Don't know how. Wanted to give her something to . . . live for. Ha ha."

"Yeah," I say, "she's been pretty excited. I'm surprised she hasn't been asking you about it already."

"Told her I'm not allowed to talk about it." Ah, a nondisclosure agreement. That's something Ginny would appreciate. I can see that Bets is hurting and I am trying to ignore that her sad news has registered in my body as relief. I also see how deeply devastated she looks, almost like she needs me.

"Bruised and broke," she says.

"Moon Boards? All that money from your commercials? I thought you were doing okay."

"Maggie," Bets says, "they're not selling. Not as many people surf at night as you might think. I haven't done a commercial in twelve years. You're the only one around here making commercials. Why don't you put me in one?"

She says it in a desperate way like she really thinks I have the power to do this, as if the next time I'm drawing fine lines on a depressed, manic, or fit woman I can just mention to my art director that my sister, the former surfing star, is available for the shoot. She looks like maybe she's even deeply hurt and offended that I haven't done this yet.

Ginny appears at her doorway. I don't know how long she's been there and I'm doubting Bets knows either. Who knows what she heard? Bets and I catch each other's eyes, afraid. I ask Ginny if she would like to go out for shrimp shumai and she says "Naptime." I ask Bets if she would like to go out for coffee or take a walk along the river before she goes. I even ask if she can spend the night, and she says, "Gotta get back." My phone dings one, two, three times. Two are my art director telling me they'll have changes—later; one is Leo, asking if he can use the car. I ask Bets if she has time to see Leo; he doesn't even know she's in town. She gives Ginny a very large hug, which Ginny does not reciprocate.

"See you on TV. I'm having a party," Ginny says.

Bets doesn't say anything. I'm looking at her, trying to catch her eyes to say, Really, you're gonna leave this one to me, too? But she won't look at me. Instead, Bets steps back to look directly at our middle sister and she says, "Gin-Gin, I'm not gonna be on *Dancing with the Stars*. Sorry to have to tell you this."

Ginny takes a minute to take this in.

"I was gonna be. I mean. You saw the promo—I really was. It's just . . . it turns out I'm not much of a dancer and I'm not much of a star either, I guess."

Ginny's quiet for a bit. Then, "It's a dumb show anyway. I was only gonna watch cuz of you, but I didn't wanna tell you it's a dumb show."

"Yeah," Bets says. "Super dumb."

They both let out deep breaths and the shared disappointment is penetrable.

Gin-Gin and Rascal watch and Philomena waves as we pull away. The car is beeping because Bets hasn't buckled herself in. As we turn the block, she slides herself forward and reaches behind to click the belt and then slides herself back. Beeping stops. No comment. We're quiet as we drive through the sweet neighborhood, past the high school on the hill, the cemetery. Gosh, I could probably count on one hand how many times I've been alone with my big sister.

"That's cute," she says as we pass the local ice-cream place. They've got a giant bright blue pig out front. As we cross over the Quaker Bridge, she looks both ways up and down our little river. "Nice," she says. Up the hill and into the land of tall trees, "These trees are taller than I remember," she says. Well, it's been years since she's been to our place. They are taller. And then, to my own surprise, I pull over to the side of the windy, hilly road. I take a space right next to the aqueduct entrance, the trail where I walk Coyote on most days. I turn off the car. I don't know what I'm doing, and I hope I'll figure it out.

"What's up?" Bets says, kind of nervous, I can tell. "You know I've gotta get back, I'd love to take a walk, but I really do . . ."

I didn't pull over to take a walk, I know that much. I see a man I know coming this way between the rock walls, his dog's name is Buster. I don't know what the man's name is.

"I don't understand," I finally say.

"Huh?" Bets says. "It's a surfing intensive."

"Why? Why do you never come here? Why don't you visit or stay? I could take you places. I could take you to get ice cream at that place. We'd hang out at Ginny's. Take her out for drives. We could do so many things. It's been years, Bets. I need to know why."

"I just told you, Magpie, it's been a tough time."

"For five years? Ten?"

"Yeah, sure. You wouldn't . . ."

"Wouldn't what? Understand? Do you think I don't know about tough times?"

"Like I said, my girlfriend broke up with me. I'm broke. I'm lucky I didn't break something at those rehearsals, but I needed a break and I just can't get one. I need to hang up my surfboard someday. Don't know how I'll ever do that."

"Come clean with me, Betsy. Why the suitcase?"

"What suitcase?" she looks to the backseat as if to confirm. "I've got nothing."

"RIDE, it said, with a dino." Looked like a suitcase one of my boys would have loved when they were in their teens, I don't say. But it did.

"What now? A girl can't have a suitcase?"

"You came for Ginny's birthday for one hour—two at the most. You said you were catching the red-eye back. You didn't even stay one night. Why the suitcase then? I need to understand."

"Okay, okay, that's fair. I'd gone to an intensive. This Omega thing. A workshop to prepare myself."

Omega. Omega. She went to fricking Omega?

"It's a spiritual learning center," she says.

Yes, I know that. I've studied their catalogue several times over the last few years, salivating over workshop options that would raise and inspire me. But I couldn't do it. I couldn't afford it. I could justify using the Ginny fund for a couple of massages over two years but for a platinum-priced getaway? Couldn't do it.

"Omega's expensive," I say. "How'd you pay for it?"

"My girlfriend did."

"What's her name?"

"Oh," she says and gets quiet.

"Hard to say her name?"

"No. O. For Olivia."

"Ooooh," I say. "O. That's cool. I bet she's cool."

"She is cool. She's more than that."

"Of course," I say.

"So you had to go to a spiritual workshop to prepare yourself for seeing your family for a birthday celebration. Is that right? Are we really that awful, that scary to you?"

At this point Bets starts shaking her leg again. She's blinking hard, like she's trying to blink herself out of here. "Yes," she finally says, "you are. You are intimidating. Like what you're doing right now, bullying—"

"Bullying!" I try not to show my outrage as I don't want to appear . . . bullying.

"Yes, Baby Sister . . . You're just . . . You've always been . . . You were always so . . ." She pauses there, leaves me hanging. ". . . so perfect. And then a really talented artist on top of it, like really good at something. And then you became a successful artist with the perfect husband and perfect kids."

"Ha," I say, but I will not digress. "What about for Ginny? I know you love her, Betsy, I've never doubted that. So why can't you actually spend time with her, help her out once in a while? Don't tell me she intimidates. I'd think you'd be able to ignore my . . . whatever—to spend time with our sister with special needs." I really lay that one hard and I feel kind of bad about it, but I am tired of beating around the bush. She's quiet as a mouse, so finally, I ask, "What does O have to say about all this, huh?"

"I dropped her."

"I thought she dumped you?"

"Not O. Ginny."

"What? What do you mean?"

"I dropped her when she was one. Mom had to go to the bathroom, so she asked me to watch her. She was just laying there on the bed and there was a rainbow. Ya know? A rainbow, on the wall that kept moving? And then."

"And then, what?"

"Well, she rolled off the fricking bed and started screaming of course and Mom came running in and she was very calm, and she was just paying attention to Ginny and not even looking at me, she couldn't look at me. They probably went to the hospital. I don't remember."

I take a deep, deep, from-the-bottom-of-my-belly breath. This is something I've never heard before.

"I told you," she says. "The memories. Fucking therapy. I've been diving. Diving deep."

"No . . . ," I say. I'm shaking my head. This is something that I don't believe.

"You think I would make this shit up? You think I'm lying here?"

"No," I say. "No, no, no. Of course not. I believe you. I believe that that happened. Of course I do. But that's not the cause . . . Mom always said it was something with the birthing process. Something that happened in the womb . . . too little oxygen . . ."

"Yeah."

"I'm sure that's true, Betsy. I'm one hundred percent sure that's absolutely true." I can see she's wanting to believe me, she really is. "Look," I say. "Nobody really knows exactly what happened or why it happened, but one thing is for sure. It happened at birth! I know this, Betsy. Ginny was born this way. Trust me. I talked to Mom about it a lot. You know, we talked about this stuff. I gave birth twice. I was scared a little bit . . ."

"Well, the fall off the bed was real and it wasn't good, that's for sure."

"Babies fall all the time. Toddlers do. Toddlers try to kill themselves like twenty times a day. It's scary. You go to the ER. Nine hundred and ninety-nine times out of a thousand, they're okay. Really." Now we're both thinking about that one time, the time it's not. Okay.

"I had to drive her everywhere. You know that. Mom was always—I dunno—making dinner—and there I was, Ginny's after-school babysitter . . ."

Huh, I think. I can't imagine where she'd be taking Ginny. I mean, maybe Mom asked her to take her someplace once a week. I'm taking this in.

"Then there was that time in high school when I drove her with me to the back parking lot and I got out for a minute to berate my boyfriend who was finishing up his football practice and I ended up getting in his car with him and we drove off and had sex in the upper parking lot of White Flint Mall. He dropped me off later—I dunno how much time had passed, it was dark by then. And Ginny was still there, curled up in the passenger seat, scared out of her wits."

"Okay . . ."

"So, see? I'm a fuckup, okay? Got that?" Now Bets opens the car door and starts to step out. She actually puts one foot on the ground and then turns herself back to me. She leaves the door there open. "Remember our Bets Fetes?"

"Course I do," I say. I'm trying to be calm, to reel her in before she just takes off running or something. "Those were fun."

"That last one—the Christmas right before Dad died, we came back and you and Bill went upstairs to check on the boys and Mom and Dad were there in the kitchen, drinking their warm milks. She asked if I was drunk, and I said we all were, and he asked who drove and I said Bill did and they both just kind of shook their heads . . . They said when you guys came down to visit and I wasn't there, you didn't feel the need to go out and get drunk. It only happened when I was there."

"Okay, Bets, okay . . . Look, Bill and I . . . Well, that's just ridiculous of course."

Holy shit. This is a lot to take in. My sister is sitting right here next to me in her alternate reality. I'm not judging her reality. It's hers and only hers and everyone's got the right to their own reality. It's just. Okay. Wow.

"O really wanted to meet you guys," she says. "She said I idealized you both. You and Gin-Gin."

"What happened?"

"Like I said, she broke up with me. Right before I went into rehearsals. The timing wasn't perfect, but I can't blame her for that."

"Why?"

"She asked me to marry her. Right there on the boardwalk where we'd done our thing. That wasn't choreographed, not really. We just move well together."

"O is the firefighter?"

"Yeah."

"Wowza!"

"She's a very nice person, actually . . . So of course I said no."

"You said no to marrying this very nice person?"

"Yeah."

"So, actually, you broke up with her, not the other way around."

"One might see it that way."

"Why didn't you . . ."

"I always did better on water, Magpie. I do better when it's just me and the sea." She says this stuff like she's said it a hundred times before, I imagine her saying it to interviewers and her students now, gaining chuckles and admiration. "Standing on dry land makes me . . ."

"Makes you what, Bets?" This part, this part feels like new territory. Like she hasn't rehearsed it or isn't even sure how the sentence ends.

"Scared," she says. "Standing on dry land scares me."

We both sit there for a minute and I take my sister's hand and hold it. She squeezes mine really tight. With the other hand, I believe she's wiping a tear away, though she's looking down the trail so I'm not completely sure. This idea, though, of my biggest sister, Betsy, crying, feeling so scared and afraid and . . . . *guilty*, makes me cry, too, though I also try to hide it. I don't know why. "I'm sorry," I say, now letting go of her hand and patting it. "I held you up. Just a quick hey to Leo and I'll get you on the late train to Rockaway."

"'Kay."

I turn on the car, time to get home, Leo's probably worried about us. Ginny was going to text him that we were coming. Bets pulls her legs back in and closes the passenger door. "Actually," I say, "you're a really good dancer. The boardwalk thing. And you were really good with that tap dancer, remember that?"

"Ha," she says, still looking up at the trees as we drive up the hill, "yeah, that was fun . . ."

I miss my sister already and she hasn't even left yet. I wish that she'd at least stay for dinner, but I know she won't. Can't. I'm thinking of all the things I wish I could say to her and the one that pops into my mind is this. "Hey Bets, remember my prom night?"

She smiles real wide and says, "Oh yeah, I remember that! You went with that guy in the fedora! And man, you guys got melted butter all over Mom and Dad's nice tablecloth. I def remember that!"

She had come home to surprise me for my graduation. For prom dinner, she and Mom made dinner for me and my boyfriend and two other couples. They even brought the food out to us! Steak and lobster tails and baked potatoes! I don't know why I'm just remembering this now. It's been a while, but this is what I'm remembering. I turn onto my street.

"Who did you go with?" I ask.

"Huh?" She's got her feet up on the dashboard now. "My prom?"

"Yeah," I say. There are so many things when it comes to Bets that I just don't get, but now I'm thinking that maybe that's a result of the so many things that I just don't know.

"Tony Rivers! Remember him? He had long hair and you used to put it in pigtails whenever he came over, remember that?"

"I do! He was cute!" I say.

"He's married with eight kids now . . . Cut his hair."

When we get out of the car, Leo comes out to greet us, Coyote lumbering behind. "Where the hell have you two been?" he says. "I was worried!" Leo and Bets share a huge hug and I am grateful that he has an aunt that can hug him back. He is most happy when I ask him to drive her back to Rockaway Beach. It's less than two hours away but it's complicated, the furthest I have ever allowed him to drive. This buys us a bit more time, so I am able to give my sister some dinner after all. I get the call from my art director with the changes. I hug Bets hard before they leave.

While drawing, I reflect on what Bets said. That as a child, Ginny was her burden and responsibility. Or, at least, this is her truth. I never saw it that way. Well, why would I? I was so much younger. I just saw Ginny as a big kid and Betsy as my idol. I never really understood why she ran away from us. As I draw, I pray that Leo delivers her safely to Rockaway and himself safely home. I hug him so tight when he gets back five hours later.

Part Four

❧⚬❧

I ♥ New York

It's February now, almost three years since Ginny had "the septic." Leo is taking a gap year, working at Bets's surf shop in exchange for a bed in the attic of the bungalow she shares with three others, including O, her firefighter-in-waiting. Bets still hasn't worked up the courage to say yes, though according to Ginny, she's considering it. I'm afraid the gap year will turn to years and Ginny tells me I worry too much. "Let the waves, wave," she says. Leo says his ceiling is low, but from the tiny window below the eave, he can see the Pacific. I've barely talked to Bets since she was here last spring. It's less strained, still strange. But she seems to be there for Leo in her own way and I believe that if he went under, she'd jump in and pull him out.

Graham's a college grad and working man, now living in Brooklyn. This is nice; he comes up to visit once in a while. Not weekly, the way I had hoped, but monthly . . .

Bill has become an entertainment insurance agent star, he's started playing the banjo again, and strangely, he's gone vegan. Also, he and his girlfriend "broke up." "She was fun," he told me, "but not really the real deal, you know what I mean?" I did and I didn't, so I didn't say anything.

Theresa is now sleeping with Farzana, which no one on our little country lane saw coming.

There was a five-day power outage as a result of the early January snowstorm, but this time, Ginny had a full-powered automatic generator.

The outage turned out to be the social event of the season, with Lika going door-to-door offering use of their washer and dryer, and Ginny, there in her recliner, nodding to the people as they came and went. "Ginny is the mayor of the street!" Lika liked to say.

More like queen, I thought. And the image of a royal recliner adorned with many jewels and sparkles filled my mind. Ginny, in a purple velvet cape and golden crown, her glasses still splotchy with mayonnaise. Perhaps she would have a fine and handsome man standing next to her, whose job was solely to take off her glasses and clean them during commercials. Though not commercials that starred dogs. And Rascal, Rascal, in her royal bed, a large golden bowl of royal dog biscuits beside her, so she could indulge at any time.

I have a new client that is solely my own. A new fitness-based weight-loss program directed toward women. I tried the program and lost three pounds after a month and they said that I understand the product in a way that the male storyboard artists would not. I didn't tell them that I gained six pounds the next month and then gave up on the program completely. They say I am the perfect person to be drawing pictures of women wearing cute workout clothes and drinking protein shakes. The job pays a healthy chunk of regular money.

Separately both Philomena and Lika Dadeshkeliani tell me that they are working toward bringing their families to Westchester. Philomena says, "In two years, my Effy will open a hair salon and I will take care of my mother." Her older daughter Farida received a full ride to Stony Brook University for pre-med. "Maggie," she says, "can you help Nat and me find an apartment in your village?"

"Of course," I say.

Georgian Woman tells me the exact month and year that she plans to fly her parents west and her daughter's family east. Together they will converge here, in Croton-on-Hudson. "We would like to find small house," she says. "Not too big. Like this house. In a neighborhood without Black people. Can you help us find this house? And the schools? What do you pay for this?"

"I can help you, Lika," I say, "but we have all kinds of people here and that's the way we like it."

"I understand but I don't want my grandchildren playing with illegal ones, I don't want aliens stealing my jobs and my bread," she says.

"Lika, I will help you and your family, just as I will help Philomena and her family."

"Coming here?" she says.

"Coming here."

She throws her arms up. "She doesn't even speak the English!"

And Philomena, when she learns of Lika's similar plans, says, "Oh, her accent is very strong, nobody will understand!"

And I, I, too, will be moving into town. I'm fixing up our house in the woods and putting it on the market in the fall. I'll buy something small from which I can walk or bike to Ginny's.

Life is full of surprises and this is one of them.

⁂

I must have hit snooze and then turned it off, though I have no memory of this. All I know is it's nine fifteen and I was supposed to get up at eight for a nine o'clock briefing. Crazy Cat peeks up to see that my eyes are open and immediately begins to meow. "Meow, meow, meow," she says, running back and forth across my bladder. "Thanks a lot, Crazy Cat," I say. "Where were you an hour ago when I needed you?" I crawl out from under the covers and into my slippers and robe and it's still fricking cold and I step over Coyote to go to the bathroom.

In the bathroom, I realize something. My alarm is one thing, but there is always another thing that makes sure I get to my meetings. Coyote. Coyote always gets me up. Usually too early, and now that she's an old lady, often in the middle of the night. Sometimes she pants for a long time, even in the winter, and I will wake and say to her, "Coyote, you okay, girl?" Sometimes she'll stop for a moment, as if to answer, and then she'll just keep panting.

When I come out of the bathroom, I sit down on the floor next to my sleeping pup and before I reach out to pet her, I close my eyes and take a deep breath. With my eyes closed, I hear that there is no panting, and by now Crazy Cat is rubbing up against Coyote's back, meowing. Coyote is cold to the touch.

"Coyote? Coyote?" I say. I get on my knees so I can get down and really see her face. "Coyote," I say. I kiss her cold snout.

I cover her with the thick white Egyptian cotton blanket, though I keep her face exposed. I kiss Coyote's eyelids and Crazy Cat meows.

My morning text from Ginny: *I.AM fine .and clean. Hw u Cyote and Cazy CAT??*
I respond: *See you later.*

I wrap the whole of Coyote in the blanket and I lift her. She is light. Where has the weight gone? Her legs are stiff. It is hard to carry her down the stairs and Crazy Cat is running up and down. He knows what's up and he is crying, too. I am holding Coyote from under her belly, legs on either side. I walk sideways down the steps, Coyote's head first, each step holding my breath so I won't trip and injure her further. Is that even possible? Yes, it is. I drive her to the vet as they told me over the phone that they can have her cremated and I can pick up her ashes in a couple of days. When I arrive there, I cannot speak, and they nod in sympathy.

I don't know which boy to call first, so I ask my mother. Eeanie, meanie, miney, mo. My mother tells me to call Graham. I'm not sure if this is fair to Leo, as he was the one who lived at home with Coyote those four years while Graham was at college, but I know Graham loves her just as much, and he is more likely to make the trip for the distribution of ashes.

"I'll be there," he says. "Please wait for me."

"Of course we will," I say to my Graham-y Bear.

"Who's we?"

"Well, Ginny . . . Who else?"

"Dad?" he says. "We picked out Coyote together. He has to be there."

"Of course," I say.

I can hear him choking up on the other end. "Remember," he says, "we went to that sunken puppy den? She was our Christmas puppy, remember?"

"Yes, I do. She was."

"Dad should be there, okay?"

Leo, on the other hand, is much cooler. "Yeah," he says, "I figured she was on her way. R-I-P, Coyote. She was a great dog and we'll remember her fondly."

We'll remember her fondly? This is what the good dog gets when he's flown the coop? R-I-P? Leo was her softy. Leo was the one that laid down on top of Coyote and practically made out with her. Is this what California does to people? Make everything mellow and okay? I'm surprised he hasn't asked when I'm getting the next dog.

"Another Golden, right?" he says.

Next stop, Ginny's house. This is going to be the hardest.

"Where's your four-legged friend?" she says as I walk in the door. She looks behind me to see if Coyote is bringing up the rear. Philomena comes around and smiles and I nod to her.

Ginny asks again, "Where's your four-legged friend?" I say nothing.

Ginny is in her wheelchair, still eating breakfast. She eats breakfast for about two hours, and is coming to the end. She pauses her movie, *Mulan* this time. I bend down to pet Rascal. I feel the warmth of Rascal's face, the comfort of her breath. I go to Ginny and give her a hug and a kiss on the head and sit down next to her. "Running errands?" she says, because this is the reason that I sometimes don't bring Coyote as I don't like to leave her in the car.

I sit, and with my hands in my lap, holding on to my gloves, I say, "Coyote died."

Ginny is quiet. She wipes her mouth, and she wipes Binky Baby's mouth, and she puts down her fork.

"She died in her sleep," I say. "While I slept. When I woke up this morning, she was there on the floor next to my bed."

This is when Ginny's lips start to turn down. If she had on a big red reindeer nose, she could be mistaken for a sad clown. She takes off her glasses and closes her eyes really hard and holds them tight, as if waiting through a cold headache. Then, with her eyes still closed, she says, "The last time I saw her was on Sunday when she was eating snow."

"That's right," I say, "we FaceTimed you from the steps. Yep, that was Sunday."

"I couldn't resist her cute face," Ginny says, breaking down.

"I know. And she couldn't resist yours either."

"You need to tell Rascal," she says.

By now, Philomena is back in the room and she understands what's gone down. She sees that Ginny is crying. This is the first time that she has seen Ginny cry.

"She was a good dog!" Ginny exclaims.

I tell her that Coyote is being cremated and in a couple days I will pick up her ashes and Graham will come up from Brooklyn for the weekend and we can all go to the top of the dam to distribute Coyote's ashes because we all know how Coyote loved to play fetch in the river so much.

The next day, Philomena calls me to say that Rascal has wet herself during the night and won't get up.

A text from Ginny later: *Rascul sad bow Kyote.* Many crying emojis.

Philomena calls again. "I believe we need to call the veterinarian. She having diarrhea but is not eating."

Dr. Chan comes to the house. This is her third home visit for Rascal.

"Kidney failure," she says.

"Her BFF died," Ginny says. "Makes sense."

Ginny can make sense of anything. They were cousins, but BFFs?

Well, Coyote enjoyed the idea of visiting Rascal, but then when she got there, Rascal basically scared the shit out of her, so, yes, in our dysfunctional world, perhaps BFFs could be supposed. But is grief really the thing that's putting Rascal over the edge? Do five hundred dog treats a day and no exercise and the fact that she is ninety-nine in people years have anything to do with it?

"She is going to continue to wet and defecate on herself," Dr. Chan says. "She will not be able to get up to go outside or for you to clean her. It is time to talk about quality of life . . ."

All focus is on Ginny because we all know that Ginny is Rascal's mom. Ginny cannot pet Rascal, Ginny cannot take Rascal outside, but Ginny loves Rascal with her whole heart. All is quiet but for a low whine coming from Rascal as she leaks another brown toxic-smelling trail. Philomena quickly wipes it up.

"She had a good life," Ginny says. And the decision is made.

Then there was the question of whether the vet should put Rascal to rest here, in her own home, or at the animal hospital. Ginny chooses home.

During all of this, I am dealing with calls and texts from two different art directors and my rep. How can I explain the significance of my sister's dog? In terms of suspicion, I'm sure it's right up there with "my grandmother's funeral." But I do. I tell them like it is: my dog, my sister's dog. Let they who have never felt the ache of losing their own pet throw the first storyboard.

The creative director from Connecticut needs three boards by tomorrow night. I know if I say no, she won't call me again. May that client R-I-P.

Dr. Chan and her assistant have come prepared. While she prepares the injections, I join the assistant next to Rascal on the floor and we both pet her. While touching Ginny is a commitment to stickiness, petting Rascal is a commitment to oiliness. "Greasy little rug rat," Leo used to say. Rascal puts her head on my thigh.

"Ginny, would you like to pet her?" I ask.

"Can't," she shakes her head.

"We could lift her to you, I bet. Couldn't we, Doctor Chan?"

The doctor and assistant nod.

Ginny shakes her head more. "Can't," she says again. Or she might lose it . . .

Philomena stands next to Ginny, her hand on Ginny's shoulder. I am quite sure this is the first time they have made physical contact. Doctor Chan looks to me and nods and then we all look to Ginny, who nods. Just as the first injection goes slowly into Rascal's thick thigh, Ginny says, "I love you, Rascal. You were the best dog I ever loved." And Rascal falls gently to sleep.

∽✧∼

We meet at the small parking lot on the east side of the dam. Three cars. I have Ginny next to me, with Philomena and Georgian Woman in the backseat. This is almost as exciting as having the dogs back there. It's Saturday so it's usually Lika time, but her daughter and grandchildren are visiting, so Philomena is covering for her. This was a big sacrifice of precious time with her family, and I can see she is perturbed that Lika is here.

"Of course I come," Georgian Woman weeps. "I would not miss funeral of Rascal and Coyote for my life!"

Graham brings Lydia, his old girlfriend from college who also now lives with him and two roommates in Brooklyn. She is his girlfriend again. They never really broke up, he explains to me, they were just finding their way. I was expecting a petite girl, one of feather weight and personality. Lydia is not that. She is a solid young woman with intense eyes and presence. She is Mexican and the first child in her family to attend and graduate from college. I am pleasantly surprised by Graham's choice, and also humbled by how little I know my older son.

And Bill. Bill comes. He parks next to Graham and greets Lydia warmly. Then he takes it upon himself to push Ginny up the ramp, her two angel aides on either side.

The wind whips at the top of the dam. Once the wheelchair is parked, Lika locks the wheels and Philomena tucks in Ginny's blankets. Nobody comments on the cold, we just move quickly to the side that faces the waterfall. The top of the rail is level with Ginny's eyes. She is holding tight onto her bag. The bag is a fabric one, tied with a pink ribbon. Attached to the ribbon is a tag that says "Rascal Frederick." Graham holds tight to a similarly pink ribbon–tied bag, though his tag reads "Coyote Frederick-Mitchell." The bags are weighty and flexible, like the sandbags we used to throw into the clown's mouth at the carnival.

Lika is the expert on all things. She steps forward toward the rail, licks her finger and puts it out in front of her like a strict schoolteacher telling her class to be quiet. She closes her eyes tightly and takes a deep breath in. Beyond her, I see Philomena, now behind the wheelchair, rubbing her hands together for warmth and I imagine rolling her eyes behind the sunglasses. She has little patience for Lika's dramatics. Finally, Lika releases her breath and solemnly nods. She turns to her enraptured audience and says, "It is good."

"Okay, Graham and Ginny, you can untie the bags now," I say.

Lydia holds the bag for Graham while he negotiates the pink bow. Ginny makes a micro-attempt to untie the bag in her lap, then allows Lika to sweep it up. Of course Lika cannot untie it without help, as nobody would dare put the bags down for fear that they might blow away. She looks to Bill for help, but he is busy comforting Graham. She is forced to turn to Philomena. Philomena does not respond to her silent demand. Ginny is not the only one who's proud.

"Please," Lika says.

"For my Ginny, anything," Philomena says, and she reaches out to untie the bag.

Ginny watches it all very carefully, her eyes and nostrils running freely in the cold. I step toward her to gingerly wipe her nose. Ginny shrugs, as if to say, Thank you, but it is of no use.

Inside the fabric bags are plastic bags that are tied with plastic twists, and in these bags are the soft gray remains. Graham and Philomena both take off their gloves, but their cold and numb fingers prove to be worthless.

"You'll have to rip them open," Bill declares.

Lydia nods. "Rip and release," she says. Which is kind of funny.

"Okay," Graham says.

"Ginny, do you want to do it?" asks Philomena.

No, she shakes her head. She's a big wet mess.

"Who do you want?" Lika asks Ginny. Leave it to her to make it a competition.

"My sister," Ginny says.

Good answer, I think. "I am honored," I say.

"You were her aunt," Ginny cries quietly as I bend down to kiss her head.

Bill looks directly at Ginny and then to Graham and says, "Okay, is there anything anyone would like to say?"

They both shake their heads.

"Okay," I say, as I look around at each of them. "I would like to say . . ." And I begin my speech. "They were good dogs, Rascal and Coyote. Great dogs, really . . ." I had prepared a few words but now my brain feels as frozen as my fingers. "We all loved those dogs. Well, except you, Lydia, because you didn't know them, but if you had, I'm sure that you would have loved them both. And they, I'm confident, would have loved you."

Lydia nods. Bill, on the other side of Graham, is slightly smiling.

"I remember when we brought Coyote home. It was snowing that day. She was an early Christmas present for the boys . . . And Rascal, well, I remember when Ginny called me to tell me about her after she was delivered from the shelter . . . with Mom . . . They both loved their treats! That's for sure, right, Ginny?"

Ginny nods.

"Yup. And they had a complicated relationship. At first, we thought that Rascal might kill Coyote . . . We hooked her up to the wall. But Peace Among the Pets! And dear, dear friends they became . . . Well, I wouldn't call them kissing cousins . . . kissing cousins indicates something else entirely, but—"

"Mom," Graham says, "I think the temperature's dropped ten degrees since we've been here. Can we just . . ." He indicates throwing with a sideways tilt of his head.

They all nod hard in agreement.

Freed from my obligations, I say, "Okay then! Go!"

Okay then! Go! And suddenly, I am on this same bridge, some ten years ago, when our two now–fully grown men were growing boys on their bikes. Gosh, they were so small then. It was early, before most families got out, and the boys wanted to race without anyone else on the bridge. Bill filled the tires the night before and put the bikes on the car so we could drive here, therefore not tiring someone out before the race began.

Those were my snack-packing days. I packed Froot Loops and sliced apples, hot chocolate in a thermos and coffees. I didn't like the whole competition thing, but the boys were into it. I tried to make them promise that whoever lost wouldn't take it too badly and whoever won wouldn't boast, but Bill said, "That's not the way this racing thing works."

Graham did boast and Leo did mope, but it did start off an annual Spring Thaw race that lasted for the good six years until Graham went off to college. Even now, they still occasionally get up early and ride up here right after summer sunrise or for a Christmas Eve moonlit race.

Through all the commotion, I look over toward Bill, who is looking at me, and I wonder if he is remembering this. In fact, he smiles in what I believe is recognition.

A gust sweeps in that is stronger than the rest, as if winter is a law-abiding citizen telling us that the public distribution of ashes is illegal. Graham and I have ripped and shaken the bags and a fast-moving gray tornado swirls all around us. We're all blinking like crazy. Well. Probably not Philomena. She just looks cool.

"Rascal and Coyote got in my eyes," Ginny says.

Philomena says, "They don't want to leave you, Gin-Gin!"

"They both just jumped all over me!" says Lydia. She's laughing. I like Graham's girl.

"Let's get off this fricking bridge!" he says. We all agree vigorously and start moving as fast as we can to get off the dam bridge and back into our now-cold cars.

Back at Ginny's Hot House, we joke about how our cars are now covered in dog hair and ashes, and as we take off our coats and hats, more ashes fall off and onto the floor.

"I don't mind," Ginny says. "Philomena and Lika, you never have to wash the floors again."

Philomena and Lika face each other and both sets of brows go up. We can see Philomena's pop out above her sunglasses. Had Ginny just called them by their names? Had she actually said something directly to them? It seems she had.

Lika excuses herself to return to her hunk of a husband and visiting family. Graham, Lydia, and Bill head out to have lunch together. I get the young lovers tonight for dinner. I wish Bill could come. It just seems silly, doesn't it? Them all going out without me, then we, gathering without him? It's impractical, really. Stupid. It's what we wanted, though, right?

Ginny wheels herself to the bathroom and back, and then wheels herself to the fridge for a nice Hawaiian Punch. Philomena goes off to Face-Time. And Ginny and I are left alone. Alone with no dogs by our sides.

"Big day, Gin-Gin. You okay?"

Ginny shrugs. "I'm not the only one who lost her best friend," she says.

"Yeah," I say.

It's a sweet thing to say, a thoughtful thing. I, too, have had a loss and Ginny understands that. Coyote had been my faithful companion for fourteen years. She was ancient. A bitter distraction in her puppy-dom. I had no idea how difficult a pup could be and perhaps ours was more rambunctious than some. Then, Coyote became the third sibling, growing up and going everywhere with the boys, accompanying the whole family on hikes and races (which sometimes she would win). A family photo without Coyote in it was not a family photo. Even Crazy Cat was excused from those. Coyote was my comfort when Bill moved out, and then, when the boys were both gone. And old lady Maggie and old dog Coyote took old lady walks in the woods. But mostly, most of all, she was my connection to my boys, to the days before the divorce when things were still sweet, what I privately and only to myself refer to as our Golden Years.

Coyote was perhaps the strongest force that has kept my boys coming back. What will keep them coming back now? And now that I am going to sell the house, what history will they have here? Soon, it would all be gone.

I notice that I am crying. Right here, at Ginny's table, the table that we used to sit around in our childhood home. Ginny notices, too, because she pushes the tissues toward me.

"Your nose is running a race," she says in sympathy.

"Oh," I say as I pull out a tissue. I wipe my various faucets and say, "Sorry."

"For what?" she says with true curiosity.

"I dunno," I say. "Crying, I guess."

Ginny watches me plainly as I continue crying. "I never saw you cry since you were a baby," she says.

"Do I sound like a baby?" I say through my tears.

"I don't mind," she says. "You've seen me cry hundreds of times."

I keep crying at the truth of it. Ginny cried when the boys on the school bus called her fat, she cried when she asked our mother why she was the one that was handicapped, she cried when she got fired from Roy Rogers, she "bawled her eyes out" when our father died, she cried "half the ocean" when our mother died. She cried when I told her of our divorce, and she cried when I arrived at the hospital after she herself had almost died. So many, so many countless times.

I cry silently, privately, and rarely. Honestly, I have missed crying, and sometimes have wished I could cry more. I find myself identifying situations in which, if I were a person who cried, I would. Mostly I think I've been afraid to cry, for fear that it will take away my strength, for fear that it will empty me altogether.

It feels good to cry and I feel safe in Ginny's presence. She doesn't say the things people usually say when a person cries: "It's okay, I hear you. You okay? Are you seeing a therapist?" Or the worst one: "Don't cry." After a short while, they might indiscreetly check their phone or a nearby clock. Most people wouldn't allow me to cry like this, uninterrupted, all worked up, with no end in sight. Most people might say, "Now, that's enough. Let me get you something to drink or eat. I'm sorry but I have to go. Did you hear the one about the—" Yes, some would even resort to a joke, just to put a stop to it. Not Ginny.

"Let's go to Malibu," I hear myself say as I wipe my eyes.

Ginny says nothing. She is holding Binky Baby very tight, smothering her into her large breasts.

"Ginny, did you hear me? Let's go see Leo and Betsy in Malibu. What do you say?"

"They're in Venice Beach," she says, and, "no thank you."

"I know, I know, I know," I say. "I just like to refer to all of California as Malibu, you know that. But. Seriously, Ginny." I grab another tissue and blow my nose determinedly.

"My dog just died."

"Yes, of course, I know that. Mine did, too! We don't have to go to-morrow. But soon. Before either one of us gets another dog. It would be fun! It would be good to see those guys, wouldn't it? We haven't visited Bets in her natural habitat in forever ever. I think she'd appre-ciate it, don't ya think? Just the two of us, no Philomena or Lika. Just us two."

"I wouldn't get another dog just like that. That would be mean to Rascal."

I get up and go to the bathroom and clear my head. Yes, I think, we can do this. When I return, I get us each a glass of water.

"Naptime," Ginny says.

"Okay," I say, "well think about it, okay? I can push you up and down the boardwalk! They could take us surfing! Maybe Bets can even call up your old boyfriend!"

Ginny is already heading toward her bedroom. "I think the ashes went to your head," she says.

A sweep of desperation begins to overcome me. I stand in front of Ginny, blocking her. I can still hear Philomena talking on the phone in the basement. "Ginny, it's totally possible," I say. "We'll stay in a hotel, an Airbnb . . . But you would have to pay, okay? You have money. I do not. I'm just making ends meet—that's why I'm selling the house. I'll pay you back. You trust me, right? If you can't trust your sister, who can you trust?"

"You're acting weird," Ginny says. "You should take a nap."

"Okay, Ginny, I will," I say, dabbing my eyes one last time. "I will go home and take a nap. We can both dream about Malibu."

❧

While cooking dinner, David Bowie's "China Girl" is my track. It was the soundtrack of that summer, the one when Ginny and I went to visit our sister. The summer of Ginny's hot romance. Graham makes a fire and Lydia sets the table. She feels astonishingly familiar, as if she's always been a part of us. Some people are like that, I guess. Over dinner, I tell them about Malibu and Ginny's fond recollections of that magical night and her long-time reference to surfer dude as her Last Romance.

"Last Romance?" Graham says. "Did she have any before? And was it really romantic?"

"No!" I laugh as I pour more wine. "I believe that after I had rejected him, he tied a few more on and passed out next to her."

"Did you see them together?" he asks.

"Well, what do you mean?" I say. "I was in your aunt's bungalow . . ." I turn to Lydia, whose warmth is caught by the candlelight. "When I returned," I tell her, "there they were. Passed out like spoons in front of the bonfire."

"Was she wearing a dress?" Graham asks.

"Jesus, I don't know, it was a hundred years ago!" And then I tell Lydia, "Not quite a hundred years." Wink wink.

"Okay, 'cause I was just wondering."

"Wondering what, for goodness' sake?"

"If they had sex!" he shouts. Or at least, that's how it sounds.

"God no!" I say, starting to feel the queasiness that I feel when reading a particularly horrifying news report.

"It wouldn't be the worst thing in the world, Mom . . . If Aunt Ginny once had sex."

Lydia is very quiet through all of this, but she is not a wallflower. "This chicken is delicious, Maggie," Lydia says. "You're a really good cook." It's a generic thing to say, but I am grateful. And I can see that Lydia really does like the chicken as she is gnawing at the bones. I also see that she is not drinking the wine, which makes me wonder if I should have splurged for that fancier bottle.

"I'll pay her back after I sell the house," I say. "I'm not taking advantage of my sister."

"I didn't think you . . ." Graham stops midsentence. And then he's

quiet. And then he sighs. "Um. Mom," he says. He says this but he's looking at Lydia.

I am afraid of what he is going to say. I am afraid he is going to tell
me that I am responsible for my sister's long-ago rape, I am afraid he is
going to say that I did the wrong thing, bringing my sister here, that I
should have left her in Maryland where she belonged.

"I need to tell you something," he says. Do I detect guilt in his eyes or
am I projecting? Did he get fired from his job? Get caught selling pot?
Did he somehow steal from Ginny? He's the fancy banker after all.

"Actually, look," my handsome son says. He pulls out his phone and I
wait. Then he shows it to me. "This is a text from Ginny," he says.

It reads: *u shud tell your MOTH not to sell the hous. Famly get bigg not
small. Er.* ☺

"Huh? I don't get it," I say. Even though I can actually translate Ginny's
texts quite well. "Family get bigger not small?"

"Getting bigger, not smaller," Graham smiles, as Lydia leans back to
show the truth.

My eyes shoot down to see what I had previously thought was a cute
fuck belly and that I now understand is not a fuck belly, but the result of
fucking. Wait. What? I'm having trouble taking this in even though it's
right here before me. So, "Are you kidding?" I say.

They shake their heads. "No," they say in unison.

I'm caught between shock, surprise, pleasant surprise, and what-
the-fuck surprised. I'm guessing they are messing with me. I'm guessing
my ears are due a checkup. "Wait? What? No way. Not possible."

Graham nods affirmatively. "Mom, I'm trying to tell you . . ."

I shut my eyes tight as I try to shut it all out, clear my head, but when
I open them, they're still there, Graham and his pretty girlfriend, who I
know now is his preggy girlfriend. They are both strangely smiling. I look
over to Coyote for support and all I see is her fur-covered pillow lying
empty and limp there on the floor.

"Wow," I say. "That's big news. How far along are you, Lydia?" Although I can see, now I can see, she's pretty far.

"Over halfway there," she says.

"We're due in June," Graham says. "Late June." He's grinning like it's Christmas morning, like the time we surprised him with the Fisher-Price Cadillac that he could actually drive up and down the street. It's a stupid grin. It's an innocent grin. It's hopeful.

I think a lot of things, but I do not say them. I am determined to keep my mouth shut until I have taken time to process, or at least until I have refilled my wineglass to the almost-brim and have brought it to my lips. Then I open my mouth a little and take a few gulps.

"Mom, chill," Graham says. "We're good with this."

I nod, smiling, because I want them both to see how chill I am. So chill that I am enjoying this nice warm wine on a light snowy night. Thoughts are just thoughts and here are some of mine: Are you telling me that my sister had sex on my watch? Are you telling me that someone possibly took sexual advantage of my sister? Are you telling me that my son got a girl pregnant right after his grad-u-a-tion from college? Less than a year into his first actual job? Are you telling me, Lydia, and forgive me for I barely know you, that you, the first person in your family to graduate from college in this grand U.S. of A., just messed it all up by getting pregnant? Are you both out of your fucking minds?

I finally find a word to say so I say it. "Oh?"

"Mom?" Graham says. "Are you okay? I'm having trouble reading you."

He looks scared, he looks hurt. I don't know why. I haven't said anything. I've just been sitting here thinking thoughts and not saying them and I am very consciously remaining calm. But then I have a new thought and the thought is this: "How did Aunt Ginny know?"

"That's not important," Graham says.

My brain is a little fuzzy. And I am just wondering. "When did Aunt Ginny know?"

Then Lydia stands up and her now obvious with-child belly punches me in the face. How could I not have seen that? She starts to gently pile our dishes on top of each other and she seems to slightly bow to me as she turns toward the kitchen. I watch her pregnant bottom go.

"Mom," my young older son says to me, "it's good. Lydia and I love each other, and we want to raise our child together. And other good news, I got a promotion. They said they like what I'm doing and offered me a pretty sweet deal. I wanted to tell you all of this in person. That's the other reason we came up this weekend . . ."

Other reason? I think. Your dead dog wasn't enough? I don't know why I'm so upset. I'm on the edge of feeling betrayed and I don't even know why.

"We were thinking maybe we could stay here for a while. With you. While we save up, you know? I'd keep working in the city and can help with bills and Lydia could be here with the baby while she's applying to grad schools."

"I'm a good student," she says as she returns. "I'll get scholarships."

"Maybe you could even babysit . . . ," he says with a sheepish grin.

"Babysit?" I say, processing this. "Like, hold that baby?"

"Yeah," he laughs. "And other stuff."

I did not see this coming. I am very confused. I look at my young adult son and I see him sitting right there in his high chair. I mean, not as a young adult, but as a toddler. His high chair sat right there where he is sitting now, and he sat in it. When he wasn't climbing out of it. It wasn't that long ago. I remember chasing him around this table. He was laughing, bare-bellied, wearing his big boy underpants.

"Wait. What?! My big boy is having a baby?" I say. That high chair is in the garage now. I'm pretty sure where it's hiding. I can sand it, give it a new paint job . . .

"Yes, Mom, what we've been trying to tell you. And I can even help out with the mortgage for a while . . ." I can see that he's relieved that I am seemingly seeing it, embracing it. What do you call it? A grandchild. "So good news," he says. "Double good news, right?"

"Are you both insane?" I finally say. I hadn't meant to say it. In fact, I didn't even know I was going to say it. So I kind of laugh so he knows I'm on his side, their side, I'm just processing it all.

"Stop yelling at us," Graham says, which is strange because I am so very consciously not yelling.

Lydia volunteers that her family knows and they are very happy for them and that she's got no problem working 'til she pops and by January she'll be ready to start working on her master's, so perfect timing. The girl has confidence, I've gotta give her that. And I need another drink as I seem to have finished my glass.

I go into the kitchen, open the pantry, and pull out a bottle of port. Port, the perfect elixir for a pregnant pause, I think. Which is funny, so upon my return to the table, I sing it as a classic commercial jingle, "*The perfect elixir for a pregnant pause . . .*" I open the bottle like a happy housewife. "Graham Cracker," I ask as I pour, "how does Aunt Ginny know again? Did you tell me that?"

"Um. I told her?"

"When?"

"Last month?"

"Last month?" I say. "Like, last month, like, January?"

"Yeah," he says, looking confused or concerned.

"I think this deserves a toast!" I pour some port in Graham's empty wineglass. I plug the cork back in and say, "Now I get why you aren't drinking, Lydia. I'm relieved to know you aren't a teetotaler!" I'm trying to make light. I'm trying to go with the flow and hang ten and don't worry, be happy!

"Hey Mom," Graham-y says, putting his hand on the top of my glass, "maybe you should slow down, huh?"

And this does make me laugh, like "Ha! Speak for yourself, Graham-y Pants!"

"Oh my God, Mom," Graham says. "I knew you might be upset, but this..." He stands up and takes Lydia by the hand. "We're going upstairs," he says. "When you calm down, let me know and we can talk."

"I'm not upset, I'm happy for you guys! Really!" I say. I'm just trying to figure out why I am upset, because maybe actually I am. "I'm happy for all of us! A baby!" As I watch them go and hear them trot up the stairs, I giggle a little bit. I find it amusing that Graham told me that when I calm down we can talk, as this is something that I said to the boys when they were young, when they were out of control, something I said to Bill when he was, too. I feel kind of proud that I have taught Graham this little coping trick, and strangely, I can hear him saying it to a child, the way he just said it to me.

I hear him gently close his bedroom door. Oh dear, he's taking his girlfriend up to his bedroom! I hope he doesn't get her pregnant! I am cracking myself up!

I down my rather large port and then I down Graham's port as well.

The next thing I know I am parked in front of Ginny's house and my radio is telling me way too loud about the arrival of another snowstorm in a bombardment of fucking snowstorms. What am I doing here—at Ginny's house at 59 Beech Street? I have no idea. What time is it? The dash of my car tells me it's 9:34. Is it past Ginny's bedtime? I don't care.

I see lights are on inside and even the flickering of a TV. The front lights are not on, as they are not expecting me. Knock knock knock knock knock. Ring ring ring ring ring. I announce my arrival with vigor. I try the door and it is locked. Rude. I thought we agreed this town is safe! I will now have to unzip my coat pocket and dig out my keys, but first I will ring and knock again. And then I will text them both: *It's me. I'm here. Let me in!*

I wait and I shiver. Again, I wonder why I am here. I hear the sound of the lock being turned so I ring again.

"I'm coming," I hear my dear sister say. The doorknob turns and I turn it further and push in the door to hit Ginny's purple no-skid slipper.

I push harder to push Ginny back so I can get in. Suddenly I'm freezing my ass off. Ginny's wheelchair gets stuck I suppose, so I have to wait. "Are you okay?" she says to me.

"A bear is chasing me!" I say. "A rapist! Old Man Winter!" I'm just joking. I get in and close the door behind me.

At this point, Philomena appears in the background. She is not wearing her sunglasses. Sweet relief! The sun is down and the lights are dim. She must have been in her bedroom watching TV. She can't hear the doorbell from there with both her TV and the living room TV on and sometimes she doesn't get my texts right away due to funky cell service. She looks concerned. "Oh, I'm okay, Philomena," I say. "No worries. No bears or rapists or bare rapists that I know about. Woo! Would be a cold night for a bare rapist, wouldn't it?!"

Philomena furrows her brow and gives me a look of disapproval.

"You're acting weird," Ginny says.

"She's drunk," Philomena says.

I do not appreciate this accusation. "I did have a glass of wine with dinner, but I assure you that drunkenness is not my state." And then I move up close to Philomena to take in her truly lovely eyes. "Stop hiding your eyes from us, Philomena," I say. "Get the surgery." It's not a surgery thing, she's told me that, but I dunno, can't she do something?

I enter the living room, and look into the dining area, scanning the corners and the floors. I am looking for something.

"Very weird," says my sister.

"What are you doing, Maggie?" asks Philomena.

Suddenly I realize that I am very hot. I realize that I have entered a sauna fully dressed for a cold winter night. I take off my hat and my gloves and my coat and my scarf and my snow boots and then I take off my sweater. I leave them all there on the floor by the back door. Then I look up at Ginny and Philomena and I tell them, "I was looking for Rascal, but of course she is not here."

By now my sister has turned herself around in her chair and both she and Philomena are facing me in the kitchen. I open the refrigerator doors, which are extremely heavy. "Nice fridge," I say, ". . . water and ice-maker right on the door. So fancy."

Ginny is looking very confused.

"Hm, let's see what we have in here. I feel like I'm on *Let's Make a Deal*! Mmmm, cheesecake!" I pull it out to look at the box. "Is this sugar-free, Gin-Gin? Oh, and red velvet cake! That's seasonal, right? February is Valentine's month, right? I know that because you have your Happy Valentine's flag hanging off the front deck! With Snoopy and Woodstock on it! I love Snoopy and Woodstock. Are they friends or lovers, what do you think? Hardy har har."

I am trying to read the list of ingredients, but the print is so very small, and I am not wearing my glasses. Must have left them in my purse. Must have left my purse in the car. Or did I leave it at home? Dunno. "I can't read these," I say, "but I would bet a million dollars that each of them is packed with sugar. Right, Philomena? But at least when you go into a sugar coma, Philomena here will call 911! So it's all good!" I slam the refrigerator doors shut for effect, but they don't really make a satisfying slamming sound.

Philomena shakes her head and goes to pour a glass of water, which she then gives to me. I accept and drink the whole thing. "Refreshing," I say. Ginny continues to watch me but she is blinking her eyes so hard it looks like she's checking to see if they're working right. And of course they are not. That's what the optometrist said.

"Philomena," I say, "if you would be so kind, I have a little bit of sister business to discuss with Ginny and we'll need a bit of privacy." I say "privacy" like Queen Elizabeth with the "i" pronounced as in "bit," not "bite." Philomena nods, but before she leaves she goes to get a chair from our parents' old dining room table and she brings it into the kitchen and offers it to me. "Thank you," I say, "but I would rather stand." I wait and watch Philomena turn the corner to the bedrooms.

And then I become a very prominent lawyer. I pace the kitchen floor, directing my case directly toward Gin-Gin who is now on trial. "Ginny, Ginny, Ginny, Ginny," I say.

Ginny shakes her head and begins to back herself out of the kitchen.

"Oh no," I say. "Don't back away from me. I need to ask you a question and I need for you to answer it honestly, do you understand? Let's pretend Judge Judy is the coffeemaker."

"You are drunk," my sister says.

"So what if I am?" I say. "You're drunk all the time on sugar!"

Ginny shakes her head. Not so much in disapproval, but as if she's trying to shake this whole scene out of her.

"Now listen," I say, and I go into my prepared argument. "I learned some really big news this evening. I learned some very important news that severely impacts both me and my entire family. I learned some news that was in fact, old news. News that, while new to me, is old to you. Do you know what that news is?"

Ginny says nothing.

"I know you do. Because apparently, for no reason that I understand, my son, my first child, Graham, yes, baby Graham told his Aunt Ginny first. That was an honor, I hope you realize. Ginny, when did Graham tell you that Lydia is pregnant?"

Ginny answers with her signature, "Mm-mm-mm."

I do not like her Mm-mm-mm, so I say, "No Ginny, don't pull that Mm-mm-mm shit on me. I know you know and I want you to tell me."

"New Year's Day," she says definitively.

"New Year's Day?" I say. "That was six weeks ago!" Then I turn on my heels and put my face in Ginny's and say, "Why didn't you tell me?"

"He told me not to."

"You are so STUPID, Ginny! Not very," and then I tap on my head several times. "You are stupid, you are dumb, you have extremely poor judgment!" I spin myself around and walk away. The kitchen counter catches me, so

I lean against it. Anyway, I'm tired of being a lawyer. I quit. "I announce my resignation!" I say. "You people." And now I point at the accused who represents all those who have ever thrown wrenches into my better plans. "You people are fucking me up!" Ginny is just looking at me with her signature blank face. I need to spell it out. "F-U-C-K-I-N–ME–UP! Get it?"

Right now I just feel like crying, but I need to convey a myriad of mixed-up thoughts to my sister without that happening. "You're killing yourself with sugar, you must know that. Do you know that?" She's starting to back up her chair. "That's selfish. Do you realize that? Do you realize—that after all I've done? I do so much for you! I've been so good to you! And now our lives are all screwed! My life is screwed! Don't you get that? First I take care of my kids, then I take care of you. Fine, that's cool, I chose my path. It's been a privilege and an honor. But, really, when is it going to be Maggie time?" When I say this, I use jazz hands by my face. "When am I ever going to paint a painting again? Stretch a canvas. HA! Who do you think is going to be their live-in nanny now, huh? For Graham and Lydia's . . ."

Ginny is rolling herself away from me.

"Why would you keep something so important from me, Ginny? What were you thinking? Do you even think?"

She turns herself around to face the hallway that leads to the bedrooms. Philomena emerges from wherever and stands behind her, looking at me with what seems like sadness.

"Fine," I say. "I'm going home now." I go to the back door and pull on my snow boots.

"Oh no," Philomena says, "you are not going out there." She's got her sunglasses on again, she's the bad cop.

My scarf is climbing up my jeans and I think Rascal must have stolen my second glove so I'm looking for it on the floor.

"I told him to use protection," Ginny says. "He said it was too late. He told me not to tell you. He said he was gonna tell you."

I remember that Rascal is not there and I locate my second glove tucked into my hat. I put my gloves there sometimes so I don't lose them and this little trick does come in handy. Except when my gloves are wet!

"I don't squeal," my sister says.

Now I am trying to find both sides of the bottoms of my zipper and while doing so, I hear Ginny whispering something to Philomena. Her whispers are never quiet, but I can't hear the words because I have my hat on. I look out the back window to see the snow is falling harder. I turn around to head for the front door, but Philomena is standing there, right in front of me. She has her hand out.

"Give me the car key," Philomena says.

"What? No way. I'm going home," I say. "Sorry for the trouble." I try to move past her but she's blocking me.

"Give me the car key," Philomena says.

"I will not!" I laugh. "This is absurd!" I put my hand in my snow jacket pocket to feel that my keys are indeed there.

"You will not be driving tonight," Philomena says. "Give me the key now, Maggie."

I push past Philomena and start through the kitchen, through the dining room and toward the front door. Ginny is there, in her wheelchair of course, waiting for me. Her face looks like our father's face when he was ashamed.

"It's my key," Ginny states clearly. "Now give it to her."

Some force comes in from behind and grabs me around the waist and I hear my zipper unzip and my coat gets pulled off and my gloves go flying and I can't believe I'm being attacked like this by our sweet little angel from Ghana and I lose my balance and start to fall, not really sure where I'm landing, I just know that it's soft and lumpy. I hear another zip sound and I hear the sound of what I believe to be my keys being shook. And the next thing I know, I throw up.

I wake with an extremely intense headache. I wake with an intensely strong urge to pee. I wake with hot and sweaty feet and this leads me to the realization that I am wearing snow boots. I open my eyes and a plastic baby face is staring directly at mine. "Holy shit," I say. I know where I am now, pulling some large lumps out from underneath me. I push myself up and see that the baby is still staring at me. I turn her over before I head to the hallway bathroom where I will relieve myself of all burden.

When I emerge, I see that Ginny's bedroom door is open and she is not in her bed. I get a whiff of the usual scents that I imagine greet Philomena in the morning. Ginny must be in the bathroom. Behind me I see that Philomena's door is closed. She must be in the kitchen, preparing Ginny's breakfast.

When I return to the foyer and the creepy babies, I remember the dramatics of last night and I notice the clean floor. May God bless Philomena, I think. She certainly has a humble deal. The house is strangely quiet. I hear a car honk and remember my headache, pick up the glass of water that Philomena must have left for me on the side table, and look outside.

Blizzard, schmizzard. It's only an inch or two, nothing newsworthy. Someone has done a half-assed job shoveling the front deck and the ramp. Nice of them, though. They half-assed brushed off my car, too. Okay—Ginny's car. I notice that it is still rather dark out, which means it's earlier than I had thought. I see that the car's lights are on and it's running. Exhaust is coming out of the rear tailpipe.

"Ginny?" I say. I pick up my coat and search its pockets. My phone, yes. My keys . . . I pat down my jean pockets and my eyes take a quick scan of the floor. "GINNY!" I scream.

Running down the ramp, I slip on the ice and wipe out. Pull myself up by the banister and take slidey steps to the passenger door, which is locked. "California Girls" is playing very loud and I continue to call my sister's name. It's her CD that we keep in the car and every time we go somewhere we play it. I wipe the snow off the window with my sleeve and below it, a thin layer of ice heckles me. I try the rear door and then walk around and try the other rear and then the driver's door. Locked. I wipe the driver's door window and then use my fingernails to try to get under the ice and push it. The engine revs up. The windshield wipers start going, sending some chunks of snow and ice off and fly-aways into my face.

"Very funny, Virginia," I say.

I look in the windshield for the first time and I see Ginny there, behind the wheel, wearing her *Life's a Beach* hat. Her face looks wet and pale and her gloved hand wipes her eyes and then her nose. She revs up the engine again. The car takes a jolt.

"Go away!" Ginny yells.

"Don't, Ginny," I say, as loudly and firmly as I can.

"I'm going to California!" she yells.

This has been my greatest fear. That after all of this, she'd rather be with Betsy, and who knows? Maybe Betsy would have her. She's got Leo now. "Ginny, please don't!" I yell. "Please don't go to California! Ginny, please, turn off the car!"

"I'M NOT STUPID!"

"What?" I say. "Of course you're not, Ginny! Please!"

"Go away! Just go!"

"Turn off the car, Ginny," a calm voice with Ghanaian accent says. It's Philomena, in sunglasses, robe, and slippers standing there, directly in front it. "Or you will have to run me over," she says. The ice has fallen off of Ginny's window and I can see her seeing Philomena.

"I'm going!" Ginny revs up the engine again and honks.

Philomena does not move. The neighbor from across the street comes out with a shovel and takes us all in. Then, superhero-style, I jump on the front hood of the car. "You'll have to take me with you!" I yell.

Vroom, the car says again.

"Ginny, please don't."

Hoooooooooooonk!

The neighbor is still silently watching.

"I'm not the one who's stupid! You're the one who's stupid!" Ginny says loud enough so that I can hear her clearly, even through the icy dripping window.

"Of course you're not stupid, Ginny. Of course you're not . . . Please don't drive," I say.

Another long *Hooooooonk*, which really hurts my ears and is starting to pound at my frontal lobe. The car jolts and I fall off. Okay, maybe I jump off, I'm not sure. Philomena is still standing there, she's no chicken. I don't think the car moved far. I think the emergency brake held it there.

I'm just standing there in the middle of the road, right outside her window now. "Please, Ginny," I say, quietly pleading now. "I know you don't want to run over anyone." She's not looking at me, she's staring straight ahead, hard. "Pretty please, Gin-Gin?"

The car turns off. The Beach Boys stop.

"Thank you, dear sister," I sigh. "Thank you, Philomena," I say.

Philomena nods. Ginny is still staring straight ahead. I can't tell if she's looking at Philomena or not.

"I've got it, Philomena," I say. "Thank you so much," I say. I am excusing her from suicide duty. "I'm good, I've got it."

"You sure?" she says. Philomena isn't sure I've got it. Neither am I, actually.

"Oh yeah, we're good. Right, Gin-Gin? We're good?"

Philomena takes this as a yes and returns inside.

"Ginny, will you please get out now? Can we please go inside?"

Ginny won't budge.

"Ginny, please," I say. "Will you let me in then? I'm really cold."

Ginny stares straight ahead.

"Gin-Gin . . . Please?"

The doors unlock. I walk around the car oh so casually—I'm not sure if nosy neighbor is still there—and pull hard on the passenger door, which is still semi–iced shut. I manage to pull it open and slip inside the car.

"Thank you," I say, taking in my cold, wet sister. "Would you mind turning on the heat?"

Ginny turns the key and both the heat and the Beach Boys blast. Without thinking, I reach over and turn off the music.

"You're too controlling," Ginny says.

"Oh," I say. She's right. I put the music back on and it is very loud again. "Sorry," I say even louder, "I just wanted to talk with you."

"You were drunk last night."

"I was mad," I say. We are talking very loud to hear each other over "Fun, Fun, Fun."

"I'm sorry that I ruined your life," my sister says. There is a hard bitterness in her voice that is not the freezing temperature. I see that my sister is tearing. We both reach to turn off the music and I let her do it. Silence. Except for her heavy breathing.

"What are you talking about?" I say.

"Don't worry about me anymore. I'm fine by myself . . . I have my nannies."

"Then where are you going, Gin? The roads are icy and it's not safe . . ."

"I'm not driving anywhere!" she yells. "I'm not stupid!" Then through her tears, she says, "I just wanted to get behind the wheel, that's all. I just wanted to remember what it feels like. You wouldn't let me do it."

"Oh," I say. Oh.

"You called me stupid. You should go away. I don't need you. I'm an adult and I don't need you."

Oh? I try to piece together the things I said and did last night. I'm rubbing my hands together, my fingers are ice cubes. I don't remember calling Ginny stupid, though I've said it in the past—just not in her presence. "I'm sorry if I called you stupid," I say. "That was stupid of me. I don't think you're stupid. If I said it, it's just because I was angry. I mean, everybody is stupid sometimes and I was probably very stupid . . ."

"You were stupid. You are stupid," my sister says.

"Yeah," I say. I am also the biggest jerk in the world, I think.

"I am stupid," Ginny says.

"No, Ginny. No, you are not. Don't say that."

"I'm slow."

"You know what you are, Ginny?" I say. Ginny looks afraid to find out. "You're special."

"Special needs," she says.

"You have special needs, sure. But mostly, you are special. Just special."

She looks confused. "I'm slow. My brain doesn't work fast like everybody else's."

"Okay, so you are special and slow, and I am stupid. The special, slow, and stupid sisters," I say.

"I asked if he was using protection . . ."

Huh? What? "Oh, yeah, that was very smart of you! See? Little Graham was the one that was stupid!"

"He's a grown man. It's his choice," Ginny says.

"Yeah . . . You're right. And Graham isn't stupid . . ." I'm still trying to wrap myself around the wild and scattered emotions of it all. The heat is blasting but it's still not warm. And then a new thought enters my head. I'm embarrassed and ashamed, but I have to say it. "I think I felt left out."

"Of what?" Ginny says, wiping her nose with her sleeve.

"Out of the loop! Everybody else is in the loop!" I'm drawing a big loopy wave in the air and imagining Betsy there, riding it. "Does Bets know?" I have to know. "Does everyone know but me?"

"I doubt it," Ginny shrugs.

"Why didn't Graham tell me first? I'm his mom. Why do you guys have a whole text stream without me? Why am I always the last to know? Why would you and Graham keep such a big secret from me?" I'm shaking and I don't think it's the cold.

"Nobody wants to bother you," my sister says.

"Bother me?" I'm not sure why but this feels like the most awful, most terrible pain to my chest. An ice pick to the heart? Something cold and metal stabbed me there? I am here for people! That's my thing! Don't they see that? I, Maggie Frederick, am here for you all, always!

"You can move someplace else," she says. She takes her gloved finger and swirls it around like the whole universe. "I won't stop you."

"Ginny," I say. "I am very sorry for everything I said last night, and I am sorry for being selfish and stupid. I don't want to move someplace else. I like it here. I like being here with you."

Ginny doesn't say anything to this. But I think she believes me.

"You know what else, Ginny?" I know what else, but I am afraid to say it. I don't know why I am afraid to say it, but I will say it anyway. "I love you, Gin-Gin, and also . . . I need you. I need you very much."

She's quiet and then says, "Your sons think you drink too much."

Wait. What? This isn't where we were going. "What?" I almost laugh.

"They told me not to tell you but I'm tired of secrets."

My head is shaking and I feel the whole of me is on fire. "What did they say?" I say. Though I don't want to know. I want to cover my ears.

"You drink too much. You drink alone. You think they don't know but they do."

I feel my body want to swallow up inside of itself, and the impulse to run away. "Drink alone?" I say. "I only drink alone because I'm lone . . . Because I'm alone," I say. "Graham is never home," I continue. "Leo isn't home, Bill has a different home . . . so the only way I can drink, when I do drink, which isn't too much, by the way . . ." I am showing my shock and my rage. ". . . is when I'm alone. And that is not a problem! God knows I need a drink at night! I mean, I enjoy one! The lordesses know I deserve one!"

"I told them you're a grown-up and you can do what you want," she says. I think she's trying to figure out my face, because in their defense she says, "They can't help it if they're worrywarts."

Honk. Honk. This time it's not Ginny. It's someone else.

"Asshole!" I say. "We're not making a scene anymore! Just move around!"

"It's your son," Ginny says. She puts her window down and Graham's car has stopped in the middle of the road, parallel to us. Lydia is in the passenger seat and her window is down.

"The dynamic duo," Graham says.

Lydia smiles a very warm smile. An upside-down double rainbow smile. I want to sink into my seat, into the corner behind the driver's seat like Coyote. I don't want my older son knowing what I have done and I don't want to see him seeing what he already sees. I'm shy of the adult man that he has become.

Graham pulls up and parks in front of us. They both get out and I get out and Graham helps Ginny get out and he supports her as they walk slowly back into the house. It smells like breakfast inside and it feels warm, like home.

I don't understand Lydia's sweetness. If I were Lydia, I would run far away from this crazy woman. I don't understand Graham's forgiveness. He even brought me a large coffee and Tylenol. I don't understand why Philomena is still here and hasn't told both Ginny and me that we're both stupid, and quit. After Graham and Lydia say goodbyes, I drink my coffee as I watch Ginny soak her Eggos in fake maple syrup. I mean, she's really soaking them. They are floating there in a sea of syrup.

"You should tell our big sister," Ginny says.

Tell our big sister? What? About my awful deeds?

"If you don't want to, I will."

"Tell her what?" I say, and I'm kind of scared.

"About the baby," she says.

Oh my gosh, the baby. The baby! I don't know what the hell took over me last night but now, all of a sudden, as I look over at the bruised and sticky Binky Baby, I think . . . A baby! An actual baby. Graham's baby. My . . . grandbaby . . . I feel my head unspinning and everything realigning and clearing and I feel a sweetness, a lightness that I haven't felt in a long time.

"She's gonna be a great aunt."

"Hm?" I say, lost in thought.

"Bets," she says. "A great, great-aunt."

"Ha," I say. I see now that Ginny is excited. "Like you, Aunt Gin-Gin."

"June will be a busy month," she says.

"Yes," I say.

In June, it will be two years since Ginny officially moved to New York. In June, Bill and I will have been separated for four years, but still not divorced. In June, our first son and his girlfriend will have a teeny tiny baby. In June, Leo will return home from California and I hope will be ready to start classes at Westchester Community. In June, Ginny will be ready for a new dog, and in June, I will be ready for a grandchild.

She doesn't want to go to Malibu. "Been there already," she says.

"But isn't that your dream? To go back there?"

"Not really."

"But what about all those house searches in Southern California? What about the Realtor? What about all your threats to run away to Bets?"

"Trying to piss you off," she says.

"Okay, well, where do you want to go? Let's go someplace together. Just for fun."

"No, thank you."

"Don't you want to go anywhere?"

"Why would I want to do that?" my sister says. "I have this." She indicates her bay window. The one she can see out when she is eating, the one I can see in when I do my nighttime spying. The one where we put her little Christmas tree in the winter and her fake flowers in the summer. From her bay window she can see kids going to and from school, two school buses go by twice a day, she sees neighbors walk their dogs and snowplows and garbage trucks pass.

"You should go there," she says.

"Nah," I say. "Leo will be home soon ..."

"You should go on a trip someplace. For fun."

I don't say anything because I am taking in the way my sister is talking to me. She's talking like a wise woman, one who cares about me.

"You should go someplace. You're an independent woman. You should go someplace. Someplace you dream about."

I'm sitting back and taking her in as I sip my delicious coffee. She's offering Binky Baby a bite. She's a funny one, my sister. Still surprising me.

"I know it's cliché," I say, "but given the choice, I'd take Paris."

"Paris, France," she says.

"Yup. That one," I say.

⁂

I'm on a plane now to Paris, France, courtesy of my sister. She surprised me with a ticket on Mother's Day. The idea was to give me a getaway before the baby comes. A spring trip to Paris; this must have cost her something crazy. Graham says he got her a deal. He helped her make the arrangements, but she paid for it with her own credit card. Leo was in on it, too, and so was Bill.

"You do a helluva lot for me," she said.

The big boss is giving me a one-week holiday bonus. I swallow my pride and accept. I've always wanted to return to Paris. I came here with Bill for our five-year anniversary, and I always dreamed I'd come back. With him. Or Mr. X. Or Malick, ha ha. But here I am and I'm walking along the Seine on my own time, strolling through shops and galleries and drinking wine.

Everyone tells me not to worry, everything will be fine. Leo seems to have forgotten I'm out of the country: *Mom, an excellent deal on an old Kawasaki. Less gas than a car. Will pay you back. Love ya! . . .* As it should be.

Three days have passed without an exchange with Ginny. A record. I find that this isn't the liberating feeling I had expected, but more of an ache. I won't be home for another four days and I begin to have the uneasy feeling that Ginny might die in that short time. I feel like a kid who's waited for sleepaway camp all year and I'm finally here and I miss my parents. It feels like those days when I'd be dying for the boys to start day care or get back to school and then I'd miss them the whole day.

I FaceTime her from outside a patisserie. There's a particularly cute poodle sitting outside the entrance that I know she will appreciate. It's three o'clock in Paris, which means for her, it's nine a.m., her candy-in-bed time.

She does not pick up. She might be in the middle of ripping open a new package of Twizzlers. She could be bleaching her hair in the shower. She might have gone into a coma in the middle of the night and Philomena or Lika—I forgot what day it is—has yet to discover her there.

Four hours later, I'm standing outside the Opera National de Paris, where I'm about to see *Swan Lake* from the back row with an obstructed view, when I receive a FaceTime from Ginny. I answer it and in comes an odd angle of Ginny's living room ceiling fan.

"Bonjour, Gin-Gin!"

Ginny doesn't say anything.

"Ginny, are you there?" I say. "I can't see you." I hear something action-packed in the background—people screaming—probably at each other. *Sally Jessy*? Another episode of *Pit Bulls and Parolees*? "Ginny," I say, "can you bring the phone down so I can see your face?" The picture jumps around so that I get quick glimpses of the floor, Ginny's hot-pink sneakers, and the side table next to her recliner where she keeps her stash of necessities: lotion, a hairbrush, a large can of Hawaiian Punch, and a bag of cookies (just in case she has a low-sugar attack). There used to be dog biscuits on that chair, but no more.

"Ginny, the house looks great, but I want to see you. Can you please turn off the TV?"

More jumping around and then a ball of fuzz. What was that? Louder screaming and then quiet. A ball of fuzz on Ginny's right shoulder. Then the camera adjusts so I can see the whole of Ginny's face, her devilish grin acknowledging that the ball of fuzz is actually a furry feline.

"Oh my gosh, Ginny, is that a cat?"

"Kitten," she says.

"An actual living one?" I say. As in, not a stuffed animal.

"He's alive," she says.

"Where did he come from?"

She's looking at the kitten. He's tan. "Lika," she finally says.

"What do you mean? Is it Lika's kitten?"

"He's mine," she says. "She gave him to me."

Ginny is thoroughly enjoying springing this huge surprise. She did something. She made a life change. Without her baby sister's help or even knowledge. I'm stunned. I'm tickled.

"Does he have a name?" I ask.

"Dennis Wilson."

"Dennis Wilson? Like the *Beach Boys'* Dennis Wilson?"

"Reincarnated," she says.

"Really? How do you know?"

"He sings," she says. "Very high." The kitten jumps off her shoulder and Ginny wrestles with the phone. The visuals are bumpy. Then, the picture lands on the kitten again, now on Ginny's lap.

I giggle on and off throughout *Swan Lake*. The couple sitting next to me does not appreciate it.

⁂

Now I am back. I feel refreshed, I feel romantic. I am excited to be a grand-mère. In France, even the grandmothers look chic, and I plan to look chic as well. Bill tells me he's excited to be a grand-père and he invites me out to dinner to celebrate this.

"Vegan?" I say.

"French," he says.

Right now, though, I am sitting at Ginny's dining room table with my laptop opened and I am ordering her groceries.

For the past two-plus years, since Ginny has been in her new house, her aides have taken her grocery shopping. She would hold on to the cart and this was her exercise. In the beginning, it was twice a week and then it turned into once and then Ginny fell at the checkout counter, so they tried out one of those motorized carts and of course that was much too exciting.

So, Philomena and Lika got to doing the shopping while she napped, and they would bring back the receipts, for which they'd be reimbursed. This got complicated because it meant that I had to get cash out of Ginny's account each time they did this.

Then she would let them just take her credit card and they would do it that way. They forged her signature. And then each of them started individually telling me that the other one didn't pick up enough eggs or the chicken salad was all gone or "If she bought strawberry and milk why do I not see strawberry and milk? Do you hear what I am saying? Where is the strawberry and milk?"

So today I create an account at the same grocery store that we all know and love, and from here on in, I will get a list from all three of them on Tuesday, will place the order on Wednesday, to have it delivered on Thursday. We're grown-ups doing what grown-ups do.

I've already put Philomena and Lika's special requests in the cart. Now I will add Ginny's things. Here is her list:

Mik 6 galuns
Onyun rings frozn
Egg O pan caks
Eggo O waffls
Garlic bred
Contry cock buttr
Eggs
Shimp frozn
Cheze cake
Pumkin pie
Blak and wite cookes
Manays
French frys
Fis sticks
Wonder bred
Amercan cheze slise s
Appel saws

I order these things, no comments made, no questions asked.

She lost access to her email and needed help with Amazon, so I switched her email with them to mine. Now that I am privy to her Amazon orders, I see that her needs are supplemented. Here is this week's order:

Jell-O Tropical Punch, 24 cups
Mountain Dew Kickstart, Fruit Punch, 3 packs of 12

Benadryl Ultratabs, Allergy relief

Spam Classic 8/12 oz.

Reese's Peanut Butter Cups, 3 packs of 3

Canada Dry Ginger Ale, case of 24

Pepsi cans, pack of 18

Welch's Fruit Snacks, Variety Pack, 42

Little Debbie Oatmeal Big Pack Cream Pies, 31.78 oz., pack of 2

Lorna Doone Shortbread Cookies, 1.5oz pack, 60 Ct

Twizzlers, Twists Strawberry Flavored, Bulk, 80 oz

Reese's Peanut Butter Cups, Holiday, 3 15 oz. bags

Aunt Jemima Rich Syrup, Butter, 36 oz. x 2

Girl Scout Peanut Butter Patties, Cookies, 6.5 oz. box x 4

Depend Fix-Flex Underwear for Women, Maximum Absorbency, XL, Blush, 48 count

Mountain Dew ICE Soda Cans, 3 of 12

Purina Fancy Feast Medleys Adult Canned Cat Food, 24 cans x 4

Meow Mix Dry Cat Food, 22 oz. x 4

Cat Crack Catnip, 1 cup x 2 (Ginny tells me that the second one is for cousin Crazy Cat)

Jalousie 27 Pack Cat Toy Assortment, Cat Scratcher and Activity Center

❧

We all know what will happen. One sweet day or night I will get a call from Lika or Philomena. She will tell me that Ginny seems to have had a stroke. She will say that Ginny can't move half her face or get out of bed. I'll say I will be right there. I will get there in fifteen minutes. Because even though she lives six minutes away, I'll need to brush my teeth, put on more comfortable pants. Because I will know then as I know now that it is going to be a long day or night or whatever it is. When I arrive, Ginny will look at me. She will know who I am, I am quite confident of that. And I will tell her we love her, and we want to call an ambulance.

Dennis Wilson will be hiding under the dining room table. Binky Baby will be tucked under her pillow. Ginny's pillow. I don't know why, but this is how I see it.

Ginny will say, "No." Or maybe she won't be able to talk, and she will shake her head.

I will say, "But Ginny, we must. You had a stroke."

She might shake her head again. Or she might not even comprehend. And I will look at Philomena or Lika and she will look at me.

"What are we going to do?" I will say to her. Not to my sister, but to her aide.

"We should call 911," she will say.

A few months or maybe a year after that, I will paint a huge canvas. Like in the olden days, though this time I'll be painting fully dressed, drinking tea. It will be from my perspective, sitting on a beach chair looking out toward the ocean. The waves in the ocean will not be very large, but they are too large for me. Still, I enjoy looking at them, listening to them, their rhythmic pounding accompanied by the calls of seagulls.

From here, I will see a big woman with long wild hair in a one-piece American flag bathing suit. She will be sitting in a wheelchair, looking out toward the water. A tan and beautiful beach man will meet her there. Where did he come from? I didn't see him before. He popped out of the water, perhaps? He is wet and he is dripping, and his hair is past his shoulders. His mustache and beard glisten, too. His surfboard has washed up with him and it's bright purple. He picks it up easily with one arm and with the other, he reaches out toward my sister. Usually, she would not meet a hand halfway, but in this case she does. She reaches out and his strong and firm hand takes hers. Somehow, she stands, and then seems to float along the sand, following him.

Still, I am sitting there in my chair, watching this. I will say her name, "Ginny." I will call, "Ginny!" She will not hear me, or at least, she will not respond. Suddenly, they are in the water. She's holding on to the side of the board next to him, and he's kicking. I blink and they are past where the waves break, though her hair is not wet. It shines like Malibu Barbie's hair. He stands on the surfboard now, and she is still there, hanging on. But wait. A large fin pops up behind her. A perfectly symmetrical double-sided fin. It shines a translucent pink and purple, silver and gold. As he carries my sister further, she looks back—toward me? She lets go of the board. I stand. "Ginny," I say, but this time more to myself. And then right there alongside Dennis Wilson on his surfboard, Ginny pops up again. And look! The fins are attached to her, a part of her. An enormous wave opens up before them, and as it begins to break, they enter it.

ॐ

Bill picked a French restaurant just thirty minutes north in Cold Spring. Le Bouchon, where we used to go on date nights sometimes, a couple times for our anniversary. The last time we were there we got into a big fight. I had told him I wanted to get a Buddha sculpture for our humble garden, and he went into a riff about how Buddhas were so trendy and phony. I said that just because I wasn't a full-on Buddhist didn't make appreciating him phony. He said why can't we be real and put a sculpture of something that truly symbolizes our lifestyle and I said, "And what would that be?" and he paused for a minute before he said, "The Virgin Mary?" He was commenting on the fact that we weren't having sex. It was a stupid and sophomoric equation, and my response was equally childish. I pushed my chair back, knocking it down as I got up, walked out of the restaurant and went down to the river, leaving him there to pay the bill and get our food wrapped up and then wander the streets of Cold Spring looking for me.

It's a beautiful evening and they've just put the three tables on the front porch, and he reserved one of them. He pulls my chair out for me, which he never did before. He's wearing what look like new jeans and a black button-down and black sneakers. He shaves his head now because he thought the balding aged him. He does look younger, and he also looks fit.

I am wearing a cute dress that I bought in a cute boutique in Le Marais. I'm wearing chic ankle boots that I bought on sale at DSW, but hey—they look French. My hair is in a low ponytail that I've casually flipped to one side. On my way out, Lydia said I looked pretty.

"What a few years it's been," Bill says, toasting me.

"You can say that again," I say, toasting back.

"What a few years . . ." we both say, and we laugh at our shared corniness.

"Interesting choice," I say, nodding to the place.

"You wish we tried something new?" he says.

"No. Nah. Why travel to the city or up the river when we've got this right here?"

"Hey, pretty soon we'll be afraid to drive even this far. We'll be babysitting our grandbaby and sending Graham and Lydia here for a night out."

"Yea," I say, "pretty soon we'll be eating our food mashed."

He laughs. "Okay, I get it. Give me a break, okay?"

"Okay," I say.

Bill orders a bottle of champagne and we play a game making up baby names and after we finish the bottle, we share a chocolate mousse with Grand Marnier and then walk down to the river for a most spectacular view of the Hudson and the hills on the other side. A train starts winding its way around the mountains there, and from this distance it looks like a toy train on a toy train set. There are a few high school kids hanging out in the gazebo. A couple on a bench.

Bill and I are at the railing now, so it's just us and the lights of the train and the moon and the reflection on the water.

"Maggie?" he says as he turns to face me.

"Yes?" I say, feeling him there.

"Marriage is a funny thing, isn't it?"

"I guess," I say, turning to him. "Sometimes sad."

"But I mean, isn't that a part of it?" he says. "I mean, it's in and out and up and down. Like the water there, constantly moving."

"Except when it's stagnant," I say. "Or frozen. Sometimes the water freezes in place. Sometimes the water is so damn cold you can slip on it and break your hiney."

Bill steps back. "You're not going to make this easy, are you?" he laughs.

"What?" I smile. "Your metaphor? How 'bout this. Marriage is like a roller coaster. Sometimes it goes up, sometimes down."

"Or a good guitar solo," he says. "Sometimes it starts off heavy and hot only to diffuse itself into practical silence and then build back up to something gut-wrenchingly romantic."

"Spoken like a true . . . musician," I say.

"I was so scared for a moment that you were going to say insurance agent."

I laugh despite the fact that I am trying to play hard to get.

"Are you aware that we've been married for almost twenty-seven years?" Bill says.

"Almost four of which we've been separated," I say.

"That would be the diffused practically silent part," he says.

"And the many years before that when we were totally off-key? Screeching and out of sync?"

"It's all part of the music," he says to me, taking his hand to his bald head and sweeping back, the way he used to when he had a head full of hair.

He looks handsome. He looks like a profile picture on Match that I would definitely like. I'm leaning against the railing now, admiring him and the silhouette of the hills behind him. He's my husband. He's still my husband as we never divorced. I put my hand out to him. He takes it and turns it over to acknowledge that it no longer wears a ring. He steps in toward me and puts both of his hands on my hips. "Maggie?" Bill says. "I never stopped loving you. You know that, right? And, in fact, I believe that now I love you more."

"Hm," I say. I'm looking up at him looking down at me. Bill is tall. Our sons are tall. He always had to bend down to me. I put my hands on his upper arms to pull him closer, I lift my faux-French medium-heels up off the ground to meet him there. "And maybe I love you more, too," I say. And we kiss.

⁓

Today is a glorious day, as our mother used to say. It's an almost-summer day, one week to the baby's due date. I've stopped by Ginny's to get some sister sugar.

"She don't wet herself now," Philomena whispers to me when I arrive. "Dennis Wilson don't sit there when she smelling of urine so she stop like that." She laughs. Philomena is not wearing sunglasses. She is trying out special contacts that serve to diffuse the light. She now has violet eyes. "I tell you, she knows exactly what she is doing, your sister! You say she has disabilities, but I think only ten percent. Maybe five. Maybe less."

"Thought you had surgery," my sister says from her recliner.

"Surgery was canceled," I say. The gig fell through.

I think she's pleased to see me. She turns off the TV.

Now we are sitting on Ginny's front porch and I am sketching her and Dennis Wilson. Dennis Wilson is a soft tan tabby with subtle stripes on his tail and body. He is allowed to go outside by himself, but he likes to stay close to home and he especially likes to stay on Ginny's lap, a place that none of her big dogs was ever able to claim. Sadly, Binky Baby now lives her life in the high chair. Ginny pets Dennis Wilson as best she can. Sometimes she rests her sticky hand on Dennis Wilson and I am afraid she might suffocate him, but Ginny says that Dennis Wilson likes being held down, he is her ball and chain and she is his ball and chain and some marriages are like that.

Then suddenly she gets one of her devilish grins.

"Um hmm . . . ?" I say. I wonder if I can capture that grin.

"How's Bill?" she asks.

"Fine," I say, ". . . I guess."

"Don't you know?" she says.

"What do you mean? Last time we talked he was fine," I say.

"So are you exes with benefits?"

I'm caught off guard and I feel myself break into a sweat. "What are you talking about Ginny?"

"Do you like his apartment at Sing Sing?"

This is what she calls Ossining because she has trouble pronouncing it and also the prison is there. She's grinning as she opens up something on her phone. She shows me that she took a screenshot of my location late last night, and my location was Bill's apartment in Ossining.

"Ginny!" I feel my face blushing and I quickly put down my sketchbook, pick up my phone, and cut her off from my location.

"I can do that," she says, and she cuts me off, too.

I don't know what to say, so I get back to drawing. She's sitting there all pleased with herself. I'm trying to capture her mouth, the way it hangs partly open. "I gave up bourbon," I say unexpectedly. "And Baileys," I continue. "So many calories . . ."

My sister doesn't say anything, though I'm pretty sure she's listening. She pats Dennis Wilson who sits like a pillow on her lap.

"I'm just drinking one glass of wine a day now," I continue. "Just with dinner. No refills." Except for last night's dinner with Bill, that was an exception. Yea, on my flight back from France I decided to try to cut back a little bit. Maybe it was inspired by my wipeout on the front steps of the Sacré-Coeur after I finished a bottle by myself. Maybe it's just that I don't like that my boys told her that, don't want them thinking that . . . that I drink too much. It's not a problem, it's just. I'm cutting back. We sit in silence for a while as I draw the line where her belly meets her breasts. "It's hard," I say.

"Tell me about it," my dear sister says.

I sigh and I think I see the tip of one side of her mouth turn up. I finally get that I don't have to act like I've got it all together, because I don't. I don't have to pretend that she is troubled and I am not. I'm relieved that I don't have to be cheery all the time. I can just be myself, something Ginny's been able to do naturally all along.

I think I'm finished, so I turn the picture toward her. She doesn't say anything, nor do I really expect her to. She has already established that she isn't into art. Why draw a picture when you can just take a picture, she always says. I take a look at the sketch again.

"I think it's pretty good," I say. "I mean, the feel of it. Don't you think it looks like you and Dennis Wilson? I'm not going for a carbon copy, just a representation."

"Dennis Wilson always looks cute," she says.

"True," I say. "Hard to mess him up."

"I dunno know why you'd wanna draw me, but I understand Dennis Wilson."

"You are both very interesting," I say.

Hm. I look at the picture and decide to doll it up. Who says a sketch has to be serious? On Ginny's left, I draw a surfboard. In the background, an ocean with waves. And on the waves, a surfing dog, arms spread, balancing. I draw a palm tree to her right and a table with a coconut drink with a little umbrella sticking out. On the ground right next to Ginny's wheelchair, I draw a little drum set, with little drumsticks resting on top.

When I show this version to Ginny, she takes off her glasses and looks at it for a while.

"See?" I say. "That's Dennis Wilson's drum set. And his little drumsticks on top."

"I have eyes," she says. But still, she's staring at it. Finally, she declares, "That should go in a museum."

"Thanks," I say. And I mean it.

I mean it for so many things. Thanks for moving here to Croton-on-Hudson, even when you didn't want to. Thanks for being here for me. Like, actually, always here. Thanks for fixing the window that time and thanks for protecting me from Honey Bear. Thanks for playing with me when I was so much littler than you. Thanks for teaching me not to take my art—and everything else—so seriously. Thanks for loving me even though I'm weird, maybe because I'm weird? Thanks for telling me I drink too much. Thanks for not giving me shit about it. Thanks for teaching me how to just be, how to just sit and pet a dog or a cat and stop doing so many things. Thanks for teaching me to Ride the Waves. Thanks for putting so much in perspective. Thanks for not telling Mom and Dad about Marble. Thanks for reaching out to our sister when you knew I couldn't. Thanks for being my blood sister. Thanks for Paris. Thanks for letting me extend your life, even if it was for my own selfish reasons. Thanks for trusting me to care for you. Thanks for caring for me.

She takes off her glasses and puts her phone up to her face. I'm guessing she's going to FaceTime someone, which she sometimes does when sitting quietly with me . . . Leo, Graham, Bill? The rascally look on her face hints it's Bets. "Calling our sister," she says, "to congratulate."

"Congratulate?" I say. "What for?"

"It's a secret," she says, tapping hard on the screen. "'Nother realty show: *American Gladnater.* Don't tell her I told you."

I have to laugh. I look up at the clear blue sky. "It really is a glorious day, isn't it, Gin-Gin?"

The FaceTime is ringing.

"Glorious day," Ginny says. "Sounds like the name of a Beach Boys song."

Acknowledgments

To my agent, Stephanie Cabot, for seeing the merit of this story and giving me invaluable feedback and encouragement, I am ever grateful. I thank you and the rest of the incredible team at Susanna Lea Associates, including Noa Rosen, Helena Sandlyng-Jacobsen, and Sophia Schaefer for helping me take the Frederick Sisters to the next level, and Lauren Wendelken for making it all happen.

To my editor, Trish Todd, thank you for your faith in this story, and for your wise, thoughtful, and good-humored guidance. It has been such a pleasure. Thanks to Sean Delone, Fiora Elbers-Tibbitts, Liz Byer, Lisa Nicolas, Chelsea McGuckin, Jimmy Iacobelli, Gena Lanzi, Maudee Genao, and the whole team at Atria Books for your parts in bringing the Frederick Sisters to life and out into the world. Thank you to Libby McGuire, Lindsay Sagnette, and Dana Trocker for making Atria the beautiful publishing house that it is.

This book is dedicated to my beloved brother David Michael Zusy. Davie, you were a good man, a great big brother, and my very special friend.

This book is also dedicated to everyone everywhere who has ever cared for a loved one or someone else's loved one. I thank my personal heroes, Davie's caregivers: Osei Yaw Dapaah, Ioseb Saralidze, and Frank Dumevi. Thanks to the good folks at KEEN Greater DC, Victoria Home, Lean on We, and Croton Animal Hospital. To all others who were there for Davie, including his neighbors, who never asked for a thing in return, I thank you.

I thank my parents, Mary Jane Lloyd Zusy and Fred Zusy, for sharing their interest in the world, their love and their kindness. Mom, Dad, I feel your positive presences every day. I thank every member of our great big Zusy gang, each of whom had a special love for Davie. You are all very special to me. Extra gratitude to Mark and Amy Zusy, Suzy Zusy, Cathie Zusy, and Sam Kendall, and a shout-out to niece Katie Ortiz and my dear late sister Annie Zusy for the herd of elephants.

Thank you to my mother-in-law, Mémé Cote, and the great big Cote family, especially my sisters-in-law Lydia Cote, Melissa Griffin, and Mary Long.

To my soul sister since the age of two, fellow writer, and precious parallel life pal, Julie Langsdorf, thanks for being there every step of the way. Heartfelt thanks to these dear friends for reading, cheerleading, and soul meeting: Ann Shulman, Denise Bessette, Marcy B. Freedman, Rana Faure, Theone Masoner, Linda Timander, Vicky Thulman, Irene Glezos, Maureen Beitler, Debbie Broshi, and Bianca Mancinelli. Much gratitude to Carol Merle-Fishman. Deep appreciation to Andrea Kennedy Andrews, Beth Carulli, Megan David, Sheryl Heath, Kelly Jo Kuchar, Catherine O'Connor, Susan O'Keefe, Jennifer Pauley, Ruth Rust, Suzanne van der Wilden, Jana Wilson, Sarah Wright, Pope Brock, Andrew Suss, and all who have been present during my life and novel-writing adventures.

Loving thanks to Suzanne Shepherd for encouraging me to play. Thanks to every actor, director, writer, and theater artist I've worked with, including Karen Finley and Richard Caliban, who supported me on other Davie-inspired works. Thanks to Kirsten Bakis and the excellent group of writers at the Hudson Valley Writers' Center, including

Claire Hilbert, Rachel Kowalsky, Soyung Pak, Suzanne Samuels, and Lynne Peskoe-Yang, for sharing your thoughts and encouragement as I worked on this.

Thank you to Layce, Goldie, and Coby, the inspirations for Rascal, Coyote, and Crazy Cat. Thank you to Nighttime and pandemic puppy Arlo for keeping me company as I wrote this book.

To my darling daughters, Olivia Z. Cote and Nell V. Cote, you bring tremendous joy to my life. Thank you for inspiring me every day in every wonderful way.

And finally, my deepest thanks to my dear husband, John Cote, true partner in love, family, and art. John, it's so lovely riding the waves and living the dream with you.

About the Author

Jeannie Zusy has written plays, screenplays, and stories. This is her first novel. She has two young-adult daughters and lives in the Hudson River Valley with her husband and creatures.

BOOK
CLUB
FAVORITES

READER'S
GUIDE

The Frederick Sisters Are Living the Dream

Jeannie Zusy

This reading group guide for The Frederick Sisters Are Living the Dream *includes an introduction, discussion questions, ideas for enhancing your book club, and a Q&A with author* Jeannie Zusy. *The suggested questions are intended to help your reading group find new and interesting angles and topics for your discussion. We hope that these ideas will enrich your conversation and increase your enjoyment of the book.*

Introduction

Every family has its fault lines, and when Maggie gets a call from the ER in Maryland, where her older sister lives, the cracks start to appear. Ginny, her sugar-loving eldest sister, who has diabetes and intellectual disabilities, has overdosed on strawberry Jell-O.

Maggie knows her sister really can't live on her own, so she takes her sister and her occasionally vicious dog to live near her in Upstate New York. Their other sister, Betsy, is against the idea, but as a professional surfer, she is conveniently thousands of miles away.

Thus Maggie's life as a caretaker begins. It will take all her dark humor and patience—already spread thin after a separation, raising two boys, freelancing, and starting a dating life—to deal with Ginny's diapers, sugar addiction, porn habit, and refusal to cooperate. Add two devoted but feuding immigrant aides and a soon-to-be-ex–husband who just won't go away, and you've got a story that will leave you laughing through your tears as you wonder who is actually taking care of whom.

Topics & Questions for Discussion

1. Bets, Maggie, and Ginny each have their role to play as sisters. Discuss each of their relationships. Does their dynamic change throughout the story? If so, how; and if not, why do you think that is?

2. When the story starts, Bill and Maggie's relationship is essentially over. Maggie takes ownership for what finally ended their marriage, but what else happened in their relationship that led up to her affair?

3. As the story goes on, we see Maggie's drinking steadily increase. Discuss how she handles her drinking. What are some of the excuses she uses to justify her behavior?

4. Discuss the differences in approach by Philomena and Lika as they take care of Ginny. How are these women similar despite their different backgrounds?

5. Being a caretaker doesn't look the same for every person. Maggie is a caretaker for Ginny, but also for her sons and the pets in the

family. Where do you think she succeeded in taking care of her family? Were there moments where you thought she could have handled situations better? Do you see a connection between how Maggie treated Ginny and how she treated her sons?

6. If you were Maggie's friend or family member, how would you react to her relationship with Ginny? Would you have supported her caretaking decision? What does or doesn't seem to work between the sisters?

7. There are many funny scenes in the novel, in addition to its overall humorous tone. Which moments made you laugh, and how did they make you feel about the characters?

8. During the snowstorm, beginning on p. 212, Maggie realizes she can't control Ginny's care, despite her best efforts. Discuss what advice you might give Maggie about letting go when you've done all you could.

9. Although they all have various frustrations with one another, Maggie, Betsy, and Ginny clearly love each other. What are some examples of how they demonstrate their affection, albeit in perhaps untraditional ways?

10. Maggie owns the fact that she has made mistakes over the course of the novel. Discuss what some of them were. Did you empathize with her decisions or choices at all? How does author Jeannie Zusy make her sympathetic despite her mistakes?

11. The title of the book is *The Frederick Sisters Are Living the Dream*. Why do you think the author chose this? Do you think the sis-

ters are living the dream? In what ways do their dreams change throughout the book? And how do you think Maggie's job might connect to this concept of living the dream?

12. Maggie and others vacillate in their determination to break Ginny of her sugar habit. Meanwhile, it seems that Maggie and others have some of their own addictive habits. How does this inform how they all deal with Ginny? Do you think the others even see these parallels?

13. Discuss how the novel is organized and broken into four parts, each focusing on different locations and settings.

14. Each character brings something different to the story—did you relate to any particular character? If so, please explain who and why.

Enhance Your Book Club

1. In recent years there have been many more movies, TV shows, and documentaries exploring neurodivergent protagonists, such as *Atypical*, *Everything's Gonna Be Okay*, and *Ozark*. Pick one to watch for a book club screening!

2. With its big cast of characters, charming small-town New York setting, at-times-hilarious plot twists, and heart-tugging storylines, *The Frederick Sisters Are Living the Dream* seems perfect for a film or TV adaptation. Who would you cast as its main characters? What scene would you most look forward to watching?

3. Look into adult care centers in your area and volunteer your time!

A Conversation with Jeannie Zusy

The Frederick Sisters Are Living the Dream is both heartfelt and laugh-out-loud hilarious. Did you set out to write a funny novel, or did the characters you created inform its tone?

Oh, thank you! I definitely wanted to lean in to the humor. This story is about so many serious things, actually. Complex, hard things. When I was going through something similar, I found the only way I could keep myself centered was to be true to my heart and tuned in to my humor. Laughter is an excellent survival mechanism. And yes, the characters also made this happen. Ginny often cracked me up when I was writing her, and there are certain scenes, for example the one between Maggie and Lika after the Apple Store, that just totally caught me by surprise.

Sisterhood is an evergreen topic in literature. What dynamics in this relationship were you interested in exploring?

I wanted to capture the intensity, connection, and loyalty that come with sisterhood. There are no other relationships that share the same history. Sisters share bedrooms and bathrooms and an intimate knowledge of one another since childhood. The roles they play in relation to one another and the rest of the family are established so early on. This is rich and wonderful territory to explore.

Tell us about your inspiration for the novel!
My brother Davie. He was very special to me and the few of us who were lucky to know and love him. He inspired me in many ways, and I admired his strength, sweetness, and dignity.

A few years ago, he was having health issues that he couldn't manage on his own. My siblings and I decided to move him to live near me and my family. It was an intense and gratifying three-year adventure. While this was happening, I was struck by how many people I knew who were in similar situations (usually with a parent). I wanted to write a novel that addressed the rewards and challenges that come with caring for a loved one. I wanted to celebrate people who have special needs and shed some light on the preciousness of every life, even a very quiet one.

I chose to fictionalize it because I wanted to give myself some flexibility and freedom. I made it about sisters because I wanted to explore that unique dynamic. Also, I wanted to write about women, specifically the overall amazingness of women in middle age, who I feel are underrepresented in today's fiction. And finally, I wanted to celebrate caregivers, many of whom are immigrants and have their own awe-inspiring stories. I honestly don't know where our country's medical system would be without them. I dedicated this book to both my brother Davie and to those who care.

Why did you choose to separate the story into four parts, designated by place or setting?
These parts were very clear to me, each symbolizing where Ginny was in her process of rejection or acceptance of her situation and ultimately her new life in New York.

Was there a character who was your favorite to write about? If so, why?
I loved writing all three sisters. I enjoyed diving deep into Maggie's

better-to-laugh-than-cry point of view. Ginny was super fun to write. She's a woman who is not afraid to speak her mind, and sometimes she surprises with her gentleness and wisdom. And Bets—well, she's just so cool and complex. I also loved writing Philomena and Lika, Bill, the boys, oh my goodness, did I mention Rascal, Coyote, and Crazy Cat? I guess I just fell in love with all of them. Even Mr. X.

You've written for a couple of different media—playwriting (shorts and full-lengths), fiction—do you prefer one over the other? If so, why?
The exploration of media has been organic. As an actor, I started writing material for myself and then plays with friends in mind. This segued into screenplays and then short stories for my kids, then for adults. Several years ago, I would not have predicted that I'd start writing novels, but then I had stories to tell that couldn't fit into ninety minutes or thirty pages. My first attempt did not get published. Then I had this story, and I felt it needed to be a longer-form, and well, here we are! As far as a preferred medium, it really depends on the story and what I feel will be the most fun and satisfying way to tell it.

As a writer, what do you hope readers take away from this novel?
I hope this story will inspire compassion (including self-compassion), encourage humor, and perhaps offer a new view on the challenges and rewards of those living with special needs and an appreciation for those who care for them.

Do you have a next project in mind? And, if so, what is it?
I do. It's another heart-driven, sometimes-humorous contemporary novel. I'd also like to get back to that first novel attempt, a story inspired by my family history that takes place in the Middle East and Europe in the 1950s.

Thanks for these questions and thanks to all the readers!